"WAITING YOUR TURN, MISS LEIGHTON?"

Tess recognized him before he turned, even before she saw those mocking eyes. Beneath the scrap of a towel anchored about his waist, she could see the outline of lean hips and powerful thighs. Little beads of water slipped down his chest, glistening against his bronzed skin and tangled black hair. Tess had to fight to keep her eyes from following the silver drops down. . . .

Perdition! Was she losing her mind? Speechless with fury, she glared at the nearly naked man before her.

Ravenhurst's lips twisted into a cold smile. His eyes glittered, never leaving her flushed face as his hands moved slowly to the knot at his waist.

No! He could not . . .

With a muffled plop the towel hit the carpet.

"Is that more to your liking, Miss Leighton?" he taunted. With cool deliberation he stalked toward her. Before Tess knew it, his fingers were circling her wrists, dragging her back into the room. A moment later he kicked the door shut.

"What do you think you're doing?"

"Doing?" Ravenhurst repeated harshly, hauling her against his hard, wet body. "Doing, my dear Tess? I'm teaching you a lesson, that's what I'm doing. The first of many lessons I mean to teach you. Today I'm showing you exactly what you missed. And giving you a taste of what's yet to come."

Also by Christina Skye:

DEFIANT CAPTIVE

The
BLACK
ROSE

Christina Skye

A DELL BOOK

Published by
Dell Publishing
a division of
Bantam Doubleday Dell Publishing Group, Inc.
666 Fifth Avenue
New York, New York 10103

Map designed by Cynthia Savage

Ship detail by Christina Helmer

The trademark Dell® is registered in the U.S. Patent and Trademark Office.

ISBN: 0-440-20929-3

Printed in the United States of America

Published simultaneously in Canada

August 1991

10 9 8 7 6 5 4 3 2 1

OPM

To Christopher and Christian,
heroes both,

for your inspiration and encouragement,
and of course,
for first discovering Tess's secret passage

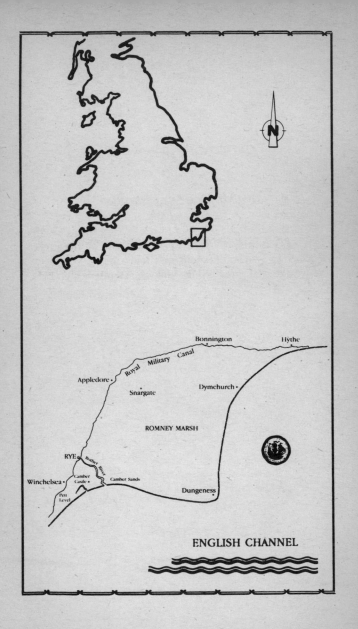

Bonnington · · · Hythe

Royal Military Canal

Appledore · Dymchurch ·

Snargate ·

ROMNEY MARSH

RYE · Rother River

Winchelsea · Camber Castle · Camber Sands

Pett Level

Dungeness ·

ENGLISH CHANNEL

A SMUGGLER'S SONG

If you wake at midnight, and hear a horse's feet,
Don't go drawing back the blind, or looking in the street.
Them that asks no questions isn't told a lie.
Watch the wall, my darling, while the Gentlemen go by!

—Rudyard Kipling

Prologue

Laces for a lady; letters for a spy.

—Rudyard Kipling

London, England
April 1810

The candles on the carved mahogany side table sputtered, their flickering dance reflected in a nearby set of crystal decanter and glasses. On the bed beside the table faint shadows danced across the snowy sheets, where two bodies moved, intertwined in the grip of passion.

By God, she was beautiful! the man thought, his eyes lingering on the voluptuous curve of breast and thigh spread for his sensual appreciation.

With cool deliberation he ran his hand across the taut nipples and lush breasts, smiling slightly as the woman beneath him shivered and arched her back. Yes, Danielle must be as near to perfection as a female could come, Dane St. Pierre, the fourth Viscount Ravenhurst decided, sliding his fingers lower to trace the hollow below his mistress's navel.

His lapis eyes narrowed. Slowly he grazed the blond tangle at the crown of her thighs.

Suddenly Lord Ravenhurst's bronzed face hardened. He fought down the image of a different pair of arms, of dancing eyes and lilting laughter.

Forget her, damn it! She was a lying schemer, an angel with a whore's heart. No one knew that better than he. He should consider himself lucky that he'd discovered the truth about her in time!

Growling a savage curse, Ravenhurst pulled his lush bed companion closer, then rolled onto his back. His eyes flickered over her face as he drew her willing body down to receive his hard shaft.

Discovering that she was wet and eager for him.

And that he was, as always, totally dead inside.

"Oh yes, Dane. Please! Now—take me now." His mistress's green eyes closed and she moved urgently against his thighs. Faint beads of sweat hung across her brow.

His face hard, Ravenhurst moved to comply. After all, he thought grimly, one did not disappoint a lady. Especially when she was as beautiful and provocative as Danielle was. "With the greatest pleasure, my dear."

Upward he drove, timing his powerful thrusts to coincide with her wild downward arch. Above him his mistress began to pant, her breath torn by jerky sobs.

A vein throbbed at Ravenhurst's temple. Desire began to crest through his veins. Groaning hoarsely, he slipped his hand between their straining bodies.

His mistress threw back her head, crying out in wild abandon at the fierce pleasure of his touch. When she collapsed onto his chest a moment later, the viscount turned swiftly, rolling onto his side to find his own release.

There he found the oblivion he sought, welcoming the savage flames that blazed for an instant then exploded into darkness and primal silence.

And there, Ravenhurst discovered, as always, that oblivion was not enough.

Not nearly enough.

Even before his ragged breathing had begun to still, he pulled away from Danielle's inert form and sat back against the cold headboard, his midnight eyes hard and unreadable.

The candles flickered. In the neighboring room a clock chimed quietly. On the wall, Dane watched the dancing shadows take on fanciful shapes.

Angry clouds.

Lashing waves.

Swift schooners with black sails.

Suddenly he was awash in memories. His hands clenched convulsively as he heard the masts collapse about him. Overhead, ten-pound shells shrieked across the port bow, while smoke poured from decks aflame. Grim-faced, Ravenhurst fought for balance, feeling pain rip through him as two hundred pounds of smoking cable plunged to the deck and tethered his wrists and arms to the fallen mast.

On the crisp sheets his fingers splayed open, white with strain. Once more he was carried back in time to that furious struggle to hack himself free of the deadly cables before they swept him overboard.

Again and again he lashed out, the knife slipping on his own blood. Halfway through the burning coils, the blade snapped. Just then a fierce gust of wind drove over the bow, filling the fallen sails and jerking him across the deck, where he was slammed nearly insensible against the port railing.

With a savage curse the viscount jerked upright. Sweat dotted his forehead and his broad, fur-matted chest. The smell and taste and feel of war at sea washed over him.

Trafalgar. Copenhagen. Corunna. Over and yet never over. Ignored but not forgotten.

Behind him the woman with jaded eyes frowned. Once again the dark dreams, Danielle thought bitterly. *Par Dieu,* she did not wish to lose her handsome viscount! He was a fierce, stormy lover and his nightmares only fed the dark flames of his passion.

Yes, he pleasured her as no man had ever pleasured his woman. And Danielle ought to know, given her extensive experience in such matters.

Yet even in the midst of savage, reckless coupling, he was gone from her, his mind somewhere apart while his powerful body found its release. She was too experienced a woman not to recognize that.

Her beautiful brow knit. Hadn't Moreton told her just last week that she was perfection itself? Yes, and that to die in her arms was to be reborn in paradise?

But it was far more than money that attached Danielle to this man, though she was careful never to let Ravenhurst know that. Such an admission would have spelled the death of their comfortable arrangement, for the viscount had made it all too clear that emotional attachments were to have no place in their relationship.

Danielle's tongue traced her rouged lips. She would catch him, she vowed. If she could not do it, no woman could. With a secret smile she began to stroke Dane's tense back and then reached up to massage the rigid muscles at his neck. He was a hero, after all. Perhaps all heroes had their nightmares. But Danielle did not dwell on the thought. She was far too practical to concern herself with idle speculations for long.

"What a fierce lover you are, my hungry panther," she whispered. "When you fill me with your shaft, I lose my breath—my very life. Such a wild hero," she whispered huskily. "Every inch rock hard. *Dieu,* but I cannot seem to get enough of you!" He would like that, Danielle thought. Men always liked to be praised in such things. And what good fortune for women like her that their wives were too stupid to know this.

The man beside her stiffened, his face twisting into a grimace.
Hero.

His mouth flattened to an angry line.

With fluid grace he rolled over and slipped from the sheets, frowning at the clothes scattered in a crazy line between bedpost and door. Oblivious to his nakedness, he strode to the side table and poured himself a glass of brandy.

For a long time he stared down at the amber spirits. "As I've told you before, Danielle, I am no hero," he said harshly. "Nelson was a hero. Collingwood, in his own quiet way, was a hero, but I am no more than a—"

What he would have said next was cut short by harsh pounding from the doorway two flights below. Anxious voices rose and fell on the quiet night air. The door banged shut. More tense words.

Something about that voice . . .

Ravenhurst stiffened and then jerked a silk dressing gown around his long, hard body. Stony-faced, he threw open the door.

"Oh, yer lordship, I didn't mean to—" The maid's dark eyes flickered over the broad chest exposed beneath his gown. Abruptly she looked away, her cheeks stained with color.

"Well, what's all the commotion about?" Ravenhurst demanded impatiently. His new title sat heavily on him, and he had not yet had time to grow comfortable with being called "your lordship." "Have the French finally invaded?" he asked mockingly.

"No, yer lordship," the girl explained nervously. " 'Tis a gem'mum below wot demands to see ye. Come 'ammerin' at the door, 'e did, nor wouldn't give 'is name proper-like, no matter 'ow 'ard I asked. Said as 'ow I was to tell yer lordship"—the girl frowned, trying to recall the exact words of the message—" 'time to strike yer colors and clear the decks.' Leastways, that's near as I recollect."

Dane's black eyebrows tightened into a scowl as he jerked the belt of his dressing gown about his lean waist. "Did the bastard, now? We'll bloody see about that!"

Ravenhurst strode out into the hall and down the stairs, his long legs taking the steps three at a time. His face was a dark mask when he threw open the door to the little drawing room at the rear of the house he maintained for his mistress.

A tall man exquisitely dressed in crimson coat and silver brocade waistcoat sat near the window, nursing a glass of brandy. His piercing turquoise eyes crinkled with humor as Dane pounded through the door.

"Ah, Ravenhurst, here you are at last," the uninvited guest drawled, placing his glass on the table at his side. "Desolated to make you, er, strike your colors at such a time," he murmured, his wicked smile revealing not the slightest hint of regret.

But that title, the Earl of Morland thought. How odd it sounded! "Captain St. Pierre" had suited his friend's hard countenance infinitely better.

"Tony! What the hell . . . ." Ravenhurst gave a snort of disgust as he noted his friend's negligent ease.

Anthony Langford, Lord Morland, pursed his lips and shook

his head disapprovingly. "Not done, you know. You've created quite a bloody stir in Whitehall, my friend. It seems the Admiralty has grown tired of having their emissaries thrown out upon their ears. So the Old Man paid me a rare visit to enlist my help." Morland smiled faintly. "I tried to resist, but you know how obdurate he can be. Which is how in due course I found myself deputed an emissary, in the assumption—erroneous I fear, judging by your stormy look—that you wouldn't throw an old friend out into the street." One fair eyebrow rose in a questioning slant. "You wouldn't, would you?"

Dane smothered a curse as he studied the man sitting entirely at ease in Dane's most comfortable chair, finishing a glass of his best brandy. They had met in the nightmare retreat at Corunna, when Dane arrived with the transport fleet to meet the retreating army. It had only been a matter of months since Ravenhurst had last seen his unflappable friend.

But it seemed like an eternity. Until this moment, the viscount had not realized just how much he'd missed Morland's irreverent wit.

Ravenhurst's eyes flickered to the cane at his friend's feet. "What's all this?"

For a moment Morland's face darkened, and then his eyes lit with their customary good humor. "Oh, no wounds earned in the service of King and country, more's the pity. Damned stupid accident with a new hunter, nothing more. I was saddened to hear about your—losses," Morland added, wanting to have the words spoken and done with.

The viscount's back stiffened. Dark tendrils of pain gripped his heart. Everyone said it would get better. So, why did it still seem like yesterday?

"I lost my own brother last year, you know," Morland said quietly. "Not the same, of course, but . . ."

Ravenhurst's lapis eyes sharpened, studying his friend's face. For the first time he noticed the traces of pain that Morland, too, tried to conceal.

Dane grimaced, refusing to allow sympathy to cloud his judgment. Friend or no friend, Morland had come from the Admiralty, and there could be nothing good in that.

With a careless shrug he turned and strode to a campaign chest before the far window. After pouring himself a liberal amount of brandy, he swung across the room with the long, fluid gait that had allowed him to stand a quarterdeck in any sort of weather.

Smiling grimly, he dropped into the chair opposite his friend and raised his glass. "Since it appears you've already helped yourself to my best brandy, I shan't offer you any more. So here's a toast instead. To a lasting peace and may it come soon."

Morland raised his glass in acknowledgment. They drank in silence, each falling into his own thoughts. And dark thoughts they were, heavy with the memory of friends fallen, of horrors seen and never forgotten.

After a long while Morland looked up, scanning Ravenhurst's face. " 'Tis peace, in a manner of speaking, that I've come to see you about tonight, Ravenhurst. Your wounds must be nearly healed by now, my friend. The wine and women are all very well, of course, but there comes a time when one must get back to the business of real life."

Dane returned his guest's gaze, his angular bronze face carefully devoid of expression. So this was to be the prologue, was it?

"You don't mean to make this any easier for me, do you?" Morland asked dryly.

A muscle flashed at Dane's jaw. He glared at the earl over the rim of his glass. No, by God, he didn't!

"Very well, since it looks as if I may soon become the fourth messenger to be thrown out into the street, I shall proceed directly to the point. The Old Man has stumbled onto something—something of crucial importance to the outcome of this wretched war."

"No more, Tony," Ravenhurst growled. "I don't want to have to throw you out too!"

Morland simply ignored him. "You are familiar with the area around Rye and Winchelsea, are you not? As I recall, you spent some time there before you went to join Nelson's fleet."

A flash of pain darkened Ravenhurst's face, and he continued to stare stonily at his friend. "What if I did? What bloody concern can that be of the Admiralty's?" Abruptly he tossed down the rest of his brandy, then moved to pour himself another. "Unless the Old Man has now vowed to clear the Channel coast of smugglers." His words were faintly slurred, and his fingers shook slightly on the crystal decanter.

Interesting, Morland thought, his blue eyes narrowing. *Very interesting.* "There are smugglers working that whole stretch of coast, of course. Bloody trade's endemic to the area. But the Admiralty's after bigger fish this time—and far more than smuggling. The Old Man's discovered that someone in the area is funnelling gold and military secrets to Napoleon. It looks like the Fox is our man."

Dane frowned, studying the brandy in his glass. Everyone knew of the Romney Fox, of course. Women whispered his name like a prayer, and the damned scoundrel was toasted in public houses from Dover to Brighton. Maybe even here in London, Dane thought cynically. Yet the notorious smuggler remained as much a phantom as the eerie lights said to dance over the Romney Marsh on moonless lights.

"Go on," Ravenhurst said flatly. His face was unreadable.

"He's using a ruined estate near Winchelsea, on the Sussex coast." Morland's voice dropped, carefully casual. "But perhaps you know the place."

"I doubt it. I was there for only a short time. As the Admiralty must certainly know," he added acidly.

Morland ignored the irritation in his friend's voice. "A great wreck of a place in the hills southwest of Rye, overlooking that whole stretch of coast as well as the marsh to the east. Been in the Leighton family for generations, so I understand, along with a very fine old inn in Rye itself. Fairleigh, I believe the place is called."

Fairleigh. A manor house in a sad state of decline, adjoined by a crumbling medieval ruin with sweeping parapets and crazy, twisting steps. Everything from Fairlight to Dungeness could be seen from the top of those walls. A lonely place, haunted by sad ghosts and a mournful wind.

Oh yes, I know the place, Dane thought harshly. The perfect place for a smuggler's tryst. The perfect spot to launch a fast cutter with a cargo of gold guineas bound for Napoleon.

And every word passed, every guinea traded meant another English soldier would die.

But Ravenhurst's chiseled features held no trace of these thoughts. "I don't believe I recognize the name," he lied coolly, swirling the brandy about in his glass. "Fairleigh, you say?"

"That's the place. There is absolutely no doubt that secrets are being passed. The Admiralty leaked a few on purpose just to be certain, and the information reached Paris in two days." Morland paused, tapping his cane thoughtfully with his forefinger. "The Admiralty sent an agent to investigate, of course. Several, in fact. Two months ago the last one washed up in Fairleigh Cove—with his throat slit."

Morland watched Dane's fingers tighten on the fine crystal goblet. So the Old Man was right about Fairleigh too. By God, was there anything the bloody old martinet did *not* know?

"All of this is lamentable, of course, but I fail to see how it involves me," Ravenhurst growled.

Morland took his time answering. His next words would have to be chosen with care, he knew. "Something big is building just now, Ravenhurst. Unfortunately, I am not at liberty to tell you what, but believe me when I say it may well turn out to be the key to Wellington's success on the Peninsula." His voice dropped then, to emphasize what he said next. "This traitor must be found before word of the new operation gets out. Found and disposed of, by any means necessary. Since you're familiar with the area, the Old Man deemed you the logical candidate for the job."

"Logic be damned!" Dane snarled, striding to the mantel and slamming down his glass. "By God, he doesn't ask much, does he? I've been five years from home, man, and six more in active service before that! I've lost my father, my brother, and my mother. I come back to find my . . ." His voice hardened. "My fiancée dead." His back rigid, he stared down at the puddles of brandy splashed like blood across the mantel. When he looked up his face was shuttered, set in harsh, forbidding lines.

Morland sat unmoving, looking deep into his friend's soul, where he saw reflected the cruel fragments of his own nightmares.

"I've lost the taste for fighting," Ravenhurst said finally. His fingers tightened, gripping the etched crystal goblet. "No, by God, I'm finished playing at games of war. The sea makes a damned cold and unforgiving mistress, Tony. So 'tis real women and fine wine for me, and nothing more serious to consider than the next night's pleasure!"

Morland steepled his fingers as he studied his friend's grim face. The keen blue eyes narrowed, sweeping over Dane's scarred wrists and the stark streaks of white hair blazing at his temples.

Morland knew, of course, that Ravenhurst had refused to discuss his role in the rout of Villeneuve's flagship at Trafalgar. He knew, too, that the officer had vehemently refused a commendation for his bravery in that encounter.

What troubled Morland more was that his friend refused to speak of what had come later—those hellish months last year after Corunna, months spent trekking home through enemy territory after he'd been blown overboard by an exploding shell. Oh, he'd turned in a report to the Admiralty upon his return, but it was the merest skeleton of the truth—all terrain and troop movements.

It was the rest that worried Morland, the flesh and tears of those long months. Those were the things not so easily forgotten.

They all carried the scars of this bloody war, Morland thought angrily.

And it was far from over.

Abruptly Ravenhurst spun around. "Damn it, Tony, I'll have nothing to do with it! Because you're my friend I've let you speak, but, by God, don't ever bring the subject up again!" He muttered a graphic curse, balling his fists and thrusting them deep within the pockets of his silk dressing gown.

Morland sighed. "I quite understand, my friend. Better than you realize, perhaps." Slowly the earl uncoiled his long frame and stood up, trying to conceal his regret. This assignment of the Old Man's might have been the perfect prescription for Dane. He'd been raking about London for almost six months now, ever since his return to town, and all he had to show for his dissipation was a new set of lines about his mouth and forehead.

But one could only ask, after all. In the end, the decision had to be Ravenhurst's.

Morland averted his face, making a great business of locating his silver-topped cane, which had dropped to the floor. When he finally straightened, his face was carefully expressionless. "So. That's that. I had to make one last attempt—for the Old Man's sake, if not for mine." *And for your sake,* Tony thought. He forced his features into a faint smile. "Go ahead and enjoy yourself, my friend. You've earned it, God knows. And give my regards to that daunting old dragon of an aunt when next you see her. I still haven't forgotten the way she trounced me at faro." He raised a dismissing hand as Dane moved to follow him to the door. "No need to see me out. You've got other matters to attend to right now, unless I'm sadly mistaken."

Morland gathered his gloves and shrugged on his greatcoat. Without another word he turned and made his way awkwardly from the room.

For a long time Dane stood listening to the echo of his friend's halting footsteps. The limp was slight but unmistakable as Morland moved down the quiet street.

With a bitter curse, the viscount tossed down the last of his brandy, then lowered his head to his hands. Bracing his forehead, he scowled down at the cold, empty grate.

So the Fox was using that great old wreck at Fairleigh for a base, was he? Dane's midnight eyes narrowed. Hard to believe. The man's reckless bravery and generosity to the local folk had reached legendary proportions, even here in London. Aye, the Fox would be a hard man to run to ground.

But now he'd tired of landing tea and brandy. Now he itched to play a deeper game—running secrets and gold to aid Napoleon's armies.

The bloody scum! Icy fury licked at Dane's blood. Every fact whispered, every guinea traded meant more English blood spilled. Didn't the scoundrel realize that? Or didn't he care?

And what of *her?* Ravenhurst wondered. If the Fox was working from Fairleigh, how could *she* not be involved?

"Tess." The word trembled in the chill air, no more than a reluctant whisper.

He'd said the name at last. The act purged him somehow, allowing him a brutal detachment—enabling him to remember all the cold, sordid details of their final encounter.

Ravenhurst's face darkened, his eyes icy lapis shards. Was she the Fox's woman now? Did they laugh together in bed about their cleverness?

And how many other men had there been to share her bed and body?

Soleil. Like a silent scream, her name echoed through his angry thoughts. With a savage curse, Ravenhurst swung his fist down against the mantel.

Layered silk whispered suddenly from the doorway. The rich fragrance of roses drifted into the room.

"Here you are, my lord," the voluptuous Danielle purred, her voice faintly chiding. "Come back to bed before you catch a chill." Her green eyes glittered; her full lips arched in a knowing smile. "There, *mon coeur,* in that big soft bed, I shall find a most unusual way to warm you."

Dane smiled slightly as he saw the lush curves clearly outlined through her diaphanous gown. "A tempting thought, *ma chérie.* I grow warmer already."

"Ah, but of a certainty I mean to make you a great deal more warm before we're finished."

But when the viscount found himself once more beside Danielle in the tumbled sheets, his hands cupping her full breasts, his lips drinking her wild moans, his heart was filled with nothing but a terrible, numbing cold.

Dead, he was. Distant and apart from his pleasure.

Only his body functioned. Just as always, he might have been watching two strangers pursue their reckless, drugging lust. Superimposed on his mistress's face he saw another pair of eyes—gray-green and stormy. Imperious. Adoring.

Danielle's lush body convulsed around him. Even then he felt a cold detachment. Moments later he threw back his head, groaning his release against his mistress's slack mouth.

Outside in the street a carriage clattered by. The candles slowly guttered out.

Then, with a muffled oath, Ravenhurst rolled them over as one. To Danielle's surprise and very great delight her lover began to move inside her again. *Par Dieu,* he had the shaft of a stallion, this one!

If there was an air of recklessness in the viscount's passionate assault, his mistress was far too wise a woman to comment upon it. Her lips curved in a smug smile and she ran a knowing hand down his hard torso, tracing the pulsing length of his manhood.

Yes, her English viscount was a man in a thousand. Danielle of all people knew exactly how rare were his talents as a lover. But then she was a woman in a thousand too. She would catch him somehow, Danielle vowed; it was only a question of time.

When his hoarse groan filled the quiet room some minutes later, Ravenhurst was pondering a very different question.

How he would enjoy making the beautiful harlot with gray-green eyes pay for what she'd done to him five years before.

PART ONE

Five and twenty ponies,
Trotting through the dark—
Brandy for the Parson,
Baccy for the Clerk. . . .

—Rudyard Kipling

1

Camber Sands
Southeast Coast of England
May 1810

The wind was fine, high, and steady. Out to sea a line of breakers roiled their white heads across the Channel between England
and France. Thin rushing lines of cloud flashed before the slivered
moon, transforming the marsh into a world of black and silver.

A smuggler's moon, so they called it here on the Romney
Marsh, where the southern shore of England teased the coast of
France. Enough light to make it easy to slip over the sand with
uncustomed tea and brandy, but too little to give His Majesty's
riding officers a clear shot at one's back.

Close to the beach, a slim figure crouched in the lee of a sand
dune, invisible amid the rustling reeds and marsh grass. The shadowy form did not move, carefully hidden in the other black
blotches on the marsh.

Near the horizon a lugger's sails billowed in the fine wind, flashing white against the dark water. Its cargo of brandy landed, the
fleet craft ran before the wind out toward open sea, its hold now
several hundred pounds lighter.

Gradually the white sails grew smaller. Still the slim shadow
waited, motionless, caught by the beauty and peace of the marsh.

Overhead came the quiet hiss of wind-driven sand. Somewhere far in the distance a lonely curlew cried.

A beautiful world, but a very deadly one.

Without warning an excise cutter slipped from one of the myriad coves notching the coast between Hastings and Rye, meaning to give chase. But the smuggler's craft was swifter and better manned, disappearing over the horizon while the excise vessel was still gathering speed.

Well pleased, the figure watching in the dunes at last began to move. As the Crown vessel tacked and began to make its way back to Rye, the slim shadow straightened and came upright, making a graceful, mocking curtsy in the direction of the returning Revenue ship.

Moonlight played over a black tricorn hat set rakishly askew. Below the hat, long quivering whiskers radiated from a dark pelt crowned by a foxy nose.

And then the tricorn went flying. Rich auburn curls spilled down over slim shoulders. The dark animal vanished, and as the fox mask fell, full lips the color of spring strawberries curved into a delighted smile.

When the moon darted from behind the clouds, its silver glow illuminated a piquant face with upturned gray-green eyes. An unforgettable face, especially now, when it was lit with triumph.

And it was most certainly a female face; the delicate brow and chiseled nose might have been the work of a Renaissance master.

The woman's slim frame shook with silent laughter as she bent down and tossed an oilskin bag of tea over her shoulder. Dressed in tight black breeches, a baggy white shirt, and high boots, she might have been a young village lad making his way home through the marsh—except for her swaying gait and the faint curve of breast and thigh revealed by her unorthodox costume.

But no one was watching this night as Tess Leighton bent her head and caught up the heavy curls that flowed like fine burgundy in the moonlight. With a defiant smile she stuffed her hair back under the tricorn and tossed her black cloak about her shoulders.

No more tears for Tess Leighton! No more poverty, she swore, her young face hard with determination. No more insults and pitying glances.

Her father was dead and the bleak past behind her. She'd made a new life for herself—a good life, no matter what others might say. Yes, she was strong and whole again. Under her deft management the fourteenth-century inn that had been in the Leighton family for generations was flourishing. Soon she would have enough money to be free of the monstrous debts her father had left.

And after that?

Theresa Ariadne Leighton froze, listening to the high, lonely notes of a kestrel. *Kee-lee, kee-lee,* it sang, winging south over the blackness of the marsh.

Yes, what then?

Her eyes darkened, emerald shifting to smoky gray.

A gust of wind caught her cloak and sent it flapping about her slim legs. Shivering slightly, she caught the heavy wool and dragged it closer about her body.

She shrugged defiantly, a wild gleam flashing in the bottomless depths of her eyes.

Why, then she'd settle down and become a fine lady, so she would! 'Twould suit her nicely to take tea before a crackling fire when her days with the free traders were done. But not for a while yet.

Her full lips quirked as she thought of the customs inspector's fury when he discovered that more contraband cargo had been slipped ashore, right beneath his eyes. She almost wished she might be there to hear Amos Hawkins's curses.

Yes, there would be no more tears for Tess. This new life was exactly what she needed.

After a final look out to sea, the woman who dared to masquerade as the Romney Fox darted to the brow of the dune, her feet whispering across the sand. A moment later her slim form vanished into the black and silver silence of the marsh.

Viscount Ravenhurst reined in his horse, frowning. For long moments he stared out over the leaden marsh, dismal in the strange half-light. A light drizzle began to fall and he jerked his collar up about his neck. In the distance he could just make out the rooftops and church spires of Rye, an inland isle surrounded by a dark, waving sea of marsh grass.

He was cold and hungry. He was also devilishly out of shape, Ravenhurst realized. He had muscles aching where he hadn't even known muscles existed. Right now all he wanted was a hot bath and a long drink—not necessarily in that order.

The rain increased, seeping unpleasantly beneath his collar and trickling down between his shoulder blades. Ravenhurst hunched his broad shoulders beneath his greatcoat and scowled, wondering why he had ever agreed to accept this wretched assignment.

Something drew his eyes to the south, where a tangled network of dikes and canals glimmered in the faint light of a half moon.

Soon even that light would be gone, he thought, studying the heavy storm clouds rolling in off the Channel.

Suddenly he stiffened. There it was again, the faintest tingling along his neck. Uneasiness—and something more.

Abruptly he straightened in the saddle, his sore muscles and aching neck forgotten as he spurred Pharaoh forward across the deserted flood plain.

"Wait, Cap'n! Over there near the reeds! I swear I saw something move!"

It was one of Amos Hawkins's men, Tess realized as she hunched down beside a low wall of marsh grass at the edge of one of the many canals crisscrossing the marsh.

In the distance she heard Hawkins's angry curses as his men pounded inland, searching for their quarry. Suddenly one of the Revenue officers let out a bellow. "There! In the reeds. It moved again!"

Tess shivered, swallowing a moan of fear. *They'd found her!*

Desperately she blinked back tears, trying to concentrate. Her ribs were aching where she had fallen during her passage through the marsh, and her feet were leaden. Her heart hammering, she crouched lower, praying that the thick foliage would conceal her.

From the far side of the river Hawkins began bellowing orders.

Tess's haunted eyes rose to the high ground in the distance, where the ragged turrets of the old priory stood silhouetted against a pale, rising moon.

Fairleigh, she thought, shivering. *What madness have you driven me to this time?*

But there was no time for regrets, no time for fear.

Not with Hawkins only minutes behind her.

So she gritted her teeth and began to move, ignoring the pain at her side and the cold creeping over her feet. Soon her slender shadow was caught up in the vast sea of shadows scudding beneath the leaden sky.

Ravenhurst's mood grew steadily blacker as he crossed Gibbett's Marsh, his greatcoat sodden, his boots squishing against the stirrups.

Abruptly his eyes narrowed. Unless he was mistaken, that solid wall of black before him was the line of warehouses along the quay.

Nearly there, thank God! Moments later the steep length of Mermaid Street was before him. Pharaoh's hooves echoed sharply as they struck cobblestone.

The city seemed deserted. Only one faint light glimmered at the top of the hill.

Frowning, Dane reined in his horse. Once again he felt that strange, jarring twinge at his spine.

Three figures slipped from the shadows. "Don't move, traveler," the man in front ordered harshly. "Keep yer hands clear o' yer coat an' state yer business in Rye." As he spoke, the man slid the muzzle of a musket from beneath his cloak, revealing a crimson uniform.

So the dragoons were out this night, were they? Ravenhurst gathered his reins loosely in one hand.

Just in case.

"My business is with the magistrate, but first I'm bound for the Angel, where I mean to stay the night."

"What sort o' business?" the dragoon demanded, moving to block Dane's path.

The fellow's surly tone set Dane's teeth on edge. He had never liked bullies—whether they were French or English. Nor did he care to stare down the muzzle of a gun.

"My business is of an official nature," he growled. "The maintenance of the Royal Military Canal, to be exact." Damn! He hadn't meant to make his presence in Rye known just yet. But these men gave him no choice.

Ravenhurst's hard lapis eyes flickered across the man's uniform. "I am Viscount Ravenhurst, the new commissioner. I trust that answers your question, Sergeant."

Something about the angry snap of command in that gravelly voice made the dragoon take an unconscious step backward. Ravenhurst did not wait for a response, spurring Pharaoh on up the lane.

His neck prickled, and he could feel the men's cold gaze upon him all the way to the top.

Twenty minutes later Tess finally reached the edge of the flood plain.

Around her all was quiet. The drizzle had nearly stopped and trailing clouds danced before the moon. Seeing no sign of Hawkins or his men, she bent over and drew in great lungfuls of air. Even though it was May, the cold was fierce. Her teeth were chattering and her feet and fingers were numb. She felt very light, weightless almost, as if she were floating over the ground.

By the time she reached the old cottage on the edge of the marsh and dropped an oilskin bag with China tea for Widow Hargate, the moon had slipped low in the sky. In the distance she could see the dark spires of St. Mary's rising above the rooftops of Rye.

Ashen-faced, she skirted Gibbett's Marsh and made for Wish Street. Her eyes dim and unfocused, she slipped between fences and darkened yards, avoiding the main streets. Her left rib throbbed where she had fallen over a rock on the marsh, and only raw willpower kept her on her feet now.

Five yards more. Four, she told herself, panting.

Soon she'd be safe. A fire. Dry clothes.

Three yards more.

Can't stop now can't stop now.

Before her the dark, narrow mouth of the Needles passage beckoned.

And then she saw the dark shape at the alley's mouth. He was a big man, his broad shoulders blotting out the moon's weak light. Unmoving, he stood at the entrance to the narrow passage, enveloped in a greatcoat and a cloud of smoke.

Dear Lord, why did he choose this place to blow a cloud? What in the name of heaven was she to do now?

From the lower reaches of the street came the angry snap of curses and the restless neighing of horses.

"Brown, take five men and scour the docks!" Amos Hawkins bellowed from the top of the street. "Boggs, go around to Mermaid Street. The rest of ye come with me. I want that bloody vermin and I don't care how ye catch him! Five hundred pounds for the man who brings me the Fox!"

Tess stifled a sob as Hawkins's eager officers thundered up the street behind her. Dear God, she was trapped!

In her panic, one weary foot struck a broken slab of cobblestone and sent it skittering down the lane. Immediately, she shrank back into the shadows, pressing herself against a darkened doorway. There she froze, her heart pounding wildly.

Too late! The man in the passage had turned, and although his face was in shadow, Tess could feel his keen eyes plumb the dark silence of the street. For long moments he stood motionless, then finally turned and braced his tall frame against the far corner of the passage.

Releasing a silent breath, she turned to scan the nearby houses, searching for a better place to hide.

Without warning a pair of iron hands seized her shoulders.

"What have we here? Hawkins's elusive prey, perhaps?"

With a wild cry, Tess twisted away, pounding furiously at those hard fingers. But her flailing fists might as well have been marsh flies.

"If so, you're a small prize," her captor growled, searching her face intently. "And a damned filthy one at that."

Tess breathed a prayer of thanks that she'd stuffed Jack's whiskered mask into the pocket of her voluminous cape before she'd left the marsh. The tricorn would conceal her hair. She only hoped that the charcoal she'd rubbed into her skin had not streaked away to nothing.

Outside the passage the drum of feet grew louder.

For a moment she swayed, and then sharp fingers caught her, pressing her back against the rough brick wall. "The Fox trains you young, doesn't he?" her captor said roughly. "By God, you can't be more than thirteen or fourteen! Just a bloody boy."

"Lemme go, ye scoundrel! I'll teach ye to go botherin' us innocent folk!" Instinctively Tess lapsed into a broad country dialect, for she knew she must keep her identity secret at all cost.

Her slim legs whipped wildly, seeking a target. With each movement her bulky cloak swept wildly about her slim body until she was suffocating in thick layers of cold, damp wool.

But the man only laughed, turning sideways and crushing her against the wall with the full weight of his massive body. "You're spirited, I'll say that for you, boy. Ten pounds of cloak and ninety pounds of fight!"

His breath was warm, tinged with the scent of brandy. Even though she knew it was useless, Tess continued to struggle. The wild movement brought her flush against the man's broad chest and the hard line of his thighs.

She felt her face flame crimson beneath the layers of charcoal.

"Stop fighting, you fool!" the stranger hissed.

Something about that gravelly voice of silk and steel cut deep into her memory, plummeting down through the layers of bitter reserve built up over long years. Down it slashed, stripping her bare as it stirred a deep wellspring of pain.

A cruel pain she had forced from her mind five years ago. A pain she had thought forgotten.

Until now.

In a daze she felt the man's rigid thighs grind against her hips and she stifled a sob.

For it had all come back to her, the memories lashing her with the sullen fury of a Channel squall.

Not a stranger's voice at all.

The voice of Dane St. Pierre, the man she had once loved with all the unbridled force of her innocent young soul.

Dear God, it could not be!

But there was no mistaking the rough timbre of that voice nor those hard cobalt eyes.

Midnight eyes. The eyes of a man who had taken her heart and stripped it into little pieces, then turned and walked out of her life without the slightest regret.

Tess froze, nearly crying out with the searing pain of those memories.

Cold and damp, her captor's fingers moved to her throat.

"Damn ye!" she croaked hoarsely. "Lemme go, ye filthy scum!" She managed to pull away and jerk her knee up toward his groin, but he turned sharply, trapping her leg with his own. Then his hard body pinned her against the wall.

"Quiet, you fool!" Ravenhurst growled, his hand digging cruelly into the soft skin at her throat. "Unless you wish Hawkins to find you!"

Outside the mouth of the passage came the stamp and neigh of restive horses.

Dane's fingers tensed warningly, his taut body forcing her back, crushing the pair of them against the wall of the passage.

Heart to heart they stood, thigh to damp thigh. Tess swayed dizzily, awash with memories, drowning in his rich scent.

She inhaled the mingled tang of sea salt and tobacco, brandy and wet wool. And beneath it the elusive man smell—clean and faintly smoky. How familiar it all was—almost as if those long years of separation had never existed.

Every taut ridge of muscle, every line of bone and sinew was molded against Tess's acutely sensitized form. Her stomach cushioned his straining thighs and her chin was wedged against his chest. Through her damp garments she could feel the heat of his skin; beneath his parted greatcoat she heard the fierce pounding of his heart.

Or was it *her* heart?

The rough, damp wool chafed her nipples, which instantly rose to taut peaks. Desire, wild and irrational, knifed through her trembling body, and she shuddered, awash in a sea of raw sensation and cruel memories.

Dane, her blood whispered. *Why did you let it end that way? And why did you ever come back?*

From the top of the lane came the sharp clatter of more hooves. "You, there! Halt, I say, in the King's name!" Quick feet tapped across the street.

"What're ye stopping for, fools?" Hawkins bellowed from the foot of the hill. "Nothing there but a bloody cat! Now, bring me those godrotting smugglers! Tonight, I say! Round up anyone with a grain of sand on his boots or a blade of marsh grass in his hair. They'll tell me what I want to know, by God, or I'll have their tongues from their heads! Now, get moving or ye'll lose yer man while ye stand there gawping!"

The horses plunged up the lane, their hooves ringing harshly in Tess's ears, and a moment later the excise force thundered past the mouth of the passage.

Finally the night grew quiet, the sharp voices trailing away to distant murmurs. Tess let her breath play out in a quiet rush.

Immediately Ravenhurst's iron fingers tightened in warning at her throat.

"Release me, ye great sapskull!" she hissed furiously, prying at his hands.

Before she knew it, she was slapped back against the wall, her captor's breath searing her chilled skin.

As her rib ground against a protruding piece of brick, she fought down a sob. *No tears!* she thought wildly. *I mustn't give myself away by a flood of weeping. Mustn't let him know I'm not the boy he takes me for!*

"Now then," her captor said silkily, his voice tinged with menace. "Let's have a look at Hawkins's elusive prey."

In vain Tess struggled, while he dragged her toward a faint square of moonlight slanting down into the narrow passage. Wild with terror, she wrenched against his grip. When she felt his arm brush her face, she bit down fiercely.

The man beside her growled with surprise as much as pain.

Cursing fluently, he forced her hands behind her back. "One more trick like that, boy, and I turn you over to Hawkins! From what I hear about the man, you'd find that little to your liking!" His keen eyes narrowed, searching her grimy face. "Your youth would do you no good at Dover jail, you fool. If the disease didn't kill you, the other men would—after they'd first used you for their unnatural pleasures, of course." Stony-faced, the tall man waited for his words to sink in.

Tess shivered. Her struggling abruptly ceased. She could never hope to win a contest of strength with him anyway. No, keen wits were what she needed now.

"That's better. No reason we can't be allies." Her captor laughed grimly. "Or neutral parties, at least while you consider my proposition."

A wild, brittle laugh escaped Tess's dry lips. Proposition? Could he have guessed his quarry was a woman?

Ravenhurst stiffened. Scowling, he turned his captive's face into the bar of moonlight, trying to discern the features hidden beneath the heavy layer of charcoal. Impatiently he jerked her cloak aside and hauled her closer.

And that is when his arm grazed soft flesh. Warm, pliant curves.

Immediately Ravenhurst's whole body froze. He knew a woman's breast when he felt one, by God!

He snapped out a cold expletive. "So the Fox welcomes women to his band, does he?" Catching her wrists in one large hand, Ravenhurst brought his other hand back to verify this startling discovery.

Tess fought wildly, terrified by what he might do next. But she was weak and dizzy from her flight and he overpowered her easily. When his hard fingers traced the curve of her breast, scarce concealed by her damp shirt, she had no strength left to resist.

His exploration was slow and ruthlessly thorough.

To her horror, Tess felt her nipple grow taut beneath those hard, probing fingers.

Her captor's breath checked. Once more his hand moved against her, but this time his touch was lingering and provocative.

His long fingers curved, cupping and teasing the furled bud with expert skill.

A little whimper escaped Tess's clenched lips. Dear God, how could this be happening to her?

With a growl of triumph, the man in the shadows anchored her hands above her head and forced her back against the wall. His full lips curved in a dark, knowing smile. "Not so young that you don't know a woman's passion, I see. I only wonder if the rest of you can feel half so good."

Grim-faced, Ravenhurst began working the buttons of her shirt free, relentlessly pushing aside the thin, damp fabric even as Tess tried to struggle against him. But he ignored her, his eyes narrowed, sweeping over the pale curves and shadowed crests faintly illumined in the moonlight.

He could see too damned little, but what he did see was more than enough to set him on fire.

Desire exploded through his groin, and his manhood strained hotly against his breeches.

By God, he wanted her, soot-faced and all, even if she was nothing but a common smuggler's doxy! But something told Ravenhurst this body of hers was young and sweet. And it had been four long weeks since he'd bedded a woman.

Yes, by God, why not?

Slowly he bent his head until his lips captured one pouting crest.

The woman in his arms trembled and moaned sharply, struggling against him.

So she felt it too, did she? Ravenhurst had heard that ragged note of passion too many times before not to recognize it now. She probably thought a little fighting would net her a higher price, he decided cynically.

His blood surging thick and hot through his veins, he took her other nipple into his mouth, nipping then suckling her fiercely. Another tremor shook her, and he smiled darkly.

God, she was a responsive little wench! Some primal instinct told him this woman would not feign or perform, as his manipulative mistress had so often done. No, this little beauty would challenge him with every breath, struggling and biting.

And then she would moan and arch beneath his teasing fingers, hot and wanton, all wet, hungry woman.

Ravenhurst's breath caught as he had a sudden urge to find out what she tasted like everywhere, starting at the dusky triangle between her thighs.

Go ahead, a dark voice whispered. *She's hot and eager, yours for the taking.*

Ruthlessly Dane anchored her head and nipped her bottom lip, then drew the soft, swollen flesh between his teeth.

Take her now!

Locked in his savage grip, Tess caught back a sob, wrenching against this unthinkable onslaught. Her cheeks burned beneath the thick charcoal. She had to get away or everything would be lost! "Take yer bloody hands off o' me!" she cried, hating the ragged note of passion in her voice. "Yer nothin' but scum, just like the rest o' yer gentry kind wot comes prowlin' here fer sport."

In the shadows Ravenhurst frowned, hearing something other than passion in her voice, something that sounded like raw fear.

"If that's fear I hear, then you're playing a damned dangerous game, my girl," he growled, fighting against the hot tide of his desire. His breath sounded harsh and uneven in his ears, and he cursed fluently beneath his breath.

What in bloody hell was wrong with him? He hadn't felt this way since he was a randy stripling! "But perhaps I could interest you in a different sort of proposition tonight."

"When pigs kin fly!" Tess spat furiously, straining sideways in a desperate attempt to escape.

But his hard thighs held her immobile against the wall. "God help you if Hawkins finds you," he growled.

"Aw, the devil fly away wi' that great black sod of an excise officer!" Tess snapped with false bravado. "Come t' think of it, the devil fly away wi' yerself too!"

"Oh yes, our friend Hawkins has a liking for a woman with some fight in her." Tess's cold-eyed captor continued harshly, just as if she hadn't spoken. "I hear he enjoys beating the spirit out of his women. Almost as much as he enjoys the things he can make them do then—the more degrading the better. No, a night with

Hawkins would not be an experience you'd relish, wench, no matter how fiery you try to appear." His eyes narrowed on her face, half-concealed beneath the jaunty tricorn. "And something tells me it would be a shame to see the light extinguished in those luminous eyes of yours."

Tess shivered, knowing that he spoke the truth about Hawkins. She remembered some of the rumors she had heard about Rye's surly customs inspector. But even if Ravenhurst was right, she refused to show any fear. "What sort of services was ye speaking of before?" she demanded, her voice sullen.

"First, let me see your face."

"Not bloody likely! Too dangerous by half. Ye'd only betray me, and then we'd both be found trussed and drowned in some lonely ditch! The Fox has eyes everywhere, don't ye know?"

"Perhaps you're right," Ravenhurst said slowly, searching her soot-darkened face.

Tess waited, frozen, praying he would not recognize her. It had been five years after all, and her features were nearly concealed by the charcoal.

After long moments her captor appeared to come to some sort of decision. "Listen hard then, woman. I'm in need of information, and I'll pay you well if you can tell me what I need to know."

"Now, why would a fine gen'lemum like yerself be asking the likes o' me fer information?"

"I have my reasons."

"Just what sort o' information ye be seeking?" she countered warily.

"How to contact the Romney Fox."

Tess's gasp exploded like thunder in the narrow space between them. "That ye can't never do!"

"I must," the man with the shadowed face growled. "You work for him. I can tell by your voice that you fear him, but you respect him too. So think hard on this. His very life depends on my talking to him. A great deal *more* than his life, in fact."

What was the madman talking about? Tess wondered wildly, struggling afresh, afraid of the ruthless determination she saw in Dane's strange, cold eyes. "Reck'n the Fox wouldn't see it that way. No, he don't meet wi' nobody. Dangerous even t' think about it an' that's a bloody fact! Now lemme go, ye villain! Before I'm seen talkin' wi' ye!"

But Tess struggled in vain against his unrelenting grip. Dear God, let it end! She couldn't keep up this masquerade much longer!

"Listen, wench, I don't ask you to tell me the man's name, nor to inform on him. Just carry a message for me. Tell him I want a meeting—at a time and place of his choosing. On his terms. But it must be soon," Ravenhurst added harshly.

"Can't be done, damn ye! Ha'n't ye ears in yer head? Too bleedin' dangerous! Besides, I dunno the Fox's name. Dunno nothin' about him—no one does! Rises like mist on the marsh, he does, and disappears just the same."

The hard fingers tightened their grip. Suddenly her captor's face was close enough for his hot breath to sear her cheek. "Listen to me, you little fool," he growled. "This is more important than a miserable smuggling run. It's more important than you or I or even your bloody Fox! Men's lives are at stake—thousands of them!" He cursed graphically, releasing one wrist to dig down into the pocket of his greatcoat.

A moment later Tess felt a cold circular shape dig into her palm. She looked down, frowning at the gold guinea she saw there.

"That's only the first, if you help me. There'll be many more—and all you have to do is carry my messages."

Tess's head was spinning. The fool didn't know it, but he'd come to the right quarter for communicating with the Fox, sure enough! If the whole situation weren't so ghastly, she might almost have laughed.

But perhaps two could play at this game of spying, Tess realized, her gray-green eyes glittering. "How much ye pay then?" she demanded warily. "If I make up my mind t' help ye, that is. Which I ain't sayin' as I will or I won't do."

Ravenhurst smiled mockingly. The money had done it, of course. It always did. "A great deal—one hundred pounds, say. Provided you perform your services satisfactorily."

Tess couldn't conceal a gasp of surprise. Such a sum would be a veritable fortune for the country wench he took her to be!

"And a pardon if you choose to leave the free traders, as you call them. Something I'd strongly advise," Ravenhurst added grimly, "for you've little future before you otherwise. If another man had caught you tonight . . ."

He didn't need to finish. Tess had been thinking the same thing herself.

"Another man might not have been content with touching you like this," Dane said hoarsely, his eyes lit with cobalt fires. His fingers found her nipple and he pulled her closer into the hard heat of his body. "Or like this," he growled, his hand slipping between them to knead her stomach. He reached lower, cradling the warm mound of her womanhood. "Aye, another man might not have stopped at all, for this wanton response of yours inflames a man beyond imagining. Something you must be well aware of," he added roughly.

Without warning his head dipped and he took her shocked mouth in a hard, scorching kiss. At the same moment his fingers tightened on the sensitive delta that her breeches made so accessible to him.

What was it about the wench that set his blood aflame? Ravenhurst wondered. He'd had women aplenty in London, but none had made his groin ache the way this one did! He could almost see how she would look with her pale thighs open to him. Yes, she would twist and fight like a little tigress.

And then she'd moan for him to fill her.

Just the way he'd have Tess Leighton moaning soon enough, he vowed grimly.

The woman in his arms struggled, cursing, certain he must recognize her any minute. Finally one straining hand broke free and flew to his face, clawing wildly as her sharp nails raked his cheek.

"You bloody little hellcat!" A muscle flashed at the hard line of Ravenhurst's jaw as he caught Tess's arm and forced her elbow behind her. Relentlessly he dragged her head back, kissing her with savage, punishing force until she stopped fighting and went limp in his arms.

Something about the ragged little sob that escaped from her swollen lips jerked Dane back from the dark grip of passion. He blinked, shocked to feel his heart pounding. God, how he wanted her! Her mouth was sweet, warm with honey that he couldn't begin to get enough of.

Suddenly all he could think of was her naked body, pale and frenzied as he took her right there in the darkness of the passage.

With a curse Ravenhurst drew back, shaking his head sharply. What in God's name was he doing? She was a common trollop and a traitor at that! Why did her body inflame him so?

"Lemme go," the woman in his arms whispered brokenly. "'Afore someone sees me wi' ye. Not sayin' as I will or I won't help ye. But I'll think on it."

There it was again. That note of blind, unreasoning panic. But there was something else about that voice, Dane thought, frowning.

Then the elusive thread of thought was lost, for all he could hear was the blood surging hot and heavy through his veins. All he could think of was the heated silk of her skin.

"Think all you want, but don't take too long," he growled. "I'll be at the Angel until my house opposite is readied. Ask for Viscount Ravenhurst."

Tess's heart lurched in her chest. Dear God, not at the Angel! Never there! It would be more than she could bear.

She swayed and would have fallen had his hands not circled her waist. In the process he brushed her rib, still throbbing from her fall upon the marsh. She stiffened, gasping with pain.

Instantly Ravenhurst's hands froze. "You're hurt? Why didn't you tell me, you little fool? Best be on your way then," he ordered grimly. "Otherwise, you'll be of no use to either of us. Have you far to go?"

"Not so far," Tess said quickly, fighting the chaos of her thoughts, unable to believe even now that this was Dane, her lover, come back after five long and barren years.

Come back to mock and torment her.

Come back to shatter her hard-won confidence and endanger the tenuous security of her new life.

Suddenly Tess's throat constricted, wedged with anger and bitterness.

Grimly she cursed herself for her weakness, for feeling anything at all for this man. It must be the shock of seeing him again, she told herself. Nothing more.

But even now she could feel the treacherous heat of desire. Haunting memories, dark and sweet, swept over her, along with the tortured dreams that always followed in their wake.

And in that moment Tess knew she hated this man.

Even more than she had once loved him.

"How do I contact you?"

Tess stiffened, called back to the present by that flat, impersonal question. "Ye don't. I can allers find ye. When—an' if—it's necessary." She grimaced, cursing the unsteadiness of her voice.

Suddenly a gust of wind rattled up the passage, sending little pebbles skittering across the cobblestones and flying into her face.

"Lemme go now," she ordered coldly, awakened at last from the dark spell of her memories. "Moon's near gone, an' I'm fair dead on my feet."

But her frowning captor did not move.

Furiously, she balled her hands into fists and drove them against his chest. "If I'm seen wi' ye, we're both lost!" she raged.

She had to get away! Her ribs were burning and she could barely stay upright.

With a raw, smothered curse Ravenhurst released her and took a quick, angry step backward. What in bloody hell was wrong with him, anyway?

Immediately the soot-faced urchin shot toward the haven of the street.

Only to discover a pair of Hawkins's dragoons posted at the next corner.

2

A shot rang out, whining angrily past Tess's ear. From the distance came an answering shout.

Desperately she turned and fled back into the narrow passage, where hard fingers dragged her into the darkness. Her heart was pounding so loudly that she could barely hear his next words.

"Leave this to me," Ravenhurst hissed.

Suddenly the night exploded into noise and curses.

"Come out, ye bloody vermin!" Amos Hawkins bellowed angrily. "I've got ye now, by God! Yer bleeding carcass ain't worth the dirt ye're standing in. So move yer arse, afore I get tired of waiting and send a few balls in just to hurry ye out."

Tess felt the hard hands release her shoulders. She watched Dane move toward the mouth of the passage, where the moon cast dancing shadows over a tense half-circle of excisemen and dragoons.

"You're out late tonight, gentlemen." Ravenhurst's tanned face was expressionless as he stepped from the darkness. His eyes narrowed on the heavy figure who sat the center horse. "Inspector Hawkins, I take it. Busy hunting foxes, Inspector?" he asked mockingly.

The squat Revenue officer's hands clenched convulsively upon the reins. The godrotting Fox had made a fool of him again! And before this damned arrogant Londoner! "My men told me they'd stopped ye down near the quay, Ravenhurst. I expect that was yer horse we found tethered over Land Gate way." Hawkins's small eyes narrowed. "So what're ye doing over here?"

"Merely enjoying the night air, Inspector. That is still permitted in England, I trust," the viscount drawled.

"Walk where ye like—Holborn or Hades—just so long as ye keep out of my way!" Hawkins snarled. "For I'll have my fox and the devil take anyone who tries to stop me. Right now the bastard's close enough I can smell him!" He hesitated slightly. "See anything odd while ye was out here, Ravenhurst?"

"I?" The single vowel resonated with mocking contempt.

Hawkins bit back a curse. "No matter. I'll have the bastard by morning. Aye, and he'll be glad to face the gallows after I'm done with him!" The inspector laughed once, a cold, flat sound. His colorless eyes flickered over the large man before him. "Now, get out of my way, Ravenhurst! This is my turf. It would be a terrible shame for a naval hero like yerself to meet with an accident on a dark night, now wouldn't it?"

Ravenhurst did not move so much as a muscle. The silence stretched out between them, the air fairly snapping with tension. Behind Hawkins a skittish horse began to dance. Somewhere in the half-circle a dragoon cleared his throat nervously.

Stony-faced, the viscount let the silence trail on until it became a deadly insult. When he finally spoke, there was an edge of menace to his voice. "I like nothing more than a good scuffle, Hawkins. I'd advise you to remember that. Remember also that I find the night air bracing, which is why I take a walk every evening. You would make a grave mistake if you tried to deprive me of that pleasure."

"If that's yer idea of pleasure, then ye're welcome to it!" Hawkins snarled. "Now, get out of my way, for I'm on the King's business!"

After a moment, Ravenhurst took a leisurely step backward, watching in silence as the excise officers swept up the High Street and disappeared around a corner.

This was precisely what Tess had been waiting for. As soon as she heard the horses plunge into motion, she fell to her knees. Her nervous fingers swept the wall, seeking an uneven brick just above the gutter. She felt a small notch, yanked out the brick, and hooked her fingers through a metal ring hidden beneath.

Now came the struggle to lift the hidden trap door.

Long heartbeats later, darkness yawned before her as she stood above the entrance to a secret tunnel which rose to her room at the Angel. It was a tunnel only she and three other people in the world knew existed.

Unfortunately, there would be no time to brush away her footprints or scatter dirt about the entrance. She was only glad the moon was thin and her pursuer had no lantern.

Her heart pounding, Tess stumbled down into the stagnant darkness, pulling the door closed behind her. Grimacing with pain, she tried to muffle the bang of the heavy metal plate as it dropped into place.

For breathless seconds she stood unmoving in the dank silence. Above her came a muffled curse, followed by the sharp stamp of feet, which halted directly overhead.

With a little ingenuity he might find the secret notch, she thought wildly. Then he would remove the brick and discover the door. If he did, all would be lost!

A boot scraped overhead. Hard fingers brushed the door.

Lungs straining, Tess waited mutely, afraid to breathe, praying that Ravenhurst wouldn't discover the false cobblestones mortared to a frame of iron and oak.

Finally, after what seemed an eternity of waiting, the steps swept off toward the mouth of the passage. Then and only then did she release the stale air blocked in her aching throat.

Too close! And she was getting far too cocky. The next time, she might not be so lucky.

As if this night, by any stretch of the imagination, could be called lucky.

Trailing her fingers along the damp earthen walls, Tess stumbled upward toward the faint light far above, where warmth and safety beckoned.

At the top of Mermaid Street Amos Hawkins savagely reined in his mount. Long and hard he cursed, blind with rage.

"Where'd the devil go?" he demanded, reaching down to cuff a nervous exciseman standing nearby. "Well, Boggs?"

"We searched the docks, but he weren't there. sir," the man added, a moment too late. For his lapse he received another blow.

Hawkins's fingers twisted convulsively in the reins. "Very well, then." His small eyes narrowed, flat and entirely colorless. "I see we'll have to try this another way."

Ravenhurst's shoulders were stiff with cold when he reined in Pharaoh before the Angel's half-timbered walls near the top of Mermaid Street. He ignored the hard-eyed gaze of a pair of Amos Hawkins's preventive officers posted across the street.

The ancient building was just as he remembered it from five years before, hung with creepers and flowering roses, its gleaming latticed windows bright and inviting. A few errant raindrops splashed onto the cobblestones as Dane passed under a narrow overhang and made his way to the stables in the rear.

Some instinct had made him ride past the old inn an hour earlier and nudge Pharaoh along the dark, rain-slick streets. Surveying enemy terrain? he asked himself. Or was it simply reliving old memories?

"Hellish night, ain't it?" A diminutive figure scuttled out of the shadows. "Seekin' a room?"

"If this is the Angel, I am." Ravenhurst smiled grimly. He must be careful to preserve the fiction that he was a stranger to this place. Until he met the Angel's mistress, at least. Surprise was always a tactical advantage.

"So it is, an' ye'll find no better lodgin's in fifty miles." The slim lad of twelve or thirteen pushed his black hat off his brow until it sat jauntily askew. Slowly he ran a hand along the neck of Dane's horse. "Prime bit o' horseflesh ye got there, mister. I'll see he's rubbed down proper. Fair to soaked, he is." He slanted a look up at Ravenhurst. "Looks like ye both are," he added.

Ravenhurst swung down from the saddle, tossed over the reins and strode into the stable. Once inside he took off his hat and shook the rain from the brim. "So we are at that. That poor beast of mine is sadly in need of a warm stall and an extra ration of oats. Aye, damned unpleasant out there on the marsh tonight."

"Came Gibbett's Corner way, did ye? Past the windmill?"

The viscount nodded, wondering at the sudden tension in the lad's voice.

"An' yer saw nothin'? Nothin' unusual?" Keen curiosity lit the boy's dark eyes. Curiosity and something else.

Regret? Dane wondered. "Ought I to have seen something? There can be few travelers foolish enough to be abroad on such a night, after all."

The lad's shoulders slumped fractionally. "Aye," he muttered, almost to himself. "Reck'n even the Fox'd think twice afore goin' out tonight."

Ravenhurst's eyes narrowed. "Who—or what—is the Fox?" he asked coolly.

"Never heard o' the Fox? Why, everyone knows the Fox! Part man an' part devil, he is! Comes sweeping' out o' the marsh like a bat from Hell! All the dragoons in England can't catch him!"

"Well, I passed no one—neither man nor devil—as I rode in," Dane said, lifting his sodden saddlebags from Pharaoh's back. "Must be this infernal weather that keeps everyone at home."

The young man snorted. "Take more 'an a bit o' rain t' clear the streets hereabouts. No, sommat else keeps the fools at home shiverin' by their hearths."

"And what might that be?"

"Gentlemen, mebbe."

"Gentlemen?" Dane's voice was carefully casual, but his mind was working rapidly. Any information could turn out to be valuable, he knew, no matter how insignificant it might seem. His months in Spain and France had taught him that.

"Smugglers, as ye'd term 'em." The young hostler cast a careful look over his shoulder before bending closer. His voice dropped. "I cud tell ye things, mister. Aye, things to make yer hair stand on end. Why, jest last week a ridin' officer tried to shoot the Fox down. Over t' end o' Watchbell Street, it were. But he vanished like a ghost, neat as ye please! Aye, only part man, he is, an' the rest's pure devil. Can't catch him! No more 'n ye cud catch those strange lights wot play upon the marsh on moonless nights," the boy added darkly.

"Does no one know the fellow's name?"

"Naw," the hostler said smugly. "Never bin caught. Never will be, neither. Like I said, he's part man an' part—"

Dane smiled thinly. "Yes, I know—part devil."

"Don't believe me, do ye? Well, I've seen him wi' me own eyes! I cud tell ye what I seen! Give ye a guided tour, like. Only charge a guinea, I would, seein' as how ye're a stranger here an' all." His young face was expectant but oddly guileless.

So the lad had a lucrative little business gulling credulous travelers, did he? There might be something to be gleaned from his wild stories at that. But it would never do to appear too interested.

"Stirring tales of derring-do upon the marsh?" Ravenhurst's voice was hard with disbelief. "I can think of better uses for my guineas than that, thank you."

Across the courtyard a door creaked open. Abruptly the boy cleared his throat and turned to lead Ravenhurst's horse back to a stall. "Aye, I'll take care o' everything, sir, just like ye asked," he called out loudly.

"And be quick about it, Jem!" A big man garbed in sober black stood upon a narrow porch at the rear of the Angel, his face set in stern lines. He ran shrewd, assessing eyes over Dane. "If you'd care to step this way, sir." He stood back, waiting expressionlessly for the new arrival to proceed him inside.

Realizing that he'd get no more from the Angel's talkative hostler that night, Ravenhurst climbed the steps at the rear of the inn. His stomach was rumbling as he stepped into a large, well-lit kitchen bustling with activity. Beside the door a large bird with emerald and scarlet plumage shrieked loudly, rocking back and forth on its wooden perch.

"Cut line, Hobhouse!" the macaw cried, ruffling its long feathers. "Ye scurvy bilge rat!"

"Quiet, Maximilian," the object of this diatribe ordered sternly. "We found him after a privateer's ship wrecked in Winchelsea cove," he explained. "I'm afraid we can do little about his execrable language. And I trust you'll forgive me for bringing you through the rear entrance, but you looked like a man who'd taken enough water this night."

"So I had. You are Hobhouse, I take it?"

The big man nodded, leading Dane from the kitchen and down a long carpeted corridor. "I am majordomo here at the Angel," he added, with pride in his voice. "I trust Jem hasn't been plaguing you with outlandish stories. He's a good lad—when his imagination doesn't run away with him, that is."

Dane raised a dismissing hand. "No need to explain. I suspected it must be something of the sort." The smells of roasted duck and fresh bread were making Dane's mouth water, and he thought lovingly of the warm bed awaiting him upstairs.

Black eyes flickered over his sodden greatcoat. "Traveled far, have you?"

Ravenhurst had the distinct impression those shrewd eyes did not miss much. "An eternity it seems. I've been on the road since midday. I'm Ravenhurst, by the way," he added. "You should have had my letter."

Was it his imagination or did the fellow's eyes narrow?

"Of course. We have been expecting you, my lord. Shall I send your meal up to your room?"

Dane nodded grimly. The very thought was heaven after the gruelling hours spent on horseback in the rain. "I'm in no state to dine in company, as you can see. My man Peale follows me by coach and should arrive within the hour."

If the Angel's shrewd majordomo found anything odd in the viscount's travel arrangements, he was careful not to show it. Long years of catering to the whims of the Quality had trained Hobhouse not to betray surprise at any eccentricities he might encounter.

And he had encountered quite a few in his days as a servant.

"Very good, my lord," he murmured, moving briskly toward the viscount's room.

After Hobhouse left, Ravenhurst wearily shrugged out of his sodden greatcoat and tugged off his water-laden boots. Scowling, he dropped the wet articles in a heap and walked to the window, sweeping back white ruffled curtains to stare out into the night.

Below him the damp cobblestones glistened faintly in the flickering lantern light.

His shoulders were aching. His wrist was acting up again. He was frozen bloody through and so hungry he could eat his horse.

But that was not what was bothering him, not really. It was something else, something that stung the back of his neck, making the tiny hairs rise.

Below the window a handful of pebbles skittered across the cobblestones. The sound echoed, pinging hollowly in the narrow space between the buildings. Dane's lapis eyes narrowed as he studied the deserted street.

That was when he recognized the dryness in his throat and the cold feeling between his shoulder blades.

Danger. Somewhere out there in the gusty, rain-swept streets. Ravenhurst knew it as surely as he drew breath. He had honed his instincts during nightmare years in battle, and he had never before had reason to doubt them.

Yes, it was danger he felt now. Vague, faceless, and cold.

Waiting for him somewhere in the night.

The wind was howling, nearly gale force by the time Tess reached her room. Chilled and stiff with exhaustion, she could barely negotiate the last steep yards of the dank passage.

The Angel dated back to the fourteenth century, and over the long years this ancient tunnel with its rough wooden steps had sheltered smugglers, dissenters, and other fugitives from the royal wrath.

Even her father had not known about this hidden route. Tess had only found it by accident one afternoon after stripping the room bare for a thorough cleaning. In the process she'd released a hidden latch and watched in amazement as the whole bookcase had swung away from the wall. Since embarking on her dangerous masquerade as the Fox, she'd had many occasions to use the passage.

When her fingers finally traced the wooden frame of the door hidden behind a bookshelf in her private quarters, Tess breathed a weary sigh of relief. Her face white with strain, she tugged a concealed latch. The heavy door swung open.

Her maid's anxious face swam before her tired eyes. "Sweet merciful Jesus, what've you gone and done to yourself now, miss?"

Grim-faced, Tess tottered forward and began stripping off her cloak.

"Oh, Miss Tess, give it up! For God's sake, give it up! It'll be the death of you. Or something far worse," the olive-skinned maid warned shrilly.

"I'll stop when I'm ready and not a second sooner, Letty." Tess's voice was muffled as she yanked her shirt over her head. "I've come too far to stop now. Not when I'm only two thousand short of having Fairleigh free and clear for life."

Grim-faced, she bent down and began to strip off her black breeches. "My father's debts must be paid, you know that as well as I do. After that there are the manor house and priory to resurrect. For five hundred years Leightons have lived at Fairleigh, and I don't mean for the house to be lost to us now."

Kicking off the sodden breeches, Tess turned to face her anxious companion, who over time had become friend as well as servant. "It's all I have, Letty, don't you see? I can't let Fairleigh go! The roof leaks and the parapets are crumbling, but it's the only home I'll ever know. And it will take fine, bright guineas to repair it. The Angel could never give me that kind of money, no matter how popular it becomes."

Her eyes worried, Letty handed Tess a thick towel to dry with. "I don't know, Miss Tess. It just doesn't seem right, your traipsing about on the marsh with that hardened pack of smugglers."

Quickly Tess dried her skin, shivering fiercely. "The right thing doesn't always fill one's stomach, I'm afraid, Letty. It took me a long time to realize that." Tess's face hardened and her fingers tightened for a moment on the thick fabric. "Maybe too long." Abruptly she shrugged and tossed down the towel, reaching for the white cambric nightgown Letty had laid out on the bed. "And there's Ashley to be supported at Oxford. He mustn't ever learn of this."

Tess's maid answered with a derisive little snort. "Seems all he does at that place is drink, play at cards, and race his curricle with the other bloods."

"And why should he not?" Tess countered. " 'Tis the leisure sort of life he was meant for, after all."

"And *you* was born to have the same sort of life," Letty answered sharply. "Begging your pardon, miss, but just you tell me why it's yourself who's running on the marsh, taking God knows what risks to keep this place stocked with brandy and tea for flush travelers." The maid snorted loudly. " 'Tain't right, that's what I say! Master Ashley should be here helping you, taking some of the weight off your shoulders."

"Oh, hush, Letty," Tess countered, her quick smile taking the sting from the words. "Only my pride's been hurt tonight. And part of my share of the cargo is even now on its way to London. Those forty kegs of fine brandy will net me enough to start repairs on the south wall at Fairleigh and pay off the last of Father's tailors."

Letty shook her head. "Well, I don't like it, not one bit, and all that fine talk of yours won't never get me to think any different."

Tess concealed a smile. Letty's grammar never slipped, except when she was very angry.

But her maid did not seem to notice. Frowning, she held out a glass to Tess. "Now, you go on and drink this, miss. The laudanum will help you sleep tonight."

Tess's eyes narrowed as she studied the dark liquid. Her hand trembled slightly.

Only twice before, after tortuous runs, had she allowed Letty to persuade her to take this route to sleep. But tonight the draught looked very tempting.

Yes, why not? At least this way she would not wake to darkness, ripped from sleep by cruel memories.

"Go on, drink it," Letty ordered.

Quickly, before she could change her mind, Tess tilted the glass and drained its distasteful contents. Yes, this was the best way. Letty was right.

Already weak with fatigue, Tess sank down onto the settee, which her maidservant had made up into a bed. Exhausted as she was, the laudanum was probably unnecessary, but Tess meant to take no chances.

Not tonight, for some instinct told her this night held dangers beyond those she had ever known.

At that moment a fierce gust of wind rattled the window, bending down the trees and dragging their bony branches across the Angel's roof. Suddenly a tile ripped free and went hurtling down to the cobblestones, where it landed with a crash.

Something cold and menacing crept down Tess's spine.

'Tis only the wind, you fool, she told herself. Perdition! Next she would be fancying faces at the window!

But she was safe now. Nothing could harm her here.

If only the shadows did not move.

If only the dark scratching things did not come looking for her in the night. . . .

One errant tear slipped down Tess's cheek, and she brushed it away roughly with the back of her hand. *Please, God, keep them away tonight,* she pleaded silently.

Her eyes were huge as she caught Letty's hand. "You won't—forget—will you, Letty?"

The maid squeezed Tess's cold fingers. "Now, don't you worry about nothing, miss. I'll see to it, the way I always do. Just you hie yourself off to sleep, young lady."

Tess sighed and slowly lay back against the flowered chintz cushions, her eyelids unbearably heavy. Like auburn veils, her long lashes fluttered and then fell. "Letty?" she mumbled a minute later. "Th-thank you . . . for not asking. Then—as well as now."

The maid cast a worried look at Tess. When her mistress's eyes did not reopen, she shook her head and slipped frowning from the room.

On the side table the candle flickered wildly.

Caught in cold, restless dreams, Tess shifted, reaching desperately for the light that was somehow always denied her.

Out of the night he came, materializing from the shadows that danced drunkenly over the inn's steep roof. Surefooted, like a cat, he crept toward the one window high above that still remained lit.

It was only an hour or two before dawn, and the Angel's other residents, he saw, were long abed.

Silently he moved through the rushing darkness, his eyes fixed on that small rectangle of light high above the eaves. Around him the wind growled, flinging gravel in his face and rattling the glass panes, but never did his path waver.

It was no more than child's play after the long years he'd spent climbing riggings in stormy seas.

And then the casement window was above him. His midnight eyes narrowed. He could almost see the woman inside freeing a row of tiny buttons and stepping out of her gown.

His revenge would be sweet and long this night, he vowed, moving inexorably toward that high, small square of light.

Near the darkened foot of the old Land Gate Amos Hawkins reined in his mount and loosed a torrent of profanity. His small eyes flashing, he studied the force of preventive officers ranged around him.

"Post a guard at both ends of Mermaid Street, Lawson. And keep yer bloody eyes open, all of ye!"

Abruptly the customs inspector's ruddy face broke into a cruel mockery of a smile. "As for myself, I reck'n I've a mind to pay a late night call on the owner of the Angel. Wouldn't want the lady to come to any harm, after all. Not with all these filthy smugglers about," he muttered, his smile widening unpleasantly.

3

Outside Tess's window the man in black waited.

A muscle flashed at his jaw as heated images flickered before his eyes. . . .

Tess slowly peeling off an exquisite chemise edged in fine lace— a gift from a satisfied lover, no doubt.

Her hair, wine-red and glorious, spilling over her naked shoulders.

Her body, so often dreamed of, white and wanton, shimmering in the candlelight.

Like a white-hot brand, desire burned a searing path to his groin. He cursed beneath his breath, unable to halt the flow of erotic images.

The casement was within reach now, and yet somehow he could not move. At his sides, his calloused, rope-scarred hands opened and closed convulsively. His breath ragged, he envisioned her ripe breasts straining for his touch.

The dusky hair curling at her silken thighs.

The moist satin petals hidden below.

Stop being a bloody fool!

Viscount Ravenhurst stiffened, fury twisting his features. His skin was hot in the cold wind; moisture beaded his brow. She was nothing but a treacherous little bitch with the heart of a whore, he reminded himself grimly.

But still the images engulfed him.

She will reach for her nightgown next, he thought. She will move slowly, enjoying the feel of the air on her naked skin. He could almost hear the fine satin rustle as it slid over her head. Something sheer and provocative, no doubt. Something that would display her pouting breasts to perfection, he thought grimly.

The man in the darkness ground out a harsh curse, able to wait no longer. Not when she was alone, only inches away, and he had already wasted too many empty nights waiting for this moment of perfect revenge.

Now he would have her, and in so doing be free of this savage, restless hunger that had plagued him for five long years.

Grim-faced, Ravenhurst pulled a thin piece of metal from his pocket and forced it between the adjoining edges of the casement, drawing the point up slowly until the closure inside blocked his progress. Then, with a flick of his wrist, he freed the latch, and the window sprang open.

Like an angry phantom he slipped a black-clad leg over the sill and slid into the candlelit room.

She was sleeping, just as he had hoped, her long hair a dark flame against the chintz cushions of the settee. But why there? the tall man wondered. And why did she sleep by candlelight?

Then these questions were forgotten, swept away by the fierce thundering of his blood. Slowly he bent down, impaling her with his heated gaze, drinking in her beauty. His lapis eyes flickered over the tight buds outlined beneath her cambric nightgown, while the haunting scent of lavender wafted around him.

Her smell—just as it had been that balmy night five years before when they had first met. Bitter memories assailed him, sharp as if it had been yesterday.

Lavender and roses. The rich scent of warm earth after a spring rain, pure and innocent.

Forget them! Ravenhurst told himself sharply. That night, like everything else about her, was nothing but a cruel illusion.

Outside in the darkness a tree branch clawed the roof. The woman on the settee stirred restlessly, one hand clutching the coverlet to her breast. A moment later her slim fingers splayed open, as if reaching for the lantern on the nearby side table.

A single tear spilled from Tess's eye, tracing a silver path down her cheek.

Ravenhurst's face grew taut. In grim silence he watched the trailing bead. Without thinking, he ran his finger over the curve of her cheek, a vein throbbing at his temple as he caught the drop and drew it to his lips.

His eyes closed, he tasted the salty tear.

Then, his eyes smoldering, the hard-faced viscount stared down at the woman sleeping before him.

Damn you, Tess Leighton! he cursed in silent fury. *Damn you for what you did that night. And damn you for being able to affect me still, after all this time. After all I know of your treachery.*

For she did haunt him still, threatening as always to worm her way back into his scarred, hardened heart.

Except this time she would fail. For this time Ravenhurst had no heart left—only a great, gaping hole where his heart should have been.

She had done that to him. And now it was time for him to repay her. After five tortured years of fantasies, Ravenhurst was about to savor the real thing.

He felt his lower body harden painfully at the thought and cursed himself for his weakness. But nothing could have made him turn away, even though he told himself the reality could never match his dark, fevered imaginings.

A gust of wind rattled the window and the light flickered crazily. His eyes like smoke, Ravenhurst knelt and began to unfasten the line of tiny buttons at Tess's bodice. To his infinite fury, his fingers trembled slightly when they grazed her skin. Smothering a curse, he forced his eyes to his task.

And then, pale and perfect, her body opened to his heated gaze.

Impossibly lovely, he thought. A hundred times more beautiful than he had imagined; a thousand times more erotic than his darkest fantasy.

A hot wave of desire ripped through him, swelling his manhood to painful proportions. He smothered a curse, fighting to control the fever her body aroused.

Her waist, so white and narrow, made him itch to span it with his hands. Full and high, her breasts taunted him, rising to dusky crimson peaks. Ruthlessly his eyes devoured her, lingering on the heart-shaped beauty mark that crowned her right breast. Another decorated her inner thigh, he saw, only inches below the tangled triangle of auburn curls.

A trickle of sweat slid slowly down his forehead.

Every second the fire in his veins raged higher, increasing his agony. Yet even then he could not tear his eyes away.

Only an illusion, he told himself. Inside, where it counted, she was ugly and hard.

And still the sight of her smooth breasts tormented him—soft and full, perfectly shaped to fill a man's hands. Just the thought of the sooty marks at her breast and thigh was enough to drive his throbbing manhood tight against his breeches.

He wanted her in every way a man could want a woman. He wanted to touch her and watch her moan, arching up to meet him again and again. He wanted her wet and hungry while he explored the mysteries of her silken body. Most of all he wanted to feel her shudder and wrap her ivory legs around him while he exploded inside her.

And that is how he meant to have her. Tonight. Right now. After that, he would strip away her deadly secrets—layer by lying layer!

"Tess." The word was a harsh caress.

The woman beside him tossed fitfully.

His eyes pools of smoke, Ravenhurst bent closer. "Tess," he whispered again, the gravel of his voice very pronounced. "I've come back. Just as I promised."

Her long lashes fluttering, the sleeping woman tossed uneasily upon the settee.

"Wake up, my love." Long, hard fingers traced the lobe of her ear, the fragile line of her jaw, the satin mystery of her neck. His touch was that of a connoisseur—expert, thorough, and totally impersonal.

At least Ravenhurst told himself it was.

His face a dark mask, he planned the night's campaign, knowing he must give her no quarter. Just as she had given Thorpe, his poor slain midshipman, no quarter, Dane reminded himself.

Just as her traitorous Fox gave no quarter.

Yes, tonight he would use all his weapons against her.

Slowly he knelt, careful not to stir the auburn tresses spread over the arm of the settee. It was then that Ravenhurst noticed the small glass on the nearby table. Bending slightly, he reached out and brought it to his nose, then sniffed sharply.

Laudanum. So that was another of her vices, he thought bitterly.

Looking down, he saw her eyelids flutter, blue veins against icy skin. Yes, by now she must be well under the influence of the drug.

Which would make his task that much easier.

Carefully he lifted the thick tendrils away from her ear, his lungs filled with the rich, tormenting scent of lavender. His fingers tightened, buried in the curling auburn strands.

Beneath him, Tess frowned. The black veil of sleep lifted for a moment. No! she thought wildly. It could not be!

Then the dark face was before her, half hidden in smoke and flame. Just as it always was. Mocking and tormenting. Gone but never gone.

She moaned, fighting the call of that rough, insistent voice.

"I've brought a message for you, love." The words came dimly, as if from the end of a long tunnel. "But first . . ." Strong fingers traced her parted lips.

Tess forgot everything but how perfect they felt.

"Open for me," the harsh voice commanded. Calloused thumbs stroked the inner edge of her sensitized mouth. "Take me inside you, Tess. All of me."

"No," she whispered desperately, slipping fast, tumbling under the drugging spell of that rough voice, under the stormy, restless magic of his stroking fingers. "No. No!"

"Shhh," the darkness answered.

"Stop," she moaned, cursing the laudanum that fogged her

thoughts. Dear God, tonight the dream was too strong! How could she fight it? "G-go away! It's—it's over."

"Tonight there will be no stopping me, Tess. Tonight I shall do what I should have done five years ago."

Then Dane's lips slanted down, hard and dominating as they cut off her ragged protests. He sealed his mouth against hers, devouring her wet curves with angry thoroughness. Wild heartbeats later his mouth opened, parting hers savagely. "More," he growled, pulling her dewy lower lip between his teeth and nipping the soft flesh.

"Stop!" Tess twisted her head wildly, trying to escape the sweet torture. "Don't—don't touch me!" Panic sharpened her voice. This—*dream*—was different from all the others!

But the strong, calloused hands only tightened, circling her shoulders with brutal force. "Give yourself to me, Tess," her vision muttered darkly, tracing her lips with his strong, sleek tongue. "Here," he whispered as their breaths mingled, hot and wet. "Here." Restless and teasing, his tongue plunged into her liquid heat. "Everywhere," he groaned thickly.

Dear God, she wanted to. Already her body was on fire for him. But some ragged vestige of reason warned Tess she must not. Somehow she knew that yielding would destroy her.

But why? a reckless voice argued. He was only a dream, after all. How could a dream hurt her?

With a little, choked sob her lips opened and she came one step closer to the forbidden, throbbing pleasure he promised.

The dream answered with a groan of his own, formed equal parts of pain and triumph. "So—damned—sweet." Like dark fire, his tongue flickered and teased, then without warning slid deep inside her mouth, plunging Tess into a sea of raw sensation. "More," he said hoarsely. "Give me what I want, Tess. All of it!"

His hands left her shoulders. She could have fought free then; dimly she knew that.

But she did not try. Perhaps she could not. She only arched her neck, shifting restlessly in a gesture as old as time. The gesture of woman seeking man, soft, aroused skin searching for its hard complement.

Yes, just this once she had to find out how the dreams ended.

A low, triumphant laugh exploded from Dane's mouth. She had forgotten nothing, by God, and tonight he would prove it! His hands clenching and unclenching, he studied her pale face.

His smoky gaze dropped. Lightly and with excruciating slowness, he brushed her proud, taunting crests.

Tess's breath came hoarse and ragged in her throat. "No!" she gasped, trying to pull away. "You're—you're only a dream."

But the cold mouth above hers only twisted into a grim smile. Ravenhurst's long fingers splayed open and took her tighter within their span, his calloused thumbs teasing and tormenting by turns. "Yes, my dear, a dream. But a dream real enough to make you tremble. Perhaps you might even call me a nightmare."

Tess's hands fluttered vainly, fighting the darkness, fighting this rush of passion, fighting herself most of all. Shameful pleasure flared wherever he touched her, making her body flow hot and wanton beneath his fingers.

Wanting more, far more.

Trust him, little fool, the darkness whispered. *Trust this pleasure he gives you.*

It had been so long, after all. So much of her life lived in dreams.

But wasn't this, too, a dream?

Darkness licked at the edges of her mind, and Tess feared she was losing her sanity. "G-go away," she rasped.

The rough hands never ceased their dark torment. "I cannot," her dream growled, inexorable, bent on conquest. "He sent me to you. I bring his message."

"W-who?"

"The Fox, of course." The gravelly voice hardened. "My sweet love. My *Soleil.*"

Tess shivered at that name from the past. Memories crowded in on her, dim but keenly painful. "How—"

"No questions! He's in danger, and you must do exactly as he asks."

"Dear God, J—when did you see—him?"

The man above her scowled. *Damn!* He'd nearly had it then!

"No, first give me the words, the secret words. Give me his *real* name." Dane's voice was taut with expectation. "The name only you know, Tess."

"But where is his rose?" Tess stiffened, suddenly wary.

"The name," her vision demanded harshly.

Frowning, she struggled to shake the dark haze from her mind. She tried to open her eyelids, but they barely stirred.

Dane cursed silently. So bloody close! John? James? "Give me the words!" he repeated.

"Go—go away. No more of your torment!" White and fragile, Tess's hands lashed at thin air.

"Oh, I'll go, love. But first I'll have his name." *And then I'll have you,* he vowed grimly.

Wrong, Tess thought disjointedly. Terribly wrong. Desperately she forced her eyes open, peering dimly at the dark face above her.

The lean, angular features blurred. *Him.* Always him. But real or a dream?

Perhaps it didn't matter. Perhaps a dream could be as dangerous as the real thing.

Mustn't speak, she thought wildly. *Mustn't give Jack away. Not ever!*

"Tell me, Tess. Trust me," her vision growled.

Oh, God, she wanted to. She yearned to give up her secrets—to let someone else bear her burdens for once. "I trusted you once," she whispered. "And then you left."

"But now I've come back, love. For you." Ravenhurst's hard fingers tightened. "For this."

Tess felt the shifting weight of a heavy body. A moment later hard, hot lips closed wetly over her nipple, tugging and stroking fiercely.

Stunned, she arched upward, straining wildly for—she knew not what. A whimper escaped her drawn lips.

"You want to trust me," her dark vision whispered. "You want this as much as I do."

She did, he was right. But Tess had learned the hard way that she could trust no one.

Not even a dream. *Especially* not a dream.

"Tell me, Tess."

"G-go away," she gasped. "Too—late!" Her lips moved again, but no sound emerged. Already the dark waves surrounded her.

"Give me his name," the rough voice from her past repeated urgently.

This time she barely heard.

Sighing, she turned her head away, drawing a hand to her flushed cheek. Slowly the last fragments of noise and color bled away around her.

She slept.

Bloody blazing hell! Once again she had tricked him, Ravenhurst thought, cursing long and fluently beneath his breath. Gripping her shoulders, he shook her savagely. "Wake up, damn it!"

Suddenly someone tried the door. Quickly Ravenhurst bent over and blew out the candle.

The door rattled gently.

But already the tall man in black was slipping toward the window. Jerking aside the curtains, he slipped one leg over the sill. "I'll be back, Tess Leighton," he whispered to the darkness. "I'll be back for Thorpe, and for all the others you and your Fox helped to kill."

A key grated in the lock outside.

Grim-faced, Lord Ravenhurst turned and tugged the window closed behind him, then dropped lightly to the roof. A cold gust knifed through his long hair.

Above him the curtains danced wildly. He froze, seeing the window swing open with a grating hiss. Smothering a curse, he pressed back against the cold roof tiles. Damn! He hadn't been able to latch the bloody thing properly.

"Fair to freezing in here," he heard a woman grumble. "Now, why is that window open?" The voice grew louder, her candle casting long shadows on the curtains. "Blown out the candle, it has. But I could have sworn I left it closed."

Dane's breath checked. He could hear the woman directly above him now, staring out into the darkness.

"Must be old age creeping up on me," he heard her mutter, and then the glass panels snapped shut with a thud. Unseen fingers drew the curtains closed.

Darkness fell around him once more.

Then he heard the maid's sharp gasp. "Dear God, Miss Tess—" Quick steps crossed to the settee.

Ravenhurst heard a glass crash onto the floor and realized the woman must have knocked it down in her distress.

For long moments he did not move, gripped by icy, unreasoning fury. His eyes smoldered, darker than midnight, promising vengeance upon the sleeping woman inside.

Far in the distance, beyond the black roofs of Rye, he could see the faint silver line of the Royal Military Canal curving to meet the coast at Hythe. Beyond lay the Channel, a grim reminder of the desperate task that had brought him here.

Next time, Ravenhurst vowed, there would be no reprieves. Next time he would have what he wanted from Tess Leighton.

And that, quite simply, was everything she had to give.

4

On the ledge outside Tess's window a pair of fantail pigeons cooed noisily in rich, liquid voices.

It was that cold, quiet hour before dawn. Twisting restlessly, Tess began to struggle back toward consciousness.

With a sigh, she pulled her pillow down over her face. Her eyes closed, she saw dim, flickering images, faint fragments of memory that teased her waking mind. Slowly she sat up, palms flat against her throbbing temples.

It made no difference. No matter how hard she tried, she couldn't seem to remember. All she felt was this lingering sense of uneasiness and regret. And yet . . .

Her pale brow furrowed in concentration. No, last night was different somehow. Last night was—was what?

More real? More compelling? As if she had touched and been touched in turn? But how—

Suddenly Tess stiffened, feeling a cold breeze play across her chest. Frowning, she looked down, wondering why the top button of her gown was undone.

Dear God, what had happened in the night?

She shivered, caught in dim currents of memory. Roaring wind. A harsh grating at the window.

The old torment. And then . . .

A savage magic. Dark words—darker hands. A raw, reckless hunger.

Him!

Dear God, was she losing her mind? Tess thought wildly, watching the stub of a candle flicker and then die. Or were the dreams growing worse? She did not move, wrapped in darkness.

Yes, my dear, a dream, she heard a cold, mocking voice answer. *But a dream real enough to make you tremble. Perhaps you might even call me a nightmare.*

With an angry cry Tess hurled her pillow across the room. Enough of this torment! No man—whether real or imagined—was going to disturb the life she had made for herself.

She refused to let the past claim her. Not when she had already paid her pound of flesh.

With haunted eyes she watched the window, looking for the first faint traces of dawn.

No, by heaven, nothing was going to stop her from succeeding. Her lips hardened to a thin line. Not even the naval officer sleeping right now in one of the Angel's soft beds, she vowed.

Her share of the smuggled cargoes would resurrect Fairleigh and pay off the last of her father's debts. Then there was the Angel's range to consider, for it was nothing short of dangerous in its present state. Only last week the dampers had locked twice, flooding the kitchen with smoke and ruining all the chef's grand efforts.

Yes, Tess swore grimly, she would give up cloak and mask when she was free of these crushing debts and not one instant sooner! Especially now that she had taken on Jack's role, for her profits would be even greater.

That the risks, too, would be greater was something she resolutely refused to consider.

The first chill rays of dawn were slanting onto the floor when Ravenhurst sat up and kicked free of the twisted bed linens. With a growled curse, he lurched to his feet and stalked toward the window, totally oblivious to his nakedness.

The room had been comfortable enough. The sheets were clean and the bed soft.

So why had he tossed and turned the whole damned night, sleep eluding him?

With a lurid curse he jerked the dainty white length of lace from the window and stared out at the quiet town, gray in the clinging mists of dawn.

Because Tess Leighton affected him still, even after all these years. He had to face that fact. It would be far more dangerous to try to deny it.

Unbidden, a vision of her naked beauty flickered before his eyes, and Ravenhurst felt himself swell with an immediate, throbbing erection. Cursing, he closed his eyes and ran his hands roughly through his hair.

No bloody wonder he hadn't had a wink of sleep all night!

He'd been so close! Only minutes more and he would have had the bastard's name.

Only minutes more and he would have had Tess too.

Scowling, Ravenhurst grabbed up his breeches and shirt from the floor, where he had dropped them the night before, refusing to listen to the mocking voice at the back of his mind.

A voice which asked which of the two things was more important to him.

"Oh, miss, they've stripped all the beds an' dumped all yer fine linens, ha'n't they just!" A rosy-cheeked maid named Nell came flying up to Tess as she descended the stairs a half hour later. "Not a single room wot they left untouched! If only I could get m' hands on that great pig of a Crown officer, I'd give 'm a piece of my mind!"

The laudanum still fogged her brain, and Tess was having trouble brushing the dark ends of sleep from her mind. But the sight of a huge mound of dirty, tangled linens dumped in the entrance hall shook her awake quickly enough.

So this was Hawkins's game, was it? Blazing with fury, she stared down at the ruined sheets. His men had been most thorough; every inch of linen was thick with mud.

Very well, if it was war he wanted, it was war the blackguard would get!

"Go fetch Letty, Nell," Tess said through clenched teeth. "Then these wretched things will have to be washed, I'm afraid. And if you should happen to see Amos Hawkins skulking about somewhere, see that he is brought to my accounts room," she added grimly.

But Tess soon discovered her travails were far from over. Entering the kitchen a few minutes later, she found Edouard, the inn's rotund and temperamental French chef, wringing his hands over a smoke-blackened tray of pastries.

As soon as the overwrought chef saw her, he halted his rain of French curses and raised his arms to the ceiling. *"Par Dieu,* she is finished, this cursed range! And me, I am finished, too, Mademoiselle Tess, for all that I dislike to tell you so. *Non,* and *non* once more! She crisps my tender, marinated pigeons in a manner most cruel. She swallows my *pâtisserie* and spits it back burned! She is a devil, your English stove, and I will fight her no longer!"

Tess bit back a sigh of frustration. Edouard's war with the dilapidated open range had been raging ever since he'd come to the Angel two years before. Excitable and difficult, he was nonetheless the best chef in all of southern England and Tess well knew it was his food that kept the Angel full of well-heeled travelers.

Even the Prince of Wales's own steward had pronounced himself impressed by the fine cuisine he had enjoyed at the inn on a recent visit. He had hinted that he might give Tess a fee for releasing the volatile chef from her employ. Fortunately, the Frenchman refused to consider the offer.

Now, however, it appeared that unless she acted quickly, she would lose him.

Straightening her shoulders, Tess tried for a sympathetic smile. "Poor Edouard," she said soothingly. "What has the wicked thing done to you now?"

"It is well that you ask. Regard there!" One large, flour-covered finger rose, pointing accusingly at the oven.

Frowning, Tess studied the ancient open range, where a thin plume of smoke even now drifted from the rear grate. "What is the problem this time? Is the smoke jack stalled again?"

"Stalled?" The chef snorted. "She is frozen forever! I reach up to turn the dampers and she showers dirt down upon me and my stuffed pigeons. And my beautiful *pâtisserie . . .*" His voice broke and he covered his face, too distraught to say more.

Tess bent down and studied the blacked oven, then turned to peer up toward the ceiling. Gingerly she pulled the chains which should have opened the flues to the chimney.

Nothing happened.

"There doesn't seem to be—"

Without warning a cloud of soot rained down upon Tess's head. Coughing wildly, she stumbled back from the oven, only to collide with the chef hovering nearby.

"Maybe now you see what I suffer here in this ruin of a kitchen," the Frenchman snapped, at the same time pressing a dampened wad of linen into her hand.

Just then a shrill cry exploded from the opposite corner of the room. "Hove to starboard!" the voice screeched. "Rocky shoals ahead!"

"Hush, Maximilian," Tess hissed at the large emerald and crimson macaw stamping upon his perch by the window.

"And that bird!" Edouard exclaimed. "I suffer much for you, mademoiselle, because of the goodness of your heart. But as to this one," he threatened, stalking toward the gaudy bird, "I will make me a nice *tarte de perroquet* with him, and *boom!*"

Hurriedly Tess stepped between her irate chef and the screeching Maximilian. "Come now, Edouard. That will not help us with our problem. Perhaps you should show me exactly what the difficulty is. We managed quite nicely last time, as I recall."

The rotund little Frenchman snorted. "Only because your Monsieur Hobhouse is a genius with his fingers to make the repairs. But this time, *par Dieu*, the brute is beyond even his skill!"

"Beat to quarters!" Maximilian cried, ruffling his feathers and puffing out his cheeks. "Enemy ships to starboard!"

A moment later the kitchen door swung open noisily on its hinges and a tall, blond gentleman in an emerald satin waistcoat peered into the room. "There you are," he said in some surprise, his green eyes sweeping Tess's soot-stained face. "Hobhouse did not seem to know what had become of you, my dear. I confess, I did not expect to find you here." The fair-haired man smiled chidingly, his bright waistcoat gleaming in the sunlight from the window.

Lord Lennox was immaculate as always, Tess noted uncomfortably, aware of exactly how disreputable she must look by comparison. After giving her cheeks a surreptitious scrub, she looked up. "How good to see you, my lord. But when did you return? You were to have remained in London for a month, as I recall."

The keen eyes darkened. "Dare I hope that means you've missed me?"

"You may hope whatever you like, my lord," Tess answered, smiling. "But now you must let me go and repair this damage, for I fear I look the worst sort of urchin."

Cool fingers grazed her flushed cheeks. "You look, my dearest Tess, enchanting—sooty cheeks and all. As you always do. I know I promised to stay away and give you time to make up your mind, but I offer you fair warning: I mean to harry you until you accept my proposal."

Tess stiffened, aware of the unnatural silence that fell over the kitchen behind her. Suddenly she felt four pairs of eyes trained upon her back.

With a clanging of silver, Edouard recalled his staff to their duties. *"Vite! Vite!"* he snapped to the trio of gawking kitchen maids. "The *pâtisserie*—or what's left of it—to Hobhouse! All the other trays to the coffee room! *Dépêchez-vous!"*

"I think, my lord, that we had better discuss this at another time," Tess said quietly.

Behind her came a muffled snort, which she resolutely ignored. Out of the corner of her eye she saw Edouard shooing the kitchen maids to the door.

Then she and Lord Lennox were alone.

Frowning, the earl studied her pale face. "You haven't been sleeping well," he murmured, his broad brow furled. "I can see it in the lines about your eyes. All of this is far too much responsibility for you, my dear. You should be dancing till dawn and doing nothing more strenuous than taking chocolate in bed when you rise at noon. And then there's all the work yet to be done at

Fairleigh." His voice dropped, becoming more urgent. "Let me bear some of the responsibility for you, Tess. I'll oversee the workmen at Fairleigh. It would give me great pleasure to see the house restored to its old grandeur. And then I'll look about for someone reliable to manage the Angel for you." Lennox's eyes were warm on her face as he took her hands in his. "Hobhouse, even—though I'm certain the curmudgeon would cheat us horribly."

Gently Tess pulled her hands free. "Dear Simon. Your offer does me great honor—"

"Honor?" the earl snapped, his eyes flashing. "I love you, damn it! Can't you see that? You drive me to complete and utter distraction!"

"Please, my lord. I—I must have time to think," Tess stammered, her hands restlessly pleating the top of her apron. "It's not just me, you understand. I have the staff to consider. And there's Ashley too."

"I hardly see how the matter affects him. He's taken no interest in Fairleigh or the Angel."

Tess sighed. "No, he hasn't, has he? But he might, if things were to change suddenly. At any rate, I must at least discuss the matter with him."

Lord Lennox raised her hand to his lips and feathered a light kiss across her palm. "I only pray you may not take too long, my dear," he said softly. Some indistinct emotion skittered across his face; slowly he bent and brushed her lips with his.

Tess stood unmoving, her thoughts awhirl.

Perdition! What kept her from accepting his offer? Lord Lennox was the catch of the county—handsome, rich, and kind. Why didn't her heart sing at his attentions?

"Hard about!" Maximilian shrieked, dancing upon his perch. "Dangerous shoals ahead!"

"Such an affecting scene."

Tess stiffened at the sound of that cool, feminine voice from the doorway.

"As always, my sister's timing is deplorable," Lennox said dryly, never taking his eyes from Tess's face.

"Quite right, my dear," Lady Patricia Lennox agreed. "I ought to have arrived much sooner." Her voice hardened. "Then I might have prevented you from making such a perfect ass of yourself."

Quickly Tess took a step backward, a hot tide of crimson flooding her cheeks. Angry words sprang to her lips.

"Please forgive my sister, Tess," Lennox said, squeezing her hands gently. "She is a spoiled, ungrateful brat, I'm afraid. What she needs is a husband who will beat her on a regular basis."

"If you say so," Tess said stiffly, wrenching free of his grasp.

"In this instance my brother is decidedly correct, Miss Leighton. But I had something else in mind for the man to provide—on a regular basis. Although a touch of savagery is never amiss."

"Patricia," Lennox hissed. "You forget yourself."

His sister's green eyes glittered. "We are all adults, I trust. There can be no harm in a little plain speaking between adults, surely." Her sharp nose twitched suddenly. "But whatever is that horrid smell? Have you a decaying fowl hidden about the kitchen, my dear?"

Tess scowled, thinking the description entirely apt for Lady Patricia herself. "Horrid smell? I perceive nothing beyond a little smoke. But since this place so offends you, Lady Patricia, I would not dream of detaining you further."

Lord Lennox's sister quirked one fair eyebrow. "One feels so out of place in a kitchen, of course. But I am waiting for you to escort me home, Simon. Or have you forgotten your promise already?"

The earl suppressed an irritated sigh. "No, I hadn't forgotten." He looked down at Tess in silent apology, gathering her hands once more into his. "Remember what I said, my dear," he murmured searchingly.

Tess could feel his sister's eyes burning into her neck. "I will give it careful consideration, I promise you, my lord."

Reluctantly Simon released her hands and walked to the door, where Lady Patricia was already making ready to leave.

"Oh, I very nearly forgot," the lushly endowed blonde said silkily, turning back toward Tess. "We are having some friends down from London next week and I should like to offer them your *pâtés garnis.* Our chef has been demanding your recipe this age, I vow. I really must send him over to speak with you. You will be a dear and help him out, won't you? You are so good about these things —I can't imagine it taking over an hour or two of your time."

Tess's eyes flashed gray-green sparks. "Indeed? But how singular. My great-great-grandmother might have asked yours the same question, when she was at the court of Charles II. Your title *was* conferred by that monarch, was it not? For services rendered in his kitchen, as I recall." Tess halted, her face a picture of exaggerated innocence. "Or was it for services rendered in his bed?"

"Why, you impertinent little slut!" Lady Patricia blazed.

"Enough, Patricia! You only receive what you deserve. Go and wait for me in the carriage!" Lennox's face was set in hard lines.

With an angry snort, his sister whirled about and stormed from the room.

"Forgive me," Tess said stiffly. "My unruly tongue again. I forget that in attacking her lineage I also attack your own. It is just that you are so different. In fact, sometimes I forget you are related at all."

Lennox's fingers skimmed Tess's still flaming cheek. "On the contrary, it is I who should beg forgiveness for my sister's behavior. You did no more than respond to her provocation. I assure you it won't happen again, however. When we are married—"

"*If* we are married," Tess corrected.

Lord Lennox's eyes darkened. "*When,*" he countered firmly. "For I give you notice, my dear. It is only a matter of time."

Strangely distracted, Tess made her way back to Hobhouse's office to confer on the day's schedule. The conversation with Lord Lennox had disturbed her more than she cared to admit, but already other problems were weighing on her mind.

Very soon she must encounter the inn's newest arrival, she knew. At that thought Tess's chin rose determinedly. Let him come then. She would teach Viscount Ravenhurst that he held no place in her heart!

As for the range, she could only pray that Hobhouse would show his customary dexterity and succeed in shoring up Édouard's fragile emotional state a while longer. Which still left the delicate matter of disposing of the high-proof brandy, Tess's share of the last runs. As prearranged, the kegs had been concealed beneath a delivery of flour and vegetables brought in by Hobhouse at dawn.

Right now the contraband was resting in a hidden recess behind her bed.

Tess's full lips curved in triumph. Tonight she would transfer the brandy into old, dusty bottles and recork them carefully. By tomorrow there would be no trace of the contraband.

But until then, she knew she would have to be very cautious. With five hundred pounds on the Fox's head, men's tongues might suddenly become very loose.

Not finding Hobhouse in his office, Tess walked slowly back to her workroom at the rear of the inn. En route, she peeked into the kitchen, surprised to see the big room empty and silent. Even Maximilian was gone, she noticed, probably carried out to entertain some revelers in the taproom. Then Tess heard shouts from the courtyard, followed by Edouard's rapid-fire directions to the staff. They were unloading a wagon of provisions, she realized, and the chef was seeing to the goods' placement in the stillroom. That mystery solved, she continued through to the small workroom where she kept her account records and received tradesmen.

Realizing she would have a few minutes of peace, Tess sat down beside the window and pulled out her account book. Swiftly she totalled the long columns. One hundred fifty pounds spent last month alone! At this rate she would never get out of debt.

Still, last night's brandy would fetch a good price in London, and there were four cargoes of tea and silk from last month for which she would soon be paid—into an anonymous account in London, of course.

Tess frowned, biting the end of her quill as she tabulated the final profit. With luck, those should net a little over two hundred pounds. This was some progress, at least, though not nearly enough.

Somewhere mid-page her eyes strayed from the long line of figures. Sunlight streamed through the window and she could see the soft outline of distant hills, lush and green after last night's rain.

A cold current of air brushed her cheek, fanning a long strand of auburn hair across her shoulder. Tess stiffened, feeling the presence of someone in the doorway.

The tension in her shoulders, the drumming in her veins told her there could be only one person standing behind her.

She had known she must face him soon. But now that the time for reckoning had come, Tess found herself no more in control than she had been in the dark alley the night before.

"Turn around, Tess," Lord Ravenhurst growled from the doorway. "Let me have a look at you. Yes, let me see if you're still the same calculating little bitch you were five years ago."

5

Tess did not turn around.

Instead, her heart constricting painfully, she closed her account book and laid her pen down beside it. Carefully she straightened a ruffle at her cuff and then brushed a tiny speck of flour from her fingers. Only then did she pivot in her chair to face the intruder.

And still the sight of his cold, bitter face and sea-dark eyes came as a shock to her.

The face of the man she had once loved.

Now the face of a brutal, implacable enemy.

He was dressed in a loose white shirt, its neck opened low to reveal bronzed skin and a lush mat of black hair. Gray breeches hugged his long, muscular thighs, disappearing beneath top boots polished to a mirror-like sheen.

But it was his face that arrested Tess. How different it is, she thought. Darker, harder. More deeply lined. Yes, long years of war had left their mark on that face. On that voice, too, which now held a rough, gravelly timbre that had not been present five years ago.

The total effect was one of harsh contrasts. Beneath that thin veneer of civilization, Tess realized, there lay a ruthless stranger—someone by nature and training both savage and unpredictable.

Right now an air of wild recklessness emanated from his confi-dent posture, from his broad shoulders pressed against the doorframe, from the big hand that rode at his hip while his lapis eyes burned across her face.

There was violence in his harsh face and violence in his cold, ruthless eyes. Everything about the man screamed "danger."

Suddenly Tess froze, seeing the streaks of white hair at his temples.

So he, too, had felt the passage of time, had he? But not nearly so much as she had suffered, Tess thought bitterly.

Now all that was past, thank God. Never would she allow herself to be hurt so deeply again.

In a flash these reflections flooded in upon Tess's raw, strained senses. She saw all of this—saw the vein throbbing at Dane's neck, saw the hard set of his jaw, saw the taut control of his posture.

But before she could react to her newfound knowledge, Ravenhurst had crossed to the kitchen and thrown the bolt that secured the outer door.

Trapping her.

"And now, my dear Tess," the viscount growled, "I believe we have some catching up to do."

"Why did you come back?" Tess hissed, her fingers clenched together tightly on her desk. "Why couldn't you just stay away, damn you?"

"Perhaps I felt it was time you had a man in your life again—a real man, that is."

"Don't flatter yourself! You meant nothing to me. And I obviously meant less than nothing to you!"

Dane's hard features twisted in a sneer. "Come, come, my dear. Is that any way to greet your long-lost lover?"

"Go to hell, St. Pierre. Or perhaps I should say Viscount Ravenhurst, as Hobhouse informs me. My congratulations on your new title. I'm certain it affords you all the opportunity for arrogance that you've ever wanted. But if you think we have any catching up to do, you are sadly mistaken. So just leave me alone!"

"Ah, but you see, leaving you alone is the *last* thing I mean to do, my love. After all, we have so much lost time to make up," Lord Ravenhurst added, his voice cold with menace. "Five years, to be precise."

Tess's hands clenched and unclenched on her desk. What cruel game was he playing at? And why in the name of heaven did he come back to torment her now, just when she was learning to forget him?

Forget him? a mocking voice asked. Forget that hard body? Forget how his eyes devoured her, with the devil's own gleam in their cobalt-blue depths? Forget how his hair smelled, rich with sea and sun and salt wind?

You could never forget him. Nor the bitter way you parted.

"I order you to leave this room!" Tess blazed. "Otherwise I shall call Hobhouse and have you thrown out."

"I should like to see him try," Ravenhurst drawled, one sable eyebrow climbing to a mocking slant. "It might prove amusing."

"Blackguard! As if I cared what might amuse you!"

The man in the doorway did not move. Tess watched a vein pound at his neck. Only his eyes moved, searing her, smoky and furious, as if he wished he might burn her into a thousand cinders.

"At one time you cared." Ravenhurst's voice hardened, dropping to a dangerous growl. "At one time my feelings meant everything to you, Tess. Or so you assured me." His full lips twisted in a snarl. "Was that, too, a lie?"

So the thought bothered him, did it? Reckless with fury, Tess tilted back her head, gray-green eyes glittering beneath a curtain of auburn lashes. "You'll never know for certain, will you?" she purred.

Dane's eyes narrowed, and Tess felt the hot, churning force of his gaze. His thighs were slightly apart, taut and braced as if he rode a pitching quarterdeck. Power emanated from that hard body, power which fed upon his dark anger until it became a wild, pulsating thing.

Then his lazy facade shattered. With a savage growl, he thundered across the room and jerked her from her chair. "Oh, I'll know, Tess Leighton. But first . . ." Seizing her hands, he hauled her against his chest.

Tess twisted in silent fury, fighting his iron grip, fighting the savage heat of his body. "Go to hell and toast your eyebrows, for all I care! But leave me alone, damn you!"

"Ah, but that's the very last thing I mean to do," the viscount snarled, his lips twisting in a cold mockery of a smile. "No, what I mean to do is pick up precisely where we left off. Beginning with that night in your father's gate house at Fairleigh. You *do* remember that night, don't you, my love?" His fingers tightened punishingly on her wrists.

Painful images swam before Tess's eyes, fragments of memory more cruel than his ruthless fingers. *Dear God, could she never put the past behind her?*

"I remember, you swine," Tess hissed. "But it seems you do not. If your memory were better, you'd remember we left off nowhere —and with nothing! Can't you get that through your thick skull? Even now?" With a choked, angry cry she drew back her foot, taking aim just as Jack had once taught her.

Instantly Ravenhurst pivoted, then drove his knee between her flailing legs. At the same moment his fingers dug into her straining hips and forced her forward until she was anchored against his thigh. His dark eyes glittered with triumph. "You wanted me to believe that, didn't you? But it won't work. I didn't believe it then, and I don't believe it now!"

Tess gasped, twisting helplessly, feeling the hard blade of his arousal through her thin skirts. She jerked her hands wildly, desperate to rake him with her nails, but his granite arms held her captive. "Then, my lord," she spat, "you are a fool whose conceit knows no bounds!"

Grim-faced, Ravenhurst cupped her slim hips and ground his rampant manhood against her. "Not conceit, my love—just raw, hard fact. You see, nothing's changed between us, Tess," he snarled. "You burned for me once and by God I'll see you burn for me again. But I warn you—one more trick like that will find you over my knee while I teach you some manners!"

"I'd like to see you try!"

Ravenhurst's fingers tightened on her hips. "Don't tempt me, little hellcat. Nothing would give me greater pleasure than leaving my palm prints all over your sweet, pouting bottom."

Wild with fury, Tess wrenched against his grip, only to find herself quickly overwhelmed. His hands were granite-hard from years of fighting cables and furling sails. She could feel exactly where the rough callouses scraped her wrists.

Still she fought, her cheeks flooding crimson. But every movement drove her more intimately against his aroused body, making her savagely aware of the rigid column of muscle digging into her thighs.

And she hated herself for that awareness.

"You're just like all the rest of your arrogant sex! It's some kind of sick game you play, isn't it? The eternal thrill of the chase! Well, I'll not be your prey, do you hear? And I'll never surrender—not to you nor to anyone else."

Slowly Ravenhurst captured her straining wrists within one powerful hand. Some dark, fleeting emotion came and went in his eyes. "Oh, far more than a game, my dear," he whispered harshly, reaching out to anchor her face in his free hand. "And cease these comparisons to the other men who've shared your bed. I'll make you forget them soon enough, I assure you."

For long moments neither of them moved, chest against chest, hip to thigh, their eyes and bodies locked in deadly combat. Between them the electric tension built, spiralling and swelling until Tess thought she would suffocate.

Yet something about the man's arrogance triggered a reckless response in her, made her want to goad and challenge this dark-faced intruder, to strip away his veneer and reveal the raw feelings he was working so hard to conceal.

Had she thought about it, she would never have followed that wild instinct. But at that moment Tess was driven by something deeper than thought, something as old as time. High color stained her cheeks as she felt the evidence of his desire at the curve of her stomach.

She did not question why she acted as she did. She did not think at all, but simply followed the call of the angry voices clamoring in her head.

For though Ravenhurst looked dangerous, his violence was still somehow leashed, and Tess wanted to find out what this stranger with the face she could not forget would look like when he exploded.

Yes, perhaps then . . .

Her lips curved up in a mocking smile. "I sincerely doubt that, my lord. No, you look a great deal too . . ." Her head tilted back as she studied him with cool deliberation. "Battered about. Weary and weak from your years at sea," she lied silkily. "No, I'm afraid you're in no condition for a fight, my lord." She ran her tongue delicately across her upper lip, taunting him. "Not with me at least."

"Am I man enough to take you on? Is that your question, Tess?"

Her small, willful chin rose as fury goaded her one dangerous step further. "Are you, my lord?" Tess purred, studying him from beneath lowered lashes. "Man enough, that is?"

And then some reckless demon made her move slightly, brushing her thighs against that straining line of male muscle.

In that moment Tess had her wish. Her eyes glittering, she watched the last shreds of Ravenhurst's iron restraint shatter. With a graphic curse he captured her legs and wrapped them about his waist, letting her taste the full force of his angry arousal. His face dark with fury, he thundered to Édouard's long, flour-strewn worktable in the kitchen, where he deposited her sprawling, careful to keep her captive against him.

"My condition," he snarled, bending down and forcing Tess closer against his hardened sex, "is more than adequate to service one devious little slut like yourself, let me assure you. And it will give me the greatest pleasure to prove it to you. Right here and now."

Her gray-green cat's eyes glittering, Tess returned Ravenhurst's fury spark for spark. "How unfortunate for you, then, that you won't have the opportunity. Now, release me immediately, before Hobhouse comes looking for me and you make an even greater fool of yourself."

"I think not. My love," Ravenhurst added, the words a curse on his lips. "You've used your time well, I see. What a very accomplished little trollop you've become. How many men did it take to teach you these squalid tricks?"

Although her heart was pounding wildly, Tess managed to

shrug in indifference. "Fifty. One hundred. What does it matter? Your bodies are all much the same in the dark, after all."

Dane found himself scowling, unprepared for the scalding jealousy that knifed through him at her words. *"How many, damn you?"*

"Does it bother you so? Then of course I must tell you. Fifty! No, thrice fifty!" Tess blazed, squirming madly against him.

Suddenly she was desperate to break away. To escape the memories that threatened to engulf her . . .

At her movements, desire, savage and blinding, ripped through Dane's groin. With each touch of her twisting body he wanted her more. But he could not allow desire to become part of his game.

Not *his* desire, at least.

Cursing darkly, Ravenhurst tightened his grip on her wrists. "Tell me, what price does an experienced whore fetch in Rye these days?"

Tess's breath caught for an instant before she schooled her face to icy indifference. "I haven't the faintest idea, my lord. Those who were fortunate enough to receive my favors would never stoop to discuss such a thing." She made a little moue of distaste. "For your information, however, I rather prefer objects. Clothing, carriages, jewelry—anything, so long as it is very fine. And very expensive, of course. As for you, my Lord Ravenhurst"—Tess lowered her lashes, her strange, uptilted eyes glittering with anger —"I sincerely doubt that you could muster my price."

The viscount's eyes narrowed to dark slits. "Oh, I can muster your price, my dear—both in guineas and in male stamina. But the question is whether I would find such a well-ripened but obviously over-handled bit of fruit at all worth the trouble."

Tess's heart slammed violently against her ribs. Faint streaks of red tinged her cheeks. But she fought down her fury, only smiling provocatively at the man bending so close to her.

For some deep woman's instinct told her this would hurt Ravenhurst the most.

"If you lack interest, my lord, then I can only wonder why you are here, determined to maul me about in this crude fashion."

Ravenhurst's fingers bit into the fragile bones at her wrists as he

studied her, captive beneath him upon the flour-covered table.
"Because it suits me to be here, wench," he countered flatly.

"Let me go, you swine! You're hurting me!"

Again, Tess thought.

"I might consider it. When you tell me all you know about the
Fox."

"What makes you think I know anything about the man?"

One dark brow rose mockingly. "Don't you?"

"And if I did," Tess continued, just as if he had not spoken,
"what makes you think I would reveal any part of it to you?"

"Because," the viscount growled, bending down until his breath
teased her cheek, "I will most certainly squeeze the life out of that
lying little throat of yours if you do not."

"I rather think you might, at that," Tess agreed coolly. "However, I shall not put you to the trouble. You see, I have not the
slightest knowledge of this notorious smuggler. He is a mystery to
me—just as he is to every other person in this district."

"Liar!" The word exploded off Ravenhurst's lips. "You can't
have lived here so long and learned nothing about the man. Amos
Hawkins must have had some reason for seeing your linens tossed
out into the street."

"Amos Hawkins is nothing but a black-hearted bully! Why do
you bring his name into this?"

"Because the man knows a traitor when he sees one. As do I."

"We harbor no traitors here at the Angel!" Tess blazed back,
struggling to break free. "What's more, I hardly see what all the
fuss is about. Free trading is a way of life here along the coast, and
has been so for over five hundred years. Indeed, if all the smugglers were jailed, there would be very few people left—whether
farmer, fisherman, or excise officer." Furious, she squirmed back
and forth but could not escape his implacable grip.

She was good, Ravenhurst thought coldly. *Damned good.* "That
sounds remarkably like sedition, my dear," he growled, forcing
her wrists flat on the table beside her. "You'd be well advised to
mind your tongue, lest people begin calling you a traitor as well as
a whore."

"Only a foul snake like yourself would be so crude! For I say no more than anyone in Rye would say—if they were honest, which they'd hardly be with an outsider like yourself. And I'll give you another truth, as well," she spat. "We don't care for strangers here, my lord. Too often they turn out to be tax collectors. Or press-gangs come to drag away our men in chains—brothers, husbands, and sons—to serve upon your cursed warships! Now, let me go, you—you—contemptible son of a worm!"

Ravenhurst's lips thinned with anger. "Not just yet, I think." Ruthlessly he pushed her down, crushing her against the flour-covered table. His eyes were opaque and unreadable as he crouched over her, the sun streaming through the mullioned kitchen windows at his back. "We are at war with France, woman. Need I remind you that a war requires men and ships of the line? Those are the only things that will protect this coast if the French should choose to land here!"

Tess could only stare back at him in patent disbelief. "An invasion?" she scoffed. "Here? You talk the worst sort of rubbish! This new military canal must thwart any French hopes on that score."

"You seem very confident of that," Ravenhurst growled. "But it is my job to see that it does so." His eyes narrowed. "And Boney might find that the barren stretches of Romney Marsh have other uses for his men than as a landing place."

Instantly Tess stiffened. "Are you insinuating we're in league with the enemy here?" she hissed.

"Why don't you tell me?"

Her eyes snapping, Tess twisted against his taut body, against his cruel fingers. "That I will, you arrogant cur. While our people may run uncustomed brandy and sail with the tide to Dieppe, they are *Englishmen* before all else! They would as little support Napoleon's military ventures as they would"—she muttered a most unladylike oath beneath her breath, searching for a comparison strong enough—"why, why—dance with the devil himself!"

Dane's lips curved slightly. "You sound very certain of that, my dear. I can only wonder how you come to know these desperate criminals so well." Abruptly his lapis eyes narrowed, probing her face. "I have heard it said that this madman takes females into his motley band. Can it be that . . ."

Tess's pulse raced as she remembered how he had studied her sooty features in just the same way the night before. Sweet heaven, what if he recognized her as the woman from the alley?

Wildly, she strained with thigh and chest, arching her back and twisting from side to side. But her struggles only forced her closer against Ravenhurst's unyielding form.

Her captor stiffened, a vein throbbing at his temple. "Stop struggling, damn it! Unless you want me to take you here and now. This table will serve as well as any bed you have upstairs, by God!"

Mute with fury, Tess glared back at him, her cheeks aflame.

Slowly Ravenhurst raised a questioning brow. "Or is all this anger merely a smoke screen to protect something—or someone—else?"

Tess's eyes darkened with fear at his cold scrutiny. "Let me go!" she cried, aware that every second brought him closer to dangerous recognition. "I—I don't know what you're talking about!"

"No?" With his long fingers Dane tilted her head back and examined her face. "By God," he said sharply.

Tess's pulse thundered in her ears. Wildly she wrenched against his hard grip, desperate to escape his gaze. "Let me go—"

"I wouldn't have believed it," he muttered, as much to himself as to her.

The look in his eyes made Tess's heart lurch sickeningly. *He knew. Damn him!* Why didn't he just get it over with then? Why did he continue to play this game of cat and mouse with her?

Her captor's eyes narrowed. "It's true then. I can see it in your face." Slowly his fingers slid down to cover the pulse throbbing at her neck.

Ashen-faced, Tess waited for his explosion of recognition.

"Yes, you are frightened. Very badly, I'd say, though you conceal it well."

A choked gasp broke from Tess's lips. "I'm n-nothing of the sort!"

"You're bloody terrified, woman," Ravenhurst said wonderingly, his eyes widening.

"Let me go, damn you!"

"But why, I ask myself? It must be something very grave to frighten a hard-eyed little trollop like yourself."

"You don't frighten me in the slightest," Tess blustered. "And I'll tell you once again—I know nothing about this man!"

Ravenhurst smiled grimly, feeling her pulse leap beneath his fingers. "In that case, prove it."

"You progress from insolence to imbecility!"

"Not at all, little hellcat. Since you say you have no knowledge of the Fox, then introduce me to someone who does."

Tess shook her head sharply. "That would be most unwise of me. And excessively unhealthy for us both."

"You'll find it a damn sight more unhealthy if you do not, woman! You may have bought off your other men with a few hours of furtive groping in your bed, but you'll find I shall not so easily be appeased."

"I wouldn't offer even a second of time in my bed to a filthy swine like you," Tess hissed.

"Oh, you'll offer me that and a great deal more besides, Tess. Before we're done you'll give me anything I want. And what I want, my sweet, is simple—every bloody thing you have to give." Grim-faced, Lord Ravenhurst slanted his chest down over her straining body, every ridge of bone and muscle engraved upon her soft skin. "And then," he whispered harshly, "you'll give me a little bit more."

"I'll give you n-nothing, bastard!" Tess sobbed, hating the ragged sound of her voice.

Ravenhurst's eyes smoked with fury as he crushed her to the table. "Shall we put it to a test then?"

"You vile, degenerate—" Suddenly Tess gasped, feeling something thick and sticky slip down the neck of her gown.

Slowly, with coolest deliberation, Dane assessed the remains of the cherry tart he had poured over her chest. "Yes, you put me much in mind of that confection."

Tess closed her eyes, tossing frantically when she saw his intent. But it was too late. Already his dark, bitter face was descending inexorably.

Then his mouth was upon her, savage and devouring, burning a path along her neck. "Stop!" she ordered shakily, all her energy given to fighting the wild swell of desire his touch provoked.

Dear God, how could her body turn traitor this way?

Again.

But with her eyes closed to him, she felt him all the more intensely: his tongue rough and wet on her tender skin; his lips nipping, then dragging bits of sweet fruit into his mouth.

"Very ripe," he whispered against her neck. "And obviously over-handled."

Tess squirmed desperately, but could not dislodge his taut frame by even an inch. "I'll make you pay for this," she swore through clenched teeth. "If it's the last thing I do, I will!"

She opened her eyes as she spoke, blinking as Dane's dark, hungry gaze raked her face.

"This is just the beginning, Tess. You know it as well as I do."

"It's the end, you sea scum. The end of nothing!"

Ravenhurst's face twisted, a hard mask of fury. "You cannot hope to fool me. Your wild pulse, your straining muscles betray you even now. Your body, at least, has not yet learned to lie!"

" 'Tis you who lie, you who are twisted. Nay, an utter madman!"

"Madmen sometimes speak the purest truths. Why don't you admit you want me?"

"I admit nothing, save that I loathe you!"

Hungry and smoldering, Ravenhurst's eyes pored over her. "Indeed? But I see I've missed the last piece of fruit. The ripest of all." Suddenly he shifted, one thigh pinning Tess's struggling legs while his other leg bent, braced on the table at her hip.

Once more his dark head descended.

And then raw torment—or was it sweet, searing pleasure?—swept through Tess as he wrapped his tongue around one perfect, budding nipple. Her heart hammering, she arched and strained against him, but the movement only drove her closer against his devouring mouth.

"Tell me, damn you," Ravenhurst growled, his lips teasing the dusky, fruit-stained peak. "I'll never let you go until I have the truth, Tess."

He would never release her, Tess realized dimly, biting back a wild moan of pleasure as his teeth tugged on her expertly. Dear God, she must escape! If he held her much longer she might . . .

"Very well, then, I will admit it," she whispered huskily. "If you give me an inch of room to breathe."

His eyes dark with triumph, Ravenhurst relaxed his grip slightly and eased away. "Well?"

"I—I had no idea . . ." Tess whispered. Abruptly she turned her face away, unable to continue.

"Tell me, damn you!" Ravenhurst's large hands circled her face, forcing her to look at him. "The truth this time!"

"N-no idea"—one trembling hand slipped along the table—"that you could be so—"

Her fingers closed to a taut fist—*"so utter and complete an example of twisted depravity!"* With an angry sob Tess caught a handful of flour and hurled it wildly upward.

White powder exploded all around them, covering Ravenhurst's face. Cursing viciously, he jerked away, brushing at his eyes.

"You . . . little . . . bitch!" he rasped. "I should have known better than—"

But he never finished his sentence.

For just then Tess drove her knee upward with all her strength, straight into his groin.

6

His features stiff with pain, Ravenhurst staggered backward and then doubled over, like a puppet whose strings had been severed.

It was almost funny really, Tess thought wildly, near hysteria. She could feel waves of laughter threatening to burst from her dry throat. Then that emotion faded, leaving only hollow fury.

"S-stay away from me!" she screamed, her voice high-pitched and ragged. "I'm no more the innocent girl I was five years ago, do you understand? I can fight now— in ways I never even dreamed existed then. So you'll get nothing more from me, your bloody lordship, nothing but more of the same!"

Before her, Ravenhurst swayed drunkenly and fell to his knees. The pain was unbearable, but he dug his fingers into his thighs and bit back a hoarse, choking groan. Then, still swaying, he forced his head up fractionally and sought her gaze.

A spark leapt from his eyes, and the murderous fury of his face made Tess shiver. But she did not stay to hear his brutal promises of vengeance. Only a fool would stay after such a hard-won escape.

With his harsh curses ringing in her ears, she flew to the door and freed the bolt, then fled blindly down the corridor.

"Only a bloody fool would—*aahhh*—trust a cunning little bitch like you," Ravenhurst muttered hoarsely as he watched his quarry escape. "But it's not a mistake I'll ever make again, by God!"

* * *

From her vantage point in the stillroom, Letty watched Tess fly out of the kitchen in a wild swirl of skirts. Neither the haunted look in Tess's eyes nor the strain on her face was lost on Letty, who watched in amazement as a grim-faced Lord Ravenhurst walked stiffly through the door a minute later.

Letty frowned and shook her head, wondering why the viscount's hair and shoulders were thickly dusted with flour.

Wondering even more why his dark eyes snapped with such murderous rage.

"I don't know what that girl's gone and done now," she muttered worriedly. "But I've a feeling she's going to regret it, and soon."

Several hours later, to the east of Rye, a little skiff bobbed gently, its prow loosing silver eddies as it made a slow progress along the Royal Military Canal. In the bow a young, wiry lieutenant bent to the oars.

Behind him, seated in the stern, sat Lord Ravenhurst, his lapis eyes trained on the landscape of the canal, crisply outlined beneath the molten sun that hung golden just above the treetops.

Not a speck of flour remained on his dark hair. Only the hard light in his eyes remained, mute testimony to the fury that fueled his search for the traitor who haunted these marshes.

"Tell me something about this smuggler whose name is on everyone's lips. The Romney Fox, I believe he's called." Even as he spoke, Ravenhurst scanned the banks, searching for points of vulnerability. "Have you any idea of the fellow's identity?"

"No, sir. That is—my lord," the young officer quickly corrected himself, unnerved in the presence of one of his idols. "No one does. He's as hard to trace as the lights that dance upon the marsh. People here say the fellow's part marsh phantom himself, but then, they're a superstitious lot. Whatever he is, he knows these coves and marshes like the back of his own hand. All these people do."

Ravenhurst frowned. He did not actually believe the southern coast would come under attack. Not now, with England's great sea battles relegated to the past, nearly forgotten. No, the war with Boney now raged on land, for the Corsican had learned a bitter lesson at Trafalgar. It was not, Dane was certain, a mistake the man would make ever again.

Napoleon was a brilliant strategist, however. If England lay unguarded, he would not hesitate to plunge his sharp talons directly into her heart.

And if he did, this canal would be of scant use, Dane thought grimly. Not with long stretches of it little wider than a ditch.

Two hundred and thirty-four thousand pounds spent on a damned ditch, for God's sake!

Ravenhurst cursed beneath his breath. Out of the corner of his eye he saw the lieutenant dart him a worried glance, fearful that he had somehow given offense. Uncomfortable with the adulation in those young eyes, the viscount cleared his throat sharply and looked away. "I was told the canal widens up ahead."

"So it does, my lord. Just beyond those trees." The silence broken, the young officer in the crisp blue uniform steeled himself to bring up the thing he'd been yearning to say all afternoon. "Begging your pardon, my lord, but I just wanted to say how pleased we were to hear the news."

"News?" Dane's brow furrowed. Had a message come from the Admiralty already?

"That we would be serving under your command, my lord. Seeing as how you're the new commissioner of the canal, I mean."

"Thank you, Mr. Taft," Ravenhurst said flatly, his frown deepening into a scowl.

But the eager lieutenant, full in the grip of hero worship, was slow to take a hint. "A great bit of luck for us that you were assigned here to Rye. We all know what—what you did at Trafalgar, aboard the *Bellerophon*. I'm only sorry I wasn't there to see action myself," the young man added bitterly.

"You are, are you?" Ravenhurst growled. "Then let me tell you something, Lieutenant. You ought to thank the good lord you weren't at Trafalgar, for a more hellish engagement has never been fought. Even under Nelson's management it was bloody, full-scale carnage fought by lumbering, dismasted ships locked gunport to gunport, bowsprit to bowsprit, entangled in each other's rigging. The idea of a frontal attack was revolutionary, of course, but it was also sheer madness. And Nelson knew that better than anyone."

The lieutenant's face paled at such heresy. An odd, choking sound came from his throat.

Ravenhurst's expression hardened as memories of that day swept over him. "There was no romance in what happened at Trafalgar, Mr. Taft, and even the heroism of that day has been greatly exaggerated. We can only hope the outcome prevented such things from ever happening again. And as for wars," he added grimly, "there are many kinds, fought in different ways. Remember that, Lieutenant."

"Yes, my lord," the young man replied, totally adrift.

"Good. Now, we'll need to bring in more elms for cover along that bank." Ravenhurst pointed up the north side of the canal, where the bare slope rose steeply, a dark scar upon the surrounding green plain. "Hawthorn hedges, too, I believe. They'll provide cover and give our men a better chance to return fire in case of attack."

"Do you really believe the French would dare such a thing?"

"It is not my business to speculate, Lieutenant," Ravenhurst said curtly. "My job is to insure the security of this area in the event Napoleon does invade. Now, how many feet does the canal measure at its widest?"

"Thirty, my lord. Give or take a few inches," came the tense rejoinder.

So the fellow was irritated, was he? Dane's lips twitched at the young officer's attempt to be precise. "And at its narrowest?"

"Not ten, my lord."

Ravenhurst's eyebrows rose. "Ten feet?" This did not agree with the information the Admiralty had given him.

"More or less. My lord," the officer added stiffly.

Dane waited.

"Except for the bit running west from Rye to Pett Level, that is," Taft corrected himself a moment later. "Built at the very last and little more than a ditch, that stretch is."

"Thank you, Lieutenant," Ravenhurst said dryly, his mind engaged in rapid calculations.

His first concern was ground cover. He would suggest that elm trees be planted every ten feet, and hawthorn hedges beyond that as a second layer of defense. The western stretch of the canal along Pett Level ought to be wider, of course, but that could hardly be helped now. Then there was the problem of the supply road north of the canal, which already required maintenance.

"Stop staring at me, Lieutenant," Dane snapped, without turning his head. "You're making me bloody nervous."

"Yes, my lord," came the muffled reply.

"So he has the good will of the local people, this Romney Fox?"

"Indeed he does. Always careful to drop off food, tea, or guineas for the destitute. He's a cool one, is the Romney Fox. One can't help almost—" The young officer flushed and bit off the words he'd been about to say.

"Almost what, Lieutenant?"

"Sir?" the man at the oars repeated uncomfortably.

"Finish your sentence, man," came the taut order.

"Well, admire the fellow. He's never harmed an officer or civilian, and his runs are a marvel of planning. Takes Hawkins by surprise every time—almost as if he were toying with him."

Ravenhurst's face hardened. "The man is a criminal, Lieutenant, as well as being in league with our enemies. Don't ever forget that. And there's nothing even faintly admirable about treason. So see you don't express such sentiments in my hearing again."

"Aye, my lord," came the stiff answer.

So the lad didn't like that order, did he? Well, he'd better learn to like it, Dane thought grimly, because there was still a war to be fought and an enemy to rout, and the Admiralty had every reason to believe this Fox fellow was deeply involved.

In short, they wanted their traitor run to ground, and Dane was bloody well going to do just that.

"What about the smugglers' haunts? Any clues as to where they might congregate to plan their runs? There must be some way these scoundrels communicate."

"They've a time-worn system of signals here along the coast, my lord. Things like lights in a window, horses tethered out front. Some say a fiddler plays a certain tune at the inns and public houses. They can muster two hundred men in an hour's time, I've heard."

"Inns, you say?" Dane's tone sharpened. "Like the Angel, perhaps?"

"I once heard it said—but not now. Miss Leighton's not the sort to hold with such comings and goings. No, there's been no sign of the wind in that quarter. But there's another spot—a low sort of place on the edge of the marsh, near Snargate. It's called the Merry Maids."

Dane's eyes narrowed. They were nearing the outskirts of Appledore now. Across the open fields a little church of weathered stone glowed crimson in the last rays of the setting sun. "Any other suspicious people I ought to know about, Lieutenant?"

"No one in particular, sir. Everyone hereabouts has a hand in 'the trade,' as they call it. And there's that brash Frenchman who's been patrolling the coasts from Fairlight to Folkestone. Brazen, he is. Just last week he was spotted lying at anchor near Winchelsea. Aye, in broad daylight."

"What sort of craft does he command?"

"The *Liberté,* my lord, a two-masted brig. She's square-rigged and as fine a seagoing vessel as you could ever hope to see. A crew to match, too, for they've slipped past every Revenue cutter that's gone after them."

"That hardly speaks well of the King's navy," Lord Ravenhurst said acidly.

"No, my lord."

"What about this new customs inspector, Amos Hawkins? What's his place in all this?"

"Rough lot, my lord. Enjoys his power a shade too much, if you know what I mean."

"I do not know, Lieutenant. If I did, I would not have asked."

Stinging from this rebuke, the young officer bent to the oars, averting his face to conceal his red cheeks. "The man likes to use his office to wrest goods from the townspeople—food, clothing, things of that sort. And there have been rumors about his beating some of the villagers who wouldn't comply . . ." His voice trailed off.

"Go on, Lieutenant. It sounds as if there's more."

"Well, the man's been making free with the local women, my lord. Treats them damned rough too. Only last month a village girl from Appledore came home covered with bruises. An honest girl, not one of the local trollops. Afraid to speak, she was—didn't want to give the name of the villain who'd done it. But her brothers finally got the name out of her. Amos Hawkins, it was." The lieutenant's voice hardened. "When they went after him, he had them shot in the back, all three of them, and had their bodies dumped in the canal. Said there'd be more of the same to anyone that opposed him."

"And the magistrate?"

"Didn't deem it proper to interfere, my lord. Oh, he made a hasty appearance, but pronounced it a falling out between the brothers, who'd drunk too much and then shot each other."

"I suppose after shooting each other they managed to throw their own bodies into the canal," Ravenhurst said coldly. "There were no witnesses?"

"None who dared come forward. I reckon Hawkins made his point well enough."

The viscount's face set in hard, chiseled lines. Were they fighting a war with France so that bullies like Hawkins could stay home and terrorize the countryside?

Not if he could bloody well help it, Ravenhurst vowed silently.

On they floated, grim-faced, neither speaking. Above them the sky darkened, azure slipping to lavender as the sun sank over the spires of Rye.

Dane tensed, his fingers knifing deep into the pockets of his greatcoat. *If Tess was indeed involved,* a ruthless voice asked, *would he turn her coldly over to such a man as Hawkins, knowing what he would do to her?*

Ravenhurst smothered a curse beneath his breath. Somehow life had seemed a great deal simpler at sea.

"Begging your pardon, your lordship," Lieutenant Taft began

tentatively. "For all the man's a criminal, I wouldn't like to see Hawkins get a hold of him."

Or her, Dane thought.

"You see, where the Fox is concerned, Hawkins has become— well, unhinged. The fellow's thrown sand in his eyes once too often, and catching the smuggler has become Hawkins's own private war."

"In that case, we'd bloody well better run our fox to ground before Amos Hawkins finds him, don't you think, Lieutenant?"

Several hours later, when the shadows lengthened and bled together into twilight, four roses reached their destination in four different cottages on the edge of the marsh.

And four men tensed when they saw the furled black petals, the Fox's secret sign. What was the bastard doing, rousing them again so soon? they wondered, to a man. Only six hours to gather carts, horses, and forty men between them.

But their irritation soon ebbed.

More runs meant more gold guineas jangling in their pockets. So who were they to complain if their Fox was an industrious sort?

Aye, when darkness fell upon the marsh they would all be waiting.

7

The sky was leaden, streaked with dark clouds. The air hung heavy with the threat of rain.

Night on the marsh.

Ghosts might well walk in such brooding stillness.

A lantern flashed once in the darkness, and then its light was quickly muzzled. High on the dunes the figure gripping the lantern eased leeward, turning to sweep sharp eyes across the waves of sand, which stretched north to the spires of Rye and east into the great black void of Romney Marsh.

Nothing moving there, Tess told herself sharply. So why this nagging sense of urgency?

From far out in the Channel there came an answering burst of light, just as quickly extinguished.

Suddenly the landscape exploded into life. A line of dark figures broke from the dunes and forty smugglers with blackened faces clambered over the shifting sand toward the beach. As if in perfect response, the trim square-rigged sails of a brig flashed into view, no more than a pale glow in the faint moonlight.

The lonely cry of a kestrel echoed over the marsh, nearly drowned out by the creaking of a score of wagons inching over the eastern rim of the dunes.

Without warning a horse and rider, masked all in black from cloak to tricorn, swept out of the night. In the moonlight the face beneath the hat was clearly visible—an odd face, with black whiskers bristling beside a sharp little nose. Only the merest trace of the rider's eyes could be seen through tiny slits. Though they glittered with wild exhilaration, no one could have told their color.

"Once again I give you my compliments on a bonny night's work, my gentlemen," the rider shouted, his voice shrill and distorted by his mask. None would recognize his real tones, but the laugh that punctuated his words was clear and hearty.

The Fox. The name was passed breathlessly down the queue, spoken in pride, gratitude, and fear, as two score faces slanted up at the rider.

"Ever known the Fox to be late, my stout lads?" the man hissed in that strange, unnatural voice. "Aye, Hawkins's yapping dogs have yet to run me to ground!" Then the humor vanished, replaced by the cold precision of command. "Raise the galleys, Mr. Jones!"

Immediately the five front men broke free of the line and scrambled to brush sand from the craft concealed near the beach. Moments later, as if by magic, four sleek galleys were revealed, their long oars swathed in canvas to muffle their strokes.

"Soon as you've taken on your cargo, steer for Hythe, Mr. White," the Fox ordered crisply. "And it's Winchelsea Beach for you this night, Mr. Smith! The rest of you bring your goods back here for loading."

By unspoken agreement real names were never used on the marsh. No, names like Smith and Jones were all anyone needed here, and for the same reason final instructions were never given in advance of a landing. It was safer this way, and all knew it, the Fox most of all, for men were weak creatures whose tongues were far too prone to slip with drink or the flush of passion.

The brig was in clear view now, her sails slack while she rode the current. In the moonlight the lettering on her stern shone clearly: *Liberté.*

None of the figures engaged in the midnight run seemed to notice any irony in that word, nor discomfort in trading with citizens of a hostile nation.

This was business, after all, a business which had kept the coastal families from starvation for four hundred years. Wars would be won and lost, nations rise and fall, but the smuggling would always remain.

A lantern flashed once from the foredeck of the French vessel and now received an answering flare from the slim figure who'd moved to a position near the end of the line. The galleys were already being launched from the shingle. In a matter of minutes they fluttered near the hull of the brig, like moths drawn to a flame.

One by one they took on their quota of kegs filled with over-proof brandy and geneva, along with chests of uncustomed tea, tobacco, and China silks. Their cargo loaded, the stout crew turned swiftly and pulled for shore, where eager fingers waited to heft the goods into waiting wagons.

Less than a half hour later the wagons were nearly full. The galleys had already turned back for their final run, which would take one of them by sea to Winchelsea and another to Hythe. The remaining two craft would return to their hiding place beneath the Camber sands.

The whole maneuver was performed with the precision of a military exercise. Indeed, the Fox prided himself on the drilling of his gentlemen and the care of his calculations, especially when dealing with a new contact, such as the captain of the *Liberté*. Even now the smuggler was careful to communicate only through intermediaries.

No, the Fox was not a man who left any detail to chance. Which was precisely why he was so successful at his trade.

Beneath him the big black horse pranced skittishly. "Gentle, Fancy," the smuggler whispered, his sharp eyes narrowing as he studied the horizon. Seeing no untoward movement there, he swept his eyes over the toiling figures. Frowning, he studied the slight figure holding the snub-nosed lantern. Something tugged at his consciousness, something he could not quite place.

His hands tightened on the reins and he cursed silently. What was it about the lad that bothered him?

But his thoughts never had a chance to run their natural course. Just then a cry went up from the dunes bordering the beach. Suddenly a line of dragoons darkened the crest of the sand.

"Halt in the King's name, ye bloody vermin!"

The Fox was already moving. "Steady, lads!" he ordered, his voice hard and commanding. "Keep your heads and make for the marsh! Leave the goods where they fall. There'll be plenty more where those came from!"

As he spoke, the big man urged his black horse between the wagons, reaching down to offer a steadying hand or a supportive tug amid the chaos of retreat.

The first of the excisemen began plowing down the dunes toward the beach. But the smugglers were quicker, bolting to the east, where the sand stopped and the dark stretches of the marsh began.

The galleys, at least, were safe at sea, the Fox saw with satisfaction. There they would continue to take on their cargo, then steer for safe coves farther west and east, as prearranged in case of just such an event.

Suddenly the Fox spurred his horse forward. The lad with the lantern was down, he saw, thrown by that brute Tom Ransley as the big smuggler jumped free of his wagon. Already the dragoons, along with the main body of excisemen headed by Amos Hawkins, were swarming toward the last figures straggling along the curve of the beach.

With a taut curse, the Fox bent down, straining to reach the slim shape stretched on the sand. The boy's head was thrown back, his floppy hat askew, revealing a pale oval face, fragile cheekbones, and wide, frightened eyes.

"Tess!" the Fox breathed in horror, his heart constricting painfully. "Sweet Jesus, lass, what daft thing have ye done this time?"

What indeed? Tess thought wildly. But the question came too late. Her adventure had turned into a nightmare. Her rib throbbed where that fool Ransley had kicked her, and she could hardly move. Around her came the angry cries of plunging horses, the bark of pistols, and the savage curses of Hawkins's men.

"There the devil is!" the squat customs inspector bellowed. "Five hundred pounds to the first man among ye who levels the bastard!" A roar went up from the company, who began elbowing each other viciously in their eagerness to cross the beach.

"Grab my hand, lass!" the Fox ordered, fighting to calm Fancy as he reached down to the slim figure kneeling in the sand. "Hurry!"

Blindly Tess fought her way to her feet. She was nearly within reach of the Fox when she glanced up to see Hawkins's heavy figure silhouetted against the moon, one arm raised as he took careful aim.

At the Fox. And Jack was too busy trying to help her to notice.

"Behind you, Fox!" she cried, the words thin and reedy. But her warning came too late.

For in the same instant, a pistol cracked and the tall, mounted smuggler crumpled over his saddle. Gasping, Tess gritted her teeth against the pain in her ribs and stumbled toward the big, pawing horse.

"Leave m-me, lass," Jack whispered. "Make for Pett Level. I canna protect ye now," he rasped, one hand gripping his chest. Already a dark pool of blood stained the white ruffled shirt beneath his black cloak.

"I can't leave you," Tess sobbed. "Not—like this."

The Fox wavered in the saddle and nearly fell. White-faced, Tess gripped the edge of the saddle and pulled herself up behind the sagging rider. Wrapping her arms tightly about Jack's waist, she held his slack frame steady while she urged the giant black horse forward. "Go, Fancy!" she cried.

This time there was no protest from the man slumped before her.

Her face grim, Tess fought to calm her whirling thoughts. *Perdition!* The sea was at her back and the galleys were all gone. Already the cursed officers were dropping to a firing stance.

The Fox moaned slightly and Tess's trembling fingers tightened. No time for panic, she told herself, dragging in a lungful of cold air. A rush of icy calm descended upon her. They'd never take her alive, nor the Fox! Damned if she'd see her friend dangle from a noose!

Since Hawkins would expect her to run before his troops, Tess decided to do exactly the opposite. With a hoarse cry she wheeled the great horse about and made straight for the ragged line of men kneeling in the sand.

Her heart in her mouth, she spurred the horse up the slope, the drumming of his great hooves deadened by the sand. Over her head whined an angry volley, and instinctively she crouched lower, pulling the Fox down to make a smaller target.

Only ten yards to go, Tess calculated.

The dragoons kneeling in the sand were already reloading.

"Get yer heads out of yer arses and fire, ye bloody fools!" Hawkins roared from his position behind the line. One of his men stumbled in his eagerness to prime his rifle and Hawkins gave him a vicious kick that sent him flying facedown into the sand. "Drop the pair of them or by God ye'll find yerselves meat for the press-gang!"

The wind was whining in Tess's ears. Her blood sang with fear and reckless determination.

Five more yards!

One of the dragoons rose. His rifle levelled as he took careful aim. Time seemed to stop.

For an agonizing eternity Tess stared down his muzzle into the mouth of Hell.

"Now, Fancy!" she screamed, and the great beast's hooves lifted, carrying them sailing over the astonished line of dragoons just as a ball whined furiously past her ear.

Behind Tess the excise officers broke into chaotic shouting as she plunged over the crest of the dunes. As soon as she was out of sight she turned the big horse sharply toward the west.

Just beyond the mouth of the Rother, narrow now at low tide, there was a small track that led through the treacherous canals and pools of Pett Level. By day it was difficult enough. But by night . . .

Tess did not hesitate. There was no other way. At least no one would attempt to follow them. There were too many dead ends, too many narrow tracks which ended abruptly in marshy pools.

No, she thought, her brow furrowed with pain, not even for the impossible bounty of five hundred pounds would the cowardly excisemen attempt Pett Level by night.

Before her the wounded man stirred, groaned once, and began to cough harshly. "What've ye done, lassie? Sweet Mother of God, if I'd known what was brewin' in that stubborn head of yers, I'd a taken my own whip to ye," the Fox rasped, his native accent very pronounced.

"That you might have tried, Jack," Tess whispered. "But even you couldn't have changed my mind."

There was no answer from the man before her. Once again he slumped, his body a dead weight against Tess's tired arms.

"Oh, Jack," she whispered hoarsely, struggling to keep him upright as she plunged across the sand.

She prayed that the skiff was still moored in the reeds at the edge of the river, where she had concealed it the day before. Her eyes narrowed as she searched the edge of the Rother, stretching like a pale ribbon of silver in the moonlight.

When she saw the outline of an oar, she swung down to tear at a concealing mat of reeds. In the saddle the wounded smuggler swayed, and Tess rushed back to anchor him. "Steady, Jack," she said urgently. With shaking fingers she pulled his bent frame from the horse, nearly stumbling beneath his weight. With precious minutes ticking off in her head, Tess half dragged, half shoved him toward the little skiff. Behind her, from the other side of the dunes, came the shouts of Hawkins's men in hot pursuit.

Once her burden was settled in the boat, Tess turned and slapped the black horse hard on the rump. "Home, Fancy!" she ordered.

Everyone knew the Fox's great black horse. This would buy them time they desperately needed, for it had taken far too long to maneuver Jack into the little skiff.

Quickly Tess pushed off, sliding down to pull against the oars, her ribs burning with every move. Gritting her teeth against waves of pain, she concentrated on keeping the boat steady. It was low tide, fortunately, and the other shore was no more than ten yards away.

With a quiet thud the boat met the far bank. Behind them Hawkins's men were spreading out to comb the sands.

A pistol cracked. "Over there, ye bloody fools! It's the Fox! This time don't let the bastard get away. Remember—five hundred pounds for the one what brings me the pair of 'em. Dead or alive!"

Lord Ravenhurst sat before the crackling fire, still a good distance from the mindless oblivion that was his fervent goal.

He shifted slightly, his wide shoulders straining uncomfortably against an ancient, fragile wing chair far too small to contain them. His greatcoat hung awry from the back of the chair, and his long, powerful legs were stretched out toward the fire. With piercing lapis eyes he assessed the half-empty glass cradled in his right hand.

He'd forgotten how cold it could be here on the coast, even in early summer. After his months of pampered luxury in London, the dampness seemed to creep into his bones, making him ache all over. Thank God Hobhouse had ordered a fire made up.

Already he was growing bloody soft and indolent, Ravenhurst thought grimly.

The flames hissed and popped companionably as the viscount stared deep into their dancing light. Before his fixed gaze the colors began to flicker and bleed together.

He smiled faintly. Maybe he was closer to oblivion than he had realized. Still smiling, he tossed down the last of his brandy and poured himself another.

Yes, he'd forgotten a great many things about this place, things like the ghosts that haunted Church Square and Watchbell Street.

Ghosts with dark, haunting eyes and silken hair.

That was when Ravenhurst realized he was not nearly drunk enough.

Tess shivered as the cold wind flung rain into her face.

Perdition! she cursed inwardly, looking off toward Camber. In minutes this deadly game would be played! Hawkins would have her right where he wanted, and the Fox would hang.

Then she stiffened, giving a silent prayer of thanks, for she saw Jupiter waiting exactly where she had tethered him, hidden behind a lush curtain of reeds.

Now, if only she could shove Jack up onto the horse! "Wake up,

Jack! You'll have to help me." She knelt over the unconscious figure in the bottom of the boat and tugged off his mask, slapping his cheeks gently.

Sweet heaven, let him come around!

Slipping one arm beneath his shoulders, Tess struggled to pull the big man upright. "Help me, Jack," she pleaded.

Her desperation penetrated the smuggler's haze of pain. "I'll try, lassie, but 'tisna much—use I'll be to ye now. Pull me f-forward a wee bit," he rasped. He managed to sit up awkwardly, wavered for a moment, and then righted himself. With grim determination he struggled to his feet, supported by Tess.

Somehow, she never knew how, they stumbled from the skiff. "Only a little farther, Jack," she whispered urgently. "Don't stop now."

With his good hand the smuggler reached toward the horse's back and pulled himself up, then slumped sideways over the saddle. Immediately Tess jumped up behind him, her cold hands steadying his back and ribs.

All the time Hawkins's wild curses drifted toward them across the river.

If only they could make the Level, they would be safe, Tess thought. No one would follow them through its canals and dikes at night.

Her arms screamed with the weight of Jack's big body, but Tess knew she could not stop. Ashen-faced, she changed her position, trying to ease the strain of his weight.

That was when she felt her fingers slip through something warm and sticky.

A cry of horror burst from her lips. "Dear God," she whispered. "I'll get Hawkins for this, Jack. I promise you I will."

Suddenly Tess caught her breath, reining in Jupiter sharply as they nearly plunged into a pool that seemed to loom up out of nowhere. Her fingers white on the reins, she carefully nudged the big horse forward, skirting the silver water while she searched for the small clump of grass that marked the safe track up to Fairleigh.

Pale pools gleamed to right and left. So beautiful, Tess thought, dizzy with pain and fatigue.

So dangerous.

By the time they reached the old sea wall, she had formed a desperate plan. Quickly she reined in Jupiter and slid down, giving the horse's neck a reassuring stroke. "Go home to Fairleigh, Jupiter," she ordered. "Follow the old track. You know the way."

The big roan turned and nickered at her, unmoving.

"Home!" she ordered fiercely.

The man known on the marsh only as the Fox began to mumble, dragging himself back with difficulty from his netherworld of pain. "Tess?" he whispered hoarsely. His cold hand reached out to catch her wrist. "Nay, lass, I willna let ye! Take the horse and leave me here. I'll never make it anyway."

"I can't, Jack," Tess said desperately. "Thomas is in the old caretaker's cottage. He'll see to you until I can make my way back." She steeled her voice to fine bravado. "Shouldn't take me much above an hour or two, I expect. Don't worry about me. I know these pools as well as I know the Angel's cellars!"

The Fox swayed for a moment, and as he did so his grip wavered. Immediately Tess wrenched free and slapped the horse's rump sharply. "Move, Jupiter!"

The big horse plunged off to the north, Jack's muffled curses echoing in the quiet air. "When I get my hands on ye, lass, I'll—I'll make ye rue this night. Just ye—wait. Aye, s-see if I bloody don't!" the Fox rasped.

His warning was cut short as a harsh spasm of coughing racked his slumped body.

Oh, God, Jack, that I already do! Tess thought, watching Jupiter plunge deeper into the marsh until horse and rider finally disappeared.

Then, satisfied at last, she turned and began to stumble down to a narrow canal nearly concealed behind a ragged tangle of water plants.

Ravenhurst heard a gentle tap at the door.

His eyes narrowed. Maybe if he ignored it, it would go away.

Frowning, he tossed down the last of his brandy and stared into the fire, struggling under the weight of responsibilities that daily grew more urgent. Even now it was as if he heard a clock ticking inside his head. *Two weeks,* it said. *Only two weeks left.*

The tapping came again, more insistent this time.

"Who in bloody hell is it?" he growled, not looking up from the fire crackling in the grate.

The door opened with a faint squeak. "Only Peale, Captain." Ravenhurst's leathery-faced valet entered quietly and put away the boots he had just come from cleaning and polishing to a mirror-like sheen.

"Don't call me Captain," the hard-eyed man before the fire muttered. "Not anymore. Now I'm just Dane." His voice hardened. "Bloody Lord Ravenhurst!"

The manservant did not reply, knowing no answer would be acceptable when the viscount was in such a mood. Peale's stiff military bearing did not waver as he completed his task, then moved to unpack Ravenhurst's last remaining case, careful to keep his eyes from flickering toward the half-empty decanter on the table beside his employer.

Since the candles were snuffed, he had to content himself with the weak light of the dying flames. But he had worked under worse conditions, the valet thought.

Far worse.

In a few minutes the case's half dozen shirts were tucked away into drawers. Frowning, Peale lingered, fingering the fine linen garments.

All brand new. All unworn. Times change, he reminded himself sternly, and one had bloody well better change with them. Just as the captain—viscount, Peale corrected himself sharply—had to change too. It was that or be washed away like so much debris on the tide.

The valet studied Ravenhurst's bent form critically. It was a hard, well-muscled body, the broad shoulders clearly outlined beneath his shirt. Gone was the weakness that had plagued the officer upon his return to England only months ago. The rippling shoulder muscles and taut torso were the result of daily boxing and fencing. When possible the viscount swam, Peale knew, but there had been precious few opportunities for that recently.

Maybe that was why his lordship had become so damnably broodish of late. That and the stream of coded documents he'd been receiving from the Admiralty, Peale thought.

The valet's eyes narrowed and he shook his head. There'd be no swimming tomorrow either. Unless he missed his guess, his employer would be nursing the very devil of a head by morning.

His face carefully expressionless, the valet who was not quite a valet finally looked up. "Will you be wishful of more brandy before I go?" he asked blandly. "Your Lordship," he added, almost as an afterthought.

"I don't need a bloody nursemaid, Peale!" Ravenhurst snapped. "We've been through a great deal together, but even Trafalgar does not give you that right!"

The grizzled manservant sighed quietly. There was nothing more he could do this night. At least when the viscount drank, he could sleep.

Most nights he simply paced the floor, back and forth, circling like an angry, restless animal.

For long minutes Ravenhurst brooded over the fire, his lapis eyes smoky. "I'm sorry, Peale," he said presently. "You didn't deserve that. I of all people should know that."

With unsteady movements Dane stood up and walked to the window. Pushing aside the crisp white curtains, he stared out at the quiet street. To the south, the mouth of the Rother stretched ghostly in the moonlight. He could just make out the glimmer of a schooner far out at sea, long past the breakers of Winchelsea harbor.

More smugglers, no doubt, God rot their souls! The curse of this whole bloody coast!

What was he doing here anyway? Dane asked himself. He ought to be out at sea pacing the quarterdeck, with the rough timbers creaking at his feet and the wind whistling through the overhead rigging.

Why in God's name was he cooped up here on land, when there was a war raging just over the horizon?

Ravenhurst's fingers tightened on the frilled white curtains at the casement. The white hair sweeping from his brow glowed starkly, silver against ebony.

No, it was time to face the real question that was bothering him. Why had fate seen fit to spare him when so many others, far better men than he, had fallen?

But maybe it did not matter, he told himself grimly. That life was gone forever. Nelson was dead. His family, too, was gone, swept away by sickness and a freak sailing accident. He could go no more to sea, not when he had a duty to his name. One day that duty would require him to marry and provide an heir to carry on the Ravenhurst line.

He scowled at the idea of a cold-blooded alliance for the sake of progeny. But he supposed he must learn to accept that, too, just as he had learned to accept so many things since his return.

Out at sea the sails of the distant schooner twinkled for a moment, then disappeared as the ship ran south before the wind. To Dieppe, no doubt, Dane thought, his fingers unconsciously twisting the cloth at the window.

Did they even now carry gold guineas to feed and arm Napoleon's war-weary troops?

Dane's features hardened as he recalled his last meeting at the Admiralty only days before.

"Had a hell of a time tracking you down, Ravenhurst," the stern, white-haired admiral had said stiffly, with the merest touch of grudging respect. "The wine and the wenching are all very well. You've earned that, of course. But don't you think it's time to get back to the business of living again? Your wounds must be long healed, after all."

Only the wounds that showed, Dane thought bitterly, staring out into the night. His left hand moved restlessly, fingering the ugly scars that ran from wrist to elbow.

Long, searing lines that gleamed silver and bloodred in the dancing firelight.

Maybe the Old Man had been right. Maybe work was what he needed after all. Something to take his mind off the specters of Trafalgar and Corunna. Lord knows, he'd tried everything else in the last months. The wine hadn't worked, nor had the empty gaiety of London.

The women had helped—but only for a while. Soon their attractions, even those of the lush Danielle, had begun to pale.

And then the Admiralty had found him.

Dane's eyes darkened as he recalled the Old Man's blunt words.

"This time it's an order," the stern-faced man had said flatly. "I know you've been released from duty since that wretched business about your family. Hell of a thing to come home to." He held up a hand as Dane made to interrupt. "No, let me have my say. I'll not send you back to sea, so don't ask. This is something a damn sight more important, though I can see from your scowl that you'll disagree about that too! This time it's a spy I'm after. The fellow's base appears to be Fairleigh, that old wreck west of Rye. You know it well, so don't tell me you don't," he'd continued inexorably. "Been in the Leighton family for generations. A vast ruin now, unfortunately. From what I hear the last Leighton was an out and out bounder—gambled away his last shilling, then took his life. Nasty business, I can tell you. His creditors descended, and by the time they'd picked over the carcass there was very little left."

The admiral had stopped then, glancing down at a handful of papers lined up neatly in the middle of his desk. "One daughter—Theresa Ariadne Leighton. Only other survivor is her brother, Ashley. The boy's up at Oxford and already making a name for himself among the wilder set." The admiral sniffed in disapproval. "The boy's brash enough to take up smuggling, I've no doubt. But it would be a damned difficult thing to arrange at such a distance. And he is rather young for such leadership, of course. But one can never say . . ."

Frowning, the silver-haired officer had returned to the subject at hand. "At any rate it's your problem, now, Ravenhurst. We have reason to believe the man behind the spying is the Romney Fox. Damned elusive scoundrel—you must have heard of him. And you can expect no help in Rye, for the fellow's a great deal too cozy with the townsfolk there."

Too cozy with *her?* Dane had asked himself, icy fingers of fury gripping his throat.

Across the room the steely-eyed admiral had studied him long and hard. "Find the Fox, Ravenhurst. Run him to ground and see if he's behind the spying and the gold shipments. If he is"—the admiral's eyes did not flicker from Dane's face—"then remove the bastard once and for all. We can't afford for Viscount Wellington's plans to reach Bonaparte, not now, when things are reaching a crucial stage on the Continent. I won't tell you when or where, for that information only a handful are privy to. But I'll tell you this, Ravenhurst. Use whatever means you require—I give you an open hand. Just see to it that the traitor is silenced. For good."

The white curtains fluttered around Dane as he stood unmoving in a faint bar of moonlight. His lapis eyes were hard and unreadable.

Even then he had tried to escape the Old Man's net. "What makes you think I have the slightest interest in your concerns or in this cursed war?" he had demanded brusquely.

"So you won't listen? Not even for a man who saved your life?" the admiral demanded sternly. "You do remember young Thorpe, do you not? The midshipman on the *Bellerophon,* who lost an arm at Trafalgar? The boy'd been on half-pay since Corunna. Did occasional jobs for us. Well, he was the one who washed up in Fairleigh's cove. Morland didn't tell you that, did he? Nor the boy's last words. 'She was waiting for me . . . the Angel . . . Tess.' "

At the sound of that name, Dane had jerked forward in his chair, his hands clenched, his face a dark mask. An acid rage began to burn through him, churning his thoughts to a dark whirlwind.

To work with the smugglers was foul enough, but to murder an innocent lad of seventeen. . . .

The bitch! The cold-blooded bitch!

Suddenly the whole business had changed, no longer King and country, navy against navy. Now it became deadly personal, a debt of revenge owed to the innocent midshipman who had once saved Dane's life, losing his own arm in the bargain.

Now it was man against man.

Or woman.

Yes, Ravenhurst vowed grimly, he would do as the admiral ordered. He would break Tess Leighton without the slightest twinge of regret.

"You have six weeks," the admiral had continued relentlessly. "Very soon Wellington will be poised for a major push in the Peninsula. Suffice it to say that we cannot let anything interfere with the success of his mission. You and I are both expendable, so long as the campaign is safeguarded."

"But I won't need six weeks," Ravenhurst had answered softly, his voice taut with menace. "I'll have your answer for you in half that time." A cruel smile played about the corners of his mouth. "Oh, yes, I'll run your Fox to ground, Admiral. When I'm done with him, he'll wish he'd never been born."

So will she.

Dane's hands twisted convulsively against the white curtains as he remembered the harsh vow he had made that day in London.

Behind him, Peale coughed discreetly. "Will you be requiring aught else, your lordship?"

"Luck, Peale," Dane muttered, his voice slightly slurred. "Maybe even a miracle."

"Miracles have been known to happen, your lordship," the servant said quietly. "And Rye is a place where one could almost believe that magic exists."

As the door closed softly, Ravenhurst continued to stare out toward the sea. With expert eyes he scanned the horizon, where ragged white clouds ran before the wind.

Yes, he would have his dark vengeance. It might just begin to repay all the bitterness the last five years had brought him.

Suddenly the quiet of the night was rent by shouting as a company of mounted dragoons and a score of excisemen clattered up the narrow street.

So Hawkins's hounds had scented their prey, had they? Ravenhurst spun around, swaying slightly, and realized he was more than a little drunk. Smiling grimly, he jerked on his great-coat and boots.

So what if he was a trifle bosky? That was bloody fine with him. In fact, it put him in a perfect frame of mind to do a little hunting of his own!

8

By the time she got to the top of the tunnel, Tess was weaving, fighting desperately to stay upright. Her brow furled with pain, she pressed the hidden latch that opened the outer door from the tunnel to her room. Then, her heart pounding, she gave silent thanks for the Angel's myriad secrets.

Once more they had saved her life.

Her side burning, she rapped on the inner door. She could feel a fine sprinkling of sweat bead her forehead under the thick charcoal, and something warm and sticky on her side. Probably blood where that imbecile Ransley had kicked her.

A moment later there came a flurry of steps, and the door sprang open.

Letty's pale, frightened face appeared in the doorway. "Thank the good Lord! I was near to dying with worry about you, miss."

Tess tried to pull off her damp cloak and grimaced, swaying wildly.

"You've been hurt!" Letty gasped.

"That swine Ransley kicked me. Oh, don't worry, he had no idea he was kicking a woman and not another of his rough fellows. But Jack—Jack took a ball in the side, damn Hawkins's black heart!" Tess's voice grew muffled as she bent to study the dried blood and angry purple bruises mottling her side.

"Oh, miss. 'Tis mad you are!"

"You might be right," Tess said through gritted teeth. "But if I am, it's a fine sort of madness." Already she was shrugging off her filthy shirt and reaching for a piece of linen to scrub the soot from her face. "Now, hurry downstairs, Letty. I've need of some of that fine port Jack brought on his last run."

"Give it up, miss, for God's sake! Before something terrible happens!" the maid cried, her voice shrill with panic.

Tess smiled grimly. "Give it up I will, Letty, and with pleasure. But not just yet—not when I'm so close to everything I've worked for. Fairleigh's walls need shoring up, and the roof is rotten. But soon I'll have enough to do all those things. Then—"

What Tess would have said next was lost as angry fists pounded at the Angel's oak double doors three stories below. The two women froze in a crazy tableau, Letty reaching for a water basin and Tess tugging off her thick woolen stockings.

"Open up in there! Crown excisemen on official business! Fetch the proprietor!"

For a moment Tess reeled. *Would this nightmare never end?*

Far below she heard Hobhouse's irate answer, which was drowned out by a babble of furious voices.

"Miss Leighton is sleeping," the loyal majordomo insisted, "and not for a passel of brutes like yourselves would I even consider waking her."

"Mebbe she'd prefer to receive Captain Hawkins in her bedroom then!" one of the men barked crudely.

Letty turned a white, shaken face toward her mistress.

"Quickly, Letty, help me into a gown," Tess ordered. "Nothing too low, else they see the bruises. A little dishevelment may be expected, thankfully, when a lady is dragged from her bed in the middle of the night."

The anxious maid heard the rising note of hysteria in her mistress's voice, an unsteadiness which was promptly stamped out.

"Hurry, Letty!" Tess said urgently. "The blue muslin. I mustn't keep our *visitors* waiting too long."

The maid's answer was muffled as she thrust her head into a tall armoire opposite the door, then emerged with gown, chemise, knitted stockings, and blue kid slippers.

Grim-faced, Letty pulled Tess's lawn chemise over her head,

frowning as she surveyed the dark bruises mottling her mistress's chest and ribs. Shaking her head disapprovingly, she handed Tess her knitted wool stockings.

Aye, Miss Tess was a beauty, all right. That slim white body was supple and strong. Ought to be married to a good man and raising a family by now, not careering about the countryside on God knows what wild errands!

And there was that strange episode last night, when she'd found the window unlatched and Tess's gown gaping open from neck to toe. Had Amos Hawkins somehow managed to get a key to Miss Tess's room? Letty shivered at the thought. No one was safe from that brute.

An angry bellow exploded below, unmistakably the voice of Amos Hawkins. "Where's her room, damn ye?"

The two women's eyes met, wide with fear.

"Oh, Miss Tess, what's to become of us?" the maid cried, wringing her hands. "We'll all be hanged for sure!"

"Nonsense, Letty! We shall come about," Tess said firmly. "Now stop fretting and hand me my gown."

Despite her brave words, Tess's fingers were trembling as she pulled the blue muslin over her head. Amos Hawkins was a stupid man, but he was dogged and vindictive. The Fox had mocked him too long, and Tess knew the man would stop at nothing to corner his elusive prey.

"Go down and tell Hobhouse to build a fire in the small salon. I'll receive our visitors there shortly. And ask him to bring tea and sherry precisely five minutes later." Tess's gray-green eyes burned with angry glints as she saw Letty's frightened look. "Don't worry, Hawkins won't try anything here under my own roof, Letty." Her full lips curved into a slightly crooked smile. "At least not with Hobhouse standing at the door."

A moment later Tess's smile faded. Suddenly she shivered, recalling her captor's warning in the Needles passage.

Yes, Amos Hawkins was not a man she wanted to meet alone on a dark night. God willing, she never would.

* * *

Five minutes later a coolly elegant Theresa Leighton descended the ancient stairway and crossed the gallery to the Angel's main wing.

Not a strand of her rich auburn hair was out of place. An angry fire burned in her magnificent eyes and her slim, elegant figure was rigid with indignation. If there was a certain tightness about her lips, it was only to be expected when she had been summoned so rudely from her bed.

Yes, she was entirely ready to do battle with Amos Hawkins, but Tess realized she would have to play this scene just right. A touch of outrage was called for, but not so much that she made Hawkins suspicious.

A fire was blazing in the grate when she swept into the quiet room at the front of the inn. Judging by the laughter down the corridor, Tess decided Hobhouse had guided Hawkins and his men into the taproom and was treating them to her best brandy. *The Fox's best brandy,* she corrected herself, smiling thinly.

If only Hawkins knew.

But maybe he did know. Maybe that was why he was here. To arrest her, she thought wildly, her heart beginning to hammer.

Stop it! Tess told herself savagely. Ashen-faced, she moved to a small rosewood side table and poured herself a glass of port.

Dutch comfort, she thought, cupping the glass with trembling fingers and draining it quickly. She coughed sharply but forced herself to swallow the sweet, fiery liquid, which burned down her throat and immediately sent a pleasant warmth radiating from the pit of her stomach. She poured herself another, and this time the alcohol did not take her by surprise.

I rather think I might begin to enjoy this taste, Tess thought grimly.

A brisk tap sounded at the door. After squaring her shoulders, Tess turned and took a deep breath. "Yes?" Thank goodness her voice did not tremble. It was cool, she noted, with just the right touch of irritation.

Hobhouse's stern face appeared at the door. "Mr. Hawkins to see you, miss," her majordomo said in frigid tones, which told exactly what he thought of this insolent intrusion.

"Stand aside, damn ye!" Hobhouse was abruptly thrust aside as the customs inspector forced his way into the room.

Her brow raised, Tess stared at the cold, leering countenance of Amos Hawkins, willing her face to remain calm.

"So here ye are, Miss Leighton," the officer snarled, darting a quick glance about the room. From there his small eyes flickered over Tess's neck and muslin-clad chest, as if to discover what lay beneath the cloth.

His look made Tess uncomfortably aware of Dane's warning. "What is the meaning of this intrusion?" she demanded furiously, pulling herself up to her full height.

"Tell him to leave," came Hawkins's sharp order.

"I'll do nothing of the—"

"Now! Or I'll have my men drag him out!"

"Very well," Tess snapped, desperate to get rid of the man. Only raw willpower kept her on her feet now.

Without warning a wave of dizziness hit her, and she braced herself on the back of a nearby wing chair. Her eyes closed for a second, then sought Hobhouse's angry face. "You may wait for me outside in the hall, Hobhouse."

Her instructions were not lost on Hawkins, who scowled and stalked over to slam the door in the majordomo's wake. "Ye don't ask me to sit down, Miss Leighton?"

"I can see no reason to do so, Mr. Hawkins, for our business will not last long enough to require it."

"Not my business, the King's business, Miss Leighton! Aye, the King's business," Hawkins repeated menacingly. "I'm out to catch my Fox this night and neither yerself nor anyone else is going to stop me. And I'll start by searching every room." His colorless eyes scoured Tess's face. "Starting with yers, m' dear. Unless ye can give me a reason why I shouldn't."

Tess felt her face flood crimson. "It is your right, of course, but you'll only be wasting your time. You'll find no smugglers here at the Angel, Inspector."

That at least was true, Tess thought. Hawkins would never find his man. Not if Tess could help it!

Nettled by her composure, the squat officer bent closer. His stubby fingers lifted a strand of auburn hair from her shoulder and twisted it sharply, dragging her head forward until it was only inches from his face. "Won't I?" His rank breath played across her cheeks and Tess had to force herself not to flinch. "In that case ye won't mind us searching, will ye? Everywhere," he added, his eyes probing her bodice. "Starting with yer rooms."

Tess jerked away, clenching her hands to keep from slapping Hawkins's leering face. The thought of his men going through her clothes and personal belongings infuriated her, but it would not do to fuel this man's suspicions. Hawkins was within his rights as His Majesty's Customs Inspector and well he knew it.

Tess only hoped Letty had remembered to dispose of her dirty shirt and breeches.

"Mundy!"

The door jerked open. Hawkins nodded curtly to the thin man outside. "Check every room, Mundy. Beginning with Miss Leighton's," he growled. "Strip the bed, dump the drawers, and empty the shelves! I want nothing missed, d' ye hear?"

Angry green sparks darted from Tess's eyes. She spun about to face Hawkins and for a moment found herself too angry to speak. Her chest was heaving, and the squat inspector seemed to take special pleasure in the sight.

"Such crudeness cannot be necessary," she snapped through clenched teeth.

"Having second thoughts, Miss Leighton? I can always call my man back. Then we can go somewhere to discuss this, somewhere more—private."

"I've nothing to say to you, Inspector. Neither in public nor in private!"

Hawkins's thick face turned a particularly ugly shade of crimson. Cursing, he caught Tess's elbow and jerked her close.

"Still chasing foxes, Hawkins?" From the doorway came a new voice, hard edged and laced with mockery.

Tess stiffened. Instantly she felt a stab of electric awareness flash down her neck and spine. Slowly she turned, to find lazy lapis eyes measuring her flushed face.

Her heart pounded wildly. She fought to conceal her surprise, to betray no more than irritation.

"Miss Leighton." The mocking lapis eyes studied her, cool and unreadable.

"Lord Ravenhurst," Tess answered coldly. Her chin rose as she pulled free of Hawkins and moved back to straighten her skirts.

The man before her smiled grimly. "We met five years ago, Inspector, did you know that? I was a callow lieutenant then. But the lady prefers not to recall the event. Ah, that such beauty could be so fickle," he added mockingly. "I am devastated, Miss Leighton."

Tess stiffened her shoulders, returning his look with disdain. "But then five years is such a long time, my lord. A great deal may change in such a period of time. Battles won. Hearts lost—and regained."

As she spoke, Tess tried to keep her eyes from his powerful, tense body. He still had the finest pair of shoulders she had ever seen, Tess thought unwillingly. And the most compelling eyes. Midnight eyes, which just now smoked with sapphire flames.

Schooling her features to aloofness, Tess glared back at this man whom she had once loved with every fiber of her being. The man who had destroyed her every hope of happiness.

Their eyes locked. In cold silence they scrutinized each other, two ruthless enemies assessing their opponent's strengths.

And weaknesses.

Slowly Tess's lips curved into a faint, insolent smile. In that instant she was glad she was dead inside, glad that she could never again feel such pain as this man had inflicted when he left.

"I don't give a damn whether ye've met or not!" Hawkins snarled, angry at being forgotten during this tense interchange. "And what I say to Miss Leighton is no bloody business of yers, Ravenhurst!"

"On the contrary, Inspector, it is very much my business. As a guest at the Angel, I find I don't care to have my possessions mauled about."

"Ye wouldn't be tryin' to tell me my business, would ye?" Hawkins sneered. "Ye're not on your quarterdeck now, and this ain't the Mediterranean. I wouldn't care if ye was a bloody duke—'tis my town ye're in, an' ye better not forget it!"

Unruffled, Dane raised the toe of his riding boot and studied it lazily. "I didn't realize Rye was yours to control, Hawkins. Things must have changed here in the last five years, far more than I realized," he drawled insolently.

"Aye, I'm the law here now! Just this night I uncovered a band of smugglers on Camber Sands. Nearly caught the bloody vermin, I did, but they piked off afore my men could round 'em up. One's wounded, though, and he'll not be hard to track. Came to me as how such a man might seek shelter at the Angel."

"You'll find no traitors here!" Tess blazed.

Cool lapis eyes swept across her face for a moment before settling on Hawkins. "What sort of man doubts a lady's word, Inspector?" the viscount drawled lazily. "Surely your men need look no further tonight."

"I did not request your assistance," Tess interrupted stiffly. Nor would she ever. For this was a different Dane St. Pierre from the one she had known five years ago. This man was hard-edged and cynical, with vengeance on his mind. A callous stranger.

She would show him soon enough that he had no place here—in either her life or her heart!

Ravenhurst strode closer and sketched Tess a mocking bow. "Surely you have not forgotten our meeting this morning in the kitchen." As he spoke, he extended his hand, then stood unmoving before her.

Aware of Hawkins's narrowed eyes, Tess reluctantly offered her fingers, which were immediately enveloped in a hard grip. Damn and blast! Why did her heart lurch so wildly at his touch?

Around her the room blurred and the years seemed to slip away. *Forget him,* she told herself. *Forget him before it is too late.*

Suddenly Hawkins snorted angrily. "Ye mean ye haven't heard of Viscount Ravenhurst, the hero of Trafalgar? Second only to Nelson in valor at sea?" he sneered. "Come to save us all from Boney, no doubt."

"A hero, indeed," Tess said coolly, ignoring Hawkins. "You

hardly find us at our best just now, my lord." The fingers around her hand tightened, suddenly hurtful.

"Oh, I'm satisfied with what I've seen so far, Miss Leighton," Ravenhurst drawled. With studied arrogance, he bent down to brush his lips across her palm. "Of course, I mean to see a great deal *more* before I'm done," he whispered darkly, just beneath the range of Hawkins's hearing. "Of the Angel and of its lovely owner."

To her dismay Tess felt her pulse leap. She tried to pull her hand away, but his fingers only tightened.

The viscount smiled faintly, watching color stain her cheeks. Only then did he release her hand.

Damn the pair of them! Tess thought.

Gray-green eyes flashing, she spun about to face Hawkins, who was frowning over this interchange. "The Angel is nearly full, Inspector! You cannot mean to roust my guests with this mad plan of yours. As if one of them might be harboring the Fox beneath his bed!"

"So ye think it's a joke, do ye? Well ye'll stop laughin' soon enough when ye see the bastard dancin' from the end of a rope!" Hawkins snarled.

"And I'll tell you once more, we harbor no traitors at the Angel!"

"I'm glad to hear it, Miss Leighton. Very glad, indeed. For I mean to make certain of just that." Hawkins's small eyes were cold with triumph. "And to do that, everything must be inspected. There's a reward of five hundred pounds on the bastard's head, remember?"

Yes, for five hundred pounds a man might stoop to any evil, Tess thought. She would have to be very careful.

"I certainly shall, Inspector, though the money is little like to benefit me." How true that, Tess thought.

"As for yerself," Hawkins snapped, scowling at the big man who leaned lazily against the door frame, "I'd advise ye to stay out of this, else I take it into my head ye're tryin' to impede the performance of my duty."

"So now you talk of duty, do you?" Dane's lazy demeanor suddenly vanished, replaced by stiff fury. "Just remember, then, that this area falls under *my* jurisdiction as commissioner of the Royal Military Canal. If the performance of what you call your *duty* brings you into conflict with my supervision of the canal—"

"Gentlemen! Gentlemen!" Tess interrupted, desperate to have the matter finished so that she could find her bed. Her vision was hazy and she was on the verge of collapse. "I'm certain no one has the slightest intention of impeding justice, Inspector Hawkins."

Hold on, she told herself. *Just a few more minutes. Can't risk bungling everything now! Too much to lose—for yourself and for Jack, who's been the best friend you've ever known.*

Her skirts swirling, Tess turned to the desk and took a large ring of keys from a drawer. Her eyes were cold as she held the ring out to Hawkins. "Since you are insistent on this ridiculous scheme, Inspector, I shall make it easy for you. Here are my keys. You are welcome to search all you like. Hobhouse will, of course, assist you as you require. Now if you will excuse me, I shall leave you."

Her head held high, Tess swept gracefully from the room, feeling the two men's eyes burn into her back. Almost done, she told herself as she crossed the corridor and blindly sought the support of the banister.

Before her the dark staircase seemed to stretch interminably. Her vision blurred. As if in a dream she began to climb, each step harder than the last. Then finally she was at her own door, her fingers straining for the latch.

She stumbled over the threshold, tugging the door shut behind her.

Darkness—must light a candle!

Can't. Too late. Always too late.

There, very slowly, Tess slumped onto the cold floor.

9

A great bar of lightning slashed the clouds out over the Channel. The wind rose, shrieking and rattling the windows. Without warning, the cold sky opened, loosing rain in torrential sheets.

Like a shadow, the black shape bent into the wind and moved unerringly toward the roof. His hand moved at the window for an instant, and then the casement opened. In silence he slipped over the sill, the curtains dancing about him wildly.

His cold eyes narrowed as he probed the darkness. What had happened to the bloody candle? A muscle flashed at his jaw as he moved along the wall, searching his way across the room. In the darkness he bumped into a table, knocking a metal candlestick to the floor.

Lord Ravenhurst cursed harshly beneath his breath, and then his foot touched something.

Something soft.

Just then a bolt of lightning lit the room. Black-clad, he stood frozen in the phosphorous flare, unable to believe the sight before him. Even when darkness closed around him once more he still did not move, did not breathe even, unable to forget the vision of Tess's pale cheeks framed in a wild tangle of glorious auburn hair. Only inches away from his boot, one white hand curled around a flower on the rug, almost as if to pluck its teal petals.

Beautiful and silent she lay, just inside the threshold, her hair an auburn stain upon the carpet. She might almost have been dead, except for the faint rise and fall of her chest.

At his sides, Dane's calloused, rope-burned hands opened and closed convulsively.

Soleil . . . my sun.

Sweet, bright flame of a woman.

Now a cold-blooded traitor who gave her body to the highest bidder.

Once again lightning slashed the sky, and this time Dane used the momentary flare to search for candle and flint. Grim-faced, he moved toward the desk where they lay.

From somewhere below angry steps began to pound up the stairs.

"Get out of my way, Hobhouse! I know where I'm going full well. Just don't try to stop me."

Ravenhurst froze. What was the bloody customs inspector up to now? Silently he slipped through the darkness toward the far wall and tugged open the armoire.

He had barely pulled the door closed when he heard Hawkins pound across the third floor landing.

"I've got my own key this time, ye fool. Now get out of my way! Take him downstairs, Mundy. And tie him up if he tries to come back up here!"

A key rattled in the lock. A moment later the door burst open. Through the armoire's narrow crack, Ravenhurst saw Hawkins enter, candle in hand, then slam the outer door and lock it. Smiling thinly, the inspector slipped the key back into his pocket and then turned to stare hungrily at the woman on the floor.

"Sleeping, are ye, my beauty?" he muttered thickly. "I'll soon have ye warm and wakeful then." He set his candle down on the side table and bent over Tess, his fat fingers yanking feverishly at the narrow buttons over her bodice.

The man in the armoire stiffened, a hot tide of rage exploding through his veins. *The filthy, cold-blooded bastard! While she slept he meant to—*

Ravenhurst's calloused hands clenched. Beneath his fingers he felt the cold metal lip of the candlestick.

Crouching by the door, Hawkins laughed in fierce triumph. Now Tess Leighton was his, by God. No one would stand in his way! Awkwardly he tugged at the tiny buttons, only to feel them slip from his grasp again and again. With a savage curse he locked his fingers in the neck of her muslin gown and sheared away a dozen buttons in one rough stroke.

Outside in the night rain lashed the windows. A fierce burst of lightning exploded overhead.

When it came, Dane was ready. As soon as the eerie light faded, he slipped from the armoire.

Hawkins barely had time to feel the candlestick crack against the back of his head. With a stunned cry, he crumpled forward onto the rug, one stubby thigh pinning Tess beneath him.

His eyes smoking, Ravenhurst tugged Hawkins's body across the room. Carefully he opened the door and listened, then dragged the unconscious customs inspector out into the corridor.

He was just closing the door when he remembered that Hawkins still carried the key to Tess's room. "I believe I'll relieve you of this," Ravenhurst whispered to the squat, unmoving figure. His lips quirked grimly as he used the purloined key to lock the door, then slipped the cold metal into his own pocket.

Damned useful it would be too.

For long moments Ravenhurst stared down at the sleeping Tess. In silence he watched her chest rise and fall, watched her pale skin glow in the light of Hawkins's candle. Grim-faced, he remembered what the brute had been about to do, the similarity to his own earlier intent escaping him.

The woman on the floor stirred restlessly, her rose lips parting as she mumbled something under her breath. Her fingers moved, stretching toward the light.

Did she have any notion of the danger she ran? Dane wondered angrily. Or had she simply become so hardened that nothing could penetrate her cold facade?

His mouth flattened to a thin, bitter line.

What business was it of his anyway? All that mattered to him was that she tell him what he needed to know, starting with the identity of the Fox.

Yes, by God, now he'd have the fellow's name!

Ravenhurst's eyes were dark and unreadable as he picked Tess up and carried her to the canopy bed. Like burgundy silk her hair spilled over his arms, filling the air with lavender.

Fire snaked through his groin. A spark leapt from his eyes. Yes, he thought grimly, and then he'd have the rest of what he wanted.

Outside in the corridor came the quick, shuffling pad of feet.

Scowling, Dane set Tess down on the bed.

"It's Hawkins! And he's out cold!" Ravenhurst recognized the tense voice of Tess's maid. "What in God's name are we to do now?" she demanded shrilly of an unseen companion.

"Carry him downstairs, I should think," came Hobhouse's cool reply.

"He'll be furious when he wakes!"

"I expect so," the Angel's majordomo said slowly, an undercurrent of keenest pleasure warming his voice. "I only wish I could shake the hand of whoever did this to him. Not that I'd put it past Tess."

The latch clicked; the door rattled gently.

"Locked," Hobhouse muttered. "Do you have your key?"

"Aye, that I do. And I don't care if he's out cold or not. I'm still going to stay with her tonight. There's no telling what that brute will do when he wakes up. Locking the door against him might not be enough now."

Dane slipped back toward the window. There was no other way out now. With careful fingers he opened the curtains and freed the latch, pushing open the leaded panes. Immediately a cold rain lashed his face. One leg over the sill, he studied the steeply angled roof bristling with chimneys.

Behind him a key grated in the lock.

"Hurry up, lest that bellowing pig come to and discover us!"

Silently Ravenhurst slid into the night. His face dark with fury, he began to map out the final course of his ruthless campaign.

"Wake up, Tess! Sweet heaven, what's happened to you?"

Tess frowned, fighting the sharp fingers that bit into her shoulders.

"Please, Miss Tess. You must wake up!"

"Go—away," Tess mumbled. Suddenly her eyes jerked open. "Letty? What—"

"I'll be asking *you* that question, miss! We found Hawkins in the hall, knocked out cold. Hobhouse took him downstairs and I came back to check on you. Can't you remember anything?"

Tess swept a trembling hand across her pale face.

Don't try to stop me!

Hawkins?

Warm, rough hands lifting her. Her ribs grinding against thick bands of muscle.

No, not Hawkins.

Her eyes widened, gray-green pools of pain. That was when Tess saw she was not on the settee but the bed. With a little choking sob she jerked up onto her knees.

A button flew off her dress and hit the carpet with a muffled *ping*. The blue muslin fell open over her chest.

"How did that happen?" Letty stared strangely at Tess.

Dear God, Tess thought. Was this Hawkins's doing too? She pressed a fist against her clenched teeth. She had to get a hold on herself or soon the nightmares would spill over into her waking life!

"I—I don't know, Letty. I must have passed out after reaching my room. I remember it was dark and . . ." Tess's brow furrowed as she saw the candle flickering on the side table.

"Hawkins must have brought it, miss. He had a key this time too. Hobhouse tried to stop him, but the officers pulled Hobhouse away. When we came back, we found him sprawled in the corridor. Out to the world . . ." The woman's voice trailed away.

Tess shivered, feeling cold fingers of fear brush her spine. How close had she come to violence at Hawkins's hands this night?

Her eyes dropped to the pewter candlestick on the floor and her breath caught sharply. Could she have used that on her squat intruder? If so, why couldn't she remember?

White-faced, she looked up at Letty, who only shrugged.

Holding her dress closed with cold fingers, Tess slid from the bed and walked to the window, watching rain lash the roof in sullen sheets. For a moment a ragged bolt of lightning shimmered out over the marsh and then disappeared.

Out of the corner of her eye, she saw something glisten on the carpet. Slowly she bent down, picking up a key which had fallen just beneath the window.

Her key. She didn't even need to test it to know it would slip effortlessly into the keyhole.

Dear Lord, what was happening to her? Asleep, she was haunted by savage dreams, only to wake to a greater horror.

But she would not give in—neither to Hawkins nor anyone else. Her shoulders stiff and resolute, Tess faced the suffocating sense of helplessness and fought it down, just as she had done so many times before. Where terror had once gripped her, now fury began to blaze. Her eyes snapping, she thought of Amos Hawkins's fat fingers probing her dress.

No more! she swore. Never would she run. Never would she give in by even a single inch—to anyone or anything! The Angel was hers, and Fairleigh too.

If smuggling was what it took to keep them, she'd spirit a cargo of brandy past the ghost of Mr. Pitt himself!

"The filthy pig! How dare he do this?"

The next morning Tess stood staring down in rage and disbelief at a mound of linens and towels slashed beyond any hope of repair. "Where is he?" she demanded as Hobhouse came to stand beside her.

"I laid him out on a table in the taproom, Miss Tess. He woke up the same way he went to sleep, I should imagine—snarling and ugly. Took himself off with much cursing and vows of retribution. He had a knot on his head the size of Maximilian's beak, by the way. I don't suppose you'd happen to know where he got it?"

"I don't remember a thing," Tess said with perfect sincerity. Then, as her eyes returned to the torn linens, she muttered a curse beneath her breath. "I only wish I'd hit the bloody swine harder!"

Twenty minutes later she tooled her little gig through the narrow streets of Rye, the wind whipping her long hair and tossing auburn strands into her eyes. Her blood still boiled at the thought of Hawkins's arrogance, but Ravenhurst's cool mockery was worse.

The man was vile! He was insolent. He was—

She slowed her horse, smiling a greeting to a pair of ancient dowagers who had been friends of her mother.

He was despicable, degenerate, and depraved! Worst of all, he was dangerous.

Tess's hands tightened on the reins. Thank God he hadn't recognized her as the soot-faced urchin from the alley. When he discovered that . . .

If, she reminded herself sharply.

And then, with a defiant little shrug, she cracked her whip and sent her horse bowling along the Winchelsea road toward Fairleigh. Her cheeks glowing, she sped through green fields dotted with fat Sussex sheep. It was a scene of timeless peace and heart-stopping beauty.

And Tess saw none of it.

Instead she saw before her a pair of cold eyes that promised deadly vengeance. But she would teach the cursed Londoner a few things, Tess swore, the first being that she was a dangerous person to provoke.

Her thoughts were still agitated when she reined in her horse and turned up the tree-lined drive to Fairleigh. Halfway up the hill, she stopped and jumped down, tossing the reins to the old servant who came ambling over the lawns.

"You can put her out to graze, Thomas. I'll be up at the priory."

To his credit, the old man asked no questions, only shook his gray head and mumbled darkly under his breath while he led Tess's roan mare away. He'd been at Fairleigh twenty years now—long enough to know that strange things went on in the hills above the priory's weathered stone walls. Thomas was wise enough not to mention them, however.

Like everyone else, the taciturn old servant had lived long enough on the marsh to know that those who ask no questions are told no lies.

* * *

The sun was warm on Tess's shoulders as she sped up to the sun-drenched walls of the priory, on the crest of the hill. She would have a look at the manor house later, but first she meant to see how Jack was faring.

Rounding a high wall of weathered stone, Tess turned around to be certain she was not being watched. Then, satisfied that she was quite alone, she bent down and tugged at a small stone near the base of the wall.

There was a faint click; a narrow crack opened above the stone. Quickly Tess reached in and released the latch hidden below.

A moment later a long rectangular section of the wall opened out into a door.

Stale, cold air whispered out of the dark passage. Somewhere far below a man coughed urgently, then broke off in a raw, grating moan.

Jack!

Her heart pounding, Tess plunged down the passage, following the faint trace of light until the long, timber-lined tunnel opened onto a room of stone. Lying in one corner, tossing restlessly on his pallet of straw, was the white-haired man known as the Romney Fox.

Without a word, Tess sank down beside her friend, gathering his cold hands between her fingers. His face was strained and pale, she saw, and his eyes glassy with fever.

"Tess? Is that you, lassie?" Jack's black eyes blinked and then narrowed on her face. "Of course it is," he added in an undertone. "No one else knows this place's secrets, save for yourself." Suddenly he stiffened, racked by another spasm of coughing.

Helplessly Tess watched, unable to do more than smooth the wool blankets around him.

Finally the coughing subsided. Slowly the white-haired smuggler opened his eyes, only to fix Tess with a furious glare. "Now then, lassie, I'll have some answers from you! What in God's name were you thinking of? That fool Hawkins might have had us both last night, and today would see us dancing from a rope! Are you so ready to meet your maker?" he demanded harshly.

Tess's fingers tightened on the blanket. "I've every intention of living to a ripe old age, Jack. And of making enough money to repair Fairleigh's faded glories. In the meantime, however, I've an inn to run and my father's creditors to be repaid. Can you tell me any other way to do it?" she countered, her gray-green eyes challenging.

The smuggler scowled. " 'Tis no life for a woman, Tess, and certainly not for a lady such as yourself."

Tess only tossed her head angrily. "Fine words, Jack, but who's to pay for those silk dresses and gloves of kid leather? Who's going to keep the Angel in brandy and new linens? Who's going to keep Ashley—"

"Ashley?" the man said with a snort. "The lad should be here helping you, lass, not raking about with that lot of ne'er-do-wells, fine school or nae. Get him home, Tess. Give up this wild masquerade."

"I can't, Jack. Not when I'm so close to everything I've ever wanted."

"So close to dying, more like! Can't you get that through that damned stubborn head of yours?"

"It's a risk I'm prepared to take."

"But I'm *not*, by God! Not when your blood would be on my hands, for I'm the one that led you into this mad scheme."

" 'Twould be on my head alone, Jack," Tess countered mutinously. "I'll not answer to you or to anyone else. I'm not your daughter, remember." Her face softened slightly. "Though I believe I love you more than ever I did my own blood sire."

Jack's fingers sought hers. For a long moment neither spoke. "When did you take this daft idea into your head?" he asked finally.

"Not quite two years ago. The same night my father . . ." She did not finish her sentence.

"The night you heard about your father's death," the Fox said slowly. "I had a feeling—but it won't do, I tell you! 'Tis one thing to share in the profits of the run. Aye, I was glad to bring tea and silks to help you and the boy. But not this!" He raked a tired hand through his thick white hair. "My God, lassie, what would your mother say if she knew I'd led you into such a life?"

Tess only shrugged her slim shoulders. "She'd be glad her daughter was holding on to Fairleigh in the only way she knew how. From all I remember of my mother, she loved this place as much as I do."

The man on the pallet closed his eyes, a faint smile lighting his face. "Aye, she did that, Tess. I'll never forget the hours she spent planting daisies and primroses in her white garden." His voice hardened then. "But she didn't love Fairleigh that much! And she'd never forgive me if . . ." His eyes opened, hard and glittering. "Give me your word, it's over. I'll not have *your* blood on my conscience, lassie. Not when I've so much on it already."

Tess shivered, realizing there were many things that she didn't know about this man, great parts of his life that he kept carefully concealed from her.

Jack's cold hands circled her wrists. He struggled to rise on one elbow. "I want your word, Tess! Now! No more runs with my gentlemen. I'll not rest until I have your promise." His fingers tightened, biting cruelly into her wrists.

"I won't give it, Jack. I can't. Not yet."

The smuggler's face darkened with anger. A moment later, coughing hoarsely, he fell back against the pallet. His hands began to shake and he released her, then dug his fingers into the woolen blanket.

Tess watched helplessly until the spasm passed. Finally he lay still, limp and exhausted, his eyes closed. "Don't worry, Jack," she whispered, smoothing the blanket about his chest. "I've learned my lesson. I'll be far more careful in the future."

But the man beside her did not answer. He had already sunk back into a tortured, restless sleep haunted by crueller ghosts than his beautiful visitor could ever imagine.

Slowly Tess stood up, rigid with fear. He was in a bad way, this time, was her Fox. Always before he'd had the devil's own luck, eluding dragoon and excise officer alike to lead the King's men a merry dance over marsh and weald. Yes, somehow he'd anticipated their every movement with an accuracy that was uncanny.

But not this time, Tess thought, looking down at his ashen face.

And all because of her. If he hadn't turned back for her, he'd be safe and far away by now.

Perdition! Angrily, Tess brushed away her tears. What good were tears, anyway? What good did regrets do now?

Her watery gaze fell on the crossed swords at the far end of the room. For a moment her eyes lit as she remembered how Jack had first taught her to fence, delighting in her grace and deftness. For Tess, it had been as if a door was thrown open in her grim, lonely existence. Yes, from the day of their meeting long ago, when Jack had stumbled wounded onto Fairleigh land, he had swept through her life like a Channel gale, teaching her to share his zest for living.

And now?

With a frown, Tess bent to touch the chased silver hilt of the épée. They were her grandfather's weapons, carefully hidden here from her father, who would otherwise have pawned them long ago. As he had pawned everything else of value at Fairleigh.

Even his own daughter.

Tess bit back a little cry and looked down to see the foil's point biting into her fingers. Her features frozen, she watched blood well up from the wound.

No regrets! No more nightmares. Her father was gone and she was free from his tyranny forever.

Propelled as if in the grip of a dream, Tess followed the tunnel to the surface, then crossed the narrow stone courtyard and climbed the uneven steps that led to the priory's half-ruined roof. Slowly she walked to a wide corner tower and leaned her elbows upon the sun-warmed rock, staring out at the sweep of land and sea spread before her.

To the south lay Rye and beyond that the Channel, its turquoise swells merging seamlessly into a perfect azure sky. The sea was calm this day, with no more than faint flecks of white far out beyond the point at Dungeness. Squinting, Tess could just make out a two-masted lugger sailing toward Winchelsea. Something about the vessel made her think of the French ship, the *Liberté,* glimpsed briefly the night before.

The captain must be a bold man to bait the Royal Navy in its own den! But there were many kinds of courage, Tess knew. Some screeched loudly, demanding admiration, while others glowed quietly through the long nights of pain and despair, unseen and unappreciated by all but a few.

That sort of courage was far harder to sustain, but it was what Tess had tried to learn as she fought to save these barren walls that she loved so well.

Even now she could not say what drew her to this wreck. The priory's days of greatness were centuries gone, while Fairleigh was in only slightly better shape. From her vantage point high on the tower, Tess could see sparrows nesting in the house's eaves and panes missing from the broad mullioned windows.

Yes, the walls had succumbed to damp rot and all the stairs were unstable, but this was her home, the only place she would ever feel safe. Fairleigh was in her blood, and she would do whatever she must to save it.

Even as a little girl Tess had made her mother repeat Fairleigh's ancient legends over and over. Tales of how the Romans had raised a sea fortress here beside a great port city. Tales of how in later years the Normans had followed, raising their keeps around the Roman masonry dotting the marshes where once the sea had lapped.

A prickle of fear slipped down Tess's spine. She thought of the oldest legend of all, a melancholy tale that had always made her mother cry. Well Tess remembered sitting crosslegged on the rich black earth while her mother tended her garden of white flowers. Unmoving and silent, Tess had listened time and again to the story of two doomed lovers who had met their death somewhere on Fairleigh's grounds.

They still walked the parapets, so it was said, on moonless nights when the wind blew sharp and cold up from the sea. Thomas claimed to have seen their ghostly shapes several times, along with the sound of weird, distant pipes.

Another sharp pang shot down Tess's spine. She shivered as blackness lapped at the edges of her mind. How could she be so stupid? It was nothing more than a child's tale, after all.

And she was no longer a child.

With a little shrug she stood up, her eyes running lovingly across the emerald hills, then sweeping down to the turquoise waters of Fairleigh Cove. Yes, this was where she belonged. This was the only home she would ever know. Neither ghosts nor excisemen nor one cursed ex-naval officer would ever drive her from this place.

For two hours Tess remained in the passage. During that time Jack did not awaken, but her patience was finally rewarded when his color gradually returned and his breathing grew less strained.

Realizing there was nothing more she could do for her friend, Tess smoothed the blankets over his restless form and turned to leave. As she emerged from the passage, a shrill cry overhead drew her eyes skyward, where a snowy gyrfalcon wheeled gracefully in the wind, its long white wings carving a cloudless sky.

Tess froze, mesmerized by the perfect beauty of the bird's soaring flight down to the sea. In that moment she felt a fierce, stabbing jealousy. How wonderful to fly that way, knowing neither worry nor boundaries!

It seemed suddenly to Tess that she had been bearing responsibility for others as long as she could remember. For years she had cared for her frail mother, protecting her from her dissolute husband's ire. With her mother's death, Ashley had fallen to Tess's care.

Then had come their father's ruin and the threat of losing Fairleigh.

Far in the distance the falcon plummeted from sight. Tess's shoulders slumped, leaden with weariness. Just for once she wondered what it would be like to lay her burdens on another's shoulders, to know the comfort of strong, supporting hands.

But she knew it was not meant to be. Not for her, at least.

And what need had she of such dreams, anyway? They were only illusions to soothe weak minds. No, she needed nothing and no one. She had learned life's bitter lessons well.

Unbidden came the memory of a pair of furious eyes the color of wintry seas.

Tess's shoulders straightened in defiance. *I'll show you, your bloody lordship,* she vowed silently.

I'll show you all!

10

Hobhouse was waiting anxiously by the front steps when Tess drove the gig around to the stables at the rear of the Angel. One glance at her majordomo's tense face told her something was very wrong.

"There's three of them waiting inside, Miss Tess. 'Tis the same three biddies who were here last week, asking for donations for their latest charity. I told them you might not be returning until very late, but they refused to leave. Said they'd put this matter off long enough."

Tess frowned. She knew with a cold certainty that the ladies in question had not come to pay her a friendly social call. On the contrary, the redoubtable Mrs. Tredwell had shown nothing but scorn for Tess—on the few occasions she'd deigned to take any notice of her, that is. To make matters worse, the woman's dissolute scamp of a son had begun nosing around the inn, contriving once to corner Tess outside the wine cellar and probe at her with his sweaty hands.

All of which made Tess harbor no illusions as to the nature of this visit.

"How's Jack?" Letty asked quietly when Tess entered the front hall.

"His color is better, I believe. Thomas will look in on him until I can get back. Now, what's this about visitors?" Tess asked crisply.

"It's that nasty Mrs. Tredwell. She's brought along her two minions, the Crabtree sisters. There she was, hovering about the foyer like some great vulture, doing her best to make everyone uncomfortable. And we all know whom she plans to sink her claws into next! A nastier piece of work I never hope to see!"

"I rather suspect she means to apply that term of abuse to me, Letty," Tess said dryly. She sighed and rubbed her shoulders, which had begun to ache. "I was hoping this confrontation could be avoided, but the old vulture is evidently intent on her kill." Tess's eyes hardened. "She'll not find it here, however. Where have you put them?" she demanded, brushing back her shining curls and twitching her skirts flat.

"In the storage alcove off the lobby," Letty said, with a grim smile.

"You didn't! There's barely room for two in that airless cubicle. Why, Letty, what a spiteful creature you are!" Tess gurgled.

"Aren't I just! And I hope their fat legs turn up all knotted and sore when they try to stand! 'Twould serve them right, the foul-minded creatures! Do you want me to stay?" she asked, her face fiercely protective.

Tess sighed. "No, just give me several minutes and then bring them along to my accounts room. But ask Hobhouse to come back and fetch me in ten minutes, saying some urgent matter requires my attention in the kitchen." Tess's expressive mouth curved in a lopsided smile. "I only hope it may not be true, for I live in constant dread of the oven's exploding."

"Hobhouse said as how he's nearly repaired the damper, Miss Tess, so never you worry about that."

"A marvel, that man." Abruptly Tess caught Letty's arm in one slim wrist. "Has—is Lord Ravenhurst about?"

"I believe he went out some while ago. Shall I send him up when he arrives?"

"Most certainly not!" Tess snapped, her eyes glittering. "Indeed, if he asks to see me, tell him that I'm occupied with my account books and can under no circumstances be disturbed."

"Very good, Miss," Letty said, her dark eyes narrowing speculatively. "I'll leave word with Hobhouse as well."

"Have I told you that you're a dear, Letty?"

Letty flashed a cheeky smile. "Not near often enough."

"Be off with you, hussy." Tess answered with a devilish grin of her own. "It won't do to keep Mrs. Tredwell waiting any longer."

"As far as I'm concerned, the old buzzard can wait forever," Letty muttered, stalking off in search of Hobhouse.

Exactly five minutes later Letty ushered three grim-faced matrons into Tess's sunny accounts room. Their leader, the redoubtable Mrs. Tredwell, was a stout woman of nearly three-score years, dressed in brown bombazine. On her head was perched an ugly little hat with three brown feathers that curled limply around her florid face. Every few seconds she scowled and brushed the feathers out of her eyes.

It was instantly clear that the hatchet-faced Mrs. Tredwell was out for blood.

Tess's blood, to be exact.

"Well, Miss Leighton, I'm delighted that you've finally returned from your *urgent business*," the matron sneered.

"I'm sorry my absence caused you inconvenience. Had you sent around a note of your intention to pay a call, I would have arranged to be present," Tess answered coolly, waving the women to be seated.

Miss Alicia Crabtree, a thin, rather plain-faced spinster of fifty, gratefully began to lower her bony frame into a wing chair by the window, but a curt command from Mrs. Tredwell stopped her midway.

"We will not stay to be seated, Miss Leighton," the woman in brown announced imperiously. With each word the long plumes over her forehead vibrated, adding emphasis to her speech. "We have been delayed quite long enough already, so I mean to come directly to the point."

"Something told me you would," Tess said dryly.

"*Humph!* That's precisely the sort of pert comment I should have expected from you, miss," the matron snapped. "You've run tame in this town for far too long, let me tell you. You flaunt your presence here at the Angel, mingling with the lowest sort of humanity and giving decent women a bad name. Even worse, you exert a pernicious influence upon our delicately nurtured daughters. Which is why we have come today."

Mrs. Tredwell's voice rose, assuming the stentorian tones of a footman announcing the arrival of a member of the royal family. "On behalf of the Lady's Rectitude Society, we insist that you remove yourself from the Angel at once and give up this unseemly position of managing an inn."

Tess's face was unreadable as she seated herself at a graceful walnut escritoire, leaving her guests to stand stiffly by the door. "And if I do not choose to comply with this—request?" she asked, her tone deceptively soft.

"Then our members are prepared to take appropriate action."

"Do you mean to pelt my lobby with rotten fruit? Or is it to be pistols at thirty paces?"

Mrs. Tredwell's face turned a very ugly shade of crimson. "Laugh, hussy. Laugh while you may. But soon you'll feel the full force of the censure that your disgraceful conduct deserves. You will not be so cool then, I assure you!"

"And what precisely *is* this disgraceful behavior I'm to be punished for, madam? Rolling up my sleeves and doing laundry with the maidservants? Or is it my unseemliness in fighting tooth and nail for something I hold dear, keeping this inn from wrack and ruin?"

"You know the answer as well as I, Miss Leighton." The limp feathers now hung straight down before the matron's face, tickling her nose. Snorting in irritation, she swatted them away. "And do not bother trying to put us off with your cleverness. We do not deign to soil our lips by reciting further examples of your shameless conduct!"

"Indeed?" Tess said silkily, a dangerous light in her gray-green eyes. "If I am not to be held guilty for my unseemly exertions on behalf of this inn, it must be for something else. Perhaps because I ordered your husband turned out into the street last week when he tried to bring a cyprian to his room."

The Crabtree sisters gasped, their hands fluttering to their throats.

"How—how dare you!" Mrs. Tredwell sputtered.

"Or is it because I ordered the same treatment for your son?" Tess continued coolly. "He grows amorous in his cups, did you know? At which time he tried to assault me in my wine cellar. It is my considered opinion, in fact, that *yours* is the family of profligates, madam. Perhaps I should convene a meeting to deal with all of you!"

"I won't stand for this, do you hear? It is nothing short of infamous!"

"I quite agree, madam. You should exert a better moral influence over the men in your family."

" 'Tis *you* I'm speaking of. And well you know it, you shameless hussy!"

"While you, Mrs. Tredwell," Tess said sweetly, "are a hatchet-faced hypocrite who terrorizes her husband and beats her scullery maids. I know this because I've had to tend the poor girls' wounds more than once. Yes, you are a fine pillar of society, indeed. You go to church on Sunday and cheat your tradesmen all the rest of the week. Fie, madam! Who are you to be giving me instructions on behavior?"

"Why you brazen little . . ." The furious matron brought one fat hand to her heaving chest. Her voice, when she was once again able to speak, was shrill with anger. "I'll not stay here and be insulted by the likes of you, Jezebel!"

"In that case, the door is directly behind you."

"You're a disgrace to this town, that's what you are! A disgrace to womankind, I say. A disgrace to your dear, departed mama! If dear, sweet Victoria could only see what you've become!"

Tess's face paled, colored only by two spots of crimson high on her cheeks. "Quiet, madam," she ordered, her voice dangerously low. "Do not say her name in my presence again. You are unfit to breathe the same air that she did, and I won't have her name sullied on your lips. Now get out, all of you," she said icily, rising to her feet. "Before I change my mind and have Hobhouse dump you in the street as you deserve!"

"Very well, Miss Leighton. Since you show yourself determined upon this wicked behavior, we shall leave and with pleasure. But the matter is far from finished, I warn you. And the consequences for you will be anything but pleasant."

Just then there was a slight rustling in the hallway. A moment later Maximilian sailed through the doorway, his long green wings pumping. He circled the room twice, then abruptly caught sight of the limp feathers dangling before Mrs. Tredwell's mottled face.

Crying shrilly, the macaw dove down for a closer look.

"Help! I'm being attacked!" the angry matron screamed.

"Nonsense, he's merely attracted by your feathers. Maximilian, come here this instant!"

But the lure of the strange brown plumage was too great. The macaw plummeted, settling on Mrs. Tredwell's bonnet. From this perch, he twisted his head back and forth, scrutinizing the ugly plumage he had decided was an avian rival intruding on his territory.

"What the devil! What the devil!" His sharp beak opened and snapped tentatively at the offending feathers.

"G-get this c-creature off of me!" Mrs. Tredwell ordered through clenched teeth.

"Maximilian! Come away immediately!" Tess was hard pressed to hold back her laughter at the sight of the matron's face, where fear warred with fury.

With a loud snap of his powerful jaws, the gaily colored macaw snapped off the end of one brown feather. Uttering a shrill cry of triumph, he flew off, trailing the limp plume from his beak. "Run out the guns!" he screeched, settling upon Tess's desk. "Rocky shoals ahead, men!"

"You saw it with your own eyes!" Mrs. Tredwell screamed, red-faced. "That savage creature tried to attack me. I'll have the magistrate down upon you for this, mark my words!"

At that moment Edouard appeared at the door, followed closely by Hobhouse and Letty. Swiftly the keen-eyed chef took in the situation. "Who makes this squealing of wild pigs? *You?*" His stubby finger stabbed the air in front of Mrs. Tredwell. "If you ruin my *gâteaux,* I swear to give you something to squeal about!"

"He's mad!" Mrs. Tredwell cried. "They're all mad!"

"And you, *par Dieu,* are one ugly old cow! Take yourself off!" the irate chef growled.

"Come, ladies!" the matron quavered, striving to salvage her lost dignity in the face of this final assault.

Stony-faced, Hobhouse and the other staff stood back, allowing the three women passage down the corridor.

But the parting shot came from Maximilian, now perched comfortably on Tess's shoulder. "What the devil!" he chanted happily. "Ugly old cow! Ugly old cow!"

11

"**N**ow that we're rid of that vulture, tell me the sad news, Hobhouse, for I can see this wretched thing is far from fixed."

Tess's grizzled majordomo knelt before her in the kitchen, frowning at the ancient open range. "The grates are cleaned now, along with the flues. A devil of a time I had with them too. I even opened up the chimney but could find no blockage there. I'm afraid this time the blasted thing's got me stumped, Miss Tess." Hobhouse shook his head and plunged sooty fingers deep into his hair, tugging restlessly. "I'm beginning to think the infernal thing is possessed, as Edouard insists."

Tess sighed. Exactly what she needed—a haunted range. No, a ruined as well as a haunted range, she corrected herself. Damn and blast! Just when she was beginning to struggle out from under these crushing debts. . . .

"Get out of my way, ye fool!"

Without warning Amos Hawkins burst through the door behind Tess. "So there ye are," he snapped. "I'll be speaking with ye, Miss Leighton," he snarled. "*Alone.* The rest of ye—get out!"

Hobhouse stiffened, digging in his legs like a terrier and glaring at the squat inspector. "Now, just a bloody minute," he growled.

"Out!" Hawkins bellowed. "Else I close this nest of thieves down, here and now!"

Tess flinched at the malice in that voice. She didn't know if it was within Hawkins's power to do as he threatened, but she didn't mean to find out. Not with twenty kegs of uncustomed brandy upstairs, where a man with a suspicious turn of mind might discover them.

"What seems to be the problem, Inspector Hawkins?" she asked coolly.

"Get 'em out of here. Then we'll talk."

Tess smiled thinly at Hobhouse and the two wide-eyed kitchen maids cowering behind him. "You may go, all of you. We'll discuss the range later, Hobhouse."

With obvious reluctance the loyal retainer ushered the rest of the staff before him and then walked stiffly from the room, deliberately leaving the door open behind him.

"Shut the bloody door," Hawkins snarled.

When Hobhouse did not comply, the inspector stomped across the floor and jerked the door closed with a bang.

"There is no need to break my door," Tess said coldly, but her heart began to pound as she faced Hawkins. Suddenly she felt very vulnerable, thinking of last night—wondering what precisely had happened.

She certainly couldn't ask Hawkins!

To cover her anxiety Tess moved toward the table. There, her face set in stern lines, she gripped the back of a chair and faced her adversary.

Something told her that offense would be her best defense.

"Well, Inspector? I trust you're pleased with yourself. Your men missed nothing. There is now not a single towel nor bed linen left whole anywhere in the Angel. But I'm sure you didn't come here to discuss your crudity."

Hawkins's beady eyes narrowed. "Ye little bitch," he snarled. "Who did it? Hobhouse? That fat little Frenchman?"

"I haven't the slightest idea what you're talking about, Inspector."

"No? The lump on the back of my head is what I'm talking about! It's a hanging offense to impede a Crown officer in the performance of his duty, Miss Leighton. Would ye like to feel the rope tighten, to feel yer feet jerked out from under ye and the air torn from yer throat?"

"More threats, Inspector?"

"Not a threat, a statement of fact." His eyes darkened, calculating. "I could close the Angel down in a minute, did you know that?"

Was he bluffing? "For what possible reason?" Tess asked icily.

"On suspicion of harboring a dangerous fugitive."

"But that would be a lie, and you know it!"

"Would it? And if not for that reason, then try this one. Brandy, my dear Miss Leighton. One hundred kegs of it, to be exact, the unseized share of the Fox's last run. Aye, we captured some of the contraband, but there was a bloody sight more that we missed. And those hundred kegs are close enough right now I can smell 'em, by God!" Hawkins's fat lips twisted into a smile. "So I'm thinking to have a look around the Angel. I wouldn't half like to turn the place into a wreck, of course, but—"

"You've already done that, damn you!"

Hawkins shrugged coldly. "As for the linens—well, the King's work demands thoroughness, ye know." Hawkins's eyes were colorless, flat with triumph. "And thorough I'll be—unless ye give me a reason not to look any farther."

Flames of fury licked at Tess's blood. The arrogant swine—he was threatening to destroy the Angel unless . . .

"My brandy was all put down in my grandfather's time, Inspector. We use no run goods here. And I would be more than happy to prove it to you." Her fingers tightened on the back of the chair, the skin at her joints gone white.

"Oh, it's proof I'll be having, Miss Leighton, one way or another. Ye can count on that," he snarled. "And we'll start in the cellars. Just me and yerself," he added darkly, "with orders that no one is to disturb us. And this time I'll finish what I started last night," he promised hoarsely, his eyes fixed on her lips.

Tess shivered before the cold savagery of his gaze. She had a fair idea of what the brute meant to do when he got her alone in the cellar. Ever since the first day he'd arrived in Rye, Hawkins had been dogging her steps, making crude suggestions of how she might avoid all these problems. Time and again she had evaded him, pretending to misunderstand.

When he had twice attempted to go further than mere threats, a vigilant Hobhouse had arrived to thwart his plans. And then last night . . .

What *had* happened then?

Tess was careful to keep her concern from her face, however. "Hobhouse will take you to inspect the wine stores, Inspector. I, unfortunately, am far too busy with this broken range to join you just now."

The next instant Hawkins's muddy boots thundered across the kitchen floor. "Then ye'll be a damn sight busier before I'm done with this place," he snarled, his bristling eyebrows locked in a scowl. "Aye, before I'm done ye'll have neither curtains nor blankets left. Nor beds nor chairs! My men'll turn every room upside down and dump the contents out into the street." His colorless eyes narrowed. "Unless ye do my bidding, that is." Abruptly his stubby fingers shot out to grip Tess's forearms as he pushed her back against a heavy oaken china cabinet. "Ice Queen, they do call ye, but I'll melt that ice, by God! I'll ram myself between yer legs and make ye pant for more," he snarled, his foul breath scorching her face.

In a black fury Tess clawed at his probing fingers. But Hawkins dug his nails into her waist and ground his thick body against hers. "Aye, bitch. I'll show ye how a dog mates in heat. On all fours, I'll take ye," he panted, stubby fingers pinching her nipples as he forced her back against the cabinet.

"Let—let me go, you filthy bastard!" Choking with pain and anger, Tess twisted wildly, but was unable to dislodge her captor. With one trembling hand she searched the shelf at her back, desperate to find any defense against him.

And then her fingers met the thick handle of Edouard's cleaver. Black rage dulling her vision, she jerked the knife from the slab of wood where the chef had driven it. Her heart pounding crazily, she raised the razor-sharp blade in the air above Hawkins's back.

Anything to get those foul fingers off her!

"More of the King's business, Hawkins?"

The lazy, mocking words cut through the haze of Tess's fury. She froze, her fingers tightening convulsively on the cleaver's handle.

"I only wish all our excise officers were so vigilant."

Silently the heavy implement was pulled from Tess's white, trembling fingers. A second later Hawkins swung around, cursing.

"God damn ye, Ravenhurst! One day ye'll push me one godrotting inch too far!" His face mottled with rage, he glared at the mocking intruder.

Ravenhurst merely arched one thick, dark eyebrow. "At which time I shall be more than happy to meet you, Hawkins. At any time and any place of your choosing." He bent closer, his fingers tightening on the cleaver. "Until that time I advise you to step lightly, for I'd take great pleasure in gagging that foul mouth of yours permanently."

The customs inspector froze, rigid with fury, more than a little frightened by the cold savagery of Dane's eyes. "Just like to see ye try it, Ravenhurst," he blustered, edging toward the door. There he turned to sneer at Tess. "Not finished with ye, neither! Mark my words, woman!"

With that he stamped from the room, cursing all the way down the corridor.

Tess shivered, weak and drained in the aftermath of Hawkins's assault. Slowly she sank back against the china cabinet, her knees buckling beneath her.

"I begin to wonder, Tess Leighton, if you are in full possession of your sanity," Ravenhurst growled, his cobalt eyes searching her pale face. His hair was damp and clung in thick dark waves to the spotless white linen at his neck. He looked powerful and predatory, entirely in command of the situation. "Our customs inspector makes a bad enemy, I suspect. Someday I won't be here to rescue you."

"Oh, go away and leave me alone!" Tess snapped, tears prickling at her eyes. "You're no rescuer, but a plague upon me!"

"And you are a great fool!" His eyes flashing, Ravenhurst stalked closer until his hard thigh was but an inch from Tess's hip.

"Fools do not live long, my dear. Remember that." His breath, warm with the scent of brandy, played across her cold cheeks.

Tess had the wild idea he meant to kiss her. For long seconds he bent over her, his eyes all lapis and smoke as they probed her face.

Then, with one powerful stroke, he reached around her and swung the cleaver down into its block on the shelf.

The movement strained the fabric of his shirt, revealing corded muscles beneath the fine linen. Tess's eyes were drawn inexorably to the triangle at his neck, where the garment opened to reveal bronze skin lush with springy black hair.

For one electric instant their bodies met, locked in a rigid challenge.

His hot and insistent.

Hers cold and suddenly without defenses.

Where would this nightmare end? Tess wondered desperately, jerking away. She shivered slightly, feeling as if Dane had stolen all the warmth from the room.

Behind her the keen blade pierced deep, rocking back and forth with a low hum.

As the shuddering blade gradually stilled, Ravenhurst's eyes darkened. Hard and bitter, they scoured her face, expecting nothing.

Promising even less.

What bitter experiences had carved the deep lines at his forehead and lips? Tess wondered. His next words made her wonder why she even cared.

"Why don't you marry Lennox?"

"You—you've been eavesdropping!"

Ravenhurst smiled thinly. "Oh, almost certainly."

" 'Tis my affair and mine alone!"

"An interesting choice of words, my dear. Is it only Lennox you fear, or is it *all* men?"

"You bloody—"

Ravenhurst smothered a curse. "I wonder if you realize just how dangerous your position is."

"It will take a great deal more than one brutish customs inspector to frighten me, Lord Ravenhurst," Tess snapped, her voice brittle and unnatural.

She felt as much as saw the tall man tense, his raw nerves barely held in check.

"But you forget one thing, my dear," Ravenhurst whispered, his hard mouth only inches from hers. "Hawkins is not your *only* enemy. Nor your most dangerous one."

Maximilian, who had observed this tense scenario in silence up to this point, suddenly stamped upon his perch and puffed out his emerald cheeks. "Cut line!" he cried shrilly. "Breakers on the lee. Mind your bow!"

A moment later the kitchen door swung open with a squeal of hinges. Ravenhurst stepped back just as Lord Lennox entered the room.

"So I find you here once again, my dear. Hobhouse said—" Suddenly the earl's smile froze, for he saw the tall man standing only inches from Tess.

Lazily, the viscount turned and eased his long body back against the kitchen range.

"But forgive me," Lennox said, his voice cooling slightly. "I did not realize you were engaged."

Furious, Tess reached up to brush a long strand of brandy-colored hair off her shoulder. "No, you are not intruding, Lord Lennox. I was only—only attending to some business with a lodger." Quickly she moved away from Ravenhurst. "I daresay you haven't met Lord Ravenhurst yet. He has come to oversee the Royal Military Canal and will be lodging at the Angel until quarters elsewhere can be readied."

"There you are wrong, my dear. Lord Ravenhurst and I met some years ago." Lennox smiled thinly, extending a hand to the man beside the range. "This is an unexpected pleasure, Ravenhurst. Even here in this far corner of Sussex we've heard about your exploits at sea."

Dane uncoiled his long form slowly and moved to take Lennox's hand, his dark brows rising at this praise. "Exploits that have been greatly exaggerated in the retelling, I have no doubt."

He turned to look down at Tess. "But I fear I've kept Miss Leighton from her work long enough. I shall take my leave."

His boots hammered across the wooden floor to the door.

To her fury, Tess found she had to fight an urge to follow his broad shoulders with her eyes. She conquered that urge, then turned, darting Lord Lennox a bright, brittle smile. "You are very good to come see me again so soon, my lord."

"By that I fear you mean 'very troublesome to come and annoy me again.'"

"You know me well enough to believe that if I felt so, I would have said it."

He frowned, taking her fingers in his hand. "But you are upset about something. Something to do with him?"

Tess's smile faded.

Why don't you marry Lennox? Ravenhurst's hard voice came back to mock her.

"That man? What possible interest could I have in him?" Two spots of color appeared in Tess's cheeks.

"I could not begin to say." Lennox's green eyes searched her face. "I take it you haven't changed your mind about my offer?"

Tess's slight stiffening was answer enough.

Rather sadly Lord Lennox smiled, releasing her fingers. "Then I must keep the offer open, my dear. Just don't take too long, or one day you'll find me worn and weather-beaten, wearing a streak of white hair at my temple like Ravenhurst's."

After the earl had gone Tess stood for a long time, unmoving by the window. Her cheek still tingled slightly where he had kissed her before he departed.

"Hard about!" Maximilian began to dance upon his perch. "Dangerous shoals ahead!"

"Oh shut up, you plaguey creature!" Tess answered crossly. She aimed an angry kick at the broken range, wondering how the day could possibly grow any worse.

She had her answer sooner than she expected.

From high overhead came a deep rumble. A moment later the large iron damper plate tore loose and exploded down the chimney onto the top of the boiler, dragging an angry torrent of bricks and soot in its wake.

Before going to bed that night Tess threw the sturdy new bolt Hobhouse had installed on her bedroom door. Then, with strangely unsteady fingers, she secured the shiny brass latch at her casement window.

There, she told herself firmly. No one would be stealing into her room tonight. At the same time, she wondered why the sight of these devices did so little to curb her strange, gnawing uneasiness.

Out to sea, the captain of the *Liberté* gazed north toward the silver cliffs of England. With his powerful legs locked and braced he faced the wind, oblivious to the salt spray lashing his hard features.

Her face was in his thoughts. Her body fired his blood.

Soon, my auburn-haired beauty, he swore as the wind tore through his long hair.

The stupid English in the Revenue cutter would not find their prey tonight, he knew. Yes, the *Liberté* was far too swift to be captured by such as them. Around their captain, a well-trained crew sprang to their tasks, leaving André Le Brix free to ponder his own pleasures.

And his pleasure was to think of the woman whose hair shone like the finest burgundy, whose strange eyes tilted up like a cat's.

He had seen her often in the past month, though she did not know it. Sometimes he slipped up from the harbor, heady with the success of a completed run, the tang of the sea still clinging to his hard body. In silence he stalked the narrow streets to stand beneath her window.

Watching. Waiting.

It was dangerous, of course. His crew thought him half mad, in fact. But she was a woman to drive a man mad, the *Liberté*'s captain thought. And the danger only added to his reckless excitement.

For weeks he had dreamed of her, this woman of fire. Beneath his expert touch she would moan and flow like honey.

Soon, *mon coeur,* he vowed. Oh yes, very soon I shall have you.

Twice Tess woke in the night, certain she'd heard a rattle at the keyhole or a creaking of the wooden casement. Both times she'd frozen, her breath checked, waiting for an intruder to appear.

But it was only the glass pane tapping in the wind.

At least that's what she told herself as she huddled beneath the covers, staring at the flickering candle.

Only the old oak tree scraping the roof with its long, bony fingers . . .

12

When next Tess awoke, it was to golden sunlight spilling onto her face. For a moment she blinked, puzzling over the warmth on her cheeks.

Frowning, she sat up and opened her eyes.

The night was gone, the darkness past.

This time there had been no dreams, only blessed oblivion. Strangely renewed, she stretched slowly, enjoying the heavy golden feel of the sun on her outstretched arms.

Already her mind was sorting through the tasks before her. Today she would tend to the hidden brandy from the last runs. Hobhouse would have conveyed the four-gallon tubs out to Fairleigh already, she knew. There she could let down the overproof spirits with water and then transfer the mixture to bottles without fear of being disturbed.

One problem solved, her thoughts turned to the next. Tom Ransley was beginning to grow troublesome. He suspected something, she was certain. But he could not be omitted from Jack's select inner group, at least not yet. He would be too quick to sow dissension among the others.

Then there was the difficult decision of the next run. She would have to call a meeting with the Fox's four deputies. That was what Tess liked the least, those face-to-face meetings.

More danger, more risks. But she had no choice.

It would have to be the ruined castle at Camber, she decided;

and it must be the following night. Her contact at Hythe had told Hobhouse that a cargo of tea and tobacco would be available in three days.

Three days for men to be alerted, wagons and horses assembled. Jack would still be at the priory, but he would not be roaming about in his weak condition. Yes, with a little bit of luck Tess would carry off her daring masquerade one more time. Her success, she knew, was possible only due to the strict code of secrecy Jack imposed on his men. By custom, information was parceled out in small bits, and then only to the few who required it. Even then no man could be certain what his fellows knew or did not know, and no one made the mistake of asking.

Finally, her decision made, Tess stood and began to dress. Her greenish eyes looked back at her from the mirror, glittering and reckless. Once again she felt the old elation, the wild, dizzying excitement, snake through her. She might be unmasked by Ransley or any other of Jack's men. She might even be hunted down by Hawkins, but at least she was alive and truly in control of her life at last.

Something she had once believed impossible.

With a quick trill of laughter she crossed the room, threw back the curtains, and unlatched the window, feeling warm, flower-scented air brush her face and fill the room.

A new day come. She would face its trials and she would win.

It was late in the afternoon before Tess could get away to see Jack. She was on her way downstairs to give Hobhouse some last-minute instructions when she heard faint laughter, followed by the rustling of cloth.

She halted at the second-floor landing, cocking her head to listen.

More laughter, then a low groan.

A woman's muffled shriek.

Frowning, Tess slipped across the landing in the direction of those furtive sounds, only to encounter a wall of silence.

Suddenly a door at the rear of the corridor burst open. In a split second Tess was across the hall, pressing back against the wall while she waited to see the culprits emerge.

If Mrs. Tredwell's son thought he could bring another of his lightskirts here, he would find he was sadly mistaken!

A moment later a voluptuous, red-cheeked serving maid was deposited giggling into the corridor.

"Out, baggage!" came a muffled male command.

"Ye know where t' find me, love," the woman purred, turning to rub herself wantonly against the man's chest. "Any time at all. Fer a man like yerself, I've lots more o' the same. Jest you remember that."

Her face dark with anger, Tess watched as Lucy, one of the new chambermaids, molded herself against the man in the doorway. His side was to Tess, and she could see little except straight, wet hair, for Lucy's voluminous curves all but engulfed him.

In the room beyond the pair Tess saw a tub of steaming water. Little puddles dotted the carpet, marking the man's progress to the door.

Which one was it, she wondered grimly?

The red-faced wine merchant from Brighton?

The overweight squire from Tunbridge Wells?

Or the sad-eyed cavalry officer on his way back to Dover?

She frowned as the man pivoted slightly, pulling Lucy against his chest and bending closer to mutter something in her ear.

Tess felt a hot tide of crimson stain her cheeks. She couldn't see the man's face but now she had a clear view of just about all the rest of him.

Some wild urgency held her fast, made her feast furtively on the sight of that unforgettable body. Beads of water glistened on muscles rippling at his back and shoulders. Beneath the scrap of a towel anchored about his waist, she could see the outline of lean hips and powerful thighs.

Tess's errant curiosity exploded into white-hot fury. Did the brazen fool think the Angel was a brothel?

Suddenly Lucy's practiced fingers dropped lower, stroking the taut line of flesh outlined at the man's groin.

Her green eyes flashing, Tess marched from her hiding place. *"Out, the pair of you!"*

The dark-haired figure stiffened and then slowly turned, a thin smile etched on his bronzed face. "Waiting your turn, Miss Leighton?"

Tess recognized him before he turned, even before she saw those mocking eyes.

Eyes cold and hard, the color of broken promises.

One black brow raised, Lord Ravenhurst casually cupped his companion's generous breast, which was outlined clearly beneath her damp garment. Idly his thumb circled a lush nipple, which obligingly tightened at his touch.

"Get out!" Tess rasped.

The thin smile widened fractionally. "I beg your pardon?"

"You heard me, you degenerate cur! Get out. If you wish to indulge in this sort of crude pastime, then find other lodgings. The Angel is not a bordello. And as for you, Lucy," Tess added, turning to face the jeering servant, "your employment here is terminated. See Hobhouse for your wages."

"Nothing wrong wi' havin' a bit o' fun, Miss High and Mighty!" the woman shrieked. "Jest cause ye're the bleedin' Ice Queen and don't know nothin' about—"

For an instant some dark, fleeting emotion flashed in Tess's eyes. Then her small chin rose. "Oh, but I do know, Lucy," she said silkily. " 'Tis just that I prefer to exercise a little judgment instead of prowling about like a she-cat in heat, hot for any tom that happens by."

"Why, you—" Lucy's fingers curled into fierce talons as she made for Tess's face.

"Steady, love," Ravenhurst growled, securing his companion with a hand about her ample waist. "No need to run out your guns. There's more than enough of me here for both of you," he drawled mockingly.

"I'll teach Miss Flamin' High and Mighty a lesson," Lucy hissed, struggling vainly against Dane's grip.

"Off with you, Lucy." The viscount's voice cracked like a whip. Cold with command, it was the same voice that had once made grown men flinch. Now it had the same effect on the irate chambermaid.

"A'right, m'lord, but only since it's yerself askin'." Grumbling, she flounced her grimy skirts and turned on her heel.

Speechless with anger, Tess watched the woman stalk down the stairs. Then, her fury in no sense abated, she rounded on Ravenhurst.

He was waiting for her in the middle of the room, his hands on his hips, his powerful legs braced. Little beads of water slipped down his chest, glistening against his bronzed skin and tangled black hair. Tess had to fight to keep her eyes from following the silver drops down, down to where that springy mat of dark fur narrowed and . . .

Perdition! Was she losing her mind? Speechless with fury, she glared at the nearly naked man before her.

Ravenhurst's lips twisted into a cold smile. His eyes glittered, never leaving her flushed face as his hands moved slowly to the knot at his waist.

His challenge was electric, stinging, nearly palpable.

And like some angry, half-mad marsh creature, Tess absolutely refused to back down before it.

Paralyzed, she watched his long fingers hook the straining fabric.

Dry-throated, she saw them clench and tug sharply.

No! He could not. . . .

With a muffled plop the towel hit the carpet.

"Is that more to your liking, Miss Leighton?" he taunted.

Horrified, Tess jerked her eyes away from the bronzed expanse of damp, glistening skin, away from the thick tangle of sable hair, away from the rampant blade of taut male muscle.

"You—you—" she croaked, her neck and cheeks on fire.

With cool deliberation Dane stalked toward her. Before Tess knew it, his fingers were circling her wrists, dragging her back into the room. A moment later he kicked the door shut with his foot.

"What do you think you're doing?"

"Doing?" Ravenhurst repeated harshly, hauling her against his hard, wet body. "Doing, my dear Tess? I'm teaching you a lesson, that's what I'm doing. The first of many lessons I mean to teach you. Today I'm showing you exactly what you missed. And giving you a taste of what's yet to come."

"Never, you bastard!" Tess's breath came and went in harsh gasps as she jerked free to pummel his chest. Every touch of his naked skin was like fire, tormenting her in ways she had never dreamed possible. "Swine! Snake! S-scorpion!"

"How they lied when they called you the Ice Maiden," Ravenhurst growled, dodging her flying fists. With a smothered curse, he caught her hands and forced them immobile at her sides. "For you, my dear, are a fire just waiting to happen!"

"Why did you come back?" Tess hissed. "The *real* reason, this time."

"Why, my dark angel? Because of you, of course. Because of what you did to me five years ago. You told me to go to the devil, do you remember? Well, I've been there, Tess. I've seen the face of Hell itself. And now I've come back for you—to give you a taste of what it was like." Slowly, inexorably, he drew her toward his naked body.

Tess flinched, feeling the hard outline of his manhood at her thigh; finding this savage bitterness between them worse than any nightmare.

"No—"

His rough hands bit into her wrists. "Oh, yes, Tess. I'm going to do exactly what I should have done that night in the gate house. After I'd put a ball through that bastard Chevington's heart, that is. I'm going to strip away your lies, layer by poisonous layer, until I find your heart. But it will be done on *my* terms. In my own time, in my own way. And not just yet, I think." Ravenhurst's lapis eyes burned into her ashen face. "No, I believe I want to see you bleed a little first."

Her mind reeling, Tess was not immediately aware that he had released her. She stumbled slightly, then caught her balance on the dresser by the door.

Nightmares . . . more nightmares . . .

Dimly she saw Ravenhurst turn and lower his powerful body into the steaming tub. His face was hard and shuttered as he settled himself to his comfort, then lifted one powerful leg, hooking it over the tub's copper rim.

"Too bad you dispensed with Lucy. I take it that means *you're* going to soap my back?"

Tess's mouth opened and closed, but no sound came from her throat.

"Well, woman?"

"I—I'd as soon stroke a snake!"

Ravenhurst's lips twisted. "An interesting image, my love. Do go on."

"I won't have you here at the Angel one night longer, do you hear?"

"Is it my imagination or has it turned chill in here? Perhaps you'd better close the window." One sable brow rose in a mocking slant. "After you've looked your fill, of course."

"Damn you!" Tess blazed. "You're just like all the rest! You think you can—" She bit back the words she'd been about to say. "I won't have you seducing my help!"

"Then perhaps I should try seducing *you* instead. But I've already tried that, haven't I, Tess? And just look where it got us." Ravenhurst's fingers tightened on the rim of the tub. "Only I wasn't the one doing the seducing, was I? It was you, all along. How you must have laughed at your conquest."

Tess stared back in stony silence.

"Answer me, damn it! Or are you afraid to admit the truth about yourself? That even then, though only seventeen and barely out of the schoolroom, you were already a hardened trollop."

Tess stood frozen, her eyes dark pools of pain.

But we had no schoolroom at Fairleigh, she could have told him. *No tutor. No mother. No friends of any sort. We took our food when we had it and did without too many times to count. Above all, we learned to stay out of our father's way, especially when the black moods were upon him.*

Oh, yes, Lord Ravenhurst, I was many things at seventeen, but a hardened trollop was not one of them.

But telling this cold-eyed stranger the truth about those years was the last thing Tess would ever do.

Instead she tilted her head back and smiled faintly. "Yes, you were rather amusing, my lord. For a while." She shrugged indifferently. "But only for a while, alas."

"And so you sought new prey. Just like that."

"You men do it all the time. Why should a woman not do the same?"

She heard his sharp intake of breath. Disgust hardened his features, and Tess nearly flinched.

Then her slim shoulders stiffened. Why should she care what he thought of her? "I want you out of here before nightfall, Lord Ravenhurst. Do you understand me?"

"I think I do understand. Far better than you realize. But as for leaving," the hard-faced man in the tub growled, "I wouldn't dream of it. Not when things are just beginning to get interesting."

"Play your dirty little games somewhere else, your bloody lordship! And if it's entertainment you want, try the Merry Maids. You'll find nothing to suit you here!"

Without waiting for what she was certain would be another mocking reply, Tess spun about and stormed from the room. Her heart pounding, she flung the door closed behind her. "The devil fly away with you, Dane St. Pierre!" she hissed, stamping down the stairs.

But the man in the tub only laughed harshly, his eyes cold with triumph. "How wrong you are, Tess Leighton," he whispered, his lips curving into a bitter smile. "I shall find a great deal to suit me here. And what suits me, as you will soon discover, is unravelling all your sordid secrets, inch by agonizing inch, until you lie naked before me—in body and in soul. When that happens, there will be no room left between us for games."

13

Smells of sweetness and decay hung heavy on the air of Fairleigh's dusty drawing room, where Tess crouched, curtains drawn, busy at the laborious work of letting down the overproof brandy from her last runs.

Before her stood a line of dusty, cobweb-covered bottles from Fairleigh's cellars. This, she had discovered, was the safest way to cover the evidence. To any casual observer these bottles bore every evidence of having reposed in their racks for at least fifty years.

But Hawkins was no casual observer, Tess knew, and that thought made her take special care with the task.

It was all accomplished deftly and in entirely mechanical fashion. One by one she opened the four-gallon kegs, transferred their contents to a large tub, mixed in water and caramel coloring, then poured the spirits into their new—that is to say, very old-looking—containers.

Each keg yielded six gallons of brandy, which would fetch a full four pounds in London, against a purchase price in France of only thirteen shillings.

Almost a fivefold profit. A profit great enough to make a man take grave risks.

Or a woman, if she was brave enough.

Tess had done it many times before and she would, she supposed, do it many times again. Today the thought gave her no pleasure.

When forty bottles stood on the floor before her, replete with fine French brandy, she sat back. They would net her a good price, those bottles—more than enough to repair the damage Hawkins had done to her linens.

Yes, everything was going as planned. She had seen Jack and he was improving steadily. Letty had pronounced him nearly past the danger of fever.

So why did Tess still feel tense and unsettled, the way one felt before a raging storm swept across the Channel? Why didn't her heart glow with triumph as she surveyed the fruits of her labor?

This time the wild elation was gone. It was a task completed and no more.

She took a deep breath as she recorked the last bottle, then moved to her feet.

She swayed slightly and realized the brandy fumes were making her dizzy and more than a little light-headed. Perhaps that explained her odd mood.

Once again something ghosted about the edges of her mind, something that made her feel queer and uneasy. She frowned, trying to place the errant images, but they only skittered away.

It could have been the confrontation with Mrs. Tredwell, of course. It could have been the problems with Amos Hawkins. It could have been her indecision over Lord Lennox's offer.

But it was none of those things, Tess knew.

It was something to do with one bastard of a man with lapis eyes and cruel fingers. A man who knew exactly where her weak points were, and probed them with unerring accuracy. A man who cut her no slack.

In his cold eyes she had read the raw force of his hatred—and it had horrified her.

But only for a moment.

Then the other Tess had taken over, the Tess who had repeatedly saved her mother from her father's cruel abuse. The Tess who led one hundred lawless men over marsh and weald.

The Tess who had forced herself to forget anything that made her weak.

Or at least she tried to forget.

There it was again, that strange sense of having overlooked something. . . .

Her eyes narrowed, sweeping over the dusty bottles; once again the source eluded her.

Oh well, better begin tidying up here. Thomas would be around soon with the wagon, and together they would load their secret cargo into the special compartment beneath the seat.

Still frowning, Tess bent down for the rope Thomas would need to tie the crate. Absently she studied the hastily dropped coils snaking across the dusty floor, rippling back and forth across themselves in crisscross patterns.

Like a row of X's, she thought, reaching down. Like a living creature. Like . . .

And there she froze, the thick strands rough upon her fingers.

Like a writhing, tormented creature—as rough as the scars carved into Dane's wrists.

Her mind had not acknowledged the image earlier, while she was reeling under his assault and the fiery shock of her own response to his nakedness.

But now, in her first moments of leisure since that encounter, the image exploded into Tess's consciousness.

Scars—terrible scars. How had they been earned? On a quarter-deck, with cannon shot crashing overhead as he struggled with fallen rigging? In roaring seas as he grappled for a line?

She saw them in her mind clearly now, red and angry, their edges raised and puckered. Ugly and disfiguring.

Entirely in keeping with the character of the man who wore them.

It could not have been a year since their inflicting.

All this Tess saw with sudden, chilling clarity, and wondered how she could have overlooked it before.

Dear God, Dane, what happened to us? How could something so fresh and pure be corrupted into something so dark and full of hate?

There on the floor of Fairleigh's empty drawing room, with little dust motes dancing around her feet, Tess pressed her trembling hands to her face and allowed the hot tears to spill down her cheeks.

She cried for the person she had once been and the person she had become.

She cried for a love died stillborn and for the scars it had left unhealed.

She cried, too, for the dashing officer who had faced battle once too often, and for the cold-eyed stranger who had come back from the wars in his place.

It was the first time Tess had cried since her mother's death.

The first time in nearly nine years.

Already, she realized dimly, Dane's bitter threat was proving true.

"Aye, that's the lot, Miss Tess. Covered 'em good with the firewood. Nobody going to do a lot of probing there, I'll own. Now, you'd best be changing that soiled gown and washing your hands, for you've the rank smell of a tavern about you, and that's a fact!" Old Thomas smiled grimly at Tess. "As if you'd ever listen to anything I have to say. None of you Leightons ever have."

The old servant frowned, studying Tess's pale face. For a moment it looked as if he meant to say something else, but he merely shook his head and went to bring the wagon around, muttering under his breath.

Tess ran a furtive hand across her face, wondering if Thomas had guessed why her cheeks were pale and her eyes red-rimmed. But her shoulders soon straightened, their fragility enhanced by her stiff bearing.

For now she had no more time for tears.

Tonight the Fox had a trail to lay and a trap to set.

As the moon rose that night, four flowers reached their destination on the marsh. "Camber Castle," came the whispered message, and to a man the recipients of the roses shivered. The walls half decayed, open to moon and wind and night-flying bats, the castle was a place where ghosts might indeed walk.

And a fitting place to meet, therefore.

For the Fox was, perhaps, more than half ghost himself.

"Bleedin' bunch of rubbish, I tell ye!"

His long, reddish hair lank and unkempt, Tom Ransley scowled, angrily pacing back and forth within the empty circle of stone walls at the center of the ruined Tudor castle. High above, the moon rode through the sky, faint smudges of clouds trailing over its silver face. In the distance came the lonely screech of an owl, followed by the shrill whine of hungry bats racing through the night.

The two men standing beside the wall shivered. "Hush, Tom Ransley," one hissed. "Never know when *he* might be listenin'."

"The devil take the Fox, I say! Who's he to hide his face from us, when we take the same risks as ever he does! Aye, why should he keep his name a secret?" The pale light shone on the rough edges of a scar that zigzagged across Ransley's face from temple to chin.

" 'Cause 'tis him what plans the runs, and him what brings the goods, as well ye do know." As the man beside the wall spoke, he peered nervously over his shoulder. "What was that?" he demanded suddenly.

"What was what?" Ransley asked, his own voice tense.

From the other side of the wall came a quiet crunching sound. The three men froze. After a few seconds, the noise died away.

"Just a bloody lot of owls, like as not," Ransley snarled, only to sink into silence a moment later as the sound was repeated, nearer this time.

Just beyond the black opening which yawned before them.

The three men sank back, their eyes wide.

Through the breech in the ancient stone walls there stepped a tall, rangy figure.

"Who goes there?" Ransley demanded.

"John Digby, it is. Is *he* here?" None of the nervous men had the slightest question about whom Digby meant.

"Naw, the bloody bastard's late, like always. Wantin' to make the grand entrance, that's what he is." Ransley strode out into the center of the roofless walls, eager to make up for his momentary weakness. "And us standin' here white-faced and shiverin' like a bunch of bleedin' schoolboys!"

"Oh, shut yer mouth, Ransley," the new arrival snapped. " 'Tis guineas aplenty the Fox has brought us, yerself like the rest of us. So ye've no reason to be cursing the man now. Unless ye got something else on yer mind, that is."

With a low, graphic curse, the lank-haired smuggler strode over to pin Digby against the moss-dappled walls. "Shut yer soddin' mouth, John Digby. Unless ye look forward to the taste of my fist crammed down yer throat!"

With a growl, Digby whipped free, and a moment later the two were at each other's throats.

"Gentlemen! Gentlemen! What manner of reception is this?" From the top of the wall at their back came the crunch of gravel. Those low, harsh tones could belong to only one man.

The Fox.

As always, he was garbed all in black, from tricorn to high boots. His long cloak swirled about him as he stood with legs apart, arms crossed over his chest.

The long, slim whiskers of his mask gleamed faintly in the moonlight. "Take your hands off Brother Digby, Tom Ransley," the shadowy figure growled, his voice disguised by his heavy mask. "Else I escort you from here and deal with you personally. The gentlemen do not raise hands against one another. 'Tis one of the vows you took when you joined our band," the Fox reminded.

Scowling, the big man pushed his rangy opponent aside. "Ye take yer bloody time about comin', don't ye, Fox?" he snarled, aiming a thick mouthful of saliva at the dark ground between the Fox and himself.

Suddenly a ray of cold moonlight flashed from the pistol that appeared in the Fox's hand. It was the only hint of light about that dark figure.

"Is that in the manner of a complaint, my friend?" The smuggler's voice was silky with menace. "If so, I shall have to treat it with the seriousness it warrants." That unnatural voice from high above was frigid, devoid of any trace of emotion; the sound sent terror through the four men waiting below.

For long moments Ransley did not move, his face mottled with fury. He itched to draw out the pistol hidden deep in the pocket of his baggy pants.

But the time was not right for a challenge, he knew.

Not yet.

A look of cunning crossed the smuggler's scarred face, and he merely shrugged. "Not from me, it ain't. And a bad business it is when a man can't even make a simple comment without him bein' growled at. Aye, so it is, by God."

The Fox did not move from his position on the wall. Slowly his hands rose to his hips, giving him the appearance of a great black angel as he stood in judgment over them.

The four men below felt the force of his cold eyes cut through them, measuring them in turn. Each man wondered what secrets their leader had already guessed.

And each man stiffened, shivering secretly, expecting the dark phantom to single him out as the object of his wrath in the next moment.

Within that circle of weathered stones the uneasy silence seemed to stretch on forever.

But in keeping with his lightning changes of mood, the Fox smiled abruptly and doffed his tricorn. "Ah, well, then. A joke it was, Mr. Ransley, and as such it may be forgiven. But now, gentlemen, it's to business." Shifting one black-clad leg forward, the Fox leaned down, elbow braced on bended knee. "Listen, my brothers, and listen well. There's gold guineas aplenty if you do."

If there was the faintest hint of irony in that choice of epithet, none of the men below him seemed to notice, for their eyes were already gleaming with avarice at the plan the Fox had begun to describe.

At that same moment, on the opposite side of the marsh, Amos Hawkins stood with twenty of his excisemen arrayed in a ragged line before a dark cottage.

"Open up in the name of the Crown!"

There was no answer from within. Not that the tight-lipped customs inspector had anticipated one.

"Send in a fusillade to tell the bastards we mean business!"

A volley of angry shots splintered against the planked door and rough-hewn wooden walls.

Was it their imagination, or did they hear a shrill cry from somewhere inside?

Hawkins growled an order and the line of men lowered their guns, stirring nervously in the sudden silence after the volley.

With a snarl Hawkins cocked his own two pistols and jerked his head toward the cottage. "Break down the door!"

No one moved.

"You, Boggs! And you, too, Lawson!" he bellowed at the men nearest the door. "Move yer arses!"

Slowly the two men crossed the sharp shadows. Their fingers trembled as they reached for the rusted bolt at the door.

Was it the wind that stirred then, whining a shrill complaint in the taut silence?

"Get ready to fire, the rest of ye!" Hawkins ordered softly. "And don't let the bastard escape this time, else ye'll find yerselves fodder for the next press-gang."

Forty hands rose as one, pistols gripped tensely as they faced that ominous rectangle of darkness. There was no sound in the quiet yard on the edge of the marsh. Even the wind seemed to shrink back in fear.

With a faint click the bolt slid free. Nervously a young excise officer pushed open the door, revealing solid darkness beyond.

And then the night exploded in sound. First came a muffled scratching, which soon rose to shrill yelps as a host of furious, twitching bodies erupted from the black mouth of the cottage.

Tails bristling, whiskers flashing, paws racing, a dozen angry foxes plunged out into the night, their furious yelps splitting the air while the stunned excisemen looked on dumbly.

"What the—!" Hawkins's curse broke off as he stumbled toward the cottage. Then the furious animals were upon him, nipping at his breeches, barking and straining as they fought their way to freedom. "Get those bloody things out of here!" the inspector roared in impotent fury.

His men scrambled forward, fighting their way through the bristling pack, raising their hastily lit lanterns to peer into the silent cottage.

An empty cottage.

"Nothin' here, Mr. Hawkins."

There was a faint snicker from somewhere at the end of the line of waiting men.

With a murderous gleam in his eyes, Hawkins spun about to glare in the direction of the sound. "So the bastard thinks he's outsmarted me, does he? But I'll have him and have him soon, by God."

The squat man swung around again, cursing. He raised his pistol toward the foxes racing over the flat, dark earth toward freedom. His gun barked once; the last animal, smaller than the rest, cried out in terror and pain, then fell to the damp earth, twitching wildly.

"Aye, that's what ye'll have from me, ye bloody bastard. My bullet buried in your skull!"

Cold with sweat, Tess found her way to the ancient tunnel that snaked beneath the castle ruins. Thomas had first told her of this place, where he had played as a boy with his brother. But that brother was long dead, killed in an Indian raid in the upstart colonies.

Now only Tess and her old servant knew of this place.

Once she emerged from the tunnel, it was only a matter of feet to the edge of the narrow dike and the boat she'd left moored there.

This was what she liked least, this masquerade at close quarters, where every second brought the threat of exposure. Still, the men seemed to hold no suspicions this night.

All except for Tom Ransley, and he had a reputation for distrusting everyone.

Tess permitted herself a thin smile. Yes, it was a good plan and none could deny it. The signals would go out this very night: three horses tethered at Snargate church, and lanterns lit at every third cottage along the Rye-Appledore road.

By morning one hundred men would know a run was coming and wait for final instructions.

These the Fox always denied until the last remaining hours. By hard experience Jack had learned that traitors, too, found refuge in the night and in the darkness which tells no tales.

So Tess also reserved her final directions until several hours before a run. Then a fiddler would play at the inns, and certain village boys would begin to sing a simple nursery rhyme.

Two hours later her hundred men would be waiting for her upon the marsh.

Tess's hands were cold and her face itched beneath her heavy mask and cloak. The wind blew shrill about her shoulders as she pulled the little skiff from the reeds and bent to the oars, anxious to be back at Fairleigh and safety.

Jack would soon be well enough to travel, she knew. Before that time, Tess had a great many things to discuss with him.

But now, the moments of strain past, she felt weariness begin to set in. Her eyes glazed, she headed west by the narrow waterways crisscrossing Pett Level.

No one would follow her here.

The moon was rising and Tess's eyes flickered toward the hills to the north, where the proud turrets of Fairleigh Priory jutted dark in the moonlight. Dear Fairleigh, she thought. Home and yet never quite a home. Still, it was all the security she'd ever known and she meant to hold on to the ruined pile, no matter what.

With a surge of relief she saw the narrow track that looped west and then back toward Fairleigh. Tess was always careful to arrange her business far from home, for she wanted nothing to connect the Leighton estate with the smuggling trade.

After all, a fox never hunted near its own den, she thought, smiling grimly.

Before her gleamed the last obstacle, a flat pool of silver stretching toward a pasture of calmly grazing sheep. If all went well, she'd be back snug in her bed within the hour.

She was halfway across the freezing pool when she heard the sound of shouts carried down the wind from the east.

One glance at the dancing black shadows was enough to tell Tess that Hawkins had found her.

14

Pluto and perdition!

Fat grazing sheep dotted the water meadow, their thick fleece silver in the moonlight. Tess's fingernails dug into her palms as she fought her gnawing fear.

"Over there, sir!"

Realizing that she made a clear figure in the skiff, she rowed into a thick bank of reeds and berthed the boat. Her lips tense with strain, she slipped over the edge and down into the murky, salt-tinged pool, shivering as cold water surged up to her shoulders. Ducking her head, she began to swim underwater.

All was silent, mud and water plants swirling about her. But at long last her hand struck the bottom. Warily she surfaced and lifted her head, keeping close to the reeds at the water's edge.

The preventive officers were moving slowly, inching along the canals, afraid of a misstep. Only Hawkins's bellowing forced them on. Yet with five hundred pounds reward on her head, Tess knew the men would never give up until they'd searched every ditch and canal.

Shivering, she huddled near the bank at the meadow's edge, while above her a dozen sheep grazed peacefully in the moonlight. *So beautiful. So deadly.*

Tess gritted her lips, resolutely refusing to consider what would happen if Hawkins discovered her. To be a man caught as a smuggler was bad enough, but if these men discovered their prey was a woman. . . .

She tightened her icy fingers into fists, then thrust them deep into her pockets, fighting the terror that licked at the edges of her mind.

Then her hands closed upon a hard, round object. A chunk of rock salt, snatched up from the Angel's kitchen, to reward Thomas's favorite heifer!

With a prayer rising fervent on her lips, Tess crawled from the water and inched into the meadow.

"Well, ye fools? Do I have to do everything myself?" Behind her, the customs inspector's angry voice slashed through the night air.

"Happen we lost 'em, Mr. Hawkins," an unfamiliar voice whined.

"Lost them? Then by God, ye'll be keeping company with the deep blue sea if ye don't find them again!"

On Tess crawled, across the meadow and toward the grazing herd, her hand outstretched before her.

When she was still several feet away, the sheep began to stir, smelling salt. Soon they were huddled in a circle, sniffing and licking the precious white crystal that Tess held tight in her grasp.

And there she stayed, curled into a tight ball, concealed beneath their thick, shaggy coats.

Praying that the salt would not run out.

"He was there a minute ago, damn it! Search the bloody canals, ye fools. And don't expect to come out until ye find the bastard!"

From behind her came the slap of waves as several of the excise officers plunged into the water.

Tess's heart began to hammer. If she had stayed where she was, they would have found her already! Shivering convulsively, she inched deeper into the fleecy circle.

Hawkins's men were only yards away now, their flailing arms slapping the water. If only the salt held out. . . .

One of the men sloshed closer, and Tess's heart beat an angry tattoo in her chest. It seemed as if she'd been on the marsh for a lifetime—a lifetime of fatigue and cold. Her face taut with strain and fear, she fought to hold in her ragged breath while her lungs burned with pain.

"He's over there!"

Someone sloshed past her, moving fast. She heard a shuffling noise, and then the slap of water.

" 'Tis only a swan, you damned fools!" Hawkins bellowed. "Move on toward the seawall. We'll split up and catch the bastard between us."

They began to move east. A moment later, Tess heard one of the men curse quietly.

"Never find the Fox," the fellow said glumly. "Part devil and part man, he is. Aye, a bloody phantom what knows every twist of these canals. Cursed shame, too, for it's a lot of grog I could buy with five hundred pounds. Aye, and a lot of warm woman too."

Then, to Tess's infinite relief, they moved out of earshot.

For long minutes she waited, unmoving, until silence settled over the silver pools and only the wind came whispering down from the hills to the north. Even then she did not move, ruthlessly forcing herself to finish a mental count to five hundred.

Only then did she push warily through the screening circle of contented sheep.

Around her all was quiet, with no sign of either Hawkins or his men.

In an instant she was on her feet and running, her hands and feet strangely numb, her body hot and cold by turns. As she darted over the damp meadow, Tess prayed that the fleet roan stallion was waiting for her by the old windmill, where Hobhouse had tethered him at dusk.

The Merry Maids was full this night, drunken laughter spilling out into the dark yard as men with rough hands and rougher faces pushed their way inside. The air was acrid with smoke, spirits, and sweaty bodies, but the gin was cheap and the women cost little more.

George Jewkes smiled contentedly, surveying his noisy, smoky establishment with one eye awry in the fashion that was peculiar to him. Even the upstairs rooms were filled this night, he saw, nodding faintly at Bess, his new serving wench, who was just coming downstairs, smoothing her skirts around her ample, swaying hips.

Aye, a comely wench she was, Jewkes thought, and not for the first time. She'd drawn not a few men to the Merry Maids, the bald publican knew.

Just then the outer door burst open. A cold gust of wind lashed the crowded room. In the wind's wake trod a tall figure, broad of shoulder and narrow of waist, draped all in a black greatcoat. Lazily the stranger stood on the threshold, surveying the room's occupants before sauntering to a lone chair angled against the far wall.

The raucous din of laughter and good-natured argument dropped a level lower. Oblivious to the effect of his presence, the newcomer coolly drew off his gloves and threw them down on the table before him.

All noise in the room abruptly stilled.

George Jewkes frowned, wiping beats of sweat from his gleaming, bald head. What the devil was that cursed naval man doing here at the Merry Maids? Didn't he have enough to occupy him in Rye? The Angel's genteel taproom was the place for his likes, not this smoky retreat on the edge of the marsh, where men liked to drink freely and share secrets without fear of being overheard.

Even as he spoke, Jewkes saw Tom Ransley turn and slant a scowl in the man's direction. The publican's face paled. He wanted no trouble, especially not tonight, when he had fifty kegs of uncustomed brandy and gin hidden in an alcove under the rear stairway. And if he didn't think fast, there would certainly be trouble between Ransley and this hard-faced London lord.

Wiping his hands on his greasy apron, Jewkes quickly beckoned to Bess. "Fetch a bottle of rum and a tankard to the man in the corner," he whispered urgently. "And make sure it's a clean tankard, girl."

Bess, too, was aware of the brittle tension in the room as she elbowed her way through the crush of bodies to place a bottle and vessel on the dirty table where the dark-haired stranger sat alone. Her eyes wide and appraising, she took in the man's broad shoulders and lean, shuttered face, the hard set of his jaw in such sharp contrast to his full lower lip.

God's blood, but this is a man! she thought, feeling a warm rush of desire skitter through her. But what was the fine lord doing here at the Merry Maids, and on such a night?

Either he was a very brave man or a very stupid one.

Her expression, as she bent over to fill his tankard, was studiedly casual. "Rum, sir. Compliments o' Mr. Jewkes."

Ravenhurst's dark eyes narrowed; he saw the woman's smile did not extend to her eyes. Nor did he miss the fact that her fingers were trembling. "Now, there's an unexpected courtesy. Pray convey my thanks to Mr. Jewkes."

The woman's fingers slipped as she set the pewter tankard before him, and rum splashed over the table. "Drink it fast," she whispered, bending down before him to mop up the spill with her dirty apron. "Then go. There's them as won't take kindly to your presence here tonight."

Dane's smile widened and he negligently tossed a guinea down on the table. "Thank you, love. I appreciate your kind consideration, but a little boisterousness won't inconvenience me. Just keep the rum coming. No matter what," he added grimly.

Shaking her head, Bess turned and elbowed her way back toward the bar, the gold guinea buried deep in her pocket. Sweet angels above, with the coin she could buy herself a new pair of shoes, and a length of muslin besides. She only wished the handsome stranger had heeded her warning. Then she shrugged, putting him from her mind. He looked, after all, to be a man who could take care of himself—even in rough company such as this.

A dark scowl on his face, Tom Ransley swung around to stare fixedly at the room's newest arrival.

Mr. Jewkes was before him, however. Smiling nervously, he stepped to Dane's table. "Aye, courtesy of the house, it is, yer lordship. In memory of Trafalgar." The bald publican's voice dropped then. "But if ye've no particular business to look after, perhaps ye'll not take it amiss if I see ye to the door. We're a deal too crowded here tonight, as ye kin see, and some of the lads turn a bit rowdy when they've had a glass or two." His eyes darted nervously to right and left. "If ye know what I mean, m' lord . . ."

Dane sat back lazily in his chair, his face unreadable. "I understand you exactly—Mr. Jewkes, isn't it? But as it happens, I do have business here. And I mean to enjoy a drink or two before I return to the marsh. You wouldn't wish to turn a traveler away, would you?" His dark eyes were disarming, faintly chiding.

"No, but—"

"There's a good man." Suddenly there was a hard edge of steel to the viscount's voice.

Shaking his head nervously, the proprietor skittered back to his place by the bar. Why didn't the bloody Quality just stay where they was meant to be? No good would come of it, he thought. No good at all.

A moment later Tom Ransley pushed away from his companions and strode across the quiet room. He stopped before Ravenhurst's table, thick thumbs hooked in his wide leather belt. "Don't like outsiders here, Cap'n," he snarled. "Heroes or no. So I reck'n ye best be pikin' off."

Dane's expression did not change in the slightest. Very slowly, he raised his battered pewter tankard to the man before him, never taking his eyes from that angry face as he drained the potent spirits. "Your health, sir," he said softly.

"Don't ye understand the King's English, then? Ye're not wanted here!" His harsh curse split the air.

Ravenhurst sat slightly forward in his chair, dropping his empty tankard to the table. "Mr. Ransley, isn't it?" His voice was low and deceptively quiet, but it was a tone his crew on the *Bellerophon* knew well. Any one of them could have told Tom Ransley it would be most unwise to cross the captain when he was in such a mood. "Not wanted by whom, Mr. Ransley?"

But Tom Ransley was not so observant, nor was he a man for subtlety. He could not know that the man sitting in the chair before him was at his most dangerous precisely when he spoke in such soft tones. "By me, for one. And by the rest of us here, to a man!" he thundered. "Is that clear enough for ye?"

"Extremely clear. Also most ill considered."

"Just what d' ye mean by that?"

"What do you choose to make of it?"

"I won't go sparrin' words with yer bloody sort. Clear out, I said!"

"I rather think I've a notion to rest awhile, Mr. Ransley. You, of course, are entirely welcome to take yourself off anytime you choose, however," Dane replied silkily.

"The devil I do!" Ransley's face twisted in a snarl. "I've seen yer kind before. Come pokin' about the marsh, askin' all sorts of questions and mindin' everyone's bloody business but yer own. We don't fancy it, I warn ye. Or yer bleedin' charity. We've got our own ways of gettin' by here, and they don't include handouts neither. So tell yer lady friend at the Angel we don't want her leftover food and mended linens. Take care of our own, we do. Aye, tell that to yer Miss Leighton when ye go back. Which, if ye have any wits about ye, will be this very minute." Ransley's fingers slipped lower in his pocket, searching for the handle of his pistol.

"Move another inch and you're a dead man." The threat was flat and deadly. "Now, take your hand out of your pocket. *Very slowly.*"

Ransley smothered a curse, noticing for the first time that Ravenhurst's hands were hidden beneath the table.

The smuggler's mouth set in a thin, angry line; slowly he raised his left hand and opened his fingers to display an empty palm.

"Very good. Now I believe I'd like to finish my tankard in peace, Mr. Ransley." Dane's black brows slanted upward. "Unless you have some objection, that is."

At that moment Dane had nothing but two wax tapers and an apple core in his greatcoat pocket, but the harsh set to his jaw betrayed no hint of this.

The two men's eyes locked, muddy brown probing cold lapis. Around them the background noise ebbed, and an eerie silence gripped the room. Stiff-legged, bristling with anger, Ransley tried to stare Ravenhurst down.

And failed.

"Why not?" Ransley finally snarled. "No soddin' difference to me. Seein' as how ye're a *hero* and all that." Muttering a curse, he shot a mouthful of saliva onto the floor near Dane's polished black boot.

Only with the greatest effort of self-control did Ravenhurst restrain himself from responding to this insult. His fingers tightened in his pocket, mutilating the tapers into misshapen lumps.

God's blood, but he ached to bury his fist in the insolent bastard's face!

But he couldn't. 'Twas the King's business that brought him here, and the affair was too important to be jeopardized by a moment of personal vengeance—no matter how sweet it might be.

His blood hammering in his ears, Dane studied his antagonist from beneath lazy, half-closed lids. "Better watch yourself, Ransley. One day the wind will be against you and you'll find yourself with spit all over your face."

"Why ye—" Ransley's hand was already flashing toward his pocket when two of his friends grabbed him and began to drag him back across the room.

"Cut line, Tom," one of the men growled. "Been enough trouble tonight. We don't need no more of it."

Once back at his earlier seat, Ransley shrugged free of his companions' grip. "Need none of his lot here," he growled. "Bunch of godrottin' meddlers, they are. Let him go back to the Angel and play hare and hounds with the Ice Maiden, 'stead o' botherin' us. Reck'n he's not man enough to get her to spread her legs, though," the smuggler sneered drunkenly.

The steps came behind him, swift and silent. "Ransley?" The word was hardly more than a whisper.

The moment Ransley turned, his smile froze on his mottled face; a hard, bronzed fist smashed into his nose, sending blood streaming over his cheeks. With a faint groan the red-haired smuggler reeled and then slowly crumpled to the floor.

Ravenhurst's blood was still throbbing as he looked down at the man lying before him. A muscle flashing at his jaw, he fought against a wave of fierce, blinding rage.

Finally, lucidity returned. His temper was vile and he knew it. Because he knew that, the anger seldom got the best of him.

Except now.

"Please, Cap'n, no need for more fisticuffs." Jewkes's sweaty face floated dimly before Ravenhurst. "Words is often spoke in anger what are regretted at leisure. Better if ye take yer leave now, though. Surely ye can see that for yerself."

Scowling, Ravenhurst turned and swept up his gloves from the table. It was the cheap rum, he thought. Christ Almighty, it was enough to scramble a man's wits. The night air was what he needed, clean and sharp and stinging as it swept up from the sea.

And maybe if he was lucky, he could imagine he was on a quarterdeck once more, the rigging whistling overhead, the creak of timber in his ears. Yes, by God, he'd sleep beneath the stars tonight and purge himself at dawn with some punishing exercise in the surf. He knew just the place where the breakers would test his mettle.

Fairleigh Cove.

Smothering a curse, the hard-faced viscount jerked open the door and strode into the night, leaving more than one man to breathe easier in his absence.

15

An hour before dawn Tess slipped into the dark tunnel beneath the priory ruins. Her only witness was a solitary owl hooting mournfully from the heights of a yew tree at the top of the hill. The moon had gone down, and the dark meadows were covered with low-lying, drifting fog, which hugged the hollows like a sea of slow-moving foam.

Like the sad ghosts of ancient lovers, Tess thought, watching the pale, twisting shapes. Like cold memories of dead desires.

Grimly she stuffed her whiskered mask deep into her pocket and pulled her damp cloak close, shaking off the chilling fog along with her dark thoughts.

For she had more important things to worry about right now.

Jack, for one. She had stopped at Fairleigh to exchange her breeches for a dress, but if he saw her mask, his fury would know no bounds.

"Jack?" Tess moved to the end of the tunnel, holding the lantern high above her head. The flame cast crazy shadows across the steep passage, their ragged outlines spilling into the narrow room just beyond. "Are you asleep?"

The man on the straw pallet turned, his face pale and drawn. "Nay, not sleeping, lass. I hardly fancy my dreams would be pleasant ones this night." He sat back against the cold stone wall, patting the spot beside him. "Come and sit beside me. There's things that must be said before I go."

So he was leaving. Slowly Tess settled the lantern on an up-turned barrel. "You're going? Tonight?"

"I'm mended well enough to travel, lass. It's safer if I'm away from here."

Her mind understood, but her heart could never agree. "Of course," she mumbled. Something kept her from sitting, as Jack directed. Instead, her shoulders stiff with weariness, she turned to pace the narrow underground room.

It was so still here deep beneath the earth. The air was chill, with a vast, clinging sort of dampness that penetrated to one's very bones. Suddenly Tess was racked with despair. The room wrapped its great black arms around her and threatened to squeeze the life from her lungs. "Jack . . ." she cried urgently.

She fell into his arms, weeping, and the old smuggler was wise enough to let her cry, adding no word to interrupt her long wracking sobs. For this pain, Jack knew, was a pain long years growing.

So he only held her tightly, his fingers tense with his own unspoken emotion.

Finally Tess's tears slowed; the darkness seemed to release her. Sniffing, she sat back and scrubbed away her tears. "What a fool I am, crying about nothing. And yet there is something strange— very strange—about this place."

"Never mind, lass," the white-haired man said gruffly, patting her shoulder. "The tears had to come sometime. You've held them inside too long. 'Tisn't natural, that. But I know what you mean about this place." Jack's voice dropped suddenly. He shrugged, and when next he spoke, his voice was hard. "Now, I want the truth about this daft escapade of yours."

Tess knew a moment of panic as his stern eyes probed her face. Had he discovered the true extent of her involvement? Did he realize that she had been brash enough to usurp his own role, indeed had just come from doing so this very night?

Defiantly, she raised her chin, meeting his gaze directly. "I needed the money, Jack. For Fairleigh. And for—"

"For that harum-scarum brother of yours. That's another thing not quite natural. He should be here taking care of you, instead of the other way around."

"Nonsense. I'm four years older than he, and since our mother's death I've been—"

"I know all about that, lass, but Ashley's a man grown now. 'Tis time he stood on his own two feet. And as for the money, you well know I've enough to spare. Often enough I've offered to give you, to *lend* you"—he hastily corrected himself—"all the guineas you need to repair this wreck."

"I can only say what I've said before: Thank you, but no. We're in debt to half of England already, thanks to my father's propensity for gaming. I'll not add *you* to the list."

Jack was scowling now, his eyes cold and hard. They were shrewd eyes, eyes that had seen too many betrayals, too much of the dark side of the human heart. Things that Jack was determined Tess would never have to see.

"And I'll have no more of this wild running with the gentlemen, do you hear me? 'Twas only meant to be a game, don't you see? Something to fill the lonely hours I spent here with you and that scamp Ashley. 'Tis naught but madness, lass! What if Hawkins had caught you on the last run? What would you have done when the brute discovered you weren't the man you appeared!"

"But he didn't discover me," Tess answered crisply. Her gray-green eyes twinkled with a sudden warmth. "And I *did* help you to get away, if you'll recall."

"After nearly felling me from shock at the sight of you! Nay, I've not forgotten how you saved me, lass. But that's the only reason I haven't turned you over my knee and taken a strap to your tender bottom!" he growled.

Tess heard fear in his voice, and it stiffened her resolve. "Don't worry, Jack, I've learned my lesson. 'Tis no fine sport to go raking the moon from the water." That, at least, was true. She still shivered at how close to death they'd both come on the marsh.

And how close she'd come again this night.

But Tess prayed the Fox would ask no promises of her. If he pressed her for an oath, how could she lie?

She did not know. Maybe until the moment came she would never know. . . .

The Fox smothered a curse. "Get the lad back here, where he

belongs, damn it. Have him take some of the burden from your shoulders—"

"Oh, Jack, don't let's argue over this again. We've been through it all before. Ashley is where he belongs, in the world he was raised for. And there's no reason he shouldn't take his place in that world, even though Father's death left us without two shillings to rub together."

"No reason, you say, Tess Leighton? Aye, no reason except that you've not money enough to keep him in those fine clothes and pay his debts, except by joining the gentlemen. He'll turn out just like his father before him, if you ask me."

"Which I did not," Tess snapped, her lips clenched in anger. "Please, Jack," she pleaded then, "let's not waste time arguing. Not tonight—not when you're just about to leave." Her eyes glittered, green slipping into gray, dark with fear she was desperately fighting to conceal. "I'm always so worried you won't . . ."

The smuggler smiled roguishly. "Come back? Enough of this gloomy talk, lass. You wound me with your lack of faith, so you do! 'Twill take a great deal more than Amos Hawkins and his loutish men to stop the Fox, lass. I'm half marsh ghost, didn't you know?" he added with his usual fine bravado.

"Oh, Jack, don't tease me." Tess's fingers tightened on his arm.

With a suspicious sound somewhere between a sniff and a gruff little snort, the handsome silver-haired man reached down to pat her arm. "You'll see me again, I promise you that. Until then I'll always be keeping an eye open for you. And if I hear you've taken to the marsh again," he added sternly, "then, by God, I'll soon make you wish Hawkins *had* dispatched me to Hades!"

The lantern flickered suddenly and nearly went out.

Their eyes met, tense with the knowledge that the time for parting had come.

"It must be nearly dawn," the Fox said quietly. "Time for me to be off. I don't half fancy meeting anyone on the road tonight—not with this wound yet unhealed."

"Where will you go?" Tess breathed, even though she broke their rule in asking.

The smuggler's dark eyes turned chiding. "You know better

than to ask such things, lass. 'Tis better you don't know. That way—" He stood quickly, gathering his things. "Now I must be away," he said sharply, his voice muffled as he bent to his boots and saddlebags.

So few things, Tess thought despairingly. So few hours to remember him by, this kind, gentle man who had been more of a father to her than ever her own sire had been.

And now came the agony of waiting, never knowing when—or if—he would return.

"Don't come up." Jack's voice was taut with emotions of his own, and an appeal for her to oblige him, this once.

Tess's fingers clenched in her lap, the nails cutting deep into her tender skin until she felt blood pool up on her palms. "All—all right."

His steps echoed up the narrow tunnel, their crunching gradually growing fainter. In the distance Tess heard a whinny, followed by the rustle of scattered pebbles.

"Godspeed," she whispered to the darkness.

Then the realization hit her. *He was going. Maybe forever.* How could she let him go without seeing his face one last time?

"Jack!" she cried, scrambling up the passage after him.

He was already mounted and turning north toward the Downs. His expression was shrouded as he reined in his horse, which reared and pawed wildly at the air. With a muffled curse he bent and caught her in a last, quick embrace.

Then he was gone, the wild drum of hooves drifting back to Tess on the wind, along with Jack's final warning.

"Remember what I said, lass," he called. "And remember, too, that the Fox will be back. Aye, when you least expect him!"

Before Tess could answer, he was gone, swallowed up by the clinging fog and the sullen darkness beyond.

Tendrils of mist swirled around Ravenhurst's legs like a blanket of ghostly snow as he slipped up the hill toward the priory, drawn by the sound of muffled voices.

Once again they came, quick and tense, this time followed by the neighing of a horse.

Quickly he covered the last feet to the ruined terrace and there he stood, frozen with fury when he picked out the two dim figures at the base of the stairs.

He did not move nor even breathe, feeling his blood pound white-hot through his veins. His throat constricted and he knew the bitter taste of ashes in his mouth, unable to speak, even when the dark-garbed man on horseback fled through the fog downhill toward the coast.

Ravenhurst's paralysis only fueled his fury.

So this was where she met him, the treacherous bitch! The Admiralty had been right about that, along with everything else. The woman was most certainly in league with the smugglers, but like a fool he couldn't bring himself to believe it. Always there had been some trace of doubt in his mind, some hope that she wasn't involved, that she couldn't have known what was going on at Fairleigh in her absences.

And all the time that she feigned outraged innocence with him, she was warming the bloody Fox's bed!

But no longer, by God.

Silently Ravenhurst slipped back behind the wall, watching Tess turn and disappear around the corner of the priory. Then, his face a granite mask of rage, he dropped to the damp earth and prepared to wait.

16

Tess's fingers trembled as she pulled her thick woolen cloak closer about her shoulders. Halfway down the tunnel she stopped to brush away the tears blurring her vision, cursing herself for her weakness.

For weakness, she knew, was a luxury she could ill afford.

After all, this was no different from the other times Jack had left. He would be back, she told herself sternly. Hadn't he always come back before?

After a final swipe at her cheeks, she moved to the bottom of the passage and turned to survey the quiet stone room. He'd left nothing behind, no sign of his presence. Even the faint, elusive warmth was now gone from the empty room.

Cold, so cold, this place. And something else—something Tess could almost call *evil*. . . .

Shivering, she picked up the lantern and sped back up the passage, all the time feeling the darkness cold and probing at her back, like a silent, relentless enemy. Waiting for the moment her guard dropped.

Then she was outside, the night air clean and cold in her face. Low-lying fog swirled about her feet as she turned to tug on the cord that would reseal the passage. Had the door been solid, she could never have moved it, not even with the help of its ingenious pulley system. But clever hands had trimmed the stones centuries ago, making a thin facade that perfectly matched the surrounding wall.

With a tiny hiss, the passage closed, protected once more from inquisitive eyes. In the very next instant Tess heard a faint rustling in the fog at the far end of the terrace. Her heart pounding, she spun about and then froze, straining to penetrate the unnatural, suffocating silence.

It was that coldest hour before dawn, when all the world lay silent, even the birds deathly still. Tess blew out the flame in her lantern, unwilling to call extra attention to her presence now that the Fox was abroad and vulnerable.

She waited, white-faced. The noise was not repeated.

Drawn by some instinct she could not explain, she began to climb the sloping meadow toward the dim half circle of her mother's white garden. The scent of lilies drifted on the pure chill air, mingled with the clean tang of pine needles and sea salt. Frowning, Tess struggled to recapture the peace she had always known here at her mother's side.

But tonight, peace eluded her. The only emotion she felt was an oppressive sort of loneliness.

Behind her the fog swirled, reaching out with bony fingers.

"The very picture of innocence," a voice growled at her back.

She gasped and whirled about, her blood hammering in her ears.

Ravenhurst stood before her, a black phantom against the black night, his long legs draped in tendrils of mist. His expression was harsh and shuttered, the silver wings at his brow the only brightness in the dark mask of his face.

What had he seen? How much did he know?

Tess's chest rose and fell erratically as she fought for composure. Let him speak first, she thought dimly. Let him be the first to betray the extent of his knowledge.

Slowly his cool fingers brushed her cheek. "Yes, the very image of innocence." The strong fingers tensed fractionally. "Tears?"

" 'Tis only a bit of mist. Your imagination, as usual, deceives you."

"How flawlessly you lie, even now," Ravenhurst said, almost to himself. For long seconds he studied her face. "So, my dear, we come full circle," he said at last. "Back to this white garden of yours. Back five years in time. But perhaps that is not so very long after all, not when one has thought of little else during all that time. For I mean to close the circle, you see. Tonight. Settling this thing between us once and for all."

"There's nothing to be settled! Why can't you just let it go, as I have done?"

Ravenhurst's calloused fingers dropped lower, biting into her forearms. "I only wish I could," he growled, pulling her up the slope toward the silver blur of flowers.

"Wh-what are you doing?" Tess gasped, struggling to hide her panic. *Dear God, could he have seen Jack? And what of the tunnel?*

"Doing?" her hard-faced captor repeated coldly. "I'm ensuring that I have the truth from you. For once. Starting with that bastard's name."

"Wh-whose?"

Darkness pressed around them, heavy and silent. The only sound to be heard was the crushing of leaves beneath their feet. "The man who just came out of that cleverly concealed passage, by God. *Who is he?*" Ravenhurst's hands shifted, digging cruelly into Tess's wrists.

"None of your c-cursed business! L-let go of me, you contemptible b-bastard!" Tess strained furiously against him, twisting and kicking even though she saw her struggles had no effect.

Ravenhurst's mouth twisted into a thin smile. "I mean to do many things tonight, my dear, but letting you go is not one of them. Quite to the contrary." He laughed once, the sound raw and ugly.

"You've no right to come here spying! This is Fairleigh land— *my land!* Now, take your bloody carcass off before I—"

"Before you do what, my dear? There are only two of us here now. And this time our score will be settled, I promise you. As for my right, have you forgotten I'm the commissioner of the Royal Military Canal? Fairleigh lands march along that canal and lately have provoked my suspicions. Suspicions all too justified, judging by the charming scene I've just witnessed." With a smothered curse, Ravenhurst hauled Tess hard against his chest, burying his fingers in her hair and jerking her head back. His eyes were no more than blue shadows as he stared down into her pale face. "Give me his name, damn it!"

"V-very well," Tess gasped, thinking frantically. "He's one of the Fox's men. He-he brings me b-brandy and silks sometimes." Her teeth began to chatter. " 'Tis a b-business arrangement we have."

"*A business arrangement?*" The words, on Dane's lips, became an obscenity. "Is that what you call it? Is that all it takes to bed you, a few bottles of brandy and a length or two of silk? By God, you rate your services far too cheap, Tess Leighton. I know men in London who'd pay a king's ransom in gold to plow your silken thighs for one night." His fingers twisted deep in her hair. "In fact, you could almost name your price," he added harshly, fingering a heavy, scented strand. "Yes, for this hair, this warm, glowing skin, a man might well forget every scruple. But he would have to believe he was the first."

Her captor's fingers tightened suddenly, twisting so hard that they wrung a sob from Tess's dry lips. Suddenly Ravenhurst turned, forcing her back against the trunk of an ancient overhanging oak. His face was dark with fury as he seized her wrists and pinned them against the rough bark. "And you would know exactly how to convince him, wouldn't you? But he wouldn't be your first, would he, my *sweet* Tess? Chevington was the first. And how many others were there after him, damn you?"

His anger hit Tess like a knife. She twisted wildly, struggling to find any point of weakness so she could break free.

But the grim-faced man before her had no weakness.

"No more of your tricks, damn you. I've scars enough already." With his knee he forced her thighs apart, trapping her against the broad trunk. "Now, give me the devil's name!"

"Never!" Tess spit back, all the time fighting him. "You'll get nothing from me!"

But his wrists were like iron and his body was fed with a black fury that tripled his strength. "Oh, I'll get the name from you, Tess. Along with everything else I want this night." His hard thighs moved ruthlessly against her, crushing her against the tree as he whispered his dark promise.

"I—I don't know his real name. And as to his destination, he never tells me that. 'Tis safer that way."

"Liar." His body ground against her, a cold, angry weight. "Because he's not one of the Fox's men at all—he's the bloody Fox, himself! Oh yes, Jezebel, I watched the two of you part. You warm the Fox's bed, damn you. Tell me, does he kiss you like this, your midnight lover?"

Even as he spoke, Ravenhurst's mouth crushed down upon hers, grinding cruelly against her clenched teeth until Tess had to bite back a moan. Immediately his lips opened, surrounding her with driving, relentless heat.

He took her impersonally, molding her with the ruthless skill of an expert, teaching her how useless it was to fight him, and just how easily he could make her body betray her.

She felt every inch of him, felt his hot straining thighs, felt the puckered scars at his wrist, just as she felt the sharp bark biting into her back.

His mouth burned hot and cold against her, in ecstasy and torment, strange yet achingly familiar.

Like a spark of living flame, desire leapt from his mouth to hers, then flashed wildly along her trembling limbs.

A little sob escaped her lips.

"That's more like it, my love," Ravenhurst said harshly. "I like to hear you moan. Moan for me again, Tess. Just the way you did in the alley."

"L-let go, you—"

"You thought you'd fooled me, didn't you? And you bloody near succeeded. But when I saw you in the kitchen with flour over your face, everything fell into place. Yes, you were shocked to see me again, but you wanted me that night, didn't you? In spite of all your efforts to deny it—to me as well as to yourself. And now you're damned well going to have me!"

"N-oooo! I want only to be free of you. Forever!" With every movement Tess made, his scars ground into the tender skin at her

wrists, cruel and abrading. Sobbing wildly, she lashed out with her feet again and again, until finally one of those blows struck home.

Ravenhurst groaned hoarsely.

Suddenly she was free.

Gasping, she spun about and flung herself toward the little coppice at the top of the hill. There was a trail through the hedge. If only she could make the top. . . .

"Bitch!" Ravenhurst cried furiously, stumbling after her, one hand clutched to his throbbing knee.

Ten more feet! Tess told herself.

She could hear him behind her, his footsteps angry and unsteady. She fairly flew over the meadow, barely touching the wet grass, the ghostly fog swirling up in frothy waves around her.

Then the dim half-circle of the white garden was before her, faintly silver, just below the dark, wooded crest of the hill.

The scent of lilies drifted on the cold air. She could just make out the faint petals of the wild roses growing along the low garden wall.

Almost there; don't slow down!

The wind dragged icy fingers through her hair, which streamed out wildly behind her as she fled toward the coppice.

Then she felt the bite of solid fingers, harder hands. She screamed as they caught the trailing hem of her cloak, jerking her back and holding her immobile. She gagged, feeling the garment's cords bite into her throat. Desperately she yanked on the strings, fighting to untie the knot that held her captive.

Her fingers grew clumsy; she began to sway, dizzy from lack of air.

All the time he stalked closer, his hands gripping the hem of her cloak and dragging her toward him.

"The time for running is over, Tess. Tonight this circle closes. It will be finished between us, once and for all."

With a muffled hiss the knot gave way and the cloak fell from her shoulders. Wildly Tess plunged upward toward the dark woods, her face a stark splash of white against the night.

But she was not fast enough. And this time her ruthless pursuer did not trust to her garments. Instead he claimed her hair in a cruel grip.

Sobbing, she flailed at his unseen fingers, but met only mocking emptiness. Then his hand dropped to her narrow waist, yanking her around to face him.

"Did you fight Chevington this way?" Ravenhurst growled, his face a dark, angry blur. "Was that how it began that night in the gate house —when you were supposed to be meeting me here? Did you goad *him* like this too?"

At first Tess did not hear, too busy kicking, twisting, lashing out with her feet.

"When did you drop your pretense of resistance? When he promised marriage? Or was it gold guineas you were after?" His hands twisted savagely. "Tell me, damn you! What is a whore's price?"

"Stop!" Tess cried, refusing to listen to his cruel words. Refusing to see the brutal images that swept up from deep in her memory.

Ravenhurst's fingers tightened at her waist. "What did it take to win your surrender, little seductress?"

"It—it wasn't like that!"

A bitter laugh exploded from her captor's lips. "I only wish I were wrong. But I'll have no more lies, by God. For I saw you myself that night, Tess. With my own eyes I watched you strain and claw at him in your nakedness. Yes, you were wanton and every inch willing for Chevington to bed you that night. And I damn your black heart for it!"

Ravenhurst stiffened for a moment, uttering a crude and graphic curse beneath his breath.

For Tess it was as if she had finally come to the end of her running. The nightmares had caught her at last, reaching out with icy fingers to claw at her eyes and neck.

More images, dark with horror.

Then the raw, searing pain.

Dear God, she'd lied when she had said Ravenhurst was wrong about what had happened that long ago night. It was not in her power to say if he was wrong or right.

Because Tess didn't know herself what had happened that night.

"Yes, all in all, it was a fine performance. I must congratulate you," Ravenhurst continued ruthlessly. "I have only myself to blame for being too much of a fool to take what you so freely offered to Chevington. But I was a *gentleman,* you see. A man of honor. I would have you only with marriage." His fingers were like talons against her skin. "How you must have laughed at my nicety."

"You—you twist everything!" Tess rasped, trying to think of a way to explain.

Knowing all the while it was impossible. Especially now, when Ravenhurst seemed beyond listening to anything.

"For five long years I've gone to sleep with the sound of your laughter and the mocking memory of your silken skin. And every dawn has found me shaking the same feverish images from my mind. But no more. For tonight I'll know the real thing, by God, and I'll burn away your memory forever."

Tess choked back a moan, drowning in memories of her own, which swept out of the fog like a chilling wind.

First came the image of Dane's rough tenderness all through those last weeks they had spent together. In spite of that, her terror at his leaving had grown until she pleaded to know him as a woman knows a man—just once, before he left for Trafalgar.

His refusal had been harsh and absolute.

Then, finally, had come that terrible night in the gate house. Tess closed her eyes, shuddering. Remembering . . .

Her skin aflame. The scorch of hot breath and clawing fingers. Worst of all her own body, hungry and gnawing like some terrible, frenzied animal.

All of this whirled through her mind in an instant, perceived only in fragments, like glowing embers of sensation. Feeling it all again, Tess shivered, closing her eyes to the dim images she could not bear to face.

Dear God, what had actually happened that night? And why couldn't she remember?

Because you're too weak to face the truth, a dark voice whispered.

"Very affecting, my dear, but it won't work. Not this time. We've gone too far for reprieves." Grim-faced, Ravenhurst buried his fingers deep in her russet hair.

It was the bitter cynicism of his voice that finally jerked Tess back to the present. "Let me go, damn you! It's over, can't you see that?"

But Ravenhurst did not release her. "Over?" he repeated bitterly. *"Over?* By God, I only wish it were, woman! Do you know what they yet call me in London? Ravenhurst, the Devil of Trafalgar. Nelson was the day's Angel, you see, and I its Devil. Yes, I truly had the devil's own luck that day. Nothing seemed to harm me as I watched in the smoke while my men were torn to pieces before me. Even when I caught a shell hissing on the deck and threw it back into the water, I stood unscathed. Which is why I'm called a hero now. But the truth is, it's been my curse to live while my men died around me." Ravenhurst's fingers tightened in Tess's hair. He forced her head back so she would meet his gaze head on. "My curse to live, Tess, knowing all the while it was not courage that drove me that day at Trafalgar but complete and total indifference to my own fate." His eyes smoldering, the viscount scowled down at her white face. "You see, it's easy to be brave when one cares for nothing or no one. Especially for oneself. And I have *you* to thank for that."

Tess did not move, could not move, hypnotized by the torment in those lapis eyes, horrified by his ruthless revelation. She shivered, her heart constricting with pain and regret. But then her chin rose; almost immediately she began to struggle against this weakening.

For this man was her enemy, and she must never forget that.

Tess's lips clenched, her face taut with anger. "You would speak of bravery, you arrogant slime? Then look around you, for it's war we wage right here in Kent and Sussex! 'Tis a war of disease and poverty, of grinding, relentless hunger. You can see its toll in the children's pinched faces, in the eyes of women old long before their time." Her eyes flashed, alive with green sparks. "It's a war fought every second of every day, and it's impossible to win. But we fight it here the only way we can, and if smuggling is the answer for some, then I say more's the bloody power to them! And God help us if this coast loses in the fight, for it will spell the end of England long before any triumph of Napoleon does!"

A muscle flashed at the tense line of Ravenhurst's jaw. *She was good,* he thought. *Damnably good.*

Then the image of a young midshipman's battered body flashed before his eyes.

Abruptly his strong fingers tightened, twisting deep in Tess's burgundy mane. "By God, you really believe that, don't you?" Turning, he began dragging her back toward the white flowers. "That twisted notion of being right must make everything you do here so much easier."

Tess struggled, gasping, until every movement sent pain searing through her scalp.

"Give it up!" Ravenhurst ordered harshly. " 'Tis not my goal to school you by pain—not unless you force me to it, at least."

"You want it this way, don't you? Because it makes you feel more like a man. A hero, you call yourself? Oh, God, why did you ever come back?"

"Why, Tess?" her captor asked grimly. "I never meant to, you know. Not after the things I saw in the gate house. I was afraid if ever I saw you again I might—" Abruptly his voice fell away to a curse. "No, something more important brought me back. Not even the smuggling or the spying could have done it. But the gold shipments were something else. Gold buys food and weapons for Napoleon's war-weary troops, and I've seen the effects of those weapons at very close range. And, my dear, every guinea of that gold is carried across to France in the same vessels that bring you brandy and silks."

"What new and foul lie is this?"

"Not a lie. Even now, a clandestine cargo is moving south and should reach the coast by tomorrow. Is that where your lover went? To ensure its safe arrival?"

"There are *no* such shipments. No gold goes out from these coasts!" It had to be so, Tess told herself. If the Fox had planned such cargoes, she would certainly have heard of it.

Wouldn't she?

"I expected that answer from you. At first, anyway. But before long I'll have the truth from you—down to every last wretched detail. For the day you took up with your bloody Fox was the day you sealed your fate, Tess."

"What do you care about him?" she demanded bitterly. "What harm has the Fox ever done you?"

"Ask that of the hundred seamen I saw fall in one hour at Trafalgar. Ask it of the innocent man—little more than a boy, really—who washed up in Fairleigh Cove with his throat cut. With *your* name on his lips. Maybe you can explain that."

"In Fairleigh Cove? I know nothing of such a person. But I do know one thing. The Fox would never hurt a boy. Nor betray his country!" Her voice rose, wild and brittle. " 'Tis you who lie and force your twisted tales upon me as truth. Do you think I'm one of your poor press-ganged crew, to be frightened and flogged until I cower? I'll grovel before no man, I warn you!"

Ravenhurst's wrists tightened, catapulting her full against him, crushing her heaving breasts against his chest. His smile then was no more than a faint white slash against the darkness of his face. "But you've seen so *few* of my methods, my dear. And I am a man of infinite flexibility. I shall discover soon enough which techniques work best with you."

Stony-faced, Ravenhurst pulled her down onto the low stone wall bordering the garden. Still fighting, Tess stumbled onto his lap.

"Perhaps this one first?" he growled, his voice rough and smoky. One hand captured her wrists while the other traced the defiant point of her chin, then fell lower to graze her proud, thrusting breasts. Unlike his voice, his touch was light, flicking, and electric.

Each swift spark of contact made Tess gasp as if she were struck by lightning. "You are—mad!"

"Oh, I'm quite sane, my dear. Perhaps for the first time in years. And I know all about the games you and Ashley played, as well."

"Which—games?" Tess whispered, playing for time, willing her ragged breath to still. Anything to distract her savage captor so his fingers would cease their torment. Her voice rose, cool and precise. "We had so very many, after all."

Tess felt as much as saw him stiffen.

"By God, you are thoroughly your father's daughter, aren't you? I refer to your game of seeing how fast your conquests could be made. A game meant to include Chevington and myself that night. Only you and Ashley miscalculated and I arrived earlier than expected." Ravenhurst's face hardened as he watched her eyes fly open in shock and denial. "Don't bother denying it. I had the story from your own father's lips!"

"My—father—told you this?" Tess asked numbly, beginning finally to understand.

About herself. About the hard-faced man beside her, as cold and relentless as the devil himself.

"He told me, all right. Everything about his two *charming* children. And what he neglected to say, I soon saw with my own eyes. Do you moan for your Fox as you moaned for Chevington?" Ravenhurst demanded savagely. "Do you rake him with your nails when he plunges inside you?"

"Why do you ask? Since you claim to know everything, you must know that, too, surely. And since you know the terrible truth, you can have no more reason to stay here and plague me with these pointless questions." Her voice, Tess was glad to hear, did not waver. If only she could still her ragged pulse so well . . .

"Only one reason, my dear. The Fox's name, along with the names of all his men."

"I'll tell you nothing, do you hear? Not now or ever, no matter what you do to me. So release me! Or by all the saints I'll claw your eyes out the first chance I get!"

Ravenhurst's laugh as he bent over her was cold and very cruel. "Do you really think you'll want to claw my eyes out? I'm willing to wager you feel quite differently. Yes, you'll be begging me to stay before I'm done with you." As if to underscore his promise, he pressed his lips to the tender skin behind her ear, nipping and then stroking with his tongue. A moment later his teeth caught her ear and performed the same searing torment upon its lobe.

The next instant his fingers circled one furled nipple and closed to explore its pouting tip.

Flames burst through Tess's body. She gasped, hating him and at the same time fearing his ruthless touch. But already somewhere deep in the back of her mind she was praying he would not stop.

Heaven help her, it must never be! Choking down a sob, Tess tossed her head from side to side in a vain effort to dislodge his tormenting lips.

"Yes," Dane whispered hoarsely against her neck. "I feel the wild heat of your pulse. Already your straining body tells me everything your lying lips seek to deny. You want me, Tess. And you'll want me a great deal more before I'm finished with you!"

Tess shuddered, awash in a firestorm of sensation, racked by anger, fear, and a strange desperation.

What had he done to her? Why was her resolve melting?

How could I ever have loved him? she asked herself, over and over. *This man is my enemy, and I must fight him. He is a cold-blooded stranger.*

Dane's lips drank in her every desperate movement. His teeth nipped commandingly; his tongue bathed her in dark fire.

Around them the fog rose and fell in silent, ghostly waves.

Before I'm done with you.

It was then that Ravenhurst's bitter promise penetrated the chaos of Tess's thoughts. Sweet heaven, what did he mean?

As if in answer, his long fingers anchored her twisting wrists. "Fight me, little hellcat," he urged hoarsely. "Battle me with tooth and claw. I would have it no other way, for your fury only fuels my desire. But know that before the sun rises you'll be purring beneath me, begging for more. And offering me anything I choose to take. Every secret of your silken body." Like molten flame his tongue dipped into the sensitive recesses of her ear, proving the truth of his words. "Every name of your traitorous brethren."

"N-never!"

"Open for me," he murmured hoarsely, turning to sweep the

soft swell of her lips with his tongue. "Let me taste you now. Give me your dark honey."

A moan that was part sob escaped from deep in Tess's throat, and Ravenhurst found his entrance at that moment, shocking her with the relentless sweep of his velvet tongue.

"By God, you're sweet," he whispered against her opened mouth. "More," he demanded.

"Don't d-do this, Dane!" Dimly Tess realized her hands were on his tensed shoulders, digging, kneading.

Whether to drag him closer or force him away, she refused to think.

"The more you give, the more I'll take. Your mouth is like brandy, a fever in my blood. And before the night is out, you'll know that fever too, I promise you."

"Dane—" Her voice was raw, pleading.

"Dear God, how I've waited to hear you moan like this, to hear my name tremble on your lips." He growled, long and low, sealing off further protests with his lips. Sleek and hot, his tongue played over hers until Tess began to understand that she might never be free of this man.

No matter how she struggled with him. Even more fiercely with herself.

But she was losing, and they both knew it.

With ruthless precision Ravenhurst shifted, pursuing his advantage. A moment later his teeth found the hard furled bud beneath her cambric gown.

Madness! Tess screamed silently, mind and body aflame. At the same moment she prayed this sweet fire would never end.

Madness! Dane thought, remembering another woman, another night of pure enchantment. A night he had never been able to forget.

His breath caught as the woman beside him moaned in pleasure. And suddenly the fabric between them was an intolerable barrier.

With a dark groan he gripped the neck of her gown and in one fierce blow tore the thin cambric away, exposing her silver body to his hungry gaze. "Sweet Jesus, you're beautiful," he muttered hoarsely, his face set in harsh lines. "More beautiful even than I remembered. Purr for me, brandy cat," he whispered against her taut skin a moment before he drew her nipple into his mouth.

"Never," Tess moaned, but even as she spoke she felt her quivering nerves explode under the dark flame of his touch. "Stop!" she gasped, crying out at this new assault. But he did not stop, and she knew she would have to plead for her release.

And it must be soon, before she had no words left.

"Please, Dane, I beg you—this is wrong. All w-wrong!"

But the man with the midnight eyes did not hear. Inch by inch he staked his claim. Nerve by flaring nerve he bent her to his will, until only the shredded remnants of Tess's pride kept her from moaning in wild pleasure.

Before I'm done with you.

Once more his angry threat came back to haunt her.

She was no more than another military objective to this hardened officer, Tess realized dimly. No more than the conquest of a hostile terrain. No, she must never falter, nor surrender an inch.

If she showed any sign of weakness he would be quick to use it against her.

"You're mad!" she cried, writhing against his hungry mouth.

"Quite likely. But I'll have this—and much, much more." Suddenly Ravenhurst froze, his breathing harsh and strained in the silence around them.

What was he doing? Was she once again to play him for a fool?

With narrowed eyes he studied her, willing his heated, hungry body to order, banking the fire in his veins with the sullen ice of contempt.

For what both of them had become in the long years since that enchanted night they met.

Yes, tonight he would teach her that two could play the game of desire and deceit. That two could use their bodies for a darker purpose. It was a lesson she had learned long ago, it appeared, from her gamester father.

"Yes, a king's ransom and more, a man would give," Dane whispered, his fingers dropping where his eyes had feasted, teasing the cool satin of her skin while he struggled to calm his feverish thoughts. "Until he'd throw everything away just to have you one more time."

His harsh words swirled in Tess's fevered brain, sound without meaning. He was so much like the man she'd adored, his face with the same outline, his body so fierce and familiar.

How could she find the strength to resist what she had once loved so well?

What could have happened to make him this way? she wondered, before bitter reason returned. Perdition, why did she even care, when all that mattered was that she escape?

Now, before her traitorous body could betray her further!

Fight him, Tess told herself wildly, clawing her way up out of the molten sea of pleasure he'd forged around them. This cold predator had nothing in common with the gallant lieutenant who had wooed her and won her five years before.

That man, Tess realized suddenly, was dead. As dead as the love she'd once felt for him.

Now this torment of the senses was all that was left, this sullen storm, this brutal mockery of love.

"Let me go, you black-hearted bastard! Just because *you're* dead doesn't mean—"

"Dead?" Ravenhurst's laugh was sharp with bitterness, at himself as much as at her. Had Tess not been so frantic, she might have heard the raw pain at its depths. "I think I have been, in truth, until this very moment. Until I came to see you for what you really are." His hand found her buttock and forced her against his taut thighs, against his angry, throbbing man's heat. "Now I'm as far from dead as a man can be, I assure you."

"You are the devil himself. You fly out of the night like a bat from hell!" she raged, her hands yanking in vain against his iron grip.

Suddenly she felt him shift, felt him turn and press her down along the top of the wall until his straining muscles ground against her and the ridge of stones bit into her back.

"I'll make you rue this night, damn your soul!" Arching wildly, she fought to dislodge his heavy, tensed body. But the movement only served to draw her skirts up her calves.

Suddenly an iron thigh scissored between her kicking legs. "Keep rubbing against me like a she-cat and I'll not take the time I meant with you," Ravenhurst said hoarsely. "I'll take you hard and fast, by God. Right here on this wall!"

With a ragged gasp, Tess strained away from the hard blade of muscle which scorched her thigh, fighting the mad fury of his lust.

Dead, she told herself wildly. The man she had loved—the only man she could ever love. *Gone forever.* This brute was no more than a twisted wreck, a grim shadow of that other person, after all his joy and honor had been stripped away.

"Devil!" she screamed wildly, twisting closer to his iron hands. With a sob she brought her head down and sank her teeth into his wrist.

Ravenhurst's oath was short and exceedingly crude. In the same instant he jerked her hands over her head, pinioning her completely beneath his taut, angry body so that her straining only brought more torture.

For them both, although Tess could not see that.

"What—what evil thing are you planning?"

His eyes mocked her, darker than midnight, dark as Hell itself. Eyes which had seen every dream shattered, every hope destroyed.

And that was exactly what Dane meant to do to her now.

"Pleasure, my dear. A sort I'll warrant your swaggering smuggler never took the time to show you. A pleasure so keen you'll be happy to give me the answers to a few questions."

Chilled by his grim threat, Tess made one last wild attempt at freedom. Desperation made her strong, and she caught Ravenhurst unaware, wresting one hand loose and driving savagely at the point on his right wrist where the crisscrossed trail of scars was thickest.

Her stiffened fingers found their mark; she felt him flinch, then jerk back in pain.

Wildly she wrenched against his other hand, but even thus, he was more than her equal. The night trembled around them, tense and suffocating, every noise stilled except for their choked breathing, the furious hiss and rustle of their struggle.

Then Tess felt herself spin away through space, free for one delirious moment before she landed sprawling in the damp soil of the garden below, one arm on a large stone broken from the wall.

As she had known it would.

When Ravenhurst came over the wall an instant later, Tess was ready.

With a ragged sob she hurled the limestone slab toward his head, making a ghostly slash upon the darkness, felling him instantly.

17

Stumbling, blind with fury, Tess made her way back to the Angel. Hobhouse met her at the inn's steps, his eyes keen and probing.

"What—"

Tess raised a pale, trembling hand. "Not now, Hobhouse, please. P-perhaps later." White-faced, she moved past him and crossed the spotless lobby.

At the staircase she turned, her fingers tense on the polished banister. "You will please fetch me the moment Lord Ravenhurst returns," she ordered grimly.

Groaning, Lord Ravenhurst stirred slightly, feeling fragments of pain shoot through his left temple. He shifted to one side, then opened his eyes to dense, blanketing whiteness. His cheek, he discovered, was pressed against the cold earth, and someone was pounding a drum—a very large drum—inside his head.

"What in the . . ."

He sat up, breaking through the low-lying mist into a gray, chill predawn world. Immediately he brought his hand to his temple, raw and throbbing where the heavy stone had caught him.

Cursing, he traced the ragged wound, thick with blood.

The memory of Tess's betrayal flooded over him, and he cursed again, more graphically this time. Once more the Jezebel had eluded him!

He winced, brushing a thick line of blood from his eye.

She would pay dearly for this night's work, Ravenhurst vowed, stumbling to his feet. The thought of precisely *how* he would make her pay sustained him all the way through the long march back to town.

Two hours later, dusty and grim-faced, Ravenhurst reached the Angel. Hobhouse stood on the steps, a stern sentinel.

No greeting was offered by either man. Sharp-eyed and silent, they studied one another.

Tess waited inside, halfway up the staircase. Wadded beneath her arm was a heavy bundle of clothes.

"There is no need to escort Lord Ravenhurst to his room, Hobhouse," she said coldly. "There is no need, in fact, to perform the slightest service for this man."

Her fingers tightened and she cast a pair of boots down onto the floor. They struck the polished marble with the explosive report of pistols.

"You see, Hobhouse—"

A pile of books hit Ravenhurst in the chest.

"—the viscount—"

A tangled mass of shirts struck his harsh face.

"—is just—"

A leather satchel landed somewhere near his knees.

"—*leaving!*"

One by one, Dane's possessions hit the floor while he stood watching, stiff-legged and furious. Peale looked on anxiously, several feet above Tess on the stairs. "I tried to stop her, your—"

"Now!" Tess ordered.

"By God, I'll—" Dane's threat was never completed.

Grim-faced, Hobhouse moved to block the viscount's progress. "I'll be more than happy to show the gentle—*nobleman*—out, miss." The majordomo's eyes narrowed. "I wouldn't care for any trouble, your lordship. But I'm not saying I wouldn't relish going a round or two with you right now."

For long, taut minutes the four stood unmoving in the lobby.

Then Dane's eyes hardened, focused entirely upon Tess's white face. "Enjoy your triumph while you may. It will not last long, I warn you."

And then he was gone, an anxious-looking Peale following silently in his wake.

The day passed in a gray, suffocating blur. Tess gave directions to Édouard and Letty, oversaw the replacement of the Angel's linens, and considered the next week's menus. She checked the placement of the old brandy in the inn's wine cellar. She dutifully tallied her account books.

And all the time she was a thousand miles away.

Dreaming of a time when she had been young and innocent.

When the world had seemed fine and fresh, instead of the ashen hell it had now become.

"Come quick, miss. Something's happened to Thomas out at Fairleigh." His clothing all awry, Jem scuttled through the kitchen in search of Tess.

"Calm yourself, Jem. I'm right here." Tess emerged frowning from the stillroom, brushing her hands on her apron. "What has happened to Thomas?"

"It was that south wall up at the priory. Collapsed on him, it did. One of the village boys happened to be cutting through and saw him. The boy's out in the stable now. Shall I hitch up your curricle?"

Tess was already running up to her room to change. "No, saddle the roan. He'll be faster. Letty and Hobhouse can follow in the curricle."

When Tess flew downstairs five minutes later, she carried a bundle of clean linens, ointments, and a small bottle of laudanum. Hobhouse had already sent a note around to the surgeon, asking him to pay a call to Fairleigh. But since that overworked individual might likely be hours in the process, Tess knew she must do all she could for Thomas first.

There would be no sleep for her this day, she realized, fighting to focus on the road before her. She gave the roan his head then, and let him eat up the distance. Soon they rounded Gibbett's Corner and thundered past the old windmill.

Tess blinked, seeing something in the middle of the road ahead of her. It was a farm wagon, overturned on its side, the driver nowhere to be seen.

"Steady," Tess crooned to the roan, reining in and preparing to pick her way around the obstacle. She cast a quick glance into the ditch on the side of the road, thinking the owner might have been tossed out and now lay there wounded.

Without warning a hard hand gripped her ankle and wrenched her savagely from the horse.

A thick wedge of wool was thrust over her face and mouth. She kicked wildly, trying to scream.

"What—" Her foot struck bone, and she winced, then turned to deliver another sharp blow in the same direction.

Muffled oaths. Strong fingers biting into her elbow.

She stumbled free and blindly began to run.

The next thing Tess knew she was falling, only to strike rocky soil a moment later. Stars exploded before her eyes; a queer whine filled her ears.

Then darkness rushed over her, dank and suffocating.

Just like in her nightmares.

When Tess opened her eyes again, it was night.

Or at least it seemed to be night. She couldn't be certain, for her eyes and face were still muffled in the heavy wool.

She was sitting on a chair, that much she did know, for she could feel the frame and padding beneath her. But *where?*

Around her all was silence—suffocating and total. She frowned, straining to hear, and finally made out something that might have been water dripping, far in the distance.

Almost like the chill, damp void of Fairleigh's stone tunnels, Tess thought wildly. Dear God, she couldn't have been taken *there*, surely. Not down into the tunnels!

White-faced, she stumbled to her feet and began to inch across the stone floor, at the same time attacking the wool wedged against her face.

What if it were dark? What if she were trapped here forever, captive in the darkness? She began to shiver then, blackness pressing around her. There were *things* in the dark. Invisible, silent things. Deadly things.

Stop it! she told herself, tugging feverishly at the knotted cloth around her head. *Someone brought you here. Whoever it was will come back for you.* Stiffly she made her way forward until she felt the cold ridges of a stone wall beneath her fingers.

Then magically she heard the scuff of feet, followed by the metallic clang of a key in a lock.

The door creaked open and the steps hammered closer. Warm air wafted over her neck, shocking after the dampness and cold.

A moment later she felt the unseen figure move behind her. Without warning the heavy wool, damp from her breath, was stripped away from her face. She blinked, seeing before her a large stone cellar, bare except for the chair she had been sitting in and a rickety table lit by a flickering lantern.

During the few seconds it took for her eyes to became accustomed to the light, the person behind her still had not moved. Hawkins? Tess thought wildly.

Her shoulders stiffened in defiance. "This is kidnapping, you know," she said flatly, refusing to turn around. "The magistrate will hear of it."

"I believe not, my dear." Ravenhurst sauntered forward into the lantern light. His white shirt was open at the neck, hastily tucked into a form-fitting pair of buckskin breeches. Around his forehead was wound a thick white strip of linen. The bandage, Tess saw with satisfaction, was dotted with blood.

"Hobhouse will come looking for me, you know."

Ravenhurst's lip curled in a thin smile. "Hardly likely, my dear. Not when your staff believes you to be enjoying a cozy visit with Lord Lennox and his sister."

"You bloody, despicable . . ." Tess struck wildly at Ravenhurst's face, but he only shoved her hands away.

"I told you it was not over between us. But it soon will be."

"And Thomas?" Tess demanded, knowing the answer even before she asked.

"At this moment Thomas is finishing off a fine meal of roast mutton and mince tarts, unless I miss my guess. A remarkable recovery, is it not? And sharing his meal will be a helpful village boy with sixpence fresh in his pocket. The lad was only too happy to carry a message to Jem at the Angel. Of course, he had no idea what the note said."

Angry sparks shot from Tess's eyes. "You think you've taken care of everything, don't you? But I'll scream. I'll scream until someone hears me."

"You are welcome to try, of course. But these stone cellars are wondrously well built. Laid down in the Armada's time, I should imagine. Yes, they are entirely soundproof, which is why I chose this house."

"Where have you taken me, blackguard?"

"It is really of no consequence, my dear. All you need to know is that you are where no one can find you. Except myself, of course. For you are now entirely subject to my commands."

Tess backed against the cold stone wall, watching in disbelief as Ravenhurst's long fingers moved to his shirt. She stared blindly, unable to believe this was really happening. "You can't mean to . . ."

The button was freed, and then another, revealing a dense mat of black, springy hair. "Oh, I mean it, my dear Tess. I'll have the Fox's name tonight, and the plans of his runs. One way or another, I shall find out everything I need to know, you may be certain of that. But whether by the easy way or the hard way—that choice I leave up to you." Another button sprang free. His cold eyes fixed on Tess's face, Ravenhurst began to pull the shirt from his breeches, every movement cool and lazy and deliberate.

"I have no choice in any of this, and well you know it!" Tess spat, straining wildly at her bonds until her wrists and ankles were raw.

Ravenhurst's hard eyes never left her face. "Tell me what I want to know, Tess."

"Never!"

"Give me his name," her captor repeated inexorably. "Unless

you choose to know my wrath." Suddenly his arm shot out, forcing her face up to meet his gaze. "Do you understand what I'm saying, Tess? How it will be between us?"

"You are foul, contemptible! At least Hawkins is honest in his lust. But *you* try to mask it as duty!"

"It is so simple, really. A few words will suffice."

Tess countered with a look of cold fury. "Vermin! Arrogant slime!"

Ravenhurst's face darkened, but he said nothing. His strong hands left her chin and moved to his waist. Slowly he freed the last button of his shirt, then pulled the fine linen from his broad, muscled shoulders.

It was a dream, Tess told herself, staring at his naked chest. It could not be true.

But then Ravenhurst's hands dropped to the buttons at his breeches. "Having second thoughts yet, my dear?"

"How vile you are! Worse than Hawkins, I see now. For he, at least, makes no pretense of being other than what he is—a liar and a bully."

Tess saw his jaw tense at her words. Some faint spark of emotion came and went in his cold, clear eyes.

Yes, she thought wildly, perhaps this was the way!

"Did you treat your French prisoners so?" she taunted, desperate to distract him. "Did you force the women to serve your pleasure? Did you slit their throats when they would not?"

Ravenhurst's jaw hardened. "Cease this wild babbling. You know nothing of what you're saying."

"I know enough about you to guess, however."

"Be careful what you say, then, lest you feel the force of my violence now."

"I'm not afraid of you," Tess blazed. "You are but one more bellowing male in a very long list of bellowing males who have sought to control me. What could you possibly do that would frighten me?" Her small chin rose defiantly. "Well, my lord?"

"One name, Tess. One set of signals," he said harshly.

"Never!" she spat back.

Grim-faced, Ravenhurst stalked closer. "I'll have his name, Tess. One way or another."

Slowly Tess backed away until she felt the cold ridge of the wall at her shoulders.

Then he was upon her, sweeping her up and over his shoulder before she could loose a single oath. "Since you don't choose to talk, I see I must find some other activity to loosen your tongue," he growled, carrying her toward the door.

Tess's mouth flattened to a taut line. "I'll tell you what you want to know, then," she cried, kicking her feet but meeting only emptiness. "The Fox? He's the mayor, Mr. Tredwell. He—he has four assistants. Hobhouse, you know already. Jem is another, as is Amos Hawkins. Yes, Hawkins." She laughed once, raw and hoarse. "You don't believe me? Oh, yes, I know all of them. Indeed, I ride with them upon the marsh. And I've had them all, do you hear? Shared my bed with each one of them! Shall I tell you what sort of lovers they made?"

"Stop it, Tess!" Ravenhurst grated, his fingers digging into her hips.

"Stop? Why? I thought you were after secrets this night, my lord! Now where was I? Oh yes, next are the vicar and the baker. They share the watch on Mermaid Street."

"Stop it, damn you!"

"And then there's the captain of the dragoons," she continued wildly. "I mustn't forget *him,* for he is quite insatiable. And so very—inventive in the bedroom."

Ravenhurst lurched to a halt; his fingers gripped her thighs like steel traps. "Don't, Tess!" he growled.

"You mean you don't want to hear my secrets? Don't tell me you've turned fainthearted, my lord?" Tess twisted, turning glazed, bitter eyes on her captor's face.

And recoiled at the hatred she saw blazing there.

It makes no difference, she told herself. *He is no one and nothing to me now. He's dead to me, and I to him.*

She pressed her eyes closed, unable to bear the sight of his contempt any longer. Even when Ravenhurst caught her roughly and pulled her from his shoulder, she still did not open them.

"Tricks. Always tricks," he said hoarsely. "Very well, since I see you mean to play this game through to the end."

That is when Tess began to retreat, searching for the place she used to go. The quiet place she learned to find when she couldn't bear the sound of her parents' arguing and her mother's muffled sobs. The place she went when her father locked her in the cold, silent tunnels.

It had been two years now, she thought dimly. She only hoped she remembered how. . . .

"What are you doing?" Ravenhurst demanded, his fingers tense on her cool skin.

Already Tess felt his touch receding. Already the images around her began to waver and lose their clarity.

Only then did her eyes open, two smoky, green pools in the pale oval of her face. Huge and unfocused, they met his gaze—and looked far beyond.

To another time and place.

"Look at me, damn you!" Ravenhurst growled, gripping her chin and forcing her face upward. "No more of these tricks."

But Tess did not answer, indeed heard him only faintly. She certainly did not recognize the harsh note of fear that entered his voice.

For now the scent of roses and lilies filled her lungs. The sound of the wind rushed through her mind. The white garden was before her, cool and sheltering.

Almost there. Almost safe, where no one can find me. Safe . . .

"Tess!"

Even Ravenhurst's rough, tortured cry did not pierce her abstraction. For now she was running up the hillside, the grass thick with dew beneath her feet. Before her she could see dark-veined leaves and rose petals trembling in the wind.

She did not feel him flatten his palms against her cheeks. She did not hear his harsh, checked breath.

"Very well, if that's the game you wish to play, I'll give you some time to think it over. Maybe a night down here in the cold will loosen your lying tongue," he said harshly.

His boots hammered over stone. Somewhere in the distance Tess sensed a door clanging shut.

The door of hope, she thought dimly. But only for a moment.

Then she was sinking down to the damp earth, the wind playing through her unbound hair, sorrel and foxglove soft at her feet.

18

For long minutes Dane stood staring down at the woman in his arms, his fingers unmoving upon her cheek. Her eyes did not open, nor her expression change in any way.

Grim-faced, he thought of his midshipman's broken body, of the ragged wound that had drained the lifeblood from his young throat.

Black rage washed over him and for a moment he could not see. Then his fingers flew away from Tess's cold skin as if burned.

He could not stay here now, Ravenhurst realized dimly, not feeling as he did. He did not know what he might do to her if he stayed.

Scowling, he lowered her to the cold floor and pounded to the door, returning soon after with his greatcoat. Quickly he spread it over the damp stones, then laid Tess down upon it. His eyes were cold as night as he jerked the door's solid weight closed behind him. A moment later his key grated in the lock.

In his desperation to be away from her, he took the stairs three at a time, muttering black curses with each step.

Nor did he halt the stream of ragged oaths until he had reached his sparsely furnished study and drained two very large glasses of brandy.

In his rage Ravenhurst did not hear the strange, discordant

noises that welled up far below, from the darkness of the locked
cellar.

By then it was too late anyway.

Tess felt their hairy bodies first, then the prick of their tiny,
sharp jaws. They plunged down onto her in the darkness, tracing
restless paths over her unshielded skin.

Please! Someone . . .

Another probing shape hit her leg, and she wrenched her body
into a tight ball.

Anyone!

The darkness wrapped itself around her, dense and taut, envel-
oping her, stretching to shut out all sound. She had felt the insects
there too. In the tunnels where her father had locked her, when
the drunken rages were upon him.

Light a candle, she begged silently. *Please! Just this once.*

Their tiny fangs pierced her skin; their sharp legs clamored over
her bare arms. Through her hair, in her ears, upon her eyelids.

"No more!" The cry exploded from the darkness, ragged and
terrified. Her own cry, Tess realized dimly.

Her trembling fingers tore at the cold stones, desperate to avoid
the poisonous creatures skittering up out of the night. Something
dropped onto her thigh, and she ground at it frantically, digging
her nails into her skin, trying to sweep away the relentless attack-
ers.

Her fingers curved into talons as she flayed wildly—at herself,
at the stones beneath her feet, at the damp wall above her head.

The spiders were everywhere now, an angry, relentless swarm.

No—please!

And then she began to scream.

Ravenhurst meant to stay away longer, but an hour later he was
back at the cellar door, tense and determined. For a moment his
features darkened with something that might almost have been
regret. But the emotion soon vanished.

The woman beyond that door wasn't worth his regret,

Ravenhurst told himself. Anything that happened to her now, she'd brought on herself.

A blast of damp, chill air rushed into his face as he opened the cellar door and waited at the threshold, preparing for another trick, knowing he must never underestimate her. Around him the shadows danced in the light of his flickering candle. He frowned, wondering what had happened to the lantern he had left lit upon the table.

And where in bloody hell was *she?* Could she have somehow managed to escape?

Raising his candle, he searched the shadows, his frown turning to a scowl. He plunged inside, his feet hammering across the ancient stone floor.

Then he saw her, wedged tightly against the far corner of the room, her body curled into a protective ball. Her gown was rent with jagged tears at chest and hem, and one sleeve dangled by mere threads.

But it was the queer, soft humming that caught Ravenhurst up short. As he watched, she began to rock back and forth, her hands locked around her bent knees. Her eyes, he saw, were huge and haunted; as he strode closer they stared at him, unblinking, unknowing, passing right through him.

"Get up, Tess," he ordered grimly.

The rocking did not cease, nor her odd, wordless melody.

"Stop this playacting." Grim-faced, Ravenhurst knelt before her and looked deep into her eyes, surprised when they registered no change at his presence. Muttering a curse, he gripped her arms and tried to pull her to her feet.

Her body was an unresisting weight. His thumbs tightened on the fragile bones of her hands while he dragged her against him, wondering what new sort of trick this was.

A grimace crossed her face.

"Look at me, Tess," Dane ordered harshly.

The soft humming continued, unchanged. He could feel her breath, jerky and light against his neck. He stared down at her in anger and disbelief, his hands circling her slim wrists.

It was only then that Ravenhurst noticed her fingers. Raw and swollen, they oozed blood from a dozen angry sores. Every nail was broken, dark with dirt and dried blood.

Impossible! And yet . . .

"*Soleil,*" he whispered hoarsely, regret battering him like a fist. "My wild sweet sun. What have I done to you?"

At that old epithet, Tess blinked. Some spark of emotion flickered deep in her eyes, then disappeared. Silently she shrank back from him, her eyes blind with pain.

Then her hands began to quiver. She twisted, straining to brush something from her shoulder.

Something Dane could not see.

"No—no more," she stammered. "Dear God, make them g-go away." She raised her eyes, searching but seeing nothing of what was around her, lost in another world.

"Make *what* go away?"

Once again Tess's hand moved, this time gouging a deep hole in the fabric along her neck, her broken nails carving welts in her ivory skin.

"*What is it?*"

"S-spiders," Tess gasped. "Dear God—can't you *see* them?" Her trembling fingers attacked the empty air before her. "*Here!*"

"There are no spiders," Dane said harshly.

"All—over me," she gasped, struggling desperately in his arms. "L-let me go!"

A muscle flashed at the hard line of Ravenhurst's jaw as he looked down into Tess's white face. Her eyes widened, dark and terrified. Her ragged sleeve snared a button on his shirt and tore free, leaving the bodice of her dress gaping open.

With stiff, awkward fingers Ravenhurst pulled the cloth together over her naked skin, forcing his eyes away from that erotic swell of breast and rosy nipple. He cursed, feeling desire slam through him like a lightning bolt, smoking and sparking through every painful inch of his body.

At a time like this, how could he think of . . .

In his arms, Tess stiffened and began to shiver convulsively. Stifling a curse, Ravenhurst cupped her neck and tried to draw her closer to his heat. But she fought him wildly, her muscles rigid and straining, her eyes glazed and fixed.

On things only she could see.

"Don't fight me, Tess. I only want to help you." Swiftly Dane shrugged out of his jacket, then slipped it around her shivering shoulders. Beneath the torn fabric her skin was faintly blue tinged. She felt cold, far too cold, beneath his hot fingers. "Let me do that much for you at least," he whispered.

And then, without waiting for her struggles to resume, Ravenhurst swept his trembling captive up into his arms and carried her out of her dark prison.

She was still no warmer when he set her down upon his four-poster bed. Her eyelids flickered, blue-veined, and she twisted restlessly, mumbling incoherent words beneath her breath.

Her skin was like ice, he thought, pulling the covers over her, then adding another blanket. What in God's name had happened down there in the cellar? Even now she gave no sign of noticing anything he did, only stared at the candle on the bedside table. Her hands curved out, stretching to catch its flickering light.

Was this why her room at the Angel was always lit while she slept? Ravenhurst wondered, frowning.

If so, he could have devised no better form of torture than to lock her in his darkened cellar.

Looking at her pallid face, he realized it might be a great while before he had any answers. In the meantime, those wounds must be tended.

Dane's face was grim as he filled a basin with water and carried it to the table beside the bed. With unsteady hands he pried open her cold palm and then bathed her fingers, washing away the layers of dirt and ground-in blood. That done, he wrapped each finger in a length of gauze cut from the bandage at his own forehead.

Through it all Tess held herself tense, her body curved away from him, racked by shuddering.

When he was finished, Ravenhurst came slowly to his feet, balling his hands into fists as he stood looking down at her trembling body.

Five years ago he had heard stories in the village, stories about her drunken father and the odd life that Tess and her brother lived out at that great ruin of a house high above the sea. At that time he had discounted the wild tales, but now Ravenhurst found himself wondering.

A sharp rapping echoed through the nearly empty house from a door far below. Grimacing, Dane waited for whoever it was to go away. There was no one to answer the door but himself; intending no audience for his encounter with Tess, he had sent Peale away to relatives for two days.

Silence returned, only to be broken by more pounding, harder and more insistent this time. Very soon it became apparent that his visitor did not mean to leave.

Scowling, the viscount took a last look at the white-faced woman in his bed, then turned and strode down the stairs.

As he opened the door, a statuesque figure in a crimson cloak stepped into the circle of light cast by the lantern above the entrance steps. Crimson-tipped fingers circled Ravenhurst's wrist.

"So there you are, my lord," Lady Patricia Lennox purred, her eyes faintly chiding. "I'd nearly given up finding you. Then Hobhouse told me you had left the Angel and moved into your renovated town house here." A gust of wind caught her crimson cloak, twining its thick velvet around Dane's legs. At the same moment the blond woman gasped softly and stumbled forward against his chest, her hands curving around his forearms.

Her eyes glittered as she angled her head up to him. Her lips parted slightly.

Dane did not move.

His visitor blinked, and her eyes narrowed. "Strangely enough, Hobhouse seemed surprised to see me, for he believed the Leighton chit was dining with me tonight. I cannot imagine what gave the fellow such an idea." When Dane made no answer, she pulled back slightly and drew a beribboned bottle from the pocket of her cloak. "Pray allow me to present this small token to you. In memory of past pleasures. And all those yet to come." Smiling, she held out the heavy object.

"Very thoughtful of you." Dane bowed slightly and accepted

the gift, wondering why he had never noticed before how her eyes seemed slightly chill.

"Well, aren't you going to invite me in, so that we may sample a glass together?" Lady Patricia asked, her smile wide and inviting.

"I only wish I could," Ravenhurst said smoothly. "I've just received a message from London, however, and I fear I must not delay my response."

"Surely it will wait," his visitor said silkily, her lush lips settling into a pout. "For a little while at least."

"I'm afraid not, my lady. Tomorrow, perhaps?" he added, softening the blow.

Lady Patricia scowled. "I'm afraid I have other plans for tomorrow!" Suddenly her eyes darkened and a small smile played around the corners of her rouged mouth. "But I hope you will sample my gift nonetheless. Think of me when you drink it, won't you, my lord? I dearly hope it brings you—warmth—while you go about your cheerless duties."

Then, with a soft peal of laughter, she turned and glided back to her waiting carriage, baring an exceptional expanse of leg as she lifted her silken skirts and climbed inside.

The wind caught her smoky rose scent and carried it back to Dane, whose eyes narrowed for a moment.

Too bad, he thought. Lady Patricia Lennox was a female who knew how to warm a man's bed very nicely, unless he missed his guess.

Not that he could say for certain. They had come very close to that stage on several occasions since renewing their acquaintance in London several months before. Lady Patricia's interest in him had been very flattering. The reluctance to proceed further had been all on his side, Ravenhurst supposed. Certainly the beautiful blonde had showed every sign of willingness, as long as her conditions were met.

But there would most certainly be conditions, he knew. Perhaps that was what made him hold back, unwilling to incur an obligation to this woman with the cool eyes and the heated skin.

With a shrug the viscount put Lady Patricia from his mind, his thoughts returning to the woman who already occupied his bed. Still cradling his gift, he thoughtfully climbed the stairs.

Tess gave no notice of his arrival, not even when he brushed the pale skin at her forehead. She was still far too cold, Ravenhurst thought, draping another blanket over her. And this pallor was unnatural. Maybe some spirits would help.

Putting down the bottle, he pulled a knife from his boots and pried at the cork. He paused, noticing several small cracks near the top of the cork, but the barrier seemed intact. Finally, after several attempts, he worked the cork free, shredding large pieces in the process. Cautiously he sniffed the open bottle, afraid its contents might have turned bad.

But the fumes that met his nose were rich and smoky with a faint, not unpleasant tinge of pungency. Altogether an excellent brandy, he decided, wondering if it had come from a smuggler's hold.

If so, then it was only right that he should offer it to a smuggler's woman, the viscount decided grimly, lifting Tess's head and forcing some of the brandy between her lips. He smiled, thinking of what Lady Patricia would say if she knew how her gift was being used.

The sleeping woman coughed and tried to turn away, but Ravenhurst anchored her face and made her swallow. A moment later he raised the bottle again, forcing a bit more upon her.

She fought him, choking slightly, but Dane held her still until she'd swallowed. When he angled the bottle once more against her lips, Tess fought him in earnest, but her wild blows fell unheeded upon his broad shoulders. Swiftly Ravenhurst caught her wrists against his chest, holding the bottle in place until she swallowed, once and then again.

"No," she gasped, tossing restlessly. "S-stop!"

"Hush," he answered, setting the bottle on the table and taking her in his hard embrace. "Hush, *Soleil.*"

But Tess continued to writhe against him, more urgently now. "Make them go away," she pleaded, struggling against his taut frame. "No more of their fire."

"There are no spiders. It is only you and I here now," he mut-

tered huskily, stroking her cool skin with rough, reckless fingers.
It seemed, after a time, that the heat began to return to her body.
A faint flush tinged her cheeks. The brandy must be helping, he
decided.

Her eyes opened, dim and glazed. Then the restless shifting
began again. Little desperate sobs broke from her lips.

"Don't fight me, Tess," Dane whispered, only to feel her slender
hips grind against his thighs. Desire shot through him, primal and
savage, swelling his manhood.

Growling a curse, he turned and pressed her beneath him. By
God, he wanted her, wanted her hot and hungry like this, her long
white legs surrounding him. He wanted her panting, lost to everything but desire when he filled her with his hard, swollen man's
shaft.

"Open your eyes, Tess."

Restlessly she tossed against him, mumbling beneath her breath.
Her linen-wrapped hands opened and closed, straining at his
chest.

Suddenly Dane stiffened, staring down at the stark slash of red
across her cheekbones. An image flashed through his mind, a
nearly forgotten memory from his dark months in France. Where
had it been?

He watched those bandaged fingers burrow beneath his shirt,
white against the dense mat of black hair upon his chest.

The Chat d'Or, he realized, his mouth tightening in a hard line.
And then the memories engulfed him as if it were but yesterday.

The clammy hands, the heated skin, the wild, erratic pulse. The
thunder of his heart threatening to leap from his chest.

The way hers must be hammering now.

The night came back to him then, in all its raw horror. A foul
enough thing to witness, but an unspeakable thing to experience,
as he had done.

As Tess was doing now.

So the brandy had been drugged, by God, mixed with something to strip away one's inhibitions. Something that burned a
person inside and out, until there was nothing left but quivering
nerve ends.

Roots from the Orient, perhaps.

Bitter, potent powders passed down from Mogul India.

Savage, blinding drugs that could turn a rational human being into a desperate, driven animal.

And all this was Lady Patricia's doing. Blindly, Ravenhurst stared down at the woman tossing restlessly upon his bed. Except for fate, it might have been him tossing there, caught in the searing grip of a drugged passion.

Just as he had been caught in Paris those long months ago.

"Hush, Tess," he whispered hoarsely, his eyes dark with hideous memories. "Let me put out this fire."

Lost in smoke and flame, Tess twisted beneath him, her skin burning and then icy in turn, her muscles tense, her body a wild and alien thing, beyond her control.

Fear gripped her as she felt the angry march of arachnid feet probing every corner of her body. She shifted, restless and tormented, her skin raw, consumed by a thousand hidden flames.

Dear God, no! Not again.

Nightmares. More nightmares . . .

Then, miraculously, something cool splashed across her fevered skin. She whimpered, reaching for the source of that blessed, cooling dampness.

Something—someone?—pushed her hands away. "Let me help you," she heard a gravelly voice whisper. "Let me take away the flames."

Then the tenuous thread of meaning was lost. Strange, harsh words flowed over her, dim pagan chants that fell upon her hungry, aching skin like soft rain.

She writhed, nerve and muscle aflame, locked in a demon's grip. And this time Tess realized dimly there would be no retreating. This time the peace of her white haven would be denied her.

Moaning, she felt her blood surge and boil through her limbs, turning her into some sort of mindless, devouring thing. Dear God, not one of *them*. Not one of those gnawing creatures of the night!

"So—hot," she moaned.

Suddenly the orange flames exploded, and fire shot through her, raging through her veins, fed with every agonizing burst of her heart.

Her fingers dug deep into the tangled linens.

Her hips lifted from the bed, frantic and seeking. She choked, desperate to end the torment, desperate to stretch and fill the gnawing emptiness within her.

Her skin crawled, teeming with skittering creatures. She cried out hoarsely, feeling the rasp of tiny, voracious jaws. More and more of their poison flooded through her, sparking myriad new flames to life. Her neck, her breasts, her thighs . . .

Somewhere nearby a dim voice whispered, but she could not make out the words. More of the blessed coolness struck her cheeks, her eyes, her chest.

But it was not enough, not nearly enough to match these savage flames, which threatened to devour her.

Just like before. Just like that night five years ago, when she had been brutally betrayed. When all her hope had died.

"Don't—don't hurt me," she whimpered to the darkness. *"Not —again."*

19

A raw curse exploded from Ravenhurst's lips. He threw down the damp wad of linen, knowing that it would do no good.

How much of the bloody brandy had he given her? Not more than four drinks, certainly. The blond bitch must have made her poisonous brew unbelievably potent.

The viscount's eyes hardened as he looked down at the woman beside him on the bed. Gone was the sloe-eyed temptress, gone the confident, mocking wanton. In her place lay only a frightened, suffering creature.

He thought then of another woman, slender and dark-haired, who had dared to shield him while Fouché's gendarmes combed the Paris streets in search of their English prey.

When they had caught him, along with the terrified Véronique, their heavy-jowled commandant had sworn to teach the pair the price of betraying Napoleon's cause.

They had made Dane watch as they forced an unholy mixture between the woman's lips until she, too, had panted and writhed in agony, like the woman before him.

Then the leering Frenchman had made Ravenhurst mount her, goading him with the butt of his pistol when his English captive had resisted. And all the time Véronique's wild, blind eyes had followed him. *"Mon Dieu, que je souffre,"* she had rasped. *"Chaud . . . si chaud."*

Finish it, she had pleaded hoarsely, after Dane, too, was forced to drink. Through that long night he had learned firsthand the horrors of Hell, the unspeakable cruelty that men were capable of.

The bald commandant had amused himself with his voyeurism, planning to drag Dane out to be shot in the morning. Except Véronique's heart had given out from the combination of fear and an excess of the drug. Without warning, she had simply collapsed, to breathe no more.

Seizing his moment, Dane had escaped.

But he had never forgotten the price an innocent woman had been forced to pay for helping him.

Now as he looked down at Tess, her pale hands clutching the tangled bed linens, Dane realized that she, too, had been made to suffer because of him, plunged from a nightmare into something far worse.

Knowing, too, that he alone held the means of soothing her.

His face taut with emotions held fiercely in check, Ravenhurst eased down beside her, his hand cupping her shoulder when she tried to turn away. His keen, dark eyes searched her face.

Dear God, how he wanted her. He had not meant it to be this way, but now there was no other choice.

"Don't fight me, Tess," he whispered. "Not now. Later, perhaps, but for now . . ." His voice tightened. "For now let me take you back. Let me make this night what *that* one should have been."

His lips swept over her cheeks and eyelids, teasing, feather-light. He kissed the line of her brow, the edge of her mouth. And when finally he felt her relax and curve to meet him, he could not keep the tiny smile of triumph from his lips.

Slowly, as if in a dream, he watched her arms reach out.

"Dane?"

How long he had waited to hear his name on her lips.

His eyes smoky with desire, he slanted his body down over her silken heat, feeling the same fire that consumed her. She was so soft, so open to him now, her hips shifting and hungry.

All that he had ever dreamed of . . .

Desire ripped through him. He felt himself harden and swell to painful proportions. Tensing, he fought the urge to bury himself deep within her and ease the ache at his groin.

But he knew he could not. Not yet. Not while her need was so great.

A vein pounding at his temple, he grasped her wrists and crushed her beneath him, every hard ridge of sinew and bone mated to her soft hollows and swells. She stirred restlessly but did not fight him now, not even when he began to inch down her heated skin, his mouth burning a damp trail to her taut nipples.

"Yes, Tess," he urged darkly. "Let me taste you."

Stroking and biting softly, he circled the pebbled crests again and again, teasing her until she arched her back and moaned wildly beneath him. Immediately Ravenhurst's mouth opened, surrounding her.

Ragged heartbeats later he shifted; his tongue began to tease its way along the taut muscles of her abdomen, skirting her navel.

He could feel as much as hear her panting moans now, and realized they were fueled by panic along with passion. The ragged sound made him curse roughly, damning Lady Patricia for her cunning.

Slowly his fingers brushed the dusky curls crowning her thighs. Instantly Tess froze, digging her heels into the bed and pressing her legs together.

Without speaking Dane gathered her close and soothed her with his lips and strong, persuasive hands, making no advance until she began to relax. The change was subtle; he felt it in her steadied breathing, in the play of her light, searching fingers upon his shoulders.

"Open for me, Tess," he said urgently, feathering kisses over the corner of her mouth, groaning when her lips parted and she stroked his tongue with her own. "Hot . . . so sweet. Let me bring down the sun for you."

Then he parted her gently, before fear could return, and this time he felt her body strain with a different tension, a hunger as old as man and woman.

Little wordless cries trembled on her lips as he eased deep inside her, circling and stroking, surging and withdrawing rhythmically until she found his pace and instinctively began to match it.

A thin sheen of sweat covered her body, darkening the errant curls at her temples.

So beautiful, Dane thought dimly, inflamed by the sight of her pale waist, her proud, taut nipples, and the crowning birthmarks at her breast and thigh.

My woman, his blood sang fiercely. *Now and forever. Whether she likes it or not.*

His eyes darkened when he felt her tremors begin, radiating out from the heart of her, driving her mindless and urgent against him.

Suddenly her gray-green eyes flickered open, stark with shock and fear.

"Take it, Tess," he rasped, feeling the beginnings of her resistance. "My sweet *Soleil.*"

"N-no," she choked out, feeling her heart burst from her chest, feeling flames wrap around her thighs and neck.

But it was already too late.

For then, just as the dream-figure had promised, the sun was torn from the sky, descending in sweet fury upon her, burning away both poison and memory. Choking, she felt him drive the small fires hotter, ever hotter, into one vast inferno that glowed fiercely and then exploded, deep inside her.

Showing her how the dream was meant to end.

Grim-faced with his effort at control, Dane urged her once more toward the thing she needed so desperately, stroking her fevered skin until she found another wild, breathless release.

Around them the long years fell away and suddenly only the old sweet yearning was left, only this pure bright flame of love and desire that bound them inextricably. Past and future forgotten, he felt her shudder and cling tightly to him as if she never meant to let him go.

It was a promise made by her body, Dane knew, not by heart or mind. But it was a promise he meant to hold her to, the hard-faced man vowed silently, wooing her with his rough fingers, whispering her name like a hungry prayer, over and over, long after her trembling had ceased and she lay languid in his arms, lost in dreams.

When the restless shifting began again, he cradled her with his hands and drove deep inside her silken heat until their hot breath mingled and their bodies fused into one sleek, straining being.

All through the long hours of night he loved her, with hands and lips and tongue, urging her on with hushed cries and hoarse groans, in a bonding fierce beyond anything he had ever known.

For this thing between them was exquisite torment and fierce ecstasy, the most basic and primal of human needs. It was pleasure given and shared, delayed and savored. It was blinding brightness and dark inferno, consuming body and soul before it could finally be satiated in a firestorm of raw sensation.

When he could once again think rationally, Ravenhurst wondered if Tess was even aware of what had happened between them.

But it mattered not, he swore.

For she was his again, bound to him by laws older than those of man and country.

His, now and forever.

There would be no going back, for either of them.

Long hours later Tess began to stir restlessly. Her eyes fluttered, tightening against the sunlight that spilled through unfamiliar curtains. Something tickled her cheek and she batted it away, tugging at the heavy blankets on her chest.

The motion sent tendrils of pain through her arms and thighs, a strange, dull ache that radiated from muscles she hadn't known the human body possessed.

Her eyes flew open, then fixed blankly on the unfamiliar white ceiling overhead.

Her fingers probed the unfamiliar woolen blanket that covered her. Bandages?

A cry ripped from her throat, only to be stifled immediately when she saw the hard male thigh slanting along her hip.

Slowly, she turned, as if in a dream, to see a bronzed body lying beside her, long sable hair curving about an angular, unyielding jaw. White wings gleamed at his temples, unfurrowed now in sleep.

Dear God, what had he done?

What had *she* done? Tess wondered, feeling the unfamiliar ache at thigh and breast once again.

But now was not the time for questions, not with Lord Ravenhurst lying only inches away, not with an odd tension gathering in her thighs, a strange yearning to know what it would feel like to comb her fingers through the wiry hair above those flat male nipples. To feel his warm muscles bunch and ripple beneath her teasing touch.

Tess's hand flew to her lips. Desire coursed through her at that dark, erotic image, at the thought of that hard body cushioned by her softness, his bronzed thigh parting her.

Dear God, was she going mad?

With trembling fingers, Tess eased back the sheets and inched away from him. Slowly she slipped one foot to the floor and began to slide from the bed.

She was nearly free when she felt a rigid weight trap her leg. The next moment long, calloused fingers captured her wrist and yanked her sprawling against his chest.

"Just where in bloody hell do you think *you're* going?" growled Ravenhurst's dark, sleep-roughened voice.

20

Panting, Tess struggled to wrench free of the viscount's iron grip. But each movement sent pain biting through her wrists and fingers, already raw from the night before. A choked sob burst from her lips as she realized she had no hope of winning against this man.

Slowly Ravenhurst's hands tightened, dragging her inexorably closer until she was flush against his chest, staring up into a pair of icy lapis eyes.

"So you meant to slip away, did you?" he growled. "After all that happened between us last night?"

Wild-eyed, Tess studied him, afraid to listen, afraid even to consider what he meant. "N-nothing happened between us!"

The cobalt eyes narrowed. "You have beautiful breasts, you know, Tess Leighton. Silken thighs, exquisite hips, and—"

"Stop," she cried hoarsely. "You are vile—"

"I really think that under the circumstances I shall be forced to marry you," her captor said lazily, just as if she had not spoken.

"Marry!" she stormed. *"You?* I'd as soon marry a—a goat! A snake!"

Ravenhurst's lips tightened, settling into a hard line as he saw his dreams vanish like so much smoke blown before the wind.

Again.

They might have had so much together, he thought bitterly.

But he had forgotten just how hard she was. How ruthless and selfish.

"Oh, you'll become my wife, all right," he growled, masking his pain. "That's the only way you'll ever leave this house."

"You truly are mad, aren't you? You must be so, to think I'd ever consider marrying a—a loathsome reptile like you!"

Dane's eyes narrowed to dark slits. "Would you rather I billeted a group of officers at Fairleigh? 'Twould be a pity to think of their clumsy, booted feet trampling upon your mother's white garden, of course. Destroying all those fragile blooms—"

"Damn you for a black-hearted swine! You wouldn't dare!"

"Oh, but I would dare. And it is entirely within my rights as commissioner of the Military Canal to do so. You see, I mean to tighten your bit, my love, for you've run tame a great deal too long here. And after I've broken you—to my saddle, shall we say?—I have a great many questions that need answering. Yes, marriage will afford me the ideal opportunity to accomplish all those things."

"You filthy, cold-blooded—"

Ravenhurst pulled her a fraction closer, until the heat of his naked body threatened to scald her through the thin sheet she clutched to her breast. "Ah, but you did not feel so an hour ago, my dear. Then you were moaning and panting, rubbing yourself against me in total abandon, begging me to take you. Of course I," he added silkily, "being a true gentleman, had no choice but to oblige you."

Tess's face paled, her eyes emerald pools. "Impossible," she whispered.

Yet even as she spoke, she had a momentary flash of strong bronze fingers cupping her pale breasts. Tormenting images assailed her, darkness against light, hardness against aching softness.

She blinked, staring at Ravenhurst's rough, unshaven cheeks, realizing they were the source of the fine scratches that covered her tender skin.

At her breast. At her neck. At her thighs, where he . . .

No, she had not—he *could not*—

Desperately Tess tried to wrench free, afraid of the dark triumph she saw glittering in his eyes.

"I am desolate to correct you, but you did all that and a great deal more." Ravenhurst's cold eyes never left Tess's face as he shifted slightly, offering her a view of his back. "Those marks are yours, my dear. Love bites left by *your* sharp little teeth. And there are more on my neck and shoulders. You really couldn't get enough of me last night, it seemed. Yes, in bed you became quite the hot-blooded, abandoned little bitch." His fingers bit into her fragile wrists. "In *my* bed, that is. For now your passion will flare only for me. No more you'll ride the marsh, no more you'll moan for other men. You're mine now, Tess Leighton, do you hear me?"

Frozen, speechless with horror, Tess stared back at him, her eyes going dark and bottomless. *Dear God, it could not be true. It must be another of his lies . . .*

"No lie, Tess," he said harshly, almost as if he had read the denial in her face. "The marks of your teeth do not lie. Nor does the dull ache I doubt not that you feel right now at your thighs, where you rode me all through the long, stormy night." Dark flames flared deep in his eyes. "A night eminently satisfying to us both, my dear, full of the pleasures we shall know many times after we are wed."

With an angry cry, Tess flung herself to her feet, managing to rip free of his grasp. Her wild motion swept away the sheet that had been her only covering, revealing the silken expanse of her body to Ravenhurst's smoldering gaze.

"No and no again!" she cried angrily, oblivious to her nakedness. "A thousand times no, you monster!"

Fury smoldered across Ravenhurst's face. "I could become a monster, my dear. You are the very one who could drive me to it. Now, come here, Tess," he ordered, an edge of steel to his voice.

The auburn-haired beauty shot him a fulminating look. "The devil I do!"

"Don't make me come and get you."

"I take orders from no one, your bloody lordship. The sooner you realize that, the better!"

"Now, Tess," the viscount growled. "Unless you care to feel the hard edge of my anger."

"I care not a jot for anything you might threaten me with, you cur. You are nothing but a degenerate, depraved, detestable—"

"Determined," Ravenhurst grated, his voice promising vengeance. "Infinitely determined. To have you in my bed. To break you to my bit. To have the answers to my questions."

"Indeed, my lord?" Tess answered, her voice shrill. "And you may truly do all those things?"

Ravenhurst's dark brow quirked.

"Yes, all those things—when pigs fly! When it snows in July!"

"I shall never know with you, shall I? Where the tricks stop and the truth begins." A vein began to pound at Dane's temple. "Whether you are even capable of speaking the truth. But I'll soon have you speaking a different language, hellcat. The language of skin against skin, tongue upon tongue. By God, your body will not lie to me."

"You, scum, may take your—your *garrulous* anatomy and—"

"Too late, Tess." Slowly Ravenhurst eased the covers back from his waist, fury written on every stark plane of his face. Suddenly his hard body was revealed to Tess, every throbbing, overwhelmingly masculine inch of it.

Her heart began to slam against her ribs. "Stop! Don't take another step!"

But he gave no sign of hearing. Grim-faced, he uncoiled from the bed and began to stalk closer. Against the darkness of his face his eyes smoldered with a thousand tiny flames.

"Bastard! Black-hearted vermin," Tess cried, taking a step backward.

"I see I shall have my work cut out for me," Ravenhurst snarled. "And it appears my first task will be to scrub that filthy mouth of yours with soap."

Ashen-faced, Tess retreated another step, only to feel cold plaster at her back.

Dane's lips twisted in a cold smile of triumph.

The air between them trembled, raw with tension.

Wildly Tess searched the room for some weapon, some avenue of escape. But there was none, and her bloody captor knew it.

He was nearly within reach now. Color stained Tess's cheeks as her eyes fell upon the bronze breadth of his chest, the mat of dense black hair, the rigid blade of muscle flaring between his legs.

"S-stop," she cried in a strangled voice.

"Not just yet, my dear. Not until I've left my mark upon you." His voice hardened. "Not until you beg me *not* to stop."

Even as he spoke, Tess felt her body burn and run liquid. Dry-throated, she watched him come closer, stunned by the rippling power of that lean, predatory form.

But she must not allow him to see her weakness! To do so would betray Jack and the others.

Suddenly, far below, she heard the fierce pounding of brass against wood.

"Open up, in the King's name," an angry voice bellowed. "By order of Inspector Hawkins, we're searching this house for smugglers!"

For one frenzied moment, smoldering lapis eyes met smoky green. Hearts pounding, the two froze, listening to the crash of the door knocker and the angry cries whirling up from the street.

Ravenhurst was the first to move, bending to tug on his breeches. "Hawkins," he muttered. "The bloody swine!"

"L-let me go," Tess cried wildly. "There must be a servant's stair."

"Boarded up," the viscount said flatly. "Too unstable to be used. There's only one way out of this house, and that's down the front staircase—right past Hawkins's men."

Once again the knocker thundered. "Now, by God!" Hawkins's furious bellow exploded above the din.

Abruptly Dane's lips curved in a slight smile. So the Inspector himself was present, was he? Yes, perhaps fate had turned friendly once more.

Before Tess realized what he was about, he had caught her up in his arms and crossed to the bed, where he dumped her in an ignominious heap. "Our business is far from finished, my dear," he said grimly. "Now keep very quiet, so I can get rid of our malodorous visitor."

Curses tumbled from Tess's lips as she struggled to sit up. "How dare you! You are the very scum of the sea, a monster! The devil himself!"

The next moment the door closed with a mocking crash, and Tess found herself cursing empty space. Stiff with fury, she listened to the click of a key in the lock, then the thump of bare feet upon the stairs. All the while, she was scanning the sparsely furnished room. But there was nothing to help her, not even a knife or a pair of scissors. Nothing but his cursed bed and a single chair.

And of course, the half-filled bottle on the side table, she thought bitterly, spirits he had no doubt used to fog her senses during the long night. Frantically, she ran to test the locked door, then tried the smaller door opposite, which revealed a small closet.

Dear God, what was she to do?

White-faced, she spun about, in her desperation knocking the bottle onto the wooden floor, where it exploded in a chaos of glass fragments and puddled spirits.

Far below, a door grated on its hinges. Hawkins snapped out a furious command, which was followed by loud cries and the hammering of feet.

Tess's frantic eyes swept the room. She couldn't go down, and that left only . . .

Her heart hammering, she ran to the window, sobbing as glass shards cut into her bare feet. Tears sprang to her eyes, but she fought down her pain, knowing she had very little time left.

Swiftly she tossed back the curtains and tugged open the casement. Yes, just maybe!

With awkward, trembling fingers, she flung back the covers on the bed, tugged the sheets free, and dragged them to the window. They were now stained with blood from her feet, but she barely noticed. Frantically she knotted the two lengths together, then looped one end around the bedpost nearest the window. Murmuring a prayer, she tossed the other end out through the open casement.

A wave of disappointment crushed her as she watched the dangling cloth dance in the wind, at least twenty feet above the ground. Damn and blast! Far too short!

At that moment, heavy feet began to thunder up the staircase. *Think—think—think!*

Catching her lip between her teeth, Tess scanned the room, the locked outer door, the closet nearby. Dear God, what was she to do next?

21

Ravenhurst's face was harsh and shuttered as he wrenched open the thick oak door that fronted the street. Before him stood a score of preventive men ringing the house with Amos Hawkins at their center, a heavy, brass-mounted pistol clutched in his beefy fingers.

"About time ye answered the door, Ravenhurst." Hawkins's colorless eyes flickered over the viscount's naked chest and bare feet. "My, my—it appears we've come at a bad moment. Too bad," he jeered, his lips pulled back in a snarling smile.

Yes, he would enjoy taking this insolent bastard down a peg or two, Hawkins thought. "Seems my men have sighted a pair of ruffians slipping over yer garden wall. Appeared to be carrying tarred kegs of contraband, so they did. Reckon we'll just have to take a look around."

Ravenhurst studied Hawkins coldly. "Had anyone trespassed here, I would have known it, Inspector. Now, if you please, you will take your men and—"

"But I don't please, Ravenhurst. It's searching I've come for, and searching I mean to do. Now, get out of my way!"

The viscount did not move from the middle of the doorway. Slowly and very deliberately he crossed his arms over his chest. "You make a grave error, Hawkins. There is no one here but myself. Now take yourself off, before you goad me into doing something unpleasant in the extreme."

"Threatening an officer of the Crown, are ye? *Yer lordship?*"

"I might ask the same question of you."

"Yer jurisdiction begins at one bank of the canal and ends at the other, and ye bloody well know it! But this is Rye, and I give the orders here, so step aside," Hawkins snarled. "Or maybe ye'd enjoy watching my men split that fine door in half with their axes."

Ravenhurst's eyes hardened. For a moment he considered telling Hawkins precisely what he could do with the handle of one of those axes. Only by dint of fierce self-control was he able to stop himself. For a squabble on his stoop was not the goal Ravenhurst had in mind.

Careful, he thought. His eyelids lowered as he studied Hawkins lazily. Finally, with an indifferent shrug, he sauntered a step back from the door, a cold, mocking smile on his lips.

Red-faced with fury, Hawkins pushed past him and strode into the main hall, already snarling orders to his men. At the center of the hall the inspector halted, his colorless eyes flickering over a pair of rare Ming Dynasty blue-and-white vases crowning a Chippendale table.

A scowl twisted his mottled features. "Search the cellars, Boggs. Lawson, take the garden. The rest of ye spread out and comb this floor. I want nothing missed, do ye hear?"

Suddenly from high overhead there came a thunderous crash.

Slowly Hawkins's lips curved into an ugly smile. "I think I'll search the upper floors myself."

Behind Hawkins, Ravenhurst permitted himself the luxury of a brief smile. Good, very good, he thought. So far all was progressing nicely.

But his smile faded as he thought of the customs inspector scrutinizing Tess's half-clad body, for she would have his shirt and precious little else.

But there was nothing to be done about that now, and his plan would answer very nicely in every other regard. Yes, soon he would force her hand. Once Hawkins discovered her in that upstairs bedroom, nearly naked, Tess would be compromised beyond any hope of redemption.

Then the sloe-eyed little hellcat in his bed would have no choice but to accept his offer of marriage.

"Entertaining guests, were ye, my lord?" The inspector tossed Ravenhurst a leering smile as they neared the first floor landing.

"You'll answer to the customs inspector at Dover for this, Hawkins," the viscount answered coldly.

"No law to bar me searching a house where ruffians are sighted. I know a smuggler well enough when I see one!"

"And I know bilge when I hear it!"

"Why so testy, my lord? Something upstairs ye'd prefer to hide? Or should I say—*someone?*"

They were at the second floor landing. His face shuttered, Dane watched Hawkins grimace as he discovered the door was locked.

Snarling a curse, the customs officer took a step back and slammed his heel against the door. Wood fragments exploded over the landing; the door flew open with a deafening crack.

Ravenhurst stood rigid, waiting for Hawkins's growl of fury when he entered the room.

But no sound came.

Frowning, the viscount stalked inside. As if in a dream he saw the linens knotted to his bed, the curtains flying at the casement. In disbelief he watched Hawkins cross an empty room, crunching across scattered shards of glass as he made his way to the window.

They were the only ones there.

When he pulled his head back inside a moment later, Hawkins began to laugh, a shrill, mocking sound nearly as ugly as his face. "So," he snarled, "it looks like yer bird has flown, Ravenhurst. But not before ye had a regular tussle, from the look of that." As he spoke, Hawkins swept his thumb idly across a thick crimson stain dotting the white cloth. His eyes narrowed. "A virgin, too," he muttered thickly.

Dane's face darkened. Hardly a virgin. He of all people knew that. First had come the testimony of his own eyes five years ago. Now he had the tangible proof of her body.

But Hawkins was too busy to notice Ravenhurst's abstraction. The inspector's foot prodded a large piece of shattered glass.

Frowning, he bent down, reaching for something just beneath the corner of the bed. "Appears she left something behind," he muttered, lifting a carved tortoiseshell hairpin from the floor.

A look of cunning crossed his face as he held the ornament out to Dane. "Must have been quite a fight. But then I like a woman with a bit of spirit, myself." His glittering eyes probed Dane's angry face, and a moment later harsh laughter exploded through the room. "Bloody stunned, that's what ye look, Ravenhurst! Outfoxed ye, did the wench? Aye, who'd have thought of her climbing out a window? Perhaps she didn't care for your performance."

Dane's eyes smoldered. A blinding wave of fury swept over him. Unconsciously his fingers tightened on the carved piece of tortoiseshell.

With a tiny crack, the fragile ornament snapped under the pressure of his grip.

Damn her! But he'd get her back, Ravenhurst swore. And when he did—

Belatedly he realized Hawkins was speaking to him.

"Don't bother to see me out, yer lordship. Reckon I can find my way well enough. Aye, just like *she* did." His harsh laughter echoed down the corridor.

For long moments Ravenhurst stood in the middle of his bedroom, staring down at the scattered glass fragments glittering on the floor.

How had she managed it? His thoughts awhirl, he stalked to the open window. On the ground far below he saw one of his boots lying heel up in the mud.

Blindly he stared down at that mud-spattered piece of leather.

The stubborn little bitch! Yes, she was damned clever, he'd grant her that much. She must have been desperate indeed to attempt such a descent. The end of the sheets stopped at least—his eyes narrowed, judging the distance—twenty feet above the ground.

Grim-faced, Ravenhurst pulled in the makeshift rope and slammed the window shut, oblivious to the way the glass pane rattled dangerously at the force of his blow.

His hands clenched, he swung about and stamped downstairs to search the rear yard.

Knowing he would find nothing.

Knowing she was gone, that she had escaped his net once more, and was probably laughing at him even now.

As it happened, Tess was much closer at that moment than Ravenhurst imagined. Laughter was the farthest thing from her mind, however, as she crouched in the closet, breathlessly listening to the muffled thud of his bare feet upon the stairs.

But it had worked! Just like Hawkins, her cursed captor had accepted the evidence of the empty room. Ah, yes, men might be long on bluster and bravado, but it was the women who had the real intellect!

When the steps died away, she uncurled slowly and crept to the window, keeping well out of sight. Her lips curved in triumph as she watched Ravenhurst's tall form pace toward the back of the walled garden.

She did not wait to see more. The long hem of his shirt billowing out behind her, she spun about and ran for the stairs.

Seated in a gaudy silk armchair beside a bow window overlooking Watchbell Street, Mrs. Hermione Tredwell was making a desultory attempt to complete a complicated needlepoint design of a Madonna and child.

Without warning her needle slipped, pricking her finger. She snapped a curse beneath her breath, then glanced about quickly, reassured to see that that silly creature, Alicia Crabtree, was out of earshot.

Frowning with annoyance, she flung down the raggedly worked square of fabric and strode to the window.

Suddenly her beady eyes narrowed; her hard features froze in an expression of ludicrous disbelief. With a sharp cry she pressed forward, her fierce curiosity rewarded by stabbing pain when her nose collided with the glass.

"A—Alicia!" she gasped, pressing her fingers to her massive, quivering bosom. "My hartshorn! Immediately!"

* * *

On the opposite side of the street, Amos Hawkins sat alone at a table before the grimy window of the Three Herrings, draining his second tankard of ale.

His thick lips curled in satisfaction as he recalled the bloody viscount's look of fury when he realized his pigeon had flown.

But who was she? the inspector wondered, his beady eyes narrowing. The new serving maid at the Dog and Duck? Someone at the Angel, perhaps? Not Lucy, he was sure of that, for he had sampled her wares himself on several occasions and could personally attest to her being long past maidenhood.

Idly he glanced outside, watching a pair of dragoons swagger down the street. Suddenly he jerked forward in his chair, spilling his ale in his haste to get closer to the window.

Slim ivory thighs flashed by, scarce concealed beneath a trailing white shirt.

A woman's thighs, by God! Damned luscious ones at that!

Then she was gone, disappearing around the corner before Hawkins had time for a closer look.

For a moment he did not move, frozen in that awkward, crouching posture, disbelief written across his ruddy face.

Then he stumbled to his feet, kicking over the heavy chair in his haste to reach the door.

Viscount Ravenhurst smothered a curse. There was no one in the garden, just as he had known there would be no one. His mouth flattened to a hard line as he stalked back toward the house. At the rear door he halted, feeling a cold gust of wind whip down the hall.

Frowning, he strode along the corridor toward the open door at the front of the townhouse.

There he froze, his long fingers curled around the door frame. And there, for the first time in his life, Dane St. Pierre, the fourth Viscount Ravenhurst, found himself speechless, treated to the unforgettable sight of slim female legs flashing down the middle of Watchbell Street.

Naked legs. With his own linen shirt the sole garment covering the soft feminine curves above.

His throat went dry. A vein began to pulse at his temple. Stunned, he watched Tess Leighton dart over the cobblestones and stumble into hiding behind a yew hedge when two drunken dragoons lurched out of the Three Herrings.

Bloody blazing hell! She must have been hiding in his room all along, just waiting for him to leave—in the closet, perhaps, or under the bed.

And now she had the unbelievable audacity to run through the heart of Rye, clad in nothing but his shirt! It seemed once more he had underestimated her.

His eyes narrowed on the bush where she hid. Those twigs must be hurting her bare legs a great deal, Ravenhurst thought, smiling grimly.

She was a worthy adversary, he had to admit, and far more clever than he had imagined.

But clever or no, she would soon be his. It was only a question of time.

Gasping for air, Tess stumbled down the narrow flagstone alley that bordered the Angel, her bare feet throbbing. Tears blinded her eyes as she clambered up the rear steps to the kitchen.

When a pale, anxious Hobhouse opened the rear door a moment later, he was, for once in his long career in service, stripped of his customary aplomb.

"Sweet Jesus Almighty," the usually solemn majordomo breathed when he was finally able to speak, sweeping his stunned gaze from Tess's disheveled auburn curls down to her bare legs and feet. "What in the name of—"

Abruptly his features hardened, stiffening into a mask of anger. "I'll kill him for you, Miss Tess. I'll kill the bastard for sure—just you say the word! I'd like nothing better, in fact." As he spoke, his huge hands tightened into fists.

Grimly Tess shook her head, swaying slightly before she caught hold of Hobhouse's outstretched hand. "I think not, Hobhouse.

Death is far too good for such a loathsome snake." Her eyes darkened and she stared off into the distance for a moment, her face tight with bitterness. "No, I mean to think of something a great deal more excruciating than simple murder for our viscount."

22

Don't think. Don't remember. Slowly Tess climbed the stairs to her room, repeating the words with each step.

Now is all that matters.

She tried to tell herself it was true, saying the sentences over and over in her mind.

Inside at last, she tore at the buttons on her chest with numb fingers, desperate to rip off the garment—*his* garment—as if the very touch of it seared her skin. When the buttons resisted her bandaged fingers, she sheared them off in one wild stroke and wrenched the shirt from her body. With a choked little sob, she crumbled the white linen into a ball and flung it as far away as she could.

Even then she felt the touch of him, hard fingers. Rigid, straining arousal. Memories flooded over her, each more cruel than the last.

His unshaved jaw scraping her thighs.

His mouth hard and hungry as he explored her body, breaking her to his will, teaching her infinite delight and searing, breathless pleasure.

Until every nerve screamed, every inch of skin begged for release.

Tess's fist flew to her trembling lips, and she fought to hold back a ragged sob. To hold back the savage memories that threatened to drown her.

Thinking of all he had done to her.

Thinking of exactly what she had *begged* him to do.

Madness, just like that night five years ago. Like falling from one nightmare into another. Or being caught helpless in the body of a depraved stranger.

You, my dear daughter, are a bloody little whore. Just like your cursed mother.

"No!" Tess cried, locking her hands over her ears, haunted by her father's snarled words even now.

You throw yourself in front of every man you meet. So why not a man of my choosing, for once?

Tears slipped from Tess's eyes. Suddenly she was cast back to those bitter weeks five years ago, weeks of torment during which her father had pressed her continuously, threatening her with every sort of punishment if she did not make herself more "amiable" to his house guest.

For the fat, ruddy-faced Lord Chevington, though nearly her father's age, had won at play too often, and soon held a great many of her father's vowels. Vowels to the tune of five thousand pounds, to be exact.

For that reason, Edward Leighton had announced coldly, his daughter was to be "attentive" to their visitor's needs.

Tess had tried. Dear Lord, she had tried, fully intending to comply. But she hadn't really understood what was involved, not at first. Not until the earl had begun probing her breasts with his sweaty fingers, pressing his tongue between her lips.

White-faced, she had pushed him away and bolted.

Her father's retaliation had been swift and severe. She was to remain locked in her room, he announced, with no visitors and no food until she relented.

She had withstood too well, Tess realized now. One week had passed, the servants slipping her a bit of food when they could. Two weeks. Three . . .

Then her father had discovered a new means of attack. Rigid with fury, he had dragged Tess to the stone tunnels beneath the priory and locked her in, leaving her no hope of escape.

Blindly Tess stared out the window, remembering the terror that had followed.

No light. No human sounds of any sort deep in the ground.

Only the night sounds. Only the night creatures, with squirming bodies and sharp little jaws.

Only the spiders . . .

"Dear God," she whispered to the quiet room, swept back to those nightmare days she had spent sealed in darkness. The last trace of color bled from her face. It was all coming back to her now, too clearly, too cruelly.

Hours had passed, days perhaps. She could not say. Down there time was different, immeasurable. Or perhaps it simply ceased to exist.

When the brutal stranger who was her father had finally come for Tess, he found her silent and completely withdrawn, safe in that white haven she had made for herself.

At last she was ready to be compliant, Leighton had thought triumphantly, only to discover to his fury that she was nothing of the sort.

Then he had smiled, a very cruel sort of smile, which widened as he made her his next warning. Since *she* would not listen, her dear Ashley would suffer the same treatment next.

Moments later Leighton had the pleasure of seeing his daughter's face bleed white, her rebellious spirit broken at last. For Ashley, Tess well knew, had not the strength to endure such imprisonment. *She* had survived, but he never would.

So she had simply nodded and walked back to the house, her face carefully expressionless, refusing to give her father the added pleasure of seeing her pain.

And when that night Lord Chevington returned—to share a pleasant little dinner *en famille,* as her father explained—Tess had forced herself not to recoil from his probing fingers, to smile at his ponderous witticisms.

The night had dissolved into a long blur. Course upon course, remove after remove had slipped by, and always her father's cold face was before her, smiling thinly, forcing more and more wine upon her.

That, Tess had accepted willingly, desperate for oblivion, desperate to ignore what she knew was soon to come.

Until finally the candles began to dance madly and the silver to flash, while the room grew unbearably hot. Suddenly the voices grew distant and muffled, and the room spun around her.

That was all Tess remembered. Oh yes, fragments occasionally burst from some shadowed corner of her mind, but the details were buried deep, locked away where she could never find them.

Maybe it was better that way. Maybe it was by her choice that they remained so.

Tess's eyes fixed on her own ashen reflection in the cheval glass, on the stark terror in her face.

That night Dane St. Pierre had arranged to wait for her at her mother's white garden, where they often met in those last weeks before he left for Trafalgar.

Only her father had made a prior engagement for her, it seemed.

The next thing Tess remembered was coming awake to the harsh, grating sounds of a quarrel. Her father screaming, Dane white-faced and disbelieving as he stood swaying in the doorway.

Her trembling hands swept her brow. Dear God, her head throbbed to remember. The pain . . . her lover's look of shock and disbelief.

She could see it all, as if it were yesterday. She would carry the memory to her grave, Tess knew.

She saw the rest, too, with the keen, slow-moving clarity of a nightmare. After waking, she had sat up, frowning at the chaos around her, then looked down to see Chevington snoring loudly beside her, his fat, naked body sprawled across the blood-flecked sheets.

Her blood, she realized slowly. Her pain.

Dazed, she had turned, searching out her lover's eyes, only to recoil from the savagery and loathing she found burning there. When Dane had spun about, white-faced, Tess had not tried to stop him, only watched numbly as he stumbled from the room.

From the town.

From her life, forever.

Or so she had thought. Perhaps she had even hoped it would be so, for to see him again would only open the cruel wounds that could never heal.

Unmoving, Tess studied the face that looked back at her from the cheval glass, feeling it was someone else's face, someone else's body. Someone shamed beyond redemption.

The face of a whore—a woman who had betrayed her lover in a way beyond forgiving.

No amount of explaining could ever change that, and Tess had not had the heart to begin. Somewhere in the long years that followed, she had put it all behind her, or at least buried it so deep that the memories could no longer hurt her.

Until now, that is. Until the same thing happened again.

One silver tear slipped from her eye and inched down her cheek, but Tess did not notice. Blindly she stared down at the cuts on her fingers, at the jagged welts on her shoulders and thighs, knowing that the madness of the tunnels had descended upon her once more in Dane's cellar.

After that had come a different sort of madness, when he carried her to his bed.

Horrified, Tess relived it all, the way he had come to her with tongue and teeth and mouth, again and again. Only for her to find it was not enough, that she had to have him in the primal way of man and his mate.

Which he had done at last, pounding into her with all his fire and all his fury, past and future swept away in the searing pleasure of their first joining.

The way it should have been so long ago.

Except that he wore his bitterness like a shield now, where once love had draped him. And how could she blame him for that?

Slowly Tess turned from the cheval glass, her face a mask of pain as she slipped into the steaming tub beside the bed. With fierce, punishing strokes she began to scour her body from head to toe, knowing all the while that she would never, ever feel clean again.

Lazy clouds glinted pink and lavender in the late afternoon sun as Hobhouse opened the Angel's front door and strode purposefully up Mermaid Street. Stony-faced, he climbed the pristine marble steps to Ravenhurst's townhouse and banged the brass, lion-headed knocker.

Long minutes later the door opened. Peale's face registered the merest trace of surprise. "How may I assist you, Mr. Hobhouse?"

"You can fetch Lord Ravenhurst, that's what you can do for me, Mr. Peale," the majordomo growled.

"The viscount is, er, otherwise engaged at the moment. May I tell him—"

Hobhouse did not wait to hear more. His shoulders squared, he pushed past Peale into the house. "Show yourself, blackguard!" he thundered. "Or are you so craven that you dare to attack only defenseless females?"

A dark figure appeared at the landing above. "Go away, Hobhouse."

"Bastard! Bloody, black-hearted bastard. That's what you are! Now, do you come down here and face me or do I go up there?"

Ravenhurst did not move. "Neither choice holds any particular appeal," he said coldly.

"And you call yourself a hero?" Hobhouse sneered. "The only person I see before me is a miserable son of a—"

"Don't push me, man," Ravenhurst growled. "I'm trying to overlook the things you've said, but—"

"I'll leave when I have satisfaction, and not a second sooner, you scum."

The viscount's face darkened, settling into harsh, forbidding lines. Slowly he began to descend, each foot dropping with harsh finality upon the uncarpeted steps. "And what if I refuse to fight you?"

His lips curled with distaste, Hobhouse returned Ravenhurst's glare. "Oh, you'll fight me, you cur, I'll see to that." His voice dropped. "I don't know what you did to her, but she has no one else to defend her. No father, no mother. No one but me." Ravenhurst was in front of him now, his eyes smoldering. "So you see I reckon you got this coming." Even as he spoke, Hobhouse twisted, sending an iron fist arcing toward the viscount's jaw.

Oddly enough, Ravenhurst did not dodge the blow, even when

he saw it coming, so that Hobhouse's fist connected with savage force.

The viscount staggered, smothered a curse, and eased his hand across his throbbing mouth. "It appears that you will have your wish." Nodding curtly at Peale, Ravenhurst turned and began to stride down the hall toward the rear of the house, jerking off his bottle-green jacket as he went.

In grim silence they stalked out into the long, walled garden. With quick, precise movements Hobhouse stripped off his black jacket and began to roll up the sleeves of his spotless white shirt.

Ravenhurst waited, his face cold and expressionless.

Then, eyes smoldering, the two men began to circle.

Hobhouse was the first to land a blow, connecting with Dane's shoulder. In spite of his smaller size, he was tough and wiry and his aim was true. Although Ravenhurst did not know it, his opponent had worked out with the leading pugilist of his day, no less than Gentleman Jackson himself.

The viscount was stronger and taller, but Hobhouse was a veteran and well trained. They were, in short, well-matched opponents. Too well matched, it soon became clear, as blow after blow was given and then returned. Soon blood matted Dane's brow, while Hobhouse could only blink and peer out through eyes red-rimmed and swollen.

But neither man would give in. Above them the sky bled from lavender to violet and then lapis. A bat slashed through the darkness, screeching shrilly.

"I only wish I could kill you," Hobhouse muttered, landing a sharp right hook just below the viscount's left cheekbone.

His opponent recoiled, coughing, and spit out a mouthful of blood. "You are, I apprehend, a 'man of science,' Hobhouse. Studied with Belcher, did you?"

"Gentleman Jackson, himself," his opponent growled, his voice tight with pride.

"It won't help you much longer, for I'm twenty years younger and forty pounds heavier. Give it up, man!"

"Go to hell!" came Hobhouse's acid reply.

Grim-faced, Ravenhurst sent a bruising left hook toward the

older man's stomach, and Hobhouse grunted, staggering beneath the force of the blow. He began to weave unsteadily, struggling to see from his one good eye.

Overhead the sky faded to navy and then black as the two circled and engaged, barely able to see, their blows traded blindly.

Peale watched anxiously as Ravenhurst took a blow to the midriff and stumbled to the ground. "You are making a spectacle of yourself, my lord," he said tensely. "What honor is there in that?"

Unheeding, the viscount staggered to his feet.

Then Hobhouse's fist crashed into his temple, making him grunt with pain as stars exploded in his head. He swayed, blood trickling from his nose, the ground spinning crazily beneath him. A bat screamed past his head—or was it inside his head?

Where had that fool gone now? Ravenhurst wondered dimly, straining to see through the darkness.

Then it did not matter, for the ground was rushing up to meet him.

23

Hobhouse uttered a long, hoarse sigh of satisfaction. Swaying slightly, he looked down at the viscount's motionless body stretched out before him on the cold ground. Only then did the Angel's majordomo turn and begin to weave an unsteady course back the way he had come, a tight smile on his lips.

"Oh, don't worry, he's far from dead," he told Peale, who was hovering nearby. "More's the pity, too, for never a man so deserved to die as he does. But I'll not wear the title of murderer, not even for the likes of him. And you tell Ravenhurst this," the battered servant said coldly, raising a bruised fist before the valet's face. "Tell him I said to stay away from the Angel in general and Miss Leighton in particular." Hobhouse's voice flattened. "Or next time I *will* kill him."

With stiff pride, the weary fighter tugged on his black coat and arranged his torn, dirty shirt. Blood oozed thickly from a cut at his temple and his right eye was swollen nearly shut, but he gave no sign of noticing.

At the rear door of the townhouse he stopped, swinging around slowly. "Come to think of it, the same warning holds for you, Peale. Don't think I haven't noticed you and Letty Glossop sneaking about, smelling of April and May."

The valet's immediate stiffening was all the confirmation Hobhouse needed.

* * *

The return of the Angel's majordomo provoked a flurry of excitement. His eye swollen completely shut, he wobbled through the kitchen door, barely able to keep to his feet. Soon, however, he was basking in the adoring attention of Letty and two tittering kitchen maids, while Edouard stuffed precious chips of ice into an oiled cotton bag for a cold poultice.

Tess's fingers trembled as she bathed Hobhouse's raw temple. " 'Twould serve you right if you couldn't see for a week," she snapped, anxiety making her voice sharp. "I never thought to see such behavior—not from *you*, Hobhouse! A grown man, you are, and yet acting like a sulky, bad-tempered schoolboy. You look ghastly!"

Hobhouse stared at the range for a moment, his eyes distant and cold. "Ah, but you should have seen how *he* looked when I finished with him. Knocked the bloody bas—brute right out cold."

Tess sniffed the air suddenly. "Never tell me you've been drinking, Hobhouse?"

"Sober as a sexton, miss."

"Well then, whatever possessed you to—"

"No concern of yours," came the flat reply.

Suddenly Tess froze, her hands tense on Hobhouse's swollen forehead. "Who was it?"

"I don't believe I'll tell you that, either."

"It—it wasn't . . ." Her voice trailed away.

"Like I said, miss, I don't mean to give you his name."

A slow, wicked smile began to snake across Tess's lips. "You didn't," she whispered.

Hobhouse shifted, looking up at her with an expression of aggrieved innocence. "I don't have the slightest idea what you're talking about, Miss Tess." But an answering smile began to twitch at his mouth, and a look of unholy pleasure brightened his battered features. "I'll tell you this much, though. That's one bastard who won't be troubling folks around here anymore."

At that same moment, Lord Ravenhurst sat scowling in the kitchen of his town house while his tight-lipped valet pressed a slab of raw beef to his employer's swollen temple.

"Ouch! Damn it, man, watch where you're shoving that thing!"

"I beg your lordship's pardon," came the stiff reply.

Ravenhurst's eyes flickered. Peale never called him "your lordship" unless he had fallen from the servant's good graces. "Who gave you this idea, anyway?"

"A London acquaintance of mine."

"His employer brawls a great deal, does he?"

"My friend is his own employer, as it happens. He manages a public house near Drury Lane, and his clientele often turns unruly."

"Well, his bloody cure is worthless, you can tell him that for me."

"Very little would help that wound, I should think," Peale said stiffly. "Except, perhaps, the passage of time."

"Then why are you grinding that cursed piece of meat against my head?"

"One must do something, my lord. Now, please stop twitching about like a distempered canine."

"Have I ever told you you're a bloody pain in the—posterior, Peale?"

"On numerous occasions, I believe. *Your lordship.*"

"Don't be a prig, man."

"No, your lordship."

Ravenhurst flinched slightly, even though Peale's fingers were careful at his forehead. "In fact, if you weren't such a damned competent manservant, I'd get rid of you tomorrow."

"Thank you, your lordship." The valet's tone was arctic.

"That, Peale, was no compliment."

"In that case, I withdraw my thanks."

Ravenhurst was still muttering beneath his breath when a muffled tap from the far side of the kitchen interrupted this bickering. A moment later Lieutenant Taft came into view, hat in hand, a sheepish expression on his face.

"Sorry to barge in on you this way, your lordship, but I knocked several times and no one . . ." His words died away as he took in the ugly bruises and cuts about Ravenhurst's cheeks and jaw. "Have you caught one of them, then?" he asked eagerly. "On the marsh, was he?"

"No, damn it, I did not catch a smuggler, Lieutenant."

"But—"

Growling a curse, Ravenhurst pushed away the raw chop Peale was still trying to maneuver into position over his forehead. "Well, Lieutenant?" he snapped.

"Sir?" The young officer frowned, totally adrift.

"What dire emergency has brought you barging in here?"

With a start the young officer collected himself, then dug into his pocket to remove a slightly crumpled vellum envelope with a large and very official-looking wax seal. "Oh, yes—this just arrived for you. From the Admiralty, by the look of it."

Wincing slightly, Ravenhurst uncoiled his long frame and came to his feet. His eyes narrowed. "I believe you are correct, Lieutenant. For once," he added, tearing open the envelope.

Silently he drew out a heavy vellum sheet and began to read, his face growing steadily darker.

For long moments he did not move, and then only to refold the sheet slowly. "Prepare a bag for me, Peale—only the essentials. Enough for . . ." He looked out the kitchen window toward the rear of the garden, frowning. "Five days, I should think." Still abstracted, he turned and strode away.

"But sir—"

The viscount did not answer, already at the door. His hands tightened, crushing the heavy vellum sheet into a tight ball.

Although the night's rest did little to pacify Tess's chaotic thoughts, it did wonders for her lithe, healthy body. Her fingers had ceased to throb and her strength, she discovered, was entirely restored.

It was only the visions that would not go away, forbidden images of calloused bronzed hands lying heavy against her tender skin, memories of a dark and savage hunger that could not be assuaged.

Torment beyond telling. Pleasure beyond enduring.

Nightmares, she thought desperately. *Always the nightmares.*

Outside her window the wind began to rise. High over the wealden hills, lightning crackled in a demonic arc.

It was time to go.

Tess's face, reflected in the mirror, was sheet-white, her eyes dark hollows. With cold fingers she pulled her black cloak, mask, and high boots from the locked trunk at the foot of her bed.

"Don't go, miss." His face shuttered, Hobhouse stared at her from the doorway. "It's turning up nasty out there. Half the men won't even muster on such a night as this."

Silently Tess turned back to the mirror and tugged on her polished boots. As she did so, she felt something cold hit her fingers. Her mother's medallion, she saw, the only item of jewelry salvaged from her father's greed. An amulet whose magic she had felt protect her on many occasions.

Her fingers stilled, then ran lightly over the deeply chased face. "I must, Hobhouse. You of all people know that. If I do not appear—if the *Fox* does not appear—then my power to command will be forever lost."

Frowning, she lifted the heavy chain and made to slip the medallion back inside her shirt.

With a hollow clatter, the silver ornament fell to the floor.

Tess shivered, feeling a hint of coldness creep along her spine. Coldness and something else . . .

Don't be silly, she told herself sharply, bending to pick up the pendant. *'Tis merely that your fingers are still awkward where the wounds have not healed. 'Tis merely the cold air that stiffens your joints and makes you clumsy.*

She did not believe in omens and portents!

Tess bent to pick up the fallen necklace. When she looked up she saw Hobhouse's anxious face reflected in the mirror just beyond her own pale countenance.

"Don't go," he repeated urgently. "Not tonight."

Tess's lips set in a firm line.

Outside, the wind flung itself at the roof, rattling the casement windows and howling shrilly.

Mocking her efforts to be brave.

Mocking her for saying there were no such things as omens.

Her eyes dark with determination, Tess lifted her thick flow of auburn curls and thrust the cold medallion beneath her shirt. "I shall be back before dawn, Hobhouse. Tell Letty to listen for me at the passage."

And then, with a wild swirl of her long black cloak, she was gone.

He did not notice until a few minutes later. It was the fierce burst of lightning that first revealed the loss to him. In the storm's unearthly, phosphorescent flare Hobhouse saw something glitter beneath the corner of the bed.

Grim-faced, he bent down for a closer look.

Tess's medallion! The chain must have slipped free again when she pulled on her cloak.

He ran for the passage, calling her name hoarsely.

But he was too late. Far below he heard the *whish* of a door closing.

In his fingers the amulet grew heavy, cold emanating from its deeply indented center. Cold that pierced straight to Hobhouse's heart.

"God be with you, Miss Tess," he whispered to the dark, silent passage.

A thousand times between Mermaid Street and the cove, Tess thought of turning back. And each time she forced herself to do precisely the opposite.

There were men relying on her, after all. Families to be fed.

And somewhere a traitor conspiring with England's enemies? a hard voice mocked. *Carrying gold to feed Boney's troops?*

No, she must not think of that. It simply could not be true.

As if somehow sympathetic to her mood, the night turned wild, rain flung down in raw, sullen sheets. There was no moon to give guidance or comfort this night, only a lashing wind off the Channel.

Over Tess's head a giant arc of lightning exploded, bathing the chalk cliffs to the west in an unearthly silver flare. Quickly she reviewed her plans. The lugger's cargo tonight was China tea and

French brandy. Long-oared rowing galleys were to meet the ship beyond the breakers and take on the customary quota of tubs and chests. Only this night, Tess had made a slight revision in her usual plan.

This night two bands had been dispatched to receive cargo, one at the Dymchurch seawall and the other far to the west, at the narrow shingle below the unstable chalk cliffs.

Tess had been most careful in her instructions to both: each group thought the other was waiting inland to receive the contraband.

Only two men in each party knew the locations in advance. And one of those men would be the traitor who had told Hawkins where to wait for them before.

She shivered as icy fingers of rain stabbed her neck. Her eyes narrowed, she strained to pierce the sullen darkness, whose shadows held a hundred places to hide.

What if the traitor had already spilled his secrets? a cold voice asked. Were Hawkins's men waiting for her even now?

If so, she would know it soon enough. It was a terrible risk, but a necessary one. She had to know whom she could trust.

Frowning, Tess slipped on her whiskered mask and fought her way forward through the lashing rain. She had tethered a horse on Pett Level for her return, but the rest of her journey must be on foot. One slim figure made less of a target for a party of ambushing officers, she thought grimly.

Just then the wind caught the hem of her cloak and twisted the fabric around her legs, hobbling her so that she nearly fell.

Her face paled, but her chin rose in defiance. She would not turn back, not tonight or any night! She would show *him*. She would show them all!

Aye, they would soon learn that it took more than a few drops of rain to stay the Romney Fox.

They were waiting for her just beyond the labyrinth of canals at the edge of the Level.

Hawkins and forty men, muskets and pistols trained.

Someone had indeed betrayed her, Tess realized, but who? The foul-mouthed Ransley? Or was it John Digby? Both men had been told of the landing site here at the base of the cliffs. But where were the extra guards she had ordered posted? Why hadn't they alerted the group sooner?

As a precaution, of course, she had altered the real meeting point by some distance so that the lugger would be out of sight in the event of just such an ambush. Her men, those few who were taken, would be discovered cargoless, therefore, and it was hardly a crime in England to meet on the beach at night.

But Tess had not counted on Hawkins's ferocity.

"Shoot to kill, men!" he roared. "The more the better."

Then there was no more time to think, for the preventive force plunged forward in a human wave and the night exploded with shouts and cursing. Dark shapes scrambled over the beach, some fleeing toward the narrow steps twisting up to the top of the cliff, others stumbling west toward the gap in the rolling downs.

"Stop them, damn ye!" Hawkins pounded down to the beach, clutching a long-barreled flintlock carbine. "Force the scum back to the water!"

Two struggling shapes rushed past Tess. In an indistinct tangle of thrashing arms and legs, they tumbled to the sand nearly at her feet, so close she had to jump to avoid being felled herself.

That swift motion was her undoing.

"By God, there he is!" Even as he spoke Hawkins was lowering the muzzle of his long, lethal carbine. "Give yourself up, ye bastard, and I just might let ye live till morning!"

There were more dragoons coming down the beach now, hailed by Hawkins's shout of triumph. Soon she would be surrounded, Tess realized. Spinning about, she made for the only possible route of escape—the dark, snarling waters of the Channel.

"Fire, damn ye!"

A musket ball whined past her ear, and then another. Zigzagging sharply, Tess ran toward the edge of the beach, where the sea churned up in iron-gray plumes of spray.

Ten feet. Nine.

Yes, just maybe. God willing . . .

Something white-hot and savage ripped into Tess's shoulder and she sank her teeth deep into her lip to keep from screaming. Blindly she lurched on toward the water.

Seven feet. Six.

"Get him!" someone shouted behind her. "Five hundred pounds on the bloody Fox's head!"

Beneath her feet the texture of the sand changed, now hard packed, and dense. From here she could almost see the lines of foam tossed up by the breakers farther out.

She was ready to fling herself into the water when she saw the little skiff, nearly hidden by a rock a few yards out. In the ragged space of a heartbeat she registered the long, powerful oars, the kegs scattered in the stern.

But even as she saw it, Tess realized the vessel held no hope of rescue for her. Not with Hawkins only yards behind her. No, she must dive deep and swim underwater for as long as her breath would hold.

Praying that he sent no one after her.

Then she was at the water's edge, dragging in a last, choked breath before she flung herself forward into the pounding surf. Down she fell, blackness closing around her, so icy that her body quivered and went rigid. A moment was enough to school her muscles to clumsy order, to force her hands to dig deep, her legs to kick with a wild strength born of desperation.

Above her head she saw the outline of the bobbing skiff, heard the muffled *ping* of musket balls hitting the water. Almost free, she told herself.

And then with a deafening roar the darkness around her exploded into daylight, into a million furious suns, into a churning chaos of waves and flame. With savage force she was thrown from the water and hurled through space, the air ripped from her lungs.

A moment later darkness rushed back, pounding furiously over her, roaring in her ears, surging behind her throbbing eyes, squeezing through her veins.

This is where I die, she thought dimly.

And that was the last clear thought Tess Leighton had.

PART TWO

If you meet King George's men, dressed in blue and red,
You be careful what you say, mindful what is said.
If they call you "pretty maid," and chuck you 'neath the chin,
Don't you tell where no one is, nor yet where no one's been!

  Five and twenty ponies,
  Trotting through the dark—
  Brandy for the Parson,
  'Baccy for the Clerk;

Them that asks no questions isn't told a lie—
Watch the wall, my darling, while the Gentlemen go by!

—Rudyard Kipling

24

One by one the angry human sounds ceased. One by one the dark, cursing figures lumbered away across the sand.

The beach grew still, left once more to the creatures who knew it best.

A pair of kestrels darted down from their nest in the chalk cliffs, skimming over the waves and sailing south. A nightjar began to pipe the first tentative notes of its strange, churring song.

The wind was shrill and the air sullen, but to these creatures of the beach it was of no importance. The weather was not their enemy. Nor the darkness.

Only man was an enemy.

Engaged in digging a hole, a sand lizard paused, his head erect and wary. His long tongue darted out, twitching as he sniffed the sharp wind.

Out to sea, somewhere beyond the breakers, a black shape floated to the surface with a faint, muffled splash. Silent and unmoving, it rocked upon the fierce swells, barely visible in the midnight world of sea and cloud.

After several moments, the sand lizard turned back to his work. This was no business of his.

Slowly the dark shape drifted south, out into mid-Channel, where it was soon swallowed up by the unleashed fury of the storm.

* * *

Something was wrong.

He knew it with every raw breath he drew. He felt it in the sharp tug of the canvas overhead and the shrill creaking of the timber beneath his feet.

Legs braced, brow furrowed, the *Liberté*'s bearded captain stared north, where a bank of running, sullen clouds veiled the chalk cliffs of England.

"Mamm de Zoué," he muttered beneath his breath, enjoying the hard, angry bite of the Breton words against his tongue. Tonight their harshness suited his mood perfectly.

Mother of God, but something was very wrong.

Swiftly, with the fluid grace of a man raised from infancy to know the pitch and roll of the sea, the rugged captain crossed the deck and began to haul himself up the mainmast rigging.

Knowing it was not the slashing rain that bothered him, nor even the driving wind.

It was something out there in the darkness, something he could not see but could only feel, with all his seaman's keen instincts.

Ragged lines of lightning cut through the sky to the north, and for an instant he saw the ghostly silver curves of the English cliffs. But he saw nothing else, no sign of skiffs or smugglers' galleys. No hint of Revenue cutters.

A giant wave hit the *Liberté* broadside, sending the mast dipping dangerously. Locking his hands in the straining cable, André Le Brix wrapped his powerful legs around the mast and waited for the returning roll. Then, laboriously, he began to inch higher.

Rain whipped his face, but he pushed on grimly, narrowing the distance between himself and the topgallant yard.

A bolt of lightning exploded into the water nearby. Hearing the sizzle and pop of steam and churning water, he thanked God that it had not struck ten feet closer.

Then his cold fingers touched the rigging of the highest yard, and he was straining to pull himself up onto the rain-slick beam.

"Hard about, Padrig!" he roared against the wind's fury, knowing his seasoned first mate had probably done that already. A moment later he heard the protest of canvas and timber as the sleek brig's bow turned into the wind.

They were well past the middle of the Channel now, near enough to see the ghostly outline of the English cliffs. The captain's eyes narrowed, probing the darkness. He wished he'd thought to bring his viewing glass up with him.

But the flinty-eyed Padrig, amidships, was better prepared. When the next bolt of lightning split the night, the first mate was ready, searching the churning waves ahead with glass in hand.

"Duzé!" he cried. "There—to port."

At the same instant André glimpsed the dark, bobbing shape surrounded by scattered fragments of wood and other debris. Remnants of brandy kegs? he wondered. If so, why all the way out here?

"An Aotrou Doúe," the corsair whispered through lips suddenly dry. *God in Heaven.*

Then he was swinging from cable to cable, flying recklessly down toward the deck, which pitched eighty feet below him.

Even before his feet hit the deck his voice thundered from the rigging. "Hard a-lee, Padrig. Prepare to lower a skiff!"

First came the roar of the wind, then the crashing of a restless, turbulent darkness. Gradually Tess grew aware of the slap and pitch of fierce, relentless seas.

But it was the chattering of her teeth that woke her completely, followed by the lurch of her body as she was lifted and then slammed down, wave after wave.

I can't see, she thought, feeling the terror begin, feeling the darkness gnaw at her.

Her hands flailing, she struggled to keep afloat amid the churning seas. A narrow piece of timber brushed past and she seized it desperately.

In a flood the memories returned—the crash of splintering wood, the blinding explosion that had catapulted her from the water.

But where was she now? She could see no light around her, only an endless, sullen wall of darkness.

A wave broke over her head; choking, she clawed her way back to the surface. Over the howl of the wind she thought she heard a shout. Or was the cry only in her mind?

Her cold fingers tightened on the splintered length of timber that had saved her life. She was afloat now, but just barely so, and Tess knew nothing could help her against seas such as these. Just as certainly, she knew that her strength was waning. In a few minutes she would no longer be able to hold on. Her shoulder was throbbing, and already her fingers were growing numb.

Something brushed against her foot, something long and very powerful.

Tess bit back a sob.

Kicking wildly, she clung to the spar, trying to swim against the storm-driven swells.

Again it came, a creature down in the darkness, nudging her leg.

Then Tess screamed as searing agony ripped through her ankle. The thing was jerking her down! Sputtering, she dropped her head into the inky water, struggling to wrench free of that deadly grip. But her fingers were numb and she could feel nothing below the tops of her boots.

Again came the savage tugging, and this time Tess was pulled deep below the surface. Her lungs burning, she strained to kick back up, but in the darkness she could tell direction only by her body's buoyancy.

Then her face broke free. Wildly she choked down a lungful of air, only to feel herself wrenched down once more, both legs captured this time.

Blind with fear, she kicked and flailed, struggling against the power of her unseen enemy. Somewhere nearby she heard water slap against timbers. Against the scream of the wind she seemed to hear a faint shout.

Something—someone?—churned toward her. A muffled voice rose against the fury of the storm.

"Diaoul!" Another hoarse shout, closer this time.

Tess heard a splash; her shoulders were seized in cold, granite fingers.

"Ne me repoussez pas!" The command came in guttural French.

"Stop—stop fighting me!" This time the order came in English, so heavily accented as to be incomprehensible if Tess had not already understood the French.

"I'm—I'm caught!" she cried in French, thankful for her mother's lessons and the hours of practice with Edouard. "Something—down there. At my feet!"

Her only answer was another splash. Hard hands probed her legs, working their way to her ankles. Suddenly something wrapped around her knees and burned a raw path down her legs, dragging her ruthlessly into the depths once more.

Kicking wildly, Tess tried to pull to the surface, but the hands tightened, jerking her even deeper.

He was trying to kill her! she thought wildly.

Air—she must have air!

Then she was rising, the unseen hands beneath her, forcing her to the surface. She was close to unconsciousness when her head finally burst from the waves.

"Vous vous accrochez à quelque chose—une corde, peut-être. Laissez-moi—"

She was caught on something, had he said? So the man was French. A smuggler, perhaps? Or was he a sailor upon one of Napoleon's vessels, waiting just out of sight somewhere in the storm?

The rest of what he said was drowned out by the crash of a wave breaking over Tess's head. Once again she was jerked downward. Pain slammed into her like a fist, as something—a rope perhaps—sliced through her shredded breeches.

Then she was free, choking and sputtering to the surface. Her lungs burning, she dragged in blessed gulps of air.

But where was her rescuer?

She fought to penetrate the raging darkness around her, but in the storm she could make out nothing. Then her fingers brushed a thick coil of rope, the sort used to lash a string of bobbing, four-gallon brandy kegs and sink them below the surface, away from prying eyes.

A raw, hysterical laugh burst from Tess's lips. She had nearly been drowned by a cache of contraband sunk from a weighted line!

It was a common enough practice along the coast; when interrupted by the inopportune arrival of a Revenue vessel, a band of freetraders could hurriedly dispose of their cargo, then grapple it up later at their leisure.

Tess's wild, high-pitched laughter rose on the wind; she could feel the ragged edge of hysteria inching over her.

Another wave smashed down, dissolving all traces of humor, leaving her weak and trembling with the thought of just how close she had come to dying.

Now she was alone once more, her rescuer still somewhere below, drowning after he had saved her.

Choking, Tess caught the end of the thick coil and plunged back down into the murky depths. Deeper and deeper she went, feeling her way along the strand until her lungs were on fire and her head threatened to explode. She was just about to turn back when she felt his hands, then the heavy rope that twisted around his wrists, capturing him in its deadly embrace.

But Tess had strung such lines herself on occasion. Well she knew how iron bars were secured to the strand. With a strength born of desperation, she strained to free the rough hempen knots.

Her air nearly gone, she tore at the heavy coil, feeling the skin flayed from her fingers. Flares of light burst before her eyes, but still she struggled on, tugging desperately.

From the suffocating blackness around her came muffled, deathly sounds. Just like in the tunnels, she thought wildly. Here, too, death crept close with cold, probing fingers.

Can't give up one more try.

The strand moved; the knot parted slightly. Her lungs burning, Tess tugged on the rough coils, praying all the while.

Suddenly the rope went slack in her fingers and the water began to churn as she felt the Frenchman kick free and strain to the surface. A moment later he reached down to tug her up after him.

They broke free to raging waves and a furious, slashing wind, but never had Tess been so thankful to feel the sting of water on her face. Without his help, she would still be trapped in the frigid darkness right now.

Again, Tess considered how close she had come to dying. A tremor shook her.

"*Aman,* Padrig!" the Frenchman cried, his voice low and hoarse.

From the distance came an answering shout, and then a flood of guttural speech.

Not French, Tess thought, frowning. Not German.

Breton, perhaps? The rocky, jagged coast of Brittany jutted out into the Channel not too far to the south, Tess knew.

From somewhere to her right came the rhythmic slap of oars. Without warning she was caught and hauled from the water, her ribs slammed against a rim of wood for an instant before she fell sputtering to the bottom of a boat, fighting and straining like a landed fish. A moment later she heard the sound of her rescuer's body slapping down beside her.

Once again there came the strange, guttural speech—Breton, she was certain of that now. The oars dipped deep and she felt the boat pitch, then turn sharply.

With trembling fingers, Tess dashed the cold spray from her face, but in the storm's slashing fury she could still make out nothing. Shivering, numb with cold, she fingered her raw ankles where the submerged line had burned away a wide strip of skin.

But she was alive! Tess told herself. That was all that mattered. Suddenly the boat rocked crazily. Harsh shouting erupted nearby and booted feet hammered across a wooden deck. Without warning, someone caught her hands, hauling her upward until she fell onto a man's broad chest, the breath knocked from her lungs.

She heard a harsh gasp. Big fingers gripped her shoulders.

"*Sainte Vierge!*" came the hoarse exclamation. "By the Virgin! You?" her rescuer stammered in broken English. "I mean—you are *female?*"

Tess could not keep from laughing at the raw shock in the man's voice. The sounds rippled on her tongue, growing louder and wilder, until somehow she found herself sobbing.

The next thing she knew, she was crushed against the hard breadth of the Frenchman's body, her tear-stained cheek against his thick woolen sweater as he carried her across the pitching deck.

The captain of the *Liberté* smothered a curse. *"Bihan?"* he whispered in shock and disbelief.

She was here? But how? And why?

His blood froze as he thought of how near the reckless Englishwoman had come to dying, tossed about in the treacherous mid-Channel currents—and just how close he had come to joining her.

Anger and fear struck him speechless for a moment, his fingers tightening on her slim waist.

Diaoul, but she raised the fires of fury in him. His face hardened to a stony mask. The devil! Seconds more and the sea would have claimed her, and him along with her.

But she was strong, *Dieu merci!* Yes, thank God, for in the end she had saved him, much as his vanity hurt to admit it. For the cursed rope had snagged, trapping his wrists and snaking around his throat until it choked him. Even now he could feel the bite of its rough coils and the fiery welts where it had gashed his neck.

He would be hoarse for a week, the captain thought with a black sort of humor, knowing it could have been far worse. Now he owed this woman his very life.

For some reason he found the thought did not disturb him. *Eh bien, bihan,* for that I will repay you very well, the Frenchman decided, smiling darkly in the gloom of the passageway outside his cabin.

"Bi—bihan?" the woman in his arms whispered, breaking into his reverie. Her storm of emotion spent, she looked up at him, white-faced and weak.

But very brave, André thought, for she covered her fear well.

"Ma petite," he answered roughly. "Little one—my little one."

"You—you speak English?" Tess asked, trying to keep the tremor from her voice.

"Un peu. A little only." His voice was low and dark, his consonants hard and strange-sounding. "Better you use French."

"Vous êtes Breton?" she asked, complying.

"Oui, Breton," he said warily, surprised that she should have

discovered so quickly. His eyes narrowed. She was sharp, this one. He must never forget that.

Tess frowned, feeling his rough, oiled-wool sweater scratch her cheek. So he was from Brittany. She had not missed his moment of hesitation, nor the wariness in his voice. The man was almost certainly a smuggler, then. Wariness would be part of his stock-in-trade. Many of his fellow Bretons plied the seas between France and England, she knew, since the rocky soil of their homeland was little suited to farming.

Now she owed the man her life. What payment would such a corsair expect in return? Tess shivered suddenly and felt his calloused hands tighten on her shoulders.

Beneath her cheek the heat of his powerful body seeped out, warming her frigid skin. "Where—where are you taking me?" she asked breathlessly. Since her French was better than his English, she decided to speak in French.

The big, work-roughened fingers splayed open. For a moment he did not speak.

"To my cabin, I think, *bihan.*"

Tess gasped, balling her hands into fists and shoving wildly at his chest. Had she escaped the sea's wrath only to encounter a greater peril?

"I'll pay you to take me back. English gold guineas or French *louis d'or*—whichever you wish. One hundred pounds. T-two hundred. Only n-name your price," she rasped.

Her rescuer's granite fingers did not loosen. "No price, *bihan.* We do not turn back. There will be Revenue vessels prowling the Channel tonight, even in these stormy seas," he added grimly.

"Please!" Tess cried, panic tightening her voice. "You must take me—"

"Impossible." The word was a wall of granite, his refusal harsh and irrevocable.

Her thoughts awhirl, Tess listened to his boots crash upon wood. A door slammed back against the wall. The place he carried her was unlit, and she frowned, able to make out nothing, no detail of place or furnishing.

She seemed to drop, her back sinking into softness. A bed? *His* bed?

A moment later the rough fingers left her. She heard a faint scraping noise nearby.

"Please," she whispered. "L-light me a lantern, at least."

She heard his sharp indrawing of breath. "Lantern?" he repeated slowly.

"Do not ask me to explain. I—I cannot. Only do this one thing for me, that I beg of you!"

The corsair did not answer.

Tess felt her skin prickle, knew the first, faint brush of small, hairy bodies. *"Please!"* There was an edge of panic to her voice now. She had no strength left to hide it.

"In the name of God, *bihan,*" the Frenchman said slowly, "I have just done that very thing."

25

"**D**o not mock me, sir!" Tess cried wildly, her fingers digging into her cold cheeks. Huge and haunted, her eyes stared up into the flat, colorless void before her.

"There is no mockery in what I say, *bihan*. Look there, upon the table."

Tess looked—and saw nothing but a sullen wall of darkness. Choking, she closed her eyes, feeling stark, shapeless terror hammer at her chest. "You lie! There is no lantern—nor even any table! There is nothing here at all!"

Strong, calloused fingers swept the tangled curls from her forehead. Carefully they probed her brow, tracing the curve of her hairline.

"Open your eyes, *bihan*. Look at me," the captain commanded.

Blinking, rigid with shock and fear, Tess did as he ordered.

And absolutely nothing changed.

The wall of darkness before her did not waver, but mocked her openly now. Angry and threatening. Deadly.

"Dear God," she whispered, feeling cold fingers of fear plunge into her spine.

"Again," the hard voice ordered. "Look here."

She blinked. Was there a faint flickering of the shadows before her?

"I hold the lantern but inches from you, *bihan*. Can you see nothing?"

Her choked silence was answer enough.

"Diaoul!" the Frenchman muttered hoarsely.

Numbly Tess remembered the wrenching fury of the explosion that had tossed her from the water. Ashen-faced, she relived those long moments of terror when blackness had first engulfed her. Ripping the air from her lungs, tearing the light from her eyes.

Blinding her.

No, Tess thought wildly. It could not be! She shuddered, feeling tears prick her eyes even as the awful certainty of her condition settled over her. But like a wild and proud animal, she refused to allow anyone to witness her terrible weakness.

"Leave me," she whispered, feeling the last shreds of her self-control begin to slip.

"Gwellañ-karet . . ." His voice was harsh, taut with emotions he could not express.

This time Tess did not question the unfamiliar phrase he used. Now she was lost to everything but darkness and the wild hammering of her heart. A whimper broke from her dry lips. "Go. Just --go. P-please!"

Long heartbeats later she heard his boots squish away over the timber floor. With a hollow crash the door slammed shut.

In cold, angry waves the shadows closed in upon her. She tensed, already fighting the memories, the old fears.

But this time Tess knew she must fail.

Pressing icy fingers to her mouth, she turned her face into the pillow, trying to drown her choking sobs.

Trying, and failing.

Silhouetted against the flickering light of the cabin's single lantern, the tall, bearded Frenchman watched, silent and unmoving. His long shadow fell over the bed, slanting unseen across Tess's rigid body.

A thick beard the color of a crow's wing could not conceal the granite set to his weather-hardened face. With keen eyes narrowed, the captain of the *Liberté* kept a grim silence, watching the auburn-haired beauty on his bed thrust a trembling fist to her mouth and give way at last to wild sobs that seemed torn from her very soul.

Impossible, André thought, speechless with shock. His big hands clenched and unclenched at his sides, throbbing with pain where the cursed line had caught him. But the Frenchman thrust away his own pain, too stunned by the revelations of the last minutes to think of anything but the wounded woman before him.

Sainte Vierge, she saw nothing! It was nearly impossible to believe! Yet every stiff line of her back and shoulders, every choked sob bore witness to the fact.

Blind. His beautiful, wild sea gull. . . .

The Frenchman's eyes went black and bottomless as he stood with his back to the cabin door. So proud. Too proud, she was—just as he would be, were fate to strike him such a blow.

His thick brows knitted in a scowl. His fingers itched to hold her and soothe her, but he knew in her pain she would open herself to no one. So instead of doing the things he ached to do, the captain forced himself to turn away and lower his tall frame noiselessly into a big, battered armchair near the door. All the time his smoky eyes were fixed upon her trembling body.

Slowly her pain became his pain, her terror his. With fierce concentration he fought to draw the dark thoughts from her, to take her despair onto his broad shoulders, willing her to find solace. His face harsh with strain, he struggled against the urge to crush her to him and comfort her with the heat of his big, rugged body, burning away her fear in the dark, elemental fires he yearned to kindle within her.

But he did not, for the captain had watched this woman very well and knew all of her pride and all of her stubbornness. Now, he knew, she would never accept what he offered.

He smothered a harsh curse, his big hands balling into fists.

How many weeks he had stalked her, this reckless, haunted creature of marsh and sea—this creature so like himself! Yet somehow she seemed always to elude him, with rare cleverness and a fine bravado.

Now it seemed fate had trapped her, tossing her into his net at last. But he would find no pleasure in possessing her, he knew. For the Englishwoman would never trust him now; never would she drop her guard, not blinded and terrified as she was.

Go to her, a harsh voice urged. *Give her light and warmth. Give her the strength of your hard, sea-toughened body.*

But that was the last thing she would accept.

And so, his jaw locked in a hard line, he sat before her, silent and determined. If she needed him, at least he would be there.

I will not press you, mon coeur, the man with the bleak eyes swore silently. *Not yet, for you are proud and stubborn, nearly as untamed a creature as I. Yes, I must be careful to give you time and much space.*

To cage such a one would kill her, André knew. So he would give his sea gull freedom for now, until she came to know the sound of his rough voice, to crave the comfort of his big, strong hands.

And then he would give her all those things, along with others she did not yet realize she needed. Yes, *par Dieu,* with infinite strength and ruthless patience he would force this stubborn woman to love him. Soon she would wear the marks of his passion, just as he would wear hers.

For she was a storm in his very soul, like the raging winds that raked the rocky Breton coast. She was fury and torment, but also life force itself, the blood in his veins, the heat in his loins.

And he would have her, André swore, blind or no.

But before he could tame his reckless *Anglaise,* he knew somehow he would first have to heal her.

An hour passed, and then another. In silence the captain waited, relieved when the woman's breathing finally grew calm and steady. Her raw sobs stilled, she fell at last into an exhausted sleep.

Like a dark, radiant flame her hair spilled over his pillow. The sight of it burned his eyes, making his groin tighten and swell, making him ache to run his fingers through its rich fire.

But he could not, for it would spell the end of everything he had worked for. So he only waited, hoping that a merciful God would hear his prayers.

In the middle of that dark vigil, André heard the sound of quick steps in the passageway, then a tap at the door. He shifted quickly, and with an odd grace for one so tall, he slipped to the door and nudged it open.

Immediately his finger flew to his lips, cutting off his blond giant of a first mate in mid-question.

The captain gestured over his shoulder. "Quiet. She is sleeping," he whispered in the guttural tones of the Breton tongue, ignoring his first mate's patent curiosity. "At long last, thank the good Lord."

Something about his tone made Padrig Le Braz study his captain's face. "So this is the one," he said slowly. "This is the Englishwoman who haunts you day and night. The one who makes you curse at the crew and draws you away from us for days at a time. She has thrown a powerful spell over you, my friend. But so the witch Viviane did to Merlin in the Forest of Brocéliande. And I bid you not forget what happened to *him*," Le Braz added grimly.

"She *has* bewitched me, hasn't she?" the captain whispered, leaning his tired shoulders against the wall of the narrow passage and closing his eyes. "I find her at last, only to discover—" His eyes flashed open, dark with pain and anger. "She sees neither me nor anything else, Padrig. *Gwerhéz Vari!* By the Holy Virgin, she is blind!" His voice checked. "Blind. My *bihan*," he whispered.

A harsh silence fell over the two men standing in the darkness.

"You—you are certain of this, my friend?"

"As sure as I am of my own breath, my own heartbeat," the captain said bleakly. "Why would she lie about such a thing?"

The blond giant shrugged his shoulders. "Women! What does a man ever know of them?"

"This one, I do know, Padrig. Her, I know very well. And this woman would not lie about such a thing, believe me." Stiffly, André raised a hand to massage the aching muscles at the back of his neck. He frowned, realizing he would have to change out of his sodden clothes before he developed a lung contagion.

The *Liberté*'s first mate frowned, little liking the despair he saw cloud his captain's tired, bearded face. *"Mamm de Zoué,"* Le Braz muttered suddenly as his eyes dropped to André's hands. "Mother of God, did you not know you've cut yourself?"

At Padrig's startled question André looked down at his fisted hands. For the first time, he noticed the sweater's blood-stained sleeves. It must have been that weighted line. Strange, until now he hadn't even noticed.

"Both hands, by the look of it," the giant Breton first mate said roughly. "Now, get forward with you and let me clean those wounds before they begin to fester."

Slowly André straightened, weariness and something darker etched in every despondent line of face and body.

Yes, those are my wounds, he thought bleakly. They hurt now, but in time they will heal.

Hers, he feared, would be for always.

Beneath Tess the *Liberté* pitched and rolled restlessly, battered by wind and wave. Somewhere behind her eyes she felt a sharp, throbbing pain, which quickly coursed into her whole head.

But now weariness became her friend, drawing a curtain over her senses. Pressing cold fingers to her eyes, she allowed exhaustion to creep over her, and at some point sullen shadows gave way to the darkness of dreams. Yet even as she slipped into a fitful sleep, Tess was tormented by dim, faceless images.

The faint, flickering shadows of people and places Tess knew she would never see again.

With a reckless, barely curbed energy, André Le Brix paced back and forth along the wave-washed deck, struggling to concentrate on the exacting work of guiding the *Liberté* through the roiling seas.

"Close haul those main topgallants, Le Braz!" he thundered. "And mind the set of that jib. We've hard seas to cross before we make the Morbihan."

Immediately the first mate relayed the orders to the crew. The two-masted brig lunged forward, her neat bow churning up spray in solid gray sheets.

The sight should have brightened her captain's mood, giving him a fierce pride in his sleek, responsive vessel.

But now he could think only of the woman below in his cabin. And he was experienced enough to know that his preoccupation might mean the death of them all, ere this storm was done.

For somewhere out there in the distance lay the Isle of Ouessant, its craggy coasts jutting into the sea like deadly, taloned fingers. For good reason sailors called it the Isle of Dread.

One mistake, one miscalculation, and ship and crew would disappear forever, smashed against those granite rocks and treacherous reefs, their bones snapped like straws while the *Liberté* was splintered into uncountable pieces.

Qui voit Ouessant voit son sang. The ancient warning came back to André suddenly.

Who sees the rocks of Ouessant sees his own blood.

Blackness.

Dear God, she was sinking, choking in it.

For a moment Tess could not move, paralyzed by fear and dreams, defenseless against the shadows of her mind's creating.

A choked sob burst from her lips. She must escape! Anything was better than being locked here, left to die in this suffocating darkness.

The answer came to her then.

Yes, that must be it! The Frenchman had lied! He had lit no lantern—it had all been a trick to confuse her!

Above there would be light and air and laughter.

Yes, above!

Awkwardly she stumbled from the bed, nearly falling as a wave overtook the vessel from port to starboard, rocking it wildly. She swayed, struggling for balance as the returning roll overtook them.

But she did not fall. A moment later her fingers sought—then found—the wall.

Cautiously, she inched forward.

Toward the stairway. Toward the light.

* * *

Cursing silently, André fought to penetrate the chaos of wave and cloud before him. The storm was far from over, that much he knew. He could feel it in the protesting creak of the timbers, in the snap and tug of the close-hauled canvas overhead, in the *Liberté*'s fierce surge through churning seas.

From the deck before him came a muffled shout. He swung about, scowling, only to freeze a moment later, his eyes fixed on the slim form clinging precariously to the bowsprit. Her hands were tangled in the forestay and bobstay lines, which crisscrossed the long horizontal beam extending from the front of the ship.

"She came so quiet we did not see her," the first mate shouted as the captain thundered across the pitching deck.

"Diaoul," André whispered. The devil himself! She would be thrown off any second. She could never hold against such a storm.

Already his feet were hammering toward the bow. "Get me a line, Padrig!" he shouted over his shoulder. "Then shorten those sails and hold the ship as steady as you can. I'm going after her!"

Even as he spoke, André was inching out onto the wave-washed bowsprit, where the Englishwoman clung to the jibboom, spray flying in her face.

"Come here to me, *bihan,*" he said hoarsely. "Over here. Put out your hand and I'll help you." All the time André spoke, he was edging closer, crawling perilously along the top of the wide beam.

"Stay away!" Tess cried, a hoarse edge of madness to her voice. "You lied! There *will* be light, I know it now. If only I can—"

Just then the *Liberté* pitched sharply, rising with a steep wave and then plunging low into the trough, its bow submerged.

For long, terrifying moments, the woman disappeared from sight. Desperately André hauled himself toward the end of the bowsprit. Only a few feet more . . .

Without warning the great horizontal beam tore free of the waves, and sheets of spray lashed aft into his face. Frozen with fear, the Frenchman watched one of Tess's hands ripped free. She dangled perilously, her feet dragging the tops of the swells.

Mother of God, give her strength! As he inched farther and farther out over the water, André could hear her choked sobs. *Let me be in time.*

Then he was above her, his long fingers gripping her wrists and dragging her up onto the jibboom.

They had no time to spare. Any minute there would come another wave, and this one might sweep them both away.

"Don't fight me, *bihan,*" he ordered hoarsely, edging back along the beam, one arm wrapped around her waist. "This is no weather to go inspecting cables. In fairer seas I'll show you my vessel, and with pleasure."

But even as André spoke, his luck ran out. He saw what he most feared—a giant wave sweeping up out of the black waters before them, like the avenging hand of God.

"Hold on, sea gull! Hold on for me!"

With a savage roar the wave slammed across the *Liberté's* decks. A thousand gallons of water swept over its captain, pounding into his nose and mouth, in a fury so fierce, he was nearly ripped from the bowsprit. For an eternity of blackness he fought to hold himself—and her—to their precarious perch.

Then they were free, the cold wind lashing their faces.

They must jump, he knew it then. It would be a gamble at best, but the next time he could not hold them. And death would be there waiting.

"Put your arm around my shoulder," he ordered roughly.

This time the Englishwoman obeyed.

Grim-faced with strain, the captain rose to his knees, pressing his calves tightly to the beam. Slowly he pulled the woman up beside him until her chest met his thighs. His body taut, he pulled her choking to her knees, then awaited his moment, hoping his strength would hold.

Another giant wave began to rear up from the blackness. He felt the boat begin to dip.

The wind howled in his ears, angry and shrill, the despairing voice of all sailors ever lost at sea. Desperate ghosts, they fought him now, hungry to drag the living down to share their watery grave.

But they would not have him, André swore. Nor would they have the woman locked in his arms!

Praying to a whole host of Breton saints for one bit of luck, he pried her fingers free of the bowsprit and jumped.

26

The wind ripped at their clothes, lashing foam and salt spray in their faces. For long, wild heartbeats it seemed that they hung suspended, halfway between ship and sea. Then the Frenchman's sodden boots slapped down against the rough timbers and went skittering over the deck.

Padrig was there to catch them, his great hands outstretched, hauling them to safety just as another wave crashed over the bow and nearly washed them overboard.

"Not only is she beautiful, but she is mad, this one," the first mate muttered darkly. "Take care, my friend."

Tiredly André cracked open one eye, then struggled to his feet. "That you may be certain I will do, Padrig. Directly after I tie her up and give her the soundest beating of her life."

The giant's green eyes sparkled for a moment. "I wish I could be there to see you try, my captain. But a cable does not exist that will hold this one, I think!"

Just then a harsh cry exploded from the high rigging. "Reefs, Captain. Dead ahead!"

Instantly the two men's humor vanished, like smoke on the wind.

"Take her below, Padrig," the captain ordered tersely, already staggering back to his post at the wheel. "And this time, see that she *stays* below."

* * *

"What—what are you doing?" Tess rasped dizzily in French as she was hauled over a broad shoulder and carried across the deck.

Her body was still numb and frozen, her senses fogged. But one thing she knew: He had not lied. The light was gone from her world, and now all she had left were the nightmares.

"Padrig Le Braz, first mate, at your service. And what we are doing is going below, *Anglaise.*" The French words rumbled like thunder, deep and guttural, from the chest beneath her ear.

"Laissez-moi! Leave—leave me alone!" Tess cried wildly, struggling against her jailor. But it was useless, she soon realized, hearing the deep boom of his laughter as his boots hammered down the companionway.

Once more, Tess was deposited ignominiously on the captain's bed, her shoulder throbbing where Hawkins's ball had savaged it. At least the salt water would have scoured it clean.

"You're too small too keep and too valuable to throw back, *bihan,*" the seaman said wryly. "For some strange reason the captain seems to want you, so it's here you'll stay. *Dieu,* but he's waited long enough to have you."

"W-waited?" Tess stammered. "What—what are you talking about?"

"You never realized, did you?" There was rough satisfaction in the first mate's voice. "He is a clever one, my captain. *Mais oui,* for weeks he's tracked you, sea gull. *Dieu,* the danger he risked! But the madness was upon him and there was no turning him back. And your fat customs inspector soon discovered that our captain is not so easily caught." Padrig's voice grew thoughtful. "Nor were you easily taken, *bihan.*"

Tess's mind reeled. The Frenchman had followed her to Rye? All the time he had been planning to abduct her?

"Do they hurt?"

"Hurt?" Tess repeated blankly, her thoughts still whirling.

"Your ankles."

"I—I hardly felt them," she said slowly. "With everything else . . ."

"Yes, it must be a great shock. But life may hold far worse than this, *bihan.* André is a good man, a man who has twice saved your life. Remember that, especially now, when he is so hard. It is only his way of fighting the hold you have over him."

"But this hold is not of my choosing, don't you see?"

Tess heard him sigh and could almost see his broad shrug. "As to that, which of us ever chooses love? No, like the moments of our birth and dying, love must find us."

Tess's breath caught. *Love?* But how was it possible? This man André was a stranger. Yet it seemed he knew her very well.

"The captain is a man driven, *bihan.*" Once more she heard the first mate sigh; she could almost see him frown, trying to explain. "Still you do not see? *Diaoul!* I will try to explain it then. For a while it was enough merely to know that you were there. To know that he could catch a glimpse of you once in a while—your face at the window, your outline as you did some errand in the town. Perhaps, in a way, to him you were the island always just beyond the horizon. The one schooner he always sought, swift and sleek, to outrun all others. *Dieu,* but it is hard to put in words—" He broke off for a moment. "You were that which André could never attain, I think. For a while, just knowing you existed was enough."

A silence fell. Tess found herself waiting with growing urgency for Padrig to continue, her shoulder, her inn, and even her sightlessness temporarily forgotten. "And then?"

"Then everything changed. His feelings became something black and demanding. Distraction turned to—obsession."

Tess heard the creak of the armchair as he lowered his large body down into it. The Breton's voice, when he continued, was grave.

"Through the narrow streets he walked, waiting beneath your window when the nights were still and moonless. Madness, it was, even for such a man as André, who knows no fear of man or beast. And the risks he took—" Padrig broke off then, muttering something in Breton. "Twice he was nearly taken, once by that fat customs officer and another time by the English riding officers. All because of this wild, reckless fever that was upon him. A fever for you, *bihan.*"

"I—I never knew," Tess breathed.

"That, too, was by his choice. He never planned to go so far, I think. Not at first, anyway. And then later—"

From the deck above came a harsh shout, followed by the muffled thud of pounding feet.

The first mate smothered an oath. *"Ile de l'épouvante,"* he said flatly.

"The Isle of Dread," Tess translated. "But what—"

"The Isle of Ouessant, wrapped half the year in fog and all the rest in wild, snarling seas. And somewhere out there are the black reefs, *bihan,"* Le Braz muttered darkly, a hint of fear in his voice. "Only feet beneath the waves they crouch, baring savage teeth that will claw a man apart before he can voice a terrified scream. Even in clear, fine weather these waters are treacherous." His voice turned hard. "But in such a storm as this, with the captain so distracted. . . ."

Trapped in the darkness, Tess found her hearing grown keen and intuitive. "And you feel guilty," she said slowly. "You should be up on deck with him, not here with me." It was a statement, not a question.

"Oui, that I should, by all that is holy!" Padrig's guttural voice was harsh with anger. "But he told me to stay, and stay I will," he growled. "Unless . . ."

"Unless what?"

"Unless you give me your word you will not run again, *bihan."*

In tense silence Tess pondered his question, knowing somehow that the Breton would accept her word as her bond. Aware, too, that if she kept him here they might all die.

She drew a long breath. "Very well, I give it. Only"—her fingers twisted restlessly in the folds of the cold bed linens—"d-don't lock me in."

"You give your word? An oath before God?"

"I—I do."

"Then there is no need for locks," the first mate said simply.

Tess blinked, hearing the sound of liquid sloshing against glass.

"Though I doubt you'll do as I advise," the *Liberté's* first mate continued, "I've put a jug of St. Brieuc cider here beside you on the table, along with a filled glass. It will warm you a little, and a sweeter drink of bottled sunshine you'll never taste, sea gull."

"M-merci," Tess said flatly, knowing she could not drink, that the cider would be no more than acid and ash in her mouth.

The armchair creaked; she heard his boots thump across the wooden floor. The door opened, loosing a fierce gust of frigid wind upon the room, then snapped shut with a sharp bang.

Leaving Tess alone, once more. But just as Padrig had promised, there was no grating of a key in the lock.

Even as his boots echoed up the companionway, Tess began to shiver. Around her the darkness shifted, inching closer. At the same moment, the ship groaned and shuddered, tossed like a straw in the storm's fury.

The shadows grew solid, reaching out for her. Her lips white with strain, Tess pressed cold fingers to her mouth to keep from crying out. Outside, the wind howled shrilly, clawing the sails.

She would be caught here for the rest of her life, she thought wildly. Trapped forever, just like in the dark tunnels . . .

She froze, feeling the faint prickle of a fat, hairy leg.

No, she told herself wildly. They could not be here. That was a different darkness, a different dream.

Near the floor she heard the faint rustle of small bodies. A ragged whimper escaped her lips. Fight it, she told herself. They are only in your mind.

Ashen-faced, she drew back against the wall, drawing her legs up protectively against her chest. She began to shiver, slightly at first, then in wild, convulsive bursts.

She tried hard to resist; every shred of reason and willpower went into the struggle. But these were not creatures that could be bested by the force of logic or light.

These were beings sprung from darkness and imagination; their power was not to be confronted directly.

Shuddering, Tess found the coverlet and pulled it around her. A moment later she heard the first tiny body thump down upon the linen and whisper across the bed, creeping toward her.

The last vestige of warmth drained from her face.

Must—light a candle! she screamed in the silence of her mind.

Then her slim body froze, as Tess realized this time there would be no reprieve.

Never again would there be light to free her from her nightmares, for the light was gone from her world.

This torment would be forever.

"Hard a-lee, Le Fur! We're past the worst of it now, I'd say. Just hold her steady till we reach the Morbihan." Wearily, André reached up to his temple, raking dark, wet strands of hair from his face.

He was tired, by the devil, weary to the very bone. He was also near to freezing in these sodden garments.

But they had made it! he thought triumphantly. The black teeth of Ouessant's reef and rock were behind them.

As he motioned for the short, wiry Le Fur to relieve him at the wheel, André's gaze fell upon the giant form of his first mate, who was standing at the base of the mizzenmast, haranguing two crewmen on the proper way to shorten a topgallant sail.

A raw curse exploded from André's lips.

"What the devil are you doing up here, Le Braz?" Already the captain was pounding toward the companionway. "I told you to stay below with *her!*"

Padrig's expression turned dark; only with a fierce effort at control did he manage to keep the fury from his face. "I was needed *here*, Captain. And the woman gave her word she would not bolt again. I believed it would be enough—"

"Well you were wrong, damn you!" Grim-faced, André thundered past the frowning first mate, feeling the cold breath of fear. She slept by candlelight; he had seen it often enough as he stood in the shadows beneath her window at the Angel. How could he have forgotten?

Especially now, when she was trapped sightless in a world of cruel shadows.

He plunged down the narrow stairs. Behind him Padrig ground out a hoarse curse, but André did not even hear. His whole being was focused on the cabin at the end of the passage.

With cold fingers he flung open the door.

"Bihan," he whispered, his eyes darkening. "In the name of God, what have I done?"

Her body was rigid where she pressed against the wall, her face stark with pain and fear. Tears streaked her ashen cheeks, and welts lined her lips where she had bit down to keep from screaming.

But worst of all were her eyes. Huge and fixed, they stared blindly into empty space, dark wells reflecting an infinity of pain.

"Mamm de Zoué," the first mate breathed as he entered the room behind André.

"Rum, Padrig!" the captain snapped. "And bring me that chest from our last crossing." As he moved toward his bedraggled captive, the bearded Frenchman knew a moment of raw fear. Fear greater than any he had known in the fury of the storm. "I'm here, *bihan,*" he whispered slowly in English, his voice still rough from the pressure of the line that had wrapped around his throat. "You are alone no more, *mon coeur.*"

His face locked in hard lines, André touched her rigid knee, which was wedged against her chest.

What if she did not respond? What if he had come too late?

"Talk to me, sea gull," he said urgently, switching to rapid-fire French. "Tell me what you see in your darkness. In the telling, dreams may sometimes lose their power."

Did her slim frame quiver slightly?

"Come, little tigress, where is your fight?" he urged relentlessly. "Yes, it's a fight I want from you now. Scream at me! Swear and bite, even! Anything but this, for this is not the woman I dragged from the sea."

Did another spasm shake her? His face dark with worry, André sat down on the bed; cupping her shoulders in his hard hands, he drew her against his chest.

She did not speak. Her white fingers lay clenched and unmoving in her lap.

They were still sitting that way when Padrig returned with a jug of rum a few minutes later. Silently, André tilted some of the fiery liquid between Tess's taut lips.

She coughed and tried to twist her head away.

"Come, *me kalon*. Drink for me, my heart. It will warm you, and bring you light in your suffocating darkness." Once again André raised the glass to Tess's mouth. This time when she tried to strain away, he caught her face and held her still until she choked down the fiery spirits.

Her eyes flickered closed, and when again they opened, fury blazed in their gray-green depths.

Relief flooded through the *Liberté*'s captain. This was a beginning at least. Now, if only he could make her a bit angrier . . .

"Come, sea gull, you are slighting good rum, and that I will not tolerate, not when I and my crew have gone to such trouble to acquire it." Catching Tess's cold cheeks beneath his fingers, he forced her to swallow another mouthful. "Drink all of it!"

Tess's slim fingers shook as she tried to shove him away. Her right hand curled into a fist and she struck out wildly.

Her aim, André discovered to his chagrin, proved far too good. Shards of pain shot through his jaw where her blow struck home.

"*Diaoul!*" he rasped, turning swiftly and crushing her to his chest while he struggled to capture her flying fists. "By the devil himself!"

"L-let me go! I won't do it, do you hear? N-not again!" She was fighting in earnest now, her eyes huge with terror.

A muscle flashed at André's jaw as he studied her white, tear-streaked face and blind, tormented eyes.

Not this way, *bihan,* he answered silently. In the name of God, I swear I never meant it to be this way.

May heaven forgive me, the hard-faced corsair thought, reaching for the rum.

Only this time, the drink was for him.

Swiftly he tilted the jug, swallowing long and hard, trying to forget the dark terror he had seen in his captive's blind eyes.

"No more rum, sea gull, that much I promise." His long fingers covered her palms and pressed them flat against his chest. "And no more dreams in the darkness. Not when I am here, *me kalon*. With me you will know only starlight and midday sun. No more shadows. Only this . . ."

André's breathing was harsh and ragged in his ears as he

slanted his lips over hers, fighting to quell his wild haste, his fierce desperation. Haunted by the thought that three times he had nearly lost her, twice to wind and wave, and the last to something far worse.

Then the hot silk of her lips met his hungry tongue and he was lost, well and truly. Groaning, he wrapped his mouth around hers to taste her better, feeling as if he had been cast tumbling and churning into stormy seas.

Drowning—and knowing he never wanted to come back up again.

Mamm de Zoué, but she was a tempest that shook him in blood and bone. Even now, when their kiss was no more than scant seconds old, the Frenchman knew he would never get enough of this woman.

Suddenly all the fierce tension of the last weeks roiled and exploded within him, erupting in a savage wave of passion. His senses aflame, he stroked her, tongued her, nipped her.

With every second he grew reckless for more, until he thought he would drown in the sweet taste of her rum-laced mouth, her skin scented with lavender and sea salt.

Head on, the *Liberté*'s hard-faced captain faced the storm, feeling desire pound through him in fiery waves.

Oh yes, he would have her, his *Anglaise.* Whatever it took, he would do. And when the time came at last, his possession would be fierce and total.

For now and forever.

Darkness everywhere. Terror choking her. And yet—

Something sharp and bristly scoured Tess's cheek, and suddenly her lips were bathed in fire. She choked back a sob, struggling wildly against the madness hammering in her head.

Whimpering, she waited for the angry bite of tiny jaws, her fingers opening and closing convulsively.

Instead her hands met hot flesh and straining muscle.

More dreams, a cold voice whispered. *This dream more dangerous than all the rest.*

Frowning, Tess brought a trembling hand up to cup her throbbing cheek.

And realized dimly that her pain came from the rasp of bearded skin, not from the tiny, clawing night creatures.

A dream? If so, how sweet!

Once again, fierce and sleek, the dark fire raced across her lips, making her tremble—not with pain or even fear, but with a hunger she barely understood.

Deep within Tess an answering heat stirred to life. Her muscles tensed; she felt heavy and light at the same moment. Her emptiness grew into a raw ache.

"S-stop," she rasped, afraid of this storm he loosed upon her, afraid to feel so keenly when everything in her life had taught her that to feel opened one to pain and torment—that every pleasure carried anguish in its wake.

Without warning, Tess thought of the man who had been her first love, the man who had shattered her every hope of happiness. His kisses, too, had left her hungry and aching. Yet in the end that desire had brought her nothing but torment.

No, she must never yield!

"So cold, you are," the Frenchman whispered, his full beard grazing her lips. "But not for long, *bihan.*" His big, calloused fingers began to ease open the buttons on her damp shirt.

Tess gasped as dreams shifted and took solid shape in a stranger with hard, hungry fingers. Understanding his intent, she recoiled, going rigid in his arms.

He only pulled her closer. "Hush, my heart. Padrig's brought fine silks and velvet, and I would see you clothed all in sapphire and crimson rather than in these sodden breeches." All the while he spoke, André's strong fingers continued to move soothingly, weaving a spell upon her trembling flesh.

With a faint rustle the cold, wet shirt slipped from Tess's shoulders.

Cool wind played over her naked skin and panic rose to choke her. How could she? Shameful, it was. Madness itself! "Stop! You must not—"

He stilled her protests with the dark fury of his mouth. This time all gentleness was gone from his touch. Now he neither asked nor coaxed, but drove his hot tongue deep within her, molding her to his hard desire as he set the brand of his passion upon her.

Outside, the wind howled, lashing the unfurled canvas, sending sea spray exploding over the decks.

Or was it Tess's heart that pitched and foundered so?

Terror seized her as she felt the granite walls about her heart tremble and sway.

Don't let go! Don't allow yourself to feel, for feeling makes you weak, and weakness is deadly, the beginning of all pain.

But the strong hands whispered a different truth, their touch rich with the promise of magic. Captive in the thrall of André's hypnotic caress, Tess moaned, buffeted by this storm of new sensations he unleashed.

With exquisite agony his calloused, work-roughened fingers lifted her hair and scraped the tender skin of her neck. His bearded cheeks scrubbed her delicate jaw.

And this infinity of small torments only added to her dark stirring of pleasure. As if he knew this, André let his mouth hover until Tess whimpered with need; only then did he finally slant his face down, crushing her lips and devouring her very soul.

Was any of this real? she wondered wildly. Yet how could she stop her heart from racing when he touched her so, when her body turned strange and reckless, hungry for this sweet torment he brought her?

"No more shadows, *gwellañ-karet*. Only heat and storm, my love," the man beside her whispered hoarsely, his lips brushing the swell of her lips, the silken lobe of her ear, the vein that throbbed at her neck. "Nothing else matters but this. There is no past and there will be no future for us, only this sweet, effortless *now*. Open yourself to it, *bihan*. Share it with me."

His breath was hot, sweet with the hint of rum. His fingers, tracing electric patterns on her sensitized skin, were hard and sure.

Dangerous. Infinitely dangerous.

He knew exactly what he was doing, Tess realized. While she . . .

She was adrift, yawing like a rudderless ship.

With a little sob she tried to push him away, shoving at his hair-matted chest. Desperately she tried to clear her whirling thoughts, to summon the will to refuse him.

But the *Liberté*'s captain ignored her struggle. Cupping her bare shoulders, he began to feather tiny kisses down her neck and across her collarbone, groaning as he felt her skin heat beneath his mouth.

"Flame for me, *bihan*. I've waited so long . . ." Lower he moved, and lower, his touch all storm and wonderful torment. His beard scraped against the upper swell of her breast, sending shockwaves plunging to Tess's very toes.

"Dear God, André, you—must stop. I—I cannot think when you touch me so!"

"Perhaps there is no need to think, *bihan*," the captain muttered thickly, his voice as rich and dark as the rum he had pressed upon her earlier. "Perhaps, for now, to feel is enough. To feel this, and far more than this. Although for myself," he muttered hoarsely, "*this* is nearly more than I can bear."

Heat flooded Tess's face as she understood his meaning, for the rigid line of his aroused manhood was wedged against her thigh.

The captain laughed grimly, his finger tracing her hot cheek. "You blush, *Anglaise*. And it makes you beautiful beyond describing."

Stunned by the harsh tenderness in that gravelly voice, Tess cocked her head, desperately wishing she might see his face.

And in that moment a whole new world of sensation opened up to her.

Blind, she began to know the texture of sound and scent, the many shades of darkness. Sightless, she learned to draw upon new, exquisitely sensitive ways of sensation.

That was the first lesson the Frenchman taught her. In its wake Tess found herself reckless, wanting to savor all the other things he could show her.

"André," she said huskily, unaware that her thoughts had found expression. Her head fell back, her lips accidentally brushing his neck.

He shuddered. Tess felt his broad chest rumble as he groaned.

At first she stiffened, stunned by his immediate response. Then she began to smile, heated by this discovery of her power over him.

His fingers dug deep into her hair, tugging her head back and forcing her face up to his scrutiny. "So this pain of mine amuses you, does it?" His fingers tightened and he muttered a rough curse. "You learn quickly, sea gull. Too quickly, I think." His tall frame shifted and she felt him move away.

The cold that swept over her then was stunning. She shivered, feeling darkness press close.

But an instant later his powerful body fell hard and heavy against her, crushing her back onto his bed.

Suddenly the darkness was gone, swept away by a world of rich textures and infinite wonder. When his warm breath played over her naked skin, Tess realized he was studying the heart-shaped birthmark above her right breast. Her chest rose and fell erratically; she could almost feel the dark force of his eyes as they raked her skin.

Once more her face flooded crimson. What sort of wanton had he made her? She must stop now, before it was too late!

Wasn't it already too late? a mocking voice asked.

"André—"

"Say my name again, *Anglaise,*" he growled.

"An-André, please—"

"Yes, *mon coeur.* Pleasing is what this is all about. Pleasing you, my heart, which pleases me. Feeling a storm rage through me when you say my name just so. *Diaoul,* but I think pleasing you is the thing I shall do very best in this world."

Then he made truth of his words. His rough tongue lapped one soft pink nipple, making Tess gasp with pleasure. Shuddering, she tried to bite back a moan.

Her breath fled.

Her reason followed a heartbeat later.

His crisp beard chafed the soft swell of her breast, an exquisite counterpoint to the velvet torment of his wet, circling tongue. Then, with a growl, his lips captured her hot, aching center.

Tess whimpered, cast blind and yearning into a sea of raw sensation. Torment and pleasure flowed together. Around her the world shimmered and dissolved.

"Dieu, que tu es douce," the Frenchman whispered, his mouth never leaving her skin. "So soft. I think I could drown in your softness, *bihan."*

At the sound of those rough-tender words little suns exploded behind Tess's eyes, bathing her in golden light.

And by some strange alchemy the softness beneath his mouth swelled and grew taut, forming a perfect, furled bud. Tess knew and did not fight it, felt and did not wonder, cast adrift, awash in dark pleasures which left no room for logic or reason.

Groaning hoarsely, he closed his lips over her, drawing her deep within his mouth, his tongue moving hard and wet upon her aroused skin.

No more shadows, Tess thought dimly. Not with this man. With him only heat and storm—only desire in wild, cresting waves. Maybe, as he had said, that was truly enough.

She did not know how he had found her or why, only that this feeling between them was keen and blinding, sweeter than anything she had ever known. Almost, it was enough to make her believe in trust again.

"Tell me you want this, *mon coeur,"* André growled. "Tell me you feel this storm as I do."

Don't answer, a cold voice warned. *Trust no man.*

For a wild moment Tess thought of Ravenhurst, and a tremor passed through her.

The Frenchman missed neither the shiver nor the hesitation. "Is there another?" There was steel in his voice now, along with a dark edge of fury.

Cold tendrils—was it reason returning?—wrapped around her heart.

How could she explain that pain may bind as keen as pleasure; that first love, though long dead, must cast a shadow upon all future joys? In the end what could she say, especially when she understood it so ill herself?

The silence between them stretched out, brooding and potent;

every second that Tess hesitated allowed grim thoughts of fear and regret to rush between them.

"Do you love him?" the man above her rasped.

"No!" Sharp and swift, her answer shot back. Too swift?

Tess heard his quick intake of breath. There was the barest tensing of the hard fingers at her breast. Her heart began to hammer wildly. She could almost hear him scowl.

"I wonder."

"How can it matter? There is no past—you said so yourself."

Crushed against his lean body, Tess felt as much as heard his slow sigh. "It seems, *bihan,* that I was wrong."

"But I—I owe you my life."

"You *owe* me nothing," the hard-faced corsair answered savagely. *"Owing* is not what I want from you!" He jerked his hands away from her aching skin and did not reach for her again.

Tess was stunned by the fierce regret she felt when he did not. A moment later she felt him shift, the bed rocking as he surged to his feet. His boots hammered across the floor toward the door, where he halted.

"When I take you, *Anglaise,* it will be by your choice and your asking. At that moment there will be no other man's name on your lips, no other man's face in your thoughts, do you understand me? I will have you no other way!"

The door grated on its hinges, then crashed shut, plunging Tess into blackness and cold once more.

27

Long the explosive crash of wood upon wood echoed through the still room.

Numbly, Tess sat up and jerked on her shirt, her pulse still racing wildly in her ears. What had this man done to her? Dear God, he was a stranger. How could he exert such power over her?

Unbidden came the memory of his hard hands, ruthless and expert upon her heated skin. Even now the thought sent her blood roiling thickly through her veins.

Was this the thing that zealots raged against from their pulpits, and mothers warned their daughters against? Or was she truly going mad at last?

Her fingers traced her lips, swollen from his kisses, then jerked away as if burned. In that wild movement, she brushed against the cool rim of a jug.

The cider Padrig had left.

Sweet as bottled sunshine, he'd called it. She could use some sunshine right now, Tess thought. Anything to drive away her demons.

Her trembling fingers cupped the cold stoneware. Pressing her eyelids closed, she brought the vessel to her lips.

It was her first taste of smoky Breton cider, and the brown liquid was light and fire, all bubble and bite, just as Padrig had said.

Quickly Tess gulped down another drink. The darkness withdrew slightly, less suffocating; the terror did not hang so heavily on her now.

With a watery, defiant sniff she sat up and pulled the heavy jug onto her lap. Another gulp—she felt a heat begin in her belly, curling pleasantly through her arms and fingers. She wiggled her toes, enjoying the warmth that radiated out to their very tips.

You, my girl, are halfway to being tipsy, she thought. *Well, and so what?* she answered that censuring voice. What did it matter after all that had happened to her?

She forced down another long drink, and then the thought came to her. Why did she remain here in the dank silence? She was not one who could be commanded by anyone, not even by an arrogant captor like her Frenchman.

She would prove that to him now!

The wind was screaming as Tess crept along the companionway. She would have to be more careful this time, she decided. Once already she had made her way past the crew, but after suffering their captain's fury they were certain to be more vigilant.

With the wind lashing her auburn hair about her face, she stumbled on deck, realizing she was nearly three sheets to the wind herself. But the cider made her feel alive, as if the darkness could no longer harm her.

Overhead she heard the sharp snap of canvas sails, and somewhere to the left the crash of cable hitting the deck.

"Check that jib, Le Fur!" she heard André shout in guttural French from the bow.

Her heart pounding, Tess sank back into the companionway; when the brisk activity on deck continued uninterrupted, she edged forward once more.

And promptly tripped over a low chest of some sort, just as a wave swept beneath the boat, throwing her sideways, then onto her knees. Tess swayed dizzily, stifling a giggle. *Not tipsy, but in truth drunk as a lord!*

And loving every minute of it, she thought defiantly, shaking the wild curls from her face, enjoying the bite of the wind upon her flushed cheeks.

In that same instant, hard fingers circled Tess's waist, and she was hauled against a massive granite chest, the breath driven from her lungs.

"What in the name of all the saints are you doing up here?"

Tess hiccupped slightly. Her lips curved in an unsteady smile. "I am merely taking a turn around the deck, Captain. You did not restrict me to your cabin, as I recall." Her fisted hands fell against her hips as she glared up at the place where she imagined his face must be. "Not that it would have made the slightest difference if you had."

"You crazy little fool! In such a storm—" André's voice checked audibly and he sniffed the air. "You've been drinking," he said in disbelief. *"Diaoul,* but you're drunk!"

Tess tried to effect a nonchalant shrug. "I rather think I am. I should hope so, after all the trouble I've put into the effort. Of course, I can't really say for certain, never having attained that hallowed state. Perhaps if you'll describe—"

"Padrig!" the captain thundered, his hands clamped like a vice about her waist. *"Get—her—below!"*

But Tess found she didn't wish to return to the darkness, not when she was enjoying the fine fury of the wind, the salt tang in the air. And yes, she was even enjoying this skirmish with the *Liberté*'s high-handed captain. Why should she go back to the stagnant silence below deck?

Her hands on her hips, her shoulders set stubbornly, she faced the Frenchman, all fire and defiance. "I won't go!"

"Oh, you will, my little spitfire, or you'll feel the wrath of my hand upon your tender *derrière!"*

Tess's mouth tightened. Some mad demon made her press closer to him, rather than pull away.

The captain's smothered gasp was all the encouragement she needed to continue.

Her breasts brushed his chest; the soft curve of her belly teased his granite thighs. A dark jolt of pleasure shot through her when she felt him harden and swell at this intimate contact.

"What trick is this?" André demanded harshly, his fingers splaying apart and biting into her waist.

Tess did not answer, too awash in the storm that surged through her blood, in the lightning of his touch. Her head fell back, and her long hair blew wildly about his back and shoulders, lashed by the wind until it wrapped the two of them in its dark, living flames.

Somehow, of their own volition, Tess's moist lips parted. It was madness, of course, but suddenly she didn't care.

She smiled.

André groaned.

Then without warning she was jerked from the deck and crushed against the length of his unyielding frame, her thighs locked to his while he set the brand of his manhood upon her.

She should have been afraid, but somehow she wasn't. Instead she felt only a strange, urgent hunger. Wanting—she knew not what.

"You play a dangerous game, sea gull," André said hoarsely. "In this world of wind and sea, *I* am master. Whatever I want I take. Do I have to prove this to you? Do you wish me to take you here and now?"

Stop, fool, her last vestige of reason cautioned. But Tess did not listen, for some dark, primal instinct made her yearn to coax another raw groan from his lips. Once more she moved, sliding against that part of him which jutted and swelled in evidence of his desire.

This time his oath was long and very fluent.

Her breath fled as she was swept up into his arms. The schooner pitched sharply, tossed by a mountainous wave. Or did she only imagine it, buffeted as she was by wild, restless currents of longing?

She never knew the answer, for in the next instant there came a shrill shout from the rigging. Around her the night exploded into sound and movement.

"Hard about!" André roared in French, lapsing into rapid-fire Breton with his next breath.

From the aft deck came the roar of a cannonball and the splintering of wood. Beneath their feet, Tess felt the deck shudder.

The *Liberté* was being fired upon!

" 'Tis the cursed English Revenue vessel returned!" Padrig called, somewhere to her right.

"Damn it, Padrig, get her below!"

But before the first mate had time to react, another volley whined through the air. Suddenly Tess felt her captor's arms go rigid.

"An-André?" she gasped. "What has happened? Are you hurt?"

The Frenchman muttered darkly beneath his breath. "No, *par Dieu,* but this vessel of mine is sore wounded. We'll be lucky to make the Morbihan alive."

Dimly Tess felt giant hands lift her from him. André's voice seemed to retreat.

"Come, *bihan,*" the first mate said brusquely at her shoulder. "When lead is being traded, the deck is no place for a lady. Not even such a wild lady as yourself."

The jug was rattling on the table as Padrig opened the door to the captain's cabin. Tess felt the hull creak protestingly beneath her feet. The *Liberté* began to shift direction.

A moment later another shell exploded, and the sleek schooner bucked wildly, rocked by aftershocks.

"I must go!" Already Padrig was running back to the companionway.

Tess's fingers gripped the cold bed linens. Dear God, were they now to die at sea?

Suddenly her fingers froze. An English Revenue cutter, had Padrig said? Why had she not thought of it sooner? Yes, she must try to get up on deck before—

But her wild hope died stillborn. Even if she somehow managed to signal the English vessel, what could they do for her? Lower a boat—in these stormy seas?

Her shoulders slumped. *Impossible.*

For who would care? She was a passenger aboard a French smuggling vessel, and that made her equally a criminal. "But I just happened to be floating in the Channel when the *Liberté*'s notorious captain found me and forced me aboard."

Tess frowned, well able to imagine their disbelief at such a tale.

No, they would never believe her. And rightly so, she thought grimly, all too aware of the secret of her own identity.

A single tear slipped to her cheek, and she swept it away angrily. Dark and clouded, her eyes probed the darkness, seeing nothing. Another shell exploded high overhead, and Tess flinched as the vessel pitched and shuddered.

No, she had no choice but to stay here and wait.

Hoping she did not die in the next few minutes, alone and forgotten in the darkness.

It seemed hours before the shouting stopped.

At last the scurrying steps slowed on the deck. For the first time Tess realized her hands ached where they lay clenched in the tangled folds of the quilt.

From somewhere aft she heard André shout a guttural order.

Was it her imagination or did the wind seem to drop, the seas to pitch less wildly?

Her slim shoulders quivered, throbbing with the strain of holding them rigid for so long.

Suddenly heavy footsteps hammered down the stairs; the door burst open. Tess heard the sound of struggling bodies.

"Let me go, damn you!" André's savage shout rent the air, more furious than any howling winds.

Tess frowned, unable to understand the guttural Breton words he spoke next. But his meaning was clear enough, and she was glad she was not the recipient of such wrath.

There was a dull thump, followed by Padrig's muffled grunt of pain.

"Can you truly"—more scuffling—"be so afraid"—one of them cursed harshly—"of one little circle of lead?" Padrig rasped in French.

"I'm afraid of nothing, Le Braz," André roared, "and well you know it! Now, let me get back to the deck, where I'm needed. We are not yet so far past the reefs, and that dungheap of an English Revenue vessel might still choose to come back for a second look."

"Not after the way you gave them the slip, my captain."

Padrig's voice warmed, laced with humor. *"Dieu,* but it was a fine thing to see. Me, I will tell my grandchildren about it some day."

"You won't live to have any grandchildren if you don't let me go!"

"Nor will you live if I do!"

Tess stumbled to her feet. "Stop it!" she cried, frightened to hear more straining, punctuated by harsh gasps and the furious rustle of clothing. Then muscle struck skin and bone. André growled a sharp oath.

"A thousand pardons, *mon ami,* but you are not long for this world unless Le Fur can dig that inch of lead from your leg. Already you are thick with blood!"

"You call this a wound, Padrig? Bah! It is no more than the prick of an old woman's needle!"

"For such a small thing, there is a very great deal of blood," the first mate said dryly. "Now go and lie down like a brave fellow. Your woman has graciously left the bed to your use. You wouldn't want to hurt her feelings, would you?"

Your woman.

Tess shivered. The words sounded so natural, so right somehow.

The sharp silence that followed Padrig's deceptively innocent statement was broken by André's taut indrawing of breath. "Bah, get your wretched carcass back up on deck, Padrig. And mind you keep those sails close-hauled! There'll be more rain before morning, unless I miss my guess."

"Oh, of a certainty, I shall be most considerate of your ship," the first mate murmured.

"One last thing, Padrig," the captain said brusquely. The next words were only for his mate, delivered in rapid-fire Breton.

When he finished, Tess heard Padrig cross the floor. The door opened and then the first mate strode off, shouting for Le Fur.

Tess did not move, feeling the captain's powerful presence with every nerve of her body. He was close, she knew; she could hear his harsh, unsteady breathing.

"Bihan."

One word. And yet in that brief utterance was packed a wealth of feeling: tenderness, triumph, uncertainty, and fierce male possessiveness.

Was there a trace of regret too? Tess wondered. She cocked her head, frowning at the darkness.

"Come and help me to our bed, sea gull," André ordered.

"I—cannot help you," she snapped, ashamed that she could not. Furious, suddenly, that he should ask the one thing she could not do. "In case you have forgotten, I cannot see," she added icily.

"Ah, but you can hear me, sea gull. Most important of all, you can *feel* me. Let that sense guide you to me now."

Her anger flared. Madness! she thought. And yet . . .

Slowly she began to inch forward toward the place where she imagined he stood, his harsh breathing a beacon. She could almost see his tall, muscled frame braced in the doorway, his arrogant countenance shuttered as he studied her.

The Frenchman made no sound to help her, Tess noticed, which only strengthened her angry resolve to succeed. Her senses reached out, probing the darkness, her nerves drawn taut as a marksman's bow.

Then she felt it—a strange, wild resonance that hummed in her blood, vibrating through bone and muscle.

That was the second lesson he taught her.

She stiffened, all her senses reaching out for him.

He was very close, she knew it now. When his ragged breathing stilled, it only confirmed her guess.

She edged slightly to the right. A warm current of air drifted across her flushed cheeks, stirring an errant curl at her neck.

A moment later her fingers grazed the curve of his muscled forearm, rigid beneath the wet wool of his sweater.

"Do you believe me now?" the *Liberté*'s captain muttered roughly. "You see—and you feel—far more than you know, *bihan.*" He swayed slightly and muttered a rough curse. "And it is for me, sea gull. Remember that. Not for him."

Without warning the Frenchman's arm slipped from beneath her fingers and he collapsed with a ragged groan upon the floor.

28

"**P**adrig!" Tess cried wildly, her trembling fingers searching for André's head. Kneeling, she crouched down and struggled to pull him onto her lap. "Anyone!"

It seemed an eternity before she heard an answering shout, and the drum of feet down the companionway.

"The man has no more wit than the backside of a sow!" an unfamiliar voice barked. "Help me get the fool into bed, Padrig!"

The captain's inert body was lifted away from her the next moment. She heard the two men grunt as they lowered him to the bed.

Tess's fingers clenched and unclenched at her sides where she knelt, rigid with shock, in the middle of the room. "What—what has happened to him?"

"An English musket ball lodged in his thigh, that's what," Padrig answered grimly. "Hit while he was trying to carry you below. Then the fool refused to leave the deck. Now he's lost a great deal too much blood for my liking. Le Fur?"

"Aye, Padrig. I'm ready."

"What do you mean to do?" Tess asked faintly.

"Le Fur will dig it out, while we pray that his hands are steady. Best that it be done now, while the captain's still unconscious."

Tess's hand flew to her mouth. A wave of guilt swept over her. When it had happened, he had been trying to carry her below, to safety. Had she not been on deck, he might never have been hit.

He might be safe and well right now, standing before her, baiting her with the fire and challenge of his rough voice.

Across the room came the clatter of metal. Tess heard a faint sucking noise, and then the awful rasp of a metal blade carving human flesh. André groaned, then muttered something raggedly in an incomprehensible jumble of French and Breton laced with an occasional English curse.

The sweet-sharp smell of blood filled the room, along with the acrid tang of sweat—the smells of sickness and fear.

Death, hovering close.

Tess's breath caught as she envisioned the nightmare scene—the big man struggling, the bed drenched with his blood as Le Fur probed for the hidden ball. Tess swayed, certain she would faint.

"Merde! He's waking, curse it! Hold him down, Padrig!"

"I can't, not with this candle in my hand. *Bihan!"*

White-faced, Tess slipped to the bed.

"Can you hold this? And keep it steady?" Padrig guided her fingers around the cold metal base of a candlestick. She heard him curse. "You're not going to let me down, are you?"

"I-I'm all right," she managed to answer. "Go on—quickly! The longer he bleeds . . ." She did not need to finish.

The dull scraping resumed. André muttered hoarsely from dry lips. Ashen-faced, Tess listened to the sounds of his struggling. Sweat trickled down her forehead as her face was bathed in heat and smoke from the candle.

Please God, she prayed. *Save him.* She must not lose this man whom she had only just found.

Suddenly Le Fur grunted in triumph. *"Ici, le diable!"* More scraping—then the sharp clang of metal falling against metal. "A real beauty, by all the saints! Lodged but an inch from his bone. And the devil's own luck that it went no farther."

"Well done, Le Fur. You've still the steadiest hands I ever saw." Padrig's voice warmed slightly. "But you'd best save that ball, for if I know our captain he'll want to inspect it for himself to be sure you didn't miss any pieces." There was a rich undercurrent of amusement in the big man's voice now.

Tess bit back an exclamation of horror. How could they laugh while their captain lay wounded, near to death?

Her heart pounding, she stared wildly in the direction of those light-hearted voices. "How—how can you speak so, laughing and teasing? Any minute he might—he might—" Suddenly her voice seemed to give way. Her knees threatened to follow.

"I'll take that now, *bihan,*" Padrig said quietly, removing the candlestick from her rigid fingers. "The captain will be fine, never fear. The man has the constitution of an ox. It will take far more than an inch of English lead to put him in his grave. And as for the humor, well, that is our way. It's André's way also. Now he must rest, but since every man will be needed on deck till we're out of these waters—"

Without warning the ship bucked sharply, and Tess was thrown back against the wall. She heard Padrig stumble, his foot striking the wooden bed frame with a dull thump.

"Which leaves no one but me," she finished. "Well, I can do this much for him, at least." Her voice was steadier now.

"Are you sure you are well enough to tend him, *Anglaise?*" Anxiety tightened Padrig's voice. "He may grow feverish. He is a big man—in such a state he will be hard to control."

"I am strong enough to manage one wounded and delirious man, I assure you," Tess snapped, with more confidence than she felt. "I may be blind, but I haven't lost the use of arm and limb. Though I might soon lose them," she added grimly, "if I continue to be tossed about in this fashion."

"I will leave you then. I am needed at the helm."

Tess felt a chair drawn up to her leg, and then Padrig pushed her to sit.

"Le Fur has cleaned him up and set on new sheets. You will find water and fresh linens there, by your right hand." As he spoke, Padrig guided her fingers to a stoneware basin on the table beside the bed. "I'll send someone down to help you as soon as we're farther south and into calmer seas."

A tense silence fell. She heard Padrig clear his throat sharply. His giant hand caught her slim fingers for a moment. "Watch him well, *bihan,*" he whispered roughly. "For me. For all of us. He is a man headstrong and harsh, unyielding as the sea itself, but he is the finest captain the *Liberté* has ever known."

Tess felt a sudden ache in her throat. "I—I will, Padrig," she whispered.

"God be with you, my captain and friend," the giant Breton said softly, and then he was gone.

The hours passed more slowly than Tess could have thought possible. For a long time the Frenchman slept although his rest was never still. He shifted constantly, muttering, driven by some nameless urgency.

Tess bathed his sweat-beaded face, speaking quietly. Her words and her touch seemed to soothe him. For herself, she found a certain solace just being with him, wrapped in darkness, rocked wildly in the blackness of night and storm, the wind howling outside the porthole.

And always she pondered the things that Padrig had said.

The *Liberté*'s captain, it seemed, commanded the respect, the love even, of his crew. Could such a man be a scoundrel?

She sighed, her thoughts awhirl. The last twenty-four hours had brought too many surprises. Her world had turned on its end, and now she must struggle to change with it.

The long hours passed, night shifting into day and then into night again, all unbeknownst to Tess, wrapped in the unyielding shadows of her blindness.

But she would find the fire again, she told herself. With him.

Her eyes flickered and then closed. Her head dropped.

She slept.

"Gwellañ-karet."

Tess awoke with a start to discover she was still sitting in the armchair. She frowned, furious at herself for drifting off when she should have been watching over the captain.

From the bed at her side came a muffled groan. She reached out awkwardly, trying to find him.

"Gwellañ-karet?" It was louder this time, more urgent, a long, ragged cry torn from his dry throat.

"I'm here, André." Tess's fingers curved over his forehead, sweeping back a long comma of thick hair. His beard scraped her fingers, dense and springy, and Tess found herself smiling, thinking what a sight he must look now. Was his hair black or brown? she wondered. And what color were his eyes?

But there was no time to ask, for she could feel sweat beading up over his face. She fumbled for a clean piece of linen and then ran it across his heated skin.

His hands caught her wrist, then tightened. *"Chérie*—is it—*you* —truly?"

"Of a certainty, my captain." Tess tried for bravado and hoped she succeeded. "And here I shall stay, until you are strong enough to prove a better adversary. You can offer me no good sport, you see, weak as you are now."

"I . . . must . . . not . . ." André's teeth grated audibly and he muttered something in Breton. Tess felt his head toss restlessly on the pillow. Suddenly he tensed. "Don't trust me, sea gull," he rasped. "Someday I shall leave you. In the end, the sea takes all who challenge it—even the best and the bravest, which I am certainly not." He muttered something she could not make out and pushed at her hands.

He must be growing delirious, Tess decided.

Then his reason returned. "The French call it 'she,' did you know that, *bihan?* Ah, but to the Breton the sea is always male. Angry, ruthless, untamable—just the way you make me feel."

With a harsh breath, he sat up, his hands groping for her in the darkness. "Where are you? The candle has gone out."

"Ici, mon cher corsaire." My beloved—the endearment slipped out unconsciously.

André's rough fingers cupped her shoulders. "Am I so, sea gull? You know nothing about me. I might be the worst slime of the Paris streets, for all you know. And yet you use such a term—" His voice fell away into a groan. He stiffened, smothering a curse.

"Hush," Tess whispered, trying to push him back down on the bed, knowing this struggle did his wound no good. "Perhaps I do not need to think. Perhaps"—she smiled faintly in the darkness and repeated his words of such a short while before—"perhaps, for now, to feel is enough." Emboldened, she took his hand and pressed it to the vein pulsing at the base of her throat. "Perhaps to feel is more than enough," she added softly.

Was it indeed only a matter of hours? It seemed to Tess as if a lifetime had passed.

She could almost see his faint, answering smile; his voice warmed with the dark promise of retribution. "For that bit of impertinence, I shall make you pay most dearly, *Anglaise.*"

Beneath her fingers André's muscles bunched and then relaxed. At last he allowed her to push him down onto the bed.

"Later . . ." he added faintly.

He sighed once, and before his head met the pillow he was asleep.

The captain did not make an easy patient, as Tess soon discovered. He slept only for short intervals, then came half awake to mutter and toss restlessly. In vain Tess tried to soothe him, to hold him still, knowing that these exertions put added strain upon his wound. But he was a big man, and his dreams were harsh.

Padrig came twice with food and fresh linens, and Le Fur came also, to check on his patient. Otherwise she was left alone with the captain. Later—Tess could not say exactly how much later, for her sense of time blurred during those long hours—he pulled her roughly to his chest in delirium, burying his fingers deep in her tangled curls.

"Un rêve," he breathed, groaning.

"Not a dream," Tess whispered. "A woman. A woman of bone and blood."

His woman?

But Tess pushed that dangerous thought from her mind, along with all the others, and allowed herself to float on through the churning seas.

Toward the dawn.

Toward the sun-swept harbor he had promised her.

Long hours later Tess was woken by the hammering of feet on deck. Blinking, she searched for André's face, relieved to discover that his forehead was dry and cool beneath her fingers. She realized she did not even know what day it was, then smiled to discover that it mattered not in the least.

After stretching lazily, she drank some of the cider Padrig had left, shrugging when she found there was no food to go with it.

What need had she for food anyway? Not with this sweet molten Breton cider that floated through her veins like sunlight. She laughed softly, dizzy with the sharp, pungent drink, dizzy with the nearness of the man beside her.

You, Miss Leighton, are well on your way to becoming floored, flushed, and flummoxed, a harsh voice scolded. A voice that sounded strangely like Hermione Tredwell's.

Somehow that thought only made Tess laugh the louder.

With a wicked smile, she raised her glass to her invisible critic. If this was drunkenness, she was loving every minute of it. And the word was *foxed,* thank you.

Beside her she heard a faint rustling. The bed creaked.

"Anglaise?"

"Here," Tess whispered, instantly alert at the sound of André's rough voice. She had become entirely comfortable speaking French with him. But why did his husky rasp send shivers scurrying down her spine?

"Were you—here? All the time?"

Carefully Tess replaced her empty glass upon the table. "I was."

"Did I say—do—anything . . ."

She smiled at the uncertainty in his voice. "Outrageous? Improper? Or simply arrogant? Let me see, you tossed about a great deal and moaned rather a lot. Oh yes, you did mention something about a cargo hidden on an island off the coast. And there was something else—something about a man you had to meet with a message. I was just about to worm the location out of you when—"

With a growl, her patient sat up and seized her wrists.

"I see I'll have my work cut out taming you, *bihan.*" The Frenchman's fingers slipped to her forearms and he pulled her sprawling across his chest, her hair cast in wild disarray about his naked shoulders. "Kiss me, *Anglaise,*" he ordered roughly. "Kiss me awake with this sweet storm."

Dizzy with the cider, Tess found herself smiling even as she bent closer, brushing her fingers through the crisp fur on his chest. Very carefully, she swept her lips across his in the merest hint of a kiss.

His groan made her smile broaden. "More," he growled, tangling his fingers in her hair and holding her still. "You taste like cider. No, sweeter than any cider."

Slowly Tess slanted her face down to his, realizing that he would not press her, but wanted her to do the offering.

Owing is not what I want from you! André's words came back to her then, along with the fury in his voice when he had said them. He wanted her, Tess knew, but equally important was that she come to him of her own will, with a passion to match his own.

And that knowledge made her bold beyond imagining.

With exquisite care her fingers shifted, tracing the flat male nipples hidden amid the dense fleece of his chest. To her surprise Tess felt them pebble instantly at her touch.

The Frenchman groaned, long and hoarse, his fingers biting into her forearms.

Drunk with the raw sounds of his desire, Tess pressed closer, her heart racing. Even as her fingers skimmed his chest she brought her tongue lightly to his lips. Reckless, driven by a strange, nameless longing, she teased their shuttered center and then pressed closer, gaining entrance to the hot, sleek recess beyond.

Immediately André's lips closed around her, drawing her deep.

At his ragged groan, fire exploded through Tess's veins. Heat flared between them, passed back and forth like jagged lightning bolts on a summer's night.

Her heart began to hammer. *Maybe. Yes, maybe—just this once. Since all else was lost, what would it matter to give in this one time?*

Then her blind eyes darkened, full of pain. No, she could never surrender to this weakness. Not even once.

Once was all it took.

Her father had taught her that, in a way savage beyond imagining.

"André," she tried to say, afraid of what was happening between them, afraid of the turmoil she was feeling. But the sound became trapped, lost somewhere between their locked mouths.

"*Mamm de Zoué,*" he whispered hoarsely against her hot lips, never releasing her. Tess could feel his heart slam against his ribs. It seemed that his fingers trembled. "*Trop tôt.*" he rasped. *Too soon.*

And then his control shattered. In wild, churning waves the dark storm of his desire broke over her. His hard hands found her ribs and splayed open, his thumbs coaxing the soft buds of her nipples erect.

"*An Aotrou Doué,*" André muttered. "Just as I knew they'd be —perfect." Slowly his tongue slipped back and forth over hers, teasing and stroking.

Stormy seas, Tess thought dimly. Water too deep. So deep that she'd never come up again—and never even want to.

Then she was drowning, plummeting, shot through with an exquisite ache that was part pleasure and part pain. She whimpered, feeling a fierce tension grip her at the point where her softness cradled his hardness.

First the pleasure, then the pain, a shrill voice warned. *Let it go!*

With a ragged cry Tess struggled away, desperate to find air and space, afraid that if she opened this final door she would never be able to close it again.

Then she would never be safe from the demons. And they were always there, she knew, just beyond that door. Waiting in the darkness.

Her hands tensed. "I—I can't," she gasped, dizzy still. A moment later her clawing fingers flayed the air, meeting rigid muscle.

A harsh cry exploded from André's lips. His hands went rigid on her breasts.

A moment later Tess was thrust back roughly onto the bed. She felt one broad shoulder brush past her, the bed shaking as he strained forward to cup his injured thigh.

"As God is my witness, *Anglaise,* are you trying to kill me? If so, you'll find it beyond your powers. And you may give up any thoughts of escape, as well," the Frenchman growled. "This thing between us is far from over, I warn you!"

"She's not dead! I don't believe it, no matter what that foul, blood-sucking marsh mosquito says!"

The Angel's hostler stumbled into the kitchen, his young face tense with his effort to hold back tears. "She's up north visiting her brother, ain't she, Mr. Hobhouse, just like ye told me?" Jem's brown eyes scoured the majordomo's taut features, pleading for reassurance.

"Dead? Who is setting such tales about?" Hobhouse's face was stern. "It is nothing but some cruel joke."

" 'Tis Hawkins himself, that's who. Telling all the patrons down at the Three Herrings, he is. Says he caught the Fox upon the beach with his own two hands and saw him ripped to shreds. Says that the young miss was involved and killed, too, like as not, only her body was—was lost, washed away by the tide." Small spots of color stained the lad's cheeks. His fingers began to quiver, and he gripped the lapels of Hobhouse's jacket convulsively. "It's not true. It can't be! Only I—I want to hear ye say it, Mr. Hobhouse."

Over the boy's head, Hobhouse and Letty exchanged grim glances.

"Ye must tell me, sir. Ye wouldn't lie, I know it!"

A look of despair flashed across Hobhouse's face, but was almost instantly concealed. Squaring his shoulders, the servant looked sternly down at Jem, who was studying him with deathly determination. The boy would not go away without an answer, Hobhouse realized.

"Now then, Jem, what's all this rubbish about Miss Tess? She's gone up to visit Master Ashley at Oxford, just as I told you—whoever tells you different is a bleating fool. The fact is, the young master was taken sick without warning, and so she didn't have time to say good-bye." Hobhouse's strong fingers tipped up the boy's face, registering the brown eyes bright with unshed tears. Grimly he forced Jem to look directly into his eyes. "Now, who are you going to believe, Jem? Me, who has never lied to you before? Or that"—he hesitated, one dark brow raised as he tried to recall the boy's previous description.

"Blood-sucking marsh mosquito, sir?"

"Damned if you haven't caught his likeness exactly, lad. Just so. Now, I want an answer to my question." His voice was hard and unwavering, Hobhouse was relieved to hear—the sort of voice which could quell someone far more confident than a boy of Jem's age.

"Sorry, sir," the hostler said at last, reassured by the stiff indignation he saw in the majordomo's eyes. Slowly he let out the breath he'd been holding. "Knew the bastard—begging yer pardon, Miss Letty, but that's purely what he is—was lying." As he spoke, the boy's voice grew louder and more confident. "Aye, knew all along, I did." His hands fell abruptly from Hobhouse's now wrinkled jacket, which he made an ineffectual effort to smooth. "Sorry about that, sir."

Hobhouse was careful to make his voice sound irritated. "As well you should be, Jem. Now, enough of this busying yourself in matters that are none of your concern. You must have work to do out in the stables. And if not, I'm sure Edouard would be more than happy to—"

The boy threw up his hands protectively, already retreating toward the door. "I'm going, Mr. Hobhouse! Honest, I am. No need to threaten me with that sort of torture again. I couldn't bear to spend another afternoon with that mad Frenchman! Had me in an apron, he did!"

A moment later Jem disappeared, jerking the door closed with a sharp bang.

Immediately Hobhouse's shoulders slumped. Sighing harshly, he ran an unsteady hand through his dark hair.

Beside him, Letty made a sound halfway between a sigh and a sob, her eyes filling with tears. "Where is she? Dear God, Andrew, what could have happened to her? It's been three days now!"

"I only wish I knew, Letty." The man's eyes narrowed. "Has *he* said anything?" Hobhouse snorted when he saw the maid start in surprise. "Oh, don't bother to lie—I know well enough that you and Lord Ravenhurst's valet have been sneaking off to meet in the churchyard."

The denial died on Letty's lips. "No, nothing. The viscount is away to Dover on official business. Peale could tell me no more than that." Her shoulders slumped.

"Would not, more like," Hobhouse muttered, staring at the quiet accounts room, remembering all the hours of happiness and belonging he had felt there. Things he had never felt until he came to work for Tess Leighton.

The deep lines on his stern face relaxed for a moment.

There had been that time, just under two years ago . . .

His lips curving slightly, Hobhouse recalled how she had charmed the butcher out of demanding payment when the Angel had to close for a fortnight because of a leaking roof.

Soon after, she had crossed paths with a tight-fisted merchant in Dover who was grumbling about the expense of maintaining his imperious French chef. Yes, by Heaven, in mere minutes she had had Edouard wrapped around her little finger, pleading for a chance to make the Angel's kitchens into something quite out of the ordinary.

So he had, Hobhouse thought, with a wry smile. In ways no one had quite expected.

And as for that hatchet-faced Mrs. Tredwell, Miss Tess gave as good as she got.

Could all that be over, all that joy and rare spirit gone from the world? Hobhouse scowled, simply refusing to believe it. Grim-faced, he balled his hands into fists and shoved them deep into his pockets. There they touched metal.

Frowning, he pulled out a small circle of silver, which glinted in the sunlight—Tess's amulet, Hobhouse realized, dropped the night of her last run. Without a word he thrust the heavy ornament back into his pocket before Letty could see it.

Suddenly the amulet grew cold in his fingers—eerily cold.

Hobhouse's eyes narrowed, dark with pain.

As cold as the grave? a bleak voice asked.

29

"*Chaud . . .*"

Hours later a dry, strangled groan brought Tess jolting awake, her eyes flying open to shadows.

Why so dark? she wondered, still disoriented, trying to drive the cobwebs of sleep from her mind.

Then, as consciousness returned in all its raw torment, she froze.

Knowing the answer to her question, knowing that the cry of pain was her own. Knowing that she was blind, lost to a darkness that would last the rest of her days.

She choked back a sob and tried to turn against the pillow, only to discover a hard hand curved around her breast, a man's head next to hers. Fire stabbed through her as his fingers tensed, then softly kneaded the creamy lobe.

Tess's heart lurched at his touch. With a ragged breath she pulled free.

"Too hot," he croaked. In English, this time.

A man of mystery, of many tongues and talents, the *Liberté*'s captain, Tess thought.

Was he a scoundrel as well?

Silently she reached for the glass she had left ready on the side table, softness brushing across her wrist as she did so. She frowned, wondering at that fall of silk and lace.

Then she remembered the trunk Padrig had brought a short

while before. In its perfumed depths, Tess had found the gossamer peignoir she now wore, along with others of the same exquisite satin. Cut low in the bodice, the garment fell nearly to her ankles, its long sleeves ending in a splash of lace. Like the others, the gown must have been terribly expensive, probably designed in Paris for a lady with very expensive tastes.

Or more likely, for a woman who was no lady at all.

Like herself? Tess thought dimly, her cheeks flooding crimson. "Water. M-must have water."

Before Tess could guide the glass to André's lips, he had struggled his way upright. "English? Are you—"

"Here. Here, too, is your water." Tess's voice was cool and careful, her words in English, as his had been.

The glass was lifted from her fingers. She heard him drink deeply, then set the vessel down on the table with a sharp crack.

"You frown. Because I spoke in English, as I do now? But in my particular line of work, a man must speak many tongues, *tu comprends?* Even false ones, on occasion," he added grimly. Muttering, the captain switched to French. "Cursed, graceless tongue, English. The French tongue is infinitely more expressive." Then, in that abrupt way of his, he switched topics once again. "Does the thought of my work repel you, *me kalon?*"

Tess was silent, pondering his question, knowing that if she lied, somehow this man would know it. "No," she said finally. "One man's wrong may sometimes be another man's right. Yet, I do not believe you would willingly cause harm to another."

"But you know next to nothing about me . . . and you do not ask to know."

"Nor do you ask what *I* was doing in the middle of the Channel at midnight."

"Ah, but that I knew already, sea gull. You were running smuggled cargo. Along with the other gentlemen of Romney Marsh."

Tess's breath caught in harsh surprise. "But how—"

"I have watched you for a very long time, *bihan,*" the *Liberté*'s captain said brusquely. "I have even traded with some among your secret band upon occasion. There are those among your fellows who would know my voice, if not my face. It is a lucrative business, this smuggling of tea and silks; it brought me that very fetching wisp of nothing you are wearing right now. Ah, how well its suits you, *ma sauvage.* Its emerald fire lights your creamy skin. *Par Dieu,* you are a grave temptation like this—but no, we must talk, I fear. Even now your face is dark with unasked questions."

Tess shivered, the rough velvet of his voice caressing her like a lover's kiss. How easily he broached her defenses! Even now, when she was determined to resist him.

André muttered something beneath his breath, then shifted on the bed. "Yes, but this trade is not nearly so rich as the one in gold guineas. There is danger in such shipments, of course, and certain hanging if one is caught. But that only makes the running of gold —and certain human cargo—more lucrative, for few will dare to take such risks. It is a trade I mean to learn more of."

"Gold shipments?" Tess's shoulders grew tense. "I know nothing of such cargo. You must be thinking of another coast—Deal, perhaps. The Fox would never—" Too late, Tess realized her slip.

She caught her breath, checking herself sharply.

"And this Romney Fox, too, interests me much," André said softly.

Too softly? Tess wondered.

"You are close with him?"

"As close as any," she said tightly. "More than some."

"You guard your secrets, I see. Even from me, *bihan?*"

"You are a stranger, Captain. By your own admission, you might well be the very slime of the Paris streets. Or one of Napoleon's cleverest agents," she added flatly, coldness seeping into her voice—just as it did into her heart.

What did this Frenchman know of gold shipments from the Romney coast? Could it be true then?

Was her Fox indeed a traitor?

"Sometimes I say a great deal too much," the man beside her muttered grimly, reaching out for her cold fingers.

Very carefully, Tess pulled away. "Who told you of such things?" she demanded, desperate to know the truth, desperate to have an end to these cruel uncertainties.

André made no move to touch her again. "Not one, but many,

bihan. The trade is common knowledge on this side of the Channel. Would you hold my involvement against me?" he countered.

Unbidden came the memory of Viscount Ravenhurst's bitter words about those who smuggled gold in a time when the French currency was in collapse; by so doing, they prolonged this bitter war.

In her heart, Tess knew that a great deal of what he had said was true. Every guinea traded meant more blood spilled—both English and French.

The coldness grew, creeping along her spine.

And what of the man beside her? He was a smuggler, that much Tess knew for certain. But what else was he? A spy? A murderer, even?

Could she bear to know his dark secrets?

Tess's throat tightened, and she found she had to swallow before she could speak. "If—if I found out that you were involved in trading gold and the secrets of war, I would do everything in my power to stop you," she said flatly. "The trade in brandy and silks is different. It has been the lifeblood of these coasts for centuries, long before Napoleon and Wellington locked horns. But this sale of military secrets and speculation on gold guineas is a thing repellent, for like a sickness it feeds on the flesh of one's fellow creatures." Tess's fingers meshed, then locked rigid in her lap. "If you *have* done such things, I don't want to know about them. What you did before I met you is not my concern." Her voice wavered for a moment and then hardened. "But if you do such things ever again, Captain, I will most certainly find out. And then, believe me, you will live to rue the day you dragged me from the sea."

A taut silence gripped the room. Her heart pounding, Tess waited for André's answer, praying it would be a flat denial.

All the while she wondered whether she could believe such a denial, even if it came.

She heard his swift indrawing of breath.

A moment later his fingers snared a long strand of auburn hair and forced her close, so close that she felt his hot breath upon her cheek. "You dare to threaten me, *Anglaise*?" His voice was deceptively soft, silk upon steel.

"I do—in this matter. Perhaps in others as well," she added defiantly.

"I could break you in a second, woman. On this vessel, I am lord and master. All must obey me—even you!"

"I must obey my own conscience first."

"Even if it counters my command?" the Frenchman thundered, so fiercely that Tess felt the rumble of his words.

Still she did not waver. "Of a certainty."

"Then, *bihan,* you are either a fool or a very brave woman." His voice dropped to a hoarse growl. "Which is it?"

"If you had wanted a tame fish, then you should not have gone angling in wild waters, Captain."

"You mock me, woman?" André roared. *"Diaoul,* but you dare a great deal!" With a curse he buried his hands deep in her hair and dragged her down against his naked chest. "But a tame fish is not what I wanted, *gwellañ-karet*—in that you are most certainly correct."

His fingers tightened, forcing her head back. Tess's heart raced as she felt the molten fury of his gaze full upon her face.

Suddenly the Frenchman threw back his head and laughed, loud rumbling peals that rocked the whole bed and her along with it. "Yes, by all the saints, you are half mer-creature yourself, *bihan,* just as I am. You must be—for you do what no woman has ever dared before."

Roughly André crushed her head onto his hair-matted chest, and suddenly Tess heard a different rumbling—not from laughter but the wild drumming of his heart.

Or was it hers?

"You hear it, *Anglaise*? That *chamade,* that thunder is of your making. And this, too, is of your making." He shifted abruptly, the unyielding line of his manhood burning into her hip. His voice dropped, rough and smoky with desire. "Right now your eyes glow, hazy green slipping into gray as passion builds within you. The sight stabs me like a blade, woman." André's voice dropped, harsh with his own desire. "Yes, you are right to dare much, for I would risk all for you, I think. Perhaps I already have," he added grimly.

"What—"

"Now *I* will ask the questions, starting with this man who stays at your inn."

Unconsciously Tess stiffened. A faint tremor went through her. But André's hands were harsh and inexorable as he locked her against his hard length, alert to every quiver that shook her.

"Yes, I know of this lord," he continued harshly. "This fool from *Londres* who watches you when you are not looking. Him, too, I have had many occasions to observe. He has fire in his eyes, but ice in his heart, I think. At sea we might almost be well matched, but on land—" His voice dropped, dark and urgent. "Tell me, *me kalon,*" he demanded, drawing her full atop his rigid thighs and cupping her bottom with his hard fingers. "On land, who is the victor?" he grated, driving her against his hot, straining arousal. "On land, who will have your heart? I must know—this man, Ravenhurst or myself?"

In vain, Tess struggled away from his ruthless grip, already feeling his desire kindle an answering heat within her. "What if my heart is not for the asking?" she countered bleakly, awash in cruel memories at the mere mention of Ravenhurst's name.

"Then in that case I shall have to seize it, like the corsair that I am," the Frenchman growled. Groaning, he forced his angry sex against her soft thighs. "Yes, I'll slip into your deepest soul, sea gull. I'll claim you just as you have claimed me—fiercely and forever. I would tear the heart from your very breast to make it mine!"

He spoke with a fierce violence that made Tess shiver, for in that taut voice she heard the fury of a man who might well do all he threatened.

"What—what if I have no heart left to take?" she whispered, feeling the reckless hunger begin where his hardness seared her. Where his hands tensed and shook against her silk-clad bottom.

"Then I'll take whatever you have, sea gull. Body, mind, spirit —I'll have them all! If I have the three, perhaps I will not miss the other."

"You—you cannot know what you're saying!"

"I only wish I did not—I only wish I had any choice left. But I have none, nor have had since I first laid eyes upon you. And now —enough of this empty talking!"

The next instant, André's fingers drove into the yielding curve of her bottom, forcing her to receive his hard length thigh to thigh, chest to chest, their breath mingling as every rigid male inch of him was stamped upon her softness.

Even as she tried to fight, Tess felt white-hot embers explode with heat wherever their fevered nerves met, wherever trembling skin brushed hungry, straining muscle. When he groaned a moment later, dark and long, the sound was Tess's undoing.

"You cannot—" A wild whimper escaped her lips. "Dear God, André, I must not—"

"You can, *bihan,* and you will!" he growled. Even as he spoke, his mouth trapped her open lips, hard and punishing, stifling her breathless protests. His hand dug deep into her hair, anchoring her head as his tongue plundered the sleek silk of her mouth.

Like a lightning bolt, that touch exploded through Tess, rocking her to her very toes. Once more she whimpered, hot with a need of her own.

André caught the sound with his lips, then answered with a dark groan of his own. Slanting his head, he nipped her full lower lip, then stroked it smooth with his wet tongue. Passion flared between them like a shimmering veil of summer heat until Tess felt her body grow heavy and molten, love-slick, flowing to meet him.

"Ah, but it will be good between us, *Anglaise,*" André growled. "Good to feel you pant and part for me. Good to feel you gasp when you slip over the edge." His tongue entered her fiercely, offering her the first taste of what it would be like when he brought his straining manhood inside her.

Dimly Tess heard herself moan deep in her throat, yielding to those velvet thrusts, just as she knew she would yield to the driving power of his body. His dark words only fueled her desire and left her weak with wanting—more, much more.

And the Frenchman knew it well.

His rough fingers shoved at the flimsy garment shielding her from his gaze. Savagely he ripped the costly silk, shredding it to nothing. Tess's unbound breasts spilled full into his hungry fingers, her nipples aching for his fierce caress.

"Yes, *me kalon,* flower for me," André muttered hoarsely. "Give me your passion."

Tess moaned, buffeted by a dark storm that raged wherever his fingers coaxed and plundered.

Ruthless and so very expert, Tess thought dimly. How many times before had he done this?

"No—no more," she gasped, aflame with this torment past imagining. Shocked at the mindless creature she became in his arms.

"Much more, my heart. Let me show you that it gets far, far better."

Better? Tess thought wildly. If the feelings grew any better, she was certain she must die of them!

She must have spoken aloud, for André's chest rumbled with dark laughter. "Oh yes, *bihan,* it does get better, truly. Take my word for it." His voice dropped. "No, do not accept my word—let me prove it to you instead."

Suddenly an odd memory flickered through the maelstrom of Tess's thoughts. Something about the fierce triumph in André's voice, something that triggered other images—jagged and dark with pain.

Dane.

The fragments took shape, becoming sound.

Instantly the Frenchman went rigid. "You can whisper *his* name?" he breathed. "Has this Englishman your heart, then?"

Tess gasped, still awash in the sensory maelstrom he had unleashed, as shocked to hear that name as André had been. But what did this man know of Ravenhurst or the things that had passed between them? Had he seen all that, too, watching from the darkness?

"How—"

The next moment she found herself tossed onto her back, crushed beneath him on the bed.

"So, you think of him even now, do you?" André's voice was raw. His fingers froze, rigid above her flushed, sensitized nipples, denying Tess that which she had only come to realize she wanted so desperately. "Admit it! Admit that even now you want him, even as you lie here in *my* bed, with *my* hands upon you. Admit you thought of him while you moaned beneath my touch."

"L-let me go," Tess whispered brokenly, feeling she had stepped into a nightmare. "I did not ask for you to touch me, damn you. Nor for you to interfere in my life! I want nothing of this, do you hear? Not you—not any man!"

"Too late," the Frenchman said grimly. "Everything about you is my business now, *Anglaise;* since you interest yourself in this man, so must I. What if I should meet him on the marsh, *karet?* Yes, on a dark and moonless night, with no witnesses about? With him gone, I would have no rival for your heart."

"You—you could not!"

"That I could is beyond doubting. Whether I *would*—ah, but that is a different thing entirely. Would the man's death give you so much pain?"

"The question is not yours to ask!" She was finished with this cruel interrogation by a stranger, aching with the torment of all that might have been between them. "I'll tell you no more! By your strength you might succeed in possessing my body, but there are some things you cannot touch, no matter how hard you press me! No, never!"

"We shall see, *Anglaise,*" the captain whispered darkly. "We shall see very soon. But know this. When I take you, it will not be with another man's name upon your lips."

With a wild cry Tess struck out, catching the base of his neck and taking advantage of his momentary shock to break free. She stumbled from the bed, knocking over the side table, then sprang forward blindly, the shreds of her peignoir swirling about her ankles.

Desperately her fingers slid over the wall, meeting nothing but rough timber. *Perdition!* The latch had to be very close!

From behind her came the sound of ragged breathing, then the creak of the bed. Dear God, he was coming! Where was the damned latch?

"Don't fight me, *karet*," André rasped. "Save your energy for a better sort of contest."

"To hell with you and your contests! Stay away from me!" Tess's heart raced, hammering in her chest so loudly that she could barely hear him.

"Never." His voice came from her back, hot and drugging as rum. "Let me love you, sea gull. Let me drive his memory from you forever."

Behind her, Tess heard the rustle and slide of cloth and knew he was shedding his last garment, releasing the hard blade of his manhood.

Dear God, why did she tremble so? Why did part of her yearn to surrender to him? "Don't, André!" she whispered.

"Why not?" he growled. "Is it the Englishman who holds you? Does he stir your blood still?"

Once again this man had seen more than she had, penetrating the walls she had been so careful to build around her heart.

Was he right? Tess wondered wildly. Did memories of Dane still hold her captive?

"I'll release you from these shadows, *bihan*. Let me give you a pleasure beyond describing. Let me love you. Now."

White-faced, Tess searched the wall, wild tremors sweeping through her. Her knees felt like thick porridge, threatening to buckle at any moment. Haunted and smoky, her eyes strained to pierce the darkness around her.

Somehow she knew it was true, that this man would give her exquisite pleasure, that their joining would be fierce with magic, just as he had promised. Her blood surging thickly through her veins, Tess cursed the fate that demanded she refuse him.

But refuse him she must. For such perfect pleasure would make her infinitely vulnerable, and that was something Tess had vowed never to be again.

All these thoughts flashed over her in the span of a ragged heartbeat, and her answer came just as quickly.

"I cannot, André—don't ask me for what I cannot give!"

His bare feet whispered against the floor. "I'll have you, *bihan*," he growled. "And when I'm done, you'll think of no one but me!"

"No, André," Tess whispered, terrified by the cold cruelty in his voice. "Not that way."

"That way," he rasped. "Any way. With whatever it takes." He moved closer. Tess could feel the faint, shimmering heat of his body. "Over and over, until you stop this charade and admit your need for me."

"I—I cannot. You don't understand!"

"I understand all that I need to—and I'm done with waiting." He was nearly close enough to touch now.

To touch and be touched, Tess thought wildly, and knew in that instant she wanted all of that. Was she a fool to deny what would give them both such pleasure? "You're—you're not the first!" she cried wildly, desperate to stop him, knowing her own control was close to shattering.

He answered with a smothered curse. "But I'll be the last, by God!"

The Frenchman seized her wrists, forcing them back against the wall while he slanted his hard body against hers, drinking in her sweet woman's scent, mingled now with the tang of the sea. His breath ragged, he lowered his head to the pulse that hammered at her ear, tonguing the sensitive inches fiercely. "You can't see me, but you can feel me, can't you? My wet tongue. My rough hands. My heat against your belly. *Dieu,* how I want you, *bihan.* And how I'm going to enjoy making *you* want me."

"Don't do this, André. Don't make me feel—so much. It—it will destroy me!"

"If you do not feel, it will destroy me, *Anglaise.* I want—need to feel everything about you, all that before I could only imagine." His fingers drew ruthless waves of fire against Tess's wrists. His sleek tongue began to burn a blazing path down her chest toward the dusky buds that strained forward, hungry for his touch. "To feel you here, where your skin trembles beneath my lips. And here, where your heart thunders, just as mine does." With a low groan, he claimed those pouting crests, loosing a firestorm of sensation that seared everything in its path.

Finally André's mouth broke away. "*Diaoul,* how the sight of you gives me pleasure. But especially here—"

Without warning his wiry beard brushed the silk of Tess's belly. A raw whimper broke from her throat; her knees melted like wax at that erotic, scraping contact.

Roughness against melting softness. Hard, hungry male against yielding female.

Dizzily she tried to push him away.

Fight—don't feel—too dangerous, a wild voice warned.

But the warning came too late. Somehow all that mattered now was that he never stop.

Of their own volition, Tess's muscles tensed, her hips thrusting up to meet him, the birthmark at her inner thigh revealed to his burning gaze.

André answered with a dark groan, raw with hunger and primal, male triumph, for he recognized the moment of surrender when he saw it. *"Sainte Vierge!"* His breathing grew strained. "Open, *bihan,*" he said hoarsely, his manhood engorged at the sight of that tiny black half-circle and the dusky auburn triangle above.

But that was for later, he told himself fiercely. Now must be for *her,* to forge the bonds of their future. "Open for me, *Anglaise,*" he repeated urgently. "Now."

Dimly Tess realized his dark intent. Some shredded vestige of reason made her shudder and try to pull free.

But the hard, calloused fingers only tightened, biting into the soft skin of her thighs, holding her still. "No, this way, my wild beauty. The first time this way—for you and your pleasure. And because I want to see you, to taste you, sea gull, when you tremble beneath me in your ecstasy." Even as André spoke, his thumbs slid slowly higher. Their calloused pads circled, igniting embers of raw pleasure wherever they skimmed Tess's heated skin.

He breached the dark center of her desire.

Somehow timber and beam melted beneath her feet; cable and canvas, wave and cloud dissolved overhead. Suddenly she was falling, blind, vulnerable, and naked, the world of matter and mass scattered to nothing as she gave herself up to the dark poetry of André's voice and the demon fury of his touch.

Yielding, straining—hungry to find that nameless, sun-swept shore just out of reach.

"Say my name," he rasped, his fingers ruthlessly gentle, ruthlessly knowing. "Tell me which man you think of now."

Tess's dry lips moved, but no sound emerged. Her head fell back, the wild flame of her hair spilling about her shoulders and sweeping across his naked chest.

Sound burst forth from Tess's throat then—ragged, tormented, the voice of a stranger. "You, God help me! *You,* André!"

It was all the answer he needed. The next moment his stiff beard scraped her creamy thighs and she felt the silken probe of his tongue parting her. With fire and fierce tenderness he possessed her then, learning her slowly, coaxing her, driving her on toward a choking release.

She shuddered, swaying, and would have fallen had he not cupped her hips in one strong hand and cradled her against him, his mouth never ceasing its drugging torment.

Pain and pleasure.

Dear God, ineffable, devouring sweetness.

The hot, sleek rapture of tongue and teeth. Embers bursting, white-hot, to light her darkness.

Then the sweet tempest was upon her, a raw soundless moan ripped from her throat as her body tensed and began to convulse beneath him.

Sweet love, dark love, take me now. Were they his thoughts or hers? Perhaps both. Perhaps it did not matter.

For, gasping, Tess fell, down and down again, plunged into an endless raw pleasure so intense it seared. Branded, she felt his mark everywhere, his passion sweeping over her to become her passion, their bonding never to be forgotten.

That was when the Frenchman taught Tess his third lesson, while her skin still burned beneath his touch and her blood still sang.

She did indeed have a heart, Tess discovered, and although it was raw and bruised with tortured memories, it was whole.

And it was his for the taking.

30

Slowly, weak in the aftershocks of pleasure, Tess slid down the wall and toppled forward onto André's broad chest, dimly feeling the hard thrust of his manhood at her stomach.

"Ah, *bihan,*" he muttered darkly, thickly. "More than I dreamed. Unforgettable."

"I believe those lines were to be mine," Tess said faintly, her throat as dry as other hidden parts of her body were dewy-slick.

"Then say them, damn it," he muttered, shifting and tugging until she sprawled limply against his outstretched body.

"All you said and more," Tess whispered. She turned her face into his chest, feeling her cheeks flush at the memory of her wanton response. "Perfect. Oh, André . . ." She could not quite hold back the sleepy smile that curved her lips. "Perfect beyond imagining."

A calloused finger swept her cheek. "Not quite perfect, my little savage. But it soon will be," the *Liberté*'s captain murmured darkly, shifting in a vain attempt to forget the fiery torment left unassuaged at his own groin.

Knowing that even now their time together was growing short.

Her head slipped onto his shoulder and her body curved into his. He smiled grimly, feeling her proud soft breasts tease his bared chest. Mother of God, but this was pain, André thought, feeling his manhood swollen and taut where her silken thighs brushed against him.

He closed his eyes, trying to forget that tangle of auburn curls. Trying to forget how she had moved against him, pleading for his touch. How she had swayed, only to moan his name, mindless and hungry with passion.

Growling hoarsely, he shifted beneath her, trying to find a more comfortable position, knowing it was impossible until this fire in his loins was quenched in her dark sweetness.

In grim silence, he caught Tess to his chest and carried her to his bed, pulling a pillow beneath them as he settled at her side.

Ah, *Anglaise,* you are indeed all that I dreamed and more. Mystery upon mystery. A creature of rare fire.

His face dark, the captain fingered a warm strand of auburn hair. But why? he wondered. Why only with *her* this fever, this desperate hunger? There had been other women, of course—*Dieu,* but there had been women past counting. Yet, none of them had left him dizzy with just one look, with only the faintest touch of her sweet tongue.

And none of them mattered, he thought suddenly, realizing that what existed between them was new and fresh, entirely untainted by anything in his life before this moment.

That was the first lesson that the Englishwoman from Rye taught André Le Brix, though he had the strong feeling she would teach him a great many more in the years to come.

Beside him the auburn-haired beauty stirred slightly, murmuring as she nestled closer into his warmth, the movement sending new waves of torment into his already aching groin.

The captain frowned. She was young, he saw now, innocent and vulnerable when sleep took the tension from her slim shoulders and the wariness from her haunted eyes.

So young. So vital. While he . . .

Sometimes he felt a hundred years old. The Frenchman's face settled into harsh, bitter lines. Looking down at her hair, alight with tiny fires in its russet depths, André faced the fact that she was far too young for him, sea-rough and coarse as he was, carrying the curse of war and the blood of slain men upon his hands. No, he would have to take her back, and soon. It was too dangerous for her here.

Too dangerous for them both.

But he would not think of that now, the Frenchman decided. Now was for drifting and dreaming and perhaps forgetting. Now he would hold her and comfort her when the nightmares came— lighting her darkness, loving her awake, driving her to breathless pleasure until his name trembled on her raw lips.

Yes, he could not let her go until he had done that. Somehow he would protect her until then, André swore.

But who, he wondered bleakly, tortured by the knowledge of his own dark past, who would protect her from *him*?

The ship had settled to an easy creak and snap, the waves to a dull, steady slap against the hull, when André heard footsteps hammer down the passageway.

A heavy hand rapped at the cabin door.

Smothering a hard curse, the bearded Frenchman turned to tug the shreds of Tess's peignoir about her just as the door burst open.

"What sort of madness is this?" the *Liberté*'s first mate barked from the doorway, his eyes widening as he took in the two bodies entwined on the bed. "You are supposed to be resting, you fool! Or is it your goal to bleed to death?"

Mumbling furiously beneath his breath, the giant Breton stalked across the room and dropped a heavily laden tray down upon the table. His broad shoulders were a line of granite, stiff with reproach, his eyes now carefully averted from the nearly naked couple.

Blinking, Tess bolted upright, clutching the shredded scraps of silk to her chest.

Memory returned; her cheeks glowed crimson. *Dear God, what had she done? What had this stranger done to her?*

Without warning, the rich smell of eggs and butter and cheese wafted over her, knotting her stomach—reminding her that she had not eaten for hours.

Close at hand, Padrig slammed down silver and glasses, muttering in Breton, then switching to French. "She will be the death of you, my friend, I tell you that now! She and this dangerous obsession. Already your wound is bleeding again, opened up by what I am certain must have been very pleasurable exertions. But the next time I won't bother bringing new bandages, I warn you. You can lie in your own blood!" Worry made the big man's voice harsh.

Tess felt fresh waves of color stain her cheeks, painfully conscious of the wanton sight they must make. A hard, muscled arm slipped around her tense shoulders, and she stiffened, feeling André shake with barely repressed laughter.

Tight-lipped, she tugged the shredded gown up to her neck and dragged one arm over her chest, at the same time vainly trying to sweep her tangled hair into some semblance of order. Giving up that attempt, she swept away André's arm instead.

Behind her there came a muffled chuckle as the captain leaned back comfortably upon his elbow. "It's no good, *bihan*. You look exactly like what you are."

"And just exactly what is that?" Tess hissed.

"A woman who's just been pleasured—thoroughly, passionately, and decisively, *mon coeur*. Don't you agree, Padrig?"

The first mate snorted, muttering something in Breton, to which André responded with a rich, guttural laugh.

Fresh tongues of flame leaped through Tess's cheeks. They were laughing at her, the crude beasts! After all she had done to help this bloody smuggler in his hours of illness! Her hands clenched, she beat the air vainly, yearning to feel the Frenchman's skin beneath her fists.

"Come, sea gull, where's the shame in a thing so natural?" André protested, trying to dodge her flying fingers.

Across the room, Padrig broke into reluctant laughter. "You see, *mon ami*?" the first mate chided. "I told you she would be dangerous, this one. Have a care!"

"And you remember my answer, do you not, Padrig?"

"You boasted you would give her the soundest beating of her life, as I recall."

Tess's eyes smoldered with fury. "Oh, he did, did he?"

"Indeed he did, *bihan*. But the captain will find that a difficult task, I think. Now eat, the two of you. We will soon be at the gulf."

Tess frowned questioningly.

"The Morbihan—the little sea," André explained. "A gulf enclosed by two peninsulas, her waters dotted with a hundred islands, each more beautiful than the last. An enchanted place kissed with warm winds and the scent of flowers, bathed by temperate currents in every season. Yes, you will like it greatly, *bihan*."

Tess felt Padrig press a plate into her fingers, and she was once more assaulted with rich smells. She inhaled deeply, catching the fragrant tang of shallots and butter. "It smells wonderful, Padrig."

"Aye, Le Fur is a decent enough cook, so long as you don't ask for more than crepes and omelettes," the first mate said dryly. "But this time he's outdone himself, I think. Here are grilled carp and artichokes. The fish stew we Bretons call *cotriade*, thick with fish and potatoes and a hint of sorrel."

"What, no wine?" Tess snapped. "Certainly that would fit the scenario of this little seduction."

Padrig only laughed. "You would little enjoy our local wine, *bihan*, for to drink it one must have four men and a wall." In silence he waited for her next question.

Tess locked her lips, refusing to fall victim to their teasing again.

"Go ahead and ask him, *bihan*. Put the poor fellow out of his misery," André murmured.

"Oh, very well. Why four men?"

"One man to pour the wine, one man to drink it, two to hold him up, and when he falls, the wall to catch him."

Tess could not prevent a soft ripple of laughter. "Is it so very bad, then?"

"All that and more. The cider is very good, however, but you know that already, I think. Good, too, these Plougastel strawberries—and the oysters. Those we got from a vessel under a day out of Belon."

"Oysters, Padrig?" the captain growled behind Tess.

"Of course, *mon ami*." The first mate was all innocence. "You like them, do you not? You will most certainly need your strength when—"

"Enough!" André barked.

Tess frowned, understanding none of this raillery. "But why—"

"Never mind, *bihan,*" André said shortly. "I'll explain it to you later."

As the door closed, Padrig's booming laughter could be heard echoing up the companionway.

Stiffly, Tess concentrated on swallowing the fragrant omelette on her plate, bite by careful bite, furious at once more falling victim to their humor. Finally she could contain her curiosity no longer.

"What did he mean?" she demanded. "About needing your strength?"

"He meant, my little cat, the oysters. You still do not see, do you?" André's finger swept her cheek. "I think I shall enjoy seeing you blush, *mon coeur.* The oysters are an aphrodisiac—a stimulant to strength in love play."

Tess choked on her omelette, feeling her cheeks flame just as he had predicted they would. "You—you are disgusting, both of you! You are . . ." Words scathing enough escaped her.

"What I am is insatiable," the captain growled, "and I need no oysters to make me hard for you, *bihan.*" As if to prove his point, he hauled her back against his chest until the blade of muscle at his groin burned into her hip.

"Insolent, that's what you are!" Tess blazed, her breath coming and going in little gusts, furious at the sport they had made of her —furious, too, at how easily this stranger could work his dark magic, penetrating all her hard-won defenses.

"Infantile!" she snapped.

"Oh, not that. Not that, most clearly."

The rough male triumph in his voice only made Tess's fury rage hotter. "Just like two children you were, snickering about some overheard bit of wickedness."

"Ah, *gwellañ-karet,* how your cheeks blaze when you're angry. And your eyes—how they burn with haunting green fires." A dark sound—half growl and half groan—burst from his throat. "I want you, sea gull. Now. Beneath me. Panting and mindless when you sheathe me in sweetness and take me all the way home inside you."

His dark words struck sparks. A thousand fires skittered up

Tess's spine at that erotic image, but she fought them desperately, fury stiffening her determination to resist him.

As she had not the last time.

"Never! What—what happened before can never happen again, do you hear me?"

"Indeed?" André's voice was deceptively soft. "You find my body repulsive?"

Tess swallowed hard. *Repulsive? If he were any less repulsive, she would soon be clawing at him in eagerness!* "Not precisely. You are tolerable enough, I suppose." She managed somehow to make her voice no more than politely casual.

"Then perhaps you find the act itself distasteful?"

"On the contrary. That is—"

"Then I fear I do not understand you, *bihan.*" There was only faint curiosity in his tone.

"It must never happen again," Tess blazed, tugging the satin wisps higher on her chest. Although why she should bother to cover herself *now* was beyond her.

After all he had seen.

Dear God, after the way he had touched her.

Silence fell. The only sounds came from Tess's ragged breathing and her restless fingers bunching and unbunching the peignoir.

"You have beautiful breasts, *mon coeur.* Did you know that?"

Tess's heart did a painful flip-flop. He wasn't going to make this easy for her, was he? "That is neither here nor there, Captain," she said primly.

"Your nipples are exquisite—dusky, like pouting roses just longing to be kissed. I am desolate to contradict you, *ma belle,* but they are precisely, oh most perfectly, where they ought to be."

"Something you would know very well, of course. Since you've seen so very many female—er, anatomies." *He was enjoying this, damn him!*

"But of course," the captain said calmly, not missing the sharp note of jealousy in her voice. The sound pierced him with warmth, making him very happy. Dangerously so.

Careful, my friend, he told himself, then promptly forgot the warning.

"Oh, you—you—" With ruthless fingers Tess tugged at the hem of the shredded peignoir.

André smiled wolfishly, deciding it was time to put her out of her misery. "Now, *me kalon,* let me see your ankles."

"You must be mad! I'll do nothing of the sort!"

"Bihan," the Frenchman said warningly. "I would tend to those wounds." His voice dropped, husky with desire. "Just as you tended to mine during the long days of my delirium. Something I can never repay you for."

The gruffness in his voice made Tess's anger melt away like snow in the noonday sun. She contented herself with a little sniff as he rose from the bed and pulled the shredded emerald cloth from her legs. A rich, aromatic scent assaulted her lungs.

"Camphor and mint," André explained, gently massaging the unguent into the stinging welts left by the smuggler's rope. "It may burn for a moment, but the stinging will soon disappear, I promise. Once before I did this, while you slept—to the wound at your shoulder, too. Do you remember?"

His fingers moved back and forth, lulling, soothing, drugging her. Tess could only shake her head, speechless in the spell he wove, wrapped in a warm, sensuous cocoon.

Safe.

The word worked its way into her tired thoughts, and she smiled, knowing that it was true.

She *was* safe. For now. With him. Somehow Tess was certain of that. Yes, something told her this was a man who kept all of his promises.

Her eyelids grew heavy, then closed.

She felt him slip a soft fabric around her ankle, securing it with a knot. Her mind began to drift; a rich, potent silence enveloped her as she lay replete with food and dizzy from the touch of his masterful fingers.

"André?" she mumbled dreamily.

"Yes, *bihan?*" The captain settled back beside her, slipping his arm beneath her shoulders until her hair spilled over him like a burnished curtain. Not comfortable yet, not when desire still held him in its fevered grip. But content—for now, at least.

"You are the perfect one," Tess confided sleepily. "Everything precisely where it ought to be. I—I could feel you, too, you know."

He laughed, the sound strangely unsteady. "Ah, sea gull, you'll feel even more, I promise, every hot, hard inch of me. But not quite yet—not until this damnable wound heals a bit." He growled a curse, for Padrig had been right, and blood had again begun to seep beneath the thick linen bandage at his thigh.

But Tess did not answer, already drifting away into a bright world of cloud and sun and sea foam.

A short while later she heard Padrig return, but even then she did not move, lulled by their guttural Breton tones. Discussing wind speed and the best course of approach to the gulf, she supposed.

Gradually their voices grew fainter, then faded away altogether.

The world, as she slept then, was a bright place, awash with color and sound, a place where even the sun cast no shadows.

The scrawled, unsigned note reached the Angel four days after Tess's disappearance.

Hobhouse didn't see who delivered it, only discovering it by chance at the bottom of a large pile of bills and receipts cluttering the desk in Tess's accounts room.

Whoever had left it knew the Angel well, however, for he knew precisely where an outsider would be unlikely to look. He also knew that Monday was the day for paying the butcher and the day help, and that Hobhouse would certainly come across the missive in the pile.

His fingers trembling, Hobhouse slowly opened the single, folded sheet.

She is safe, he read, feeling a vast bubble of relief burst deep within him.

Do not search for her. Make no mention of this message. You will be told when she is to return.

That was all.

But it was enough for the man who had begun to fear—no, be honest, Hobhouse told himself—to *believe* that Tess Leighton truly was dead.

The grizzled servant's dark eyes filled with tears, which spilled in a silent rush down his ruddy cheeks.

That was how Letty found him a few minutes later when she came listlessly searching for Edouard. "Andrew?" she cried. "What is it?" Then her eyes widened, dark with shock. "Oh, no—it can't be! She isn't—"

"No, my dear Letty," Hobhouse managed to reply, recovering enough to begin hastily scrubbing the tears from his eyes. "Exactly the opposite." He crumpled the note and slipped it into his pocket. "She's well, thank God, and she'll be coming home soon."

At the maid's startled cry of happiness, Hobhouse caught her hand in warning.

"But you must tell no one. Leave the story just as we have set it about—she has gone to Oxford to see Master Ashley. Just pray that her young scapegrace of a brother doesn't show up here on our doorstep to prove us false," he added grimly.

Breathless, Letty could only nod, too happy to think of all the other questions she ought to ask.

A sharp, insistent pealing came from the bell in the front hall. Quickly Hobhouse ran his hand over his eyes, then straightened his collar. His shoulders high, his spirit restored, he marched to the door of the kitchen.

There he swung about, fixing Letty with a stern eye. "Don't go telling that Friday-faced valet of Ravenhurst's, either. I was told to tell no one. I've broken that order to tell you, but nobody else must know of this, do you understand?"

Letty nodded, regretfully revising her plan of sending around a note to her swain. But nothing could upset her now, not while she was brimming with this wonderful news.

At that moment, in the foyer of a quiet town house on Watchbell Street, Peale was ripping open a cream-colored envelope.

My dear Peale,

Work continues to hold me here in Dover. Meetings and more damnable meetings, until the words fall like a bloody French barrage. Likely to be here indefinitely. Taft will know what to do with Admiralty communications.

Ravenhurst

Peale carefully refolded the sheet, frowning. He had never liked this business with the local smugglers. Of course, he knew only a little about Ravenhurst's mission in Rye, but what he did know had been enough to make him nervous. Loyalties were fierce here, and tempers ran especially high where free-trading was concerned.

The valet only hoped the viscount would keep a clear head about him.

By the time Hobhouse strode briskly into the foyer, his face was impassive, the fires of happiness carefully banked.

His keen dark eyes took in the trim white-haired lady standing imperiously in the doorway, silver-mounted cane in hand, a mountainous pile of baggage scattered at her feet.

"There you are," the woman announced crisply, her tone disapproving. "I have been waiting"—her sharp eyes darted down to the elegant timepiece pinned to her bodice—"four and one-half minutes. I do not like waiting. I trust you will remember that in future." One white brow slanted, she waited for Hobhouse to acknowledge her directive, which he did with a slight inclining of his head. "Very well—I am the Duchess of Cranford. I will require a suite of rooms and accommodation for my staff of six. A southern exposure will suffice. I take tea below at four precisely and dinner in my rooms at eight. Do you have all that?" This storm of orders was delivered with all the cool aplomb of a seasoned military officer.

Hobhouse's expressionless facade did not waver. He bowed slightly. "Quite, Your Grace. We have had your reservation?" He was not about to let the old harridan take the field entirely uncontested.

The duchess merely swept one frail hand through the air, dismissing such technicalities with a frown. "I could not say. Brimble handles all such matters, of course." Her sharp blue eyes flickered across the hall. "Now, as it is nearing four o'clock, I shall take my tea directly." Her elegant, silver-handled cane rose, pointing to the cozy, well-lit rear parlor Tess had opened for the exclusive use of the Angel's female guests. "In *there.*"

A tall, severe-faced dragon of a maidservant appeared in the doorway behind the duchess.

"Ah, there you are, Brimble," the duchess said briskly. "See to the baggage first, if you please. Then arrange for my card to be taken around to Lord Ravenhurst's lodgings. On Watchbell Street, I believe. Mr.—" She interrupted this rapid-fire rain of orders to turn with a frown to the Angel's majordomo, one white brow raised imperiously.

"Hobhouse, Your Grace," the servant answered expression-lessly. Not by so much as a muscle did he betray his knowledge that Ravenhurst was from home. At the mention of the viscount's name, Hobhouse found all his negative impressions of this new visitor confirmed.

Any friend of Ravenhurst's was no friend of his.

Or of Tess Leighton's, he thought grimly.

"Mr. Hobhouse will advise you. After that I shall require my usual restoratives in my room, one hour before dinner."

The very superior lady's maid behind the duchess nodded crisply, at the same time managing to sniff and run disapproving eyes over the Angel's black-clad majordomo.

The new arrival was already moving toward the rear parlor. She moved smoothly, Hobhouse noticed, and stood perfectly erect without the slightest reliance upon her elegant cane.

Quality! he thought with a sharp mental shrug, consigning the whole lot of them to the devil. Who could ever hope to understand their whims and conceits? Their servants were not much better, he thought, his eyes flickering over Brimble's haughty features.

But if that Friday-faced individual hoped to put him in his place, she'd find herself sadly out, the servant vowed.

The duchess was settling herself in the parlor when a rustle of silken skirts signalled a new arrival at the Angel's entrance. A heavy floral scent engulfed Hobhouse, who immediately stiffened.

It was a scent he would have known anywhere.

"Where is she?" a throaty, faintly querulous female voice demanded.

Hobhouse turned, a look of perfect impassivity on his grizzled face. "Whom would you be speaking of, madam?"

The magnificent vision swathed in diaphanous sapphire silk frowned, tapping her embroidered slipper impatiently. "Your mistress, of course, you fool—Tess Leighton."

Was it his imagination, Hobhouse was to wonder later, or did the Duchess of Cranford's shoulders tense at the sound of that name?

"Miss Leighton is presently from home," Hobhouse replied unhelpfully. Damned if he'd bow and scrape to *that* man-eating female, either!

"So I've been told. Several times, in fact. But *where,* man?" The tapping of Lady Patricia's foot grew more insistent.

Hobhouse's hesitation bespoke his belief that this was none of the woman's business.

"Well?"

Hobhouse looked away, his eyes fixing somewhere above Lady Patricia's right shoulder. "To visit her brother in Oxford, I believe."

"Rather hasty, all this." The blond woman's voice was sharp with mockery.

"The visit had been planned for quite some time, madam," Hobhouse murmured. "Miss Leighton chose not to speak of it, however. 'Only among a few intimates' was how she put it."

Which Lady Patricia was most certainly not, the majordomo thought.

A faint tinge of crimson swept over her cheeks. "Indeed?" The tapping of her foot grew very loud. "And when, pray tell, does the Angel's so charming proprietor deign to return? From Oxford, of course?" she added maliciously.

"I could not say. My lady," Hobhouse added a moment later.

With what sounded suspiciously like a snort, the vision in sapphire swept about and made for the parlor. "I shall take tea before I leave," she snapped. "See to it, Hobhouse. Lord Lennox will be joining me shortly."

"I beg pardon, but you will perhaps allow me to seat you in a private parlor? That room is already—"

"Nonsense, Hobhouse." The Duchess of Cranford swept to the doorway, dismissing the majordomo's concern with an airy wave. "I am perfectly happy to share the room with so"—her voice trailed away for a moment, as if she were appreciating the vision before her—"so entrancing a companion."

Hobhouse bent his head slightly in acquiescence, concealing his surprise.

"Pray allow me to introduce myself," the duchess said, moving forward with one hand outstretched. "I am the Duchess of Cranford, and I absolutely insist that you join me for tea. Mr. Hobhouse will see to everything admirably, I am quite certain." Slim fingers, surprisingly strong for someone so advanced in years, swept out to press Lady Patricia's arm. "Now, you must tell me all about Rye. It is my first visit to this quaint little city, and I must confess I find myself agog with curiosity about the place."

For once in her life Lady Patricia found herself speechless, blinking beneath the full force of the duchess's considerable charm. "Yes, of course—that is—certainly, Your Grace."

A plague on the Quality! Hobhouse thought once again, shaking his head as he turned to leave. Up on their high horses one minute, and all oozing false affability the next.

Yes, who could ever fathom them!

31

When Tess awoke, André was gone and had been gone for some time, judging by the cold feel of the sheets at her side. After stretching lazily, she slipped from the bed to make a quick toilette at the basin on the side table. Searching for the towel, Tess's fingers brushed against velvet.

A dress?

Slowly she eased her fingers over the soft fabric, tracing tiny satin buttons, which marched in a line down the back. The front, it seemed, was very décolleté and hung with satin ribbons. A dress more rich than any she had ever owned. A beautiful dress—a dress that might even make Tess feel beautiful, while she wore it at least.

Smiling in anticipation of André's reaction, Tess slipped the lavish gown over her head, struggling to reach the buttons at her back. Finding that impossible, she fastened first and last and consigned all the rest to the devil.

Suddenly Tess cocked her head, sniffing sharply. There was a lingering warmth to the air now, a hint of something other than sea salt in the wind. They must be near the gulf, she thought eagerly.

Arms outstretched, she made her way to the door and climbed the stairs to the deck, pausing to enjoy the warmth of the sun upon her cheeks. Out here the air was rich with pine spice and the drifting scent of flowers. Above her head the sky was noisy with bird song.

"May I help you, miss?" It was the man known as Le Fur, Tess realized, the one who had dug the lead ball out of André's thigh.

She couldn't resist a little smile. "Did you ever show it to him?"

The crewman did not misunderstand her. "So I did, for a fact. He called it very pretty, so he did. Would you like to have a seat on this chest? Belle-Ile is before us, and we'll soon be cresting the gulf."

The wind was fine and strong in Tess's face as she sat down on the little square of wood. She heard Le Fur linger, moving about nearby. "I wish I might see it myself, for it sounds very beautiful," she said wistfully. "Could—could you describe it for me?"

"With pleasure, *bihan*. Now, let's see . . ." She heard him pause and scratch his stubbled cheeks. "Just to the right are the jagged cliffs of Belle-Ile, studded by hidden caves and narrow creeks. There the seas run jade, and cormorants fly to build their nests on high, rocky cliffs. A bit farther south the water froths and foams around a line of rocks like the devil's own teeth—the Needles, we call them. Tell me, can you feel the wind change?"

Tess nodded silently, her head cocked.

"That's because we're turning inland, slipping past the great curving arm of the Quiberon Peninsula on our left. The waves beat hard and heavy on those savage coasts. You'll like our isle much better. But first we must pass the big islands—Hoëdic, Houat, and Groix. Then twelve sparkling miles of inland waters dotted with hundreds of smaller islands. And there is ours, blanketed with flowers of crimson and orange."

Tess sat quietly, wrapped in the beauty of the scene he described, sad that she would never be able to see it for herself.

The old man cleared his voice. "There is my own white cottage, *bihan,* and unless my poor eyes are mistaken, my wife and son standing at the door." His voice trailed away.

Suddenly an electric tension stirred the tiny hairs at the back of Tess's neck. She cocked her head, listening to the flurried sounds of activity around her on deck—the crack of sails being shortened and the smack of cables.

But she did not hear the one sound she most wanted to hear.

"A lucky man, Le Fur," a dark voice whispered at her ear a moment later. "He has a wife and son waiting for him." Lightly the captain's rough-sleek tongue traced the arc of Tess's ear, his teeth nipping the sensitive lobe.

Tess immediately felt herself plunge under his sensual spell.

"Must you creep up on one that way?" She tried—without success—to keep the breathless tremor from her voice. Red-faced, she jerked to her feet, her shoulders stiff with anger.

"Just the way you creep up on me, *bihan.* The sight of you. The smell of you." His voice dropped to a husky growl. "The sweet, dusky taste of you."

At those erotic words a wanton heat flooded through her. Suddenly her throat grew dry, and she was aching for the taste of him in turn.

How could he do this to her? Tess wondered wildly. Maybe she was every bit as depraved as her father had accused her of being five years ago.

Maybe she was indeed a harlot born.

Icy fingers swept across her heart for an instant before she forced them away. She would *not* think of her father, never again! The man was dead—done with destroying her life. She would not allow his memory to wound her further!

"You shiver, *bihan.* Dare I hope it is for me?" the *Liberté's* captain asked huskily, moving behind Tess to cup her shoulders.

"It—it is merely the wind which blows chill."

"Indeed? I would have called the day a warm one." André's hands flattened against the bare, sun-warmed skin of her back. "Chill—and yet you display yourself half clothed on deck? You must expect some response to such wantonness in that case." Warm fingers slipped past the open folds at the back of her dress, moving around to cup her full breasts.

Tess's eyelids flickered shut. She fought to smother a whimper of delight at the raw fire of his touch. His fingers brushed over her, feather-light, circling and then plucking the dusky crests that swelled obediently beneath his expert strokes.

"S-stop, André. You—you must not—"

"Hush, *bihan*. No one can see us. The crew are all too busy at their work. As I should be," he added grimly. "But with such a one as you on deck, drowsy and content, only half clothed, I can think of nothing but *this.*" Abruptly his fingers splayed open, then closed fiercely, capturing her within their hard span. "Tell me what you feel, sea gull," he demanded hoarsely. "Does this arouse you as much as it does me?"

Tess's chest rose and fell in sharp, jerky bursts. She moaned, barely hearing his question, dazed by a rush of raw sensation that left her hungry and aching for more of the same torment. "Please," she whispered hoarsely.

"Oh, I *will* please you, *mon coeur*. That I promise."

From somewhere amidships, Padrig called out to André. "Ile aux Moines, Captain. Dead ahead."

Tess felt a raw curse rumble through André's broad chest as he crushed her back against him. Abruptly his hands withdrew from her flushed skin, and she felt him jab the row of tiny buttons into their holes. "Don't show yourself again on deck in such a way," he ordered hoarsely. "Other men would not refuse such an offer."

His harsh warning struck Tess like icy water. "Offer? Why you pig-headed, insufferable—"

"Man, *bihan*. *Your* man. As you are my woman. Do not forget this."

Her blood pounding with fury, Tess spun about to face him. "Not yours. Not any man's! I—"

Suddenly a ragged cry burst from her lips. She swayed, then flung a trembling hand across her face.

Explosions of light. Tendrils of fire and blinding color. Pain—wave after wave—exploding behind her eyes and roaring through her head.

"No!" Tess sobbed, grinding her teeth, driving her hands into her eyes at the cruel sensations. "Dear God."

"What is it, *bihan*?" André demanded hoarsely, catching her to him. "What's happening?"

"M-my head. Like knives. F-fire!"

Then the lights exploded, blinding and inhuman, dragging Tess down into their merciless embrace.

* * *

An eternity later she awoke to the low murmur of voices.

In her head? she wondered dimly. No, outside they were, ranged in a circle around her.

But why did they speak so low—the way people speak in a sickroom? For some reason the thought irritated her. "Speak up," she tried to say. "Don't mumble so."

But her throat was strangely dry; the only sound that emerged was a raw, choked whimper.

"*Bihan?*" Hard fingers swept the tangled mane from her face. Something cool and damp slid across her flushed brow. "Can you hear me?"

"I—I hear you," she managed. Pain made her fretful. "My eyes are damaged, not my ears. Why—why is everyone whispering?"

A stunned silence ensued, broken finally by the soft rumble of André's laughter.

Tess winced, trying to rise, only to feel the Frenchman's hard hands clamp down on her waist and hold her still. It was then that she realized she lay cradled in his lap, her head nestled against his knee. "Why—why am I down here?"

"I was just going to ask you the same question, *bihan.*"

Once again Tess tried to sit up, only to feel a dull pressure build behind her eyes. With a little whimper, she lay back against those rock-hard thighs.

"Tell me what happened."

"Like—a great burst of flame. Light—colors everywhere. And then . . ." Her voice trailed away. Even now it hurt to remember.

"Go on," he prodded.

"Then nothing. Only darkness."

And pain, Tess thought bleakly. Dull, throbbing paroxysms that shredded her very soul. But she did not mean to tell him of that. Curling her hands into fists, she fought to deny the pain that still pounded through her head.

"And now?"

"Just as before. Darkness—that's all." Tess's dry lips quivered for a moment, then she managed a smile. "Now, will you please take me to see this island you've been forever boasting about."

"You're lying, *bihan,*" the *Liberté*'s captain growled. "I want the truth, by God!".

"It is as I've told you. The feeling has passed. Why do you delay, when your crew must be anxious to be off?"

A rough murmur of disagreement went up from the unseen figures ranged nearby. Padrig's gruff voice filtered down to her. "Not that anxious. There's a doctor at Vannes, André. Shall I—"

"I need no doctor," Tess announced sharply. "What good would a mountebank do me anyway?"

"You should be seen," André growled. "Perhaps—"

"Perhaps he might wave a magic wand? Perhaps he might scatter moondust over me, restoring my vision? No, enough of these false hopes. Let me accept what must be." Tess's lip trembled and she caught it between her teeth. "Do you mean to take me to this island of yours, or do I have to find a boat and row there myself?"

A tense silence fell around her. André's thighs bunched and tensed beneath her neck. As he shifted, the hard, swollen line of muscle at his groin grazed her shoulder.

Tess's heart lurched, and she felt an answering heat sweep over her. Her tongue darted out to moisten suddenly dry lips.

A long, low curse erupted from the captain's mouth, followed a moment later by a rapid-fire stream of orders to his crew. Tess felt herself lifted roughly, locked in a pair of granite arms, and carried across the deck.

She was in the rowboat before she knew it, dipping and pitching toward shore.

"You've the temper of a crazed boar, do you know that? By all the saints, I think I shall have to beat you," André said grimly. "Unless I can find better ways of taming you. But one thing I know clearly. There is pain, *Anglaise*—I can see it in the way you flinch at the pitch of the boat, the way your lips tense and turn white. You can never hope to hide such things from me, and it is as well you learn that now. If you choose to ignore this pain, I will not argue with you. I ask only that you tell me when it grows too great to bear. Then I will give you something to make it better. And, of course, you *will* see the doctor from Vannes when he arrives tonight." André's voice was cold and unyielding, leaving no room for protest. "Stop arguing and let me tie this dampened cloth over your eyes. Perhaps it will make you more comfortable until the doctor can be summoned."

Tess nodded silently, feeling tears slip in a silent flood down her cheeks. She was ashamed of her weakness in relenting, but too tired for once to fight, content to leave the decision to this hard, enigmatic stranger. She turned away, scrubbing furtively at her cheeks. "Tell me about Padrig," she said, anxious to change the subject. "Is—is he married?"

André did not answer immediately. He sighed, long and rough, mumbling something under his breath. "Very well, stubborn creature, he is married and has been so for ten years. To a woman as tiny and exquisite as he is vast and brawny. Four sons he has already."

Was there a trace of regret in the captain's voice? "Do they resemble him?" Tess asked, wishing she might see his face.

"Exactly so, each with ruddy cheeks and piercing green eyes. And each one bigger than he is."

"What does his wife think of this work that takes him away from home for weeks at a time?"

"She accepts it, as all Breton women must. She has a great love for her husband. Yes, an odd pair they make, but never was there a rarer love." He turned, and Tess felt him looking down at her. "Except, perhaps, for mine, *bihan,*" he added roughly.

Soon they drifted into the quiet, sheltered waters of the gulf. Tess could hear the waves lap gently, the air rich with the mingled perfume of camellias, mimosas, and pine. Scattered around them, André told her, were two hundred tiny islands studding the silver gulf, and Tess could only marvel at the difference between this place and the angry, raging seas to the north.

A place of magic, she thought, listening to the lap of the waves on the hull. A place to dream.

A moment later André put down the sculls, and the hull whispered over a bank of sand.

"Come, sea gull, this day is yours. First I want to show you my home. Then I want to feed you, for you are too thin. And then"—his voice dropped to a husky whisper—"then we shall see."

The next thing Tess knew, she was bundled into his strong arms once more.

"Ah, there's Marthe now."

"Marthe?" Tess frowned, unable to keep the tension from her voice.

But the Frenchman only chuckled. "Yes, a woman very dear to my heart. I've loved her for almost two decades."

Tess stiffened, her fingers shoving at his chest.

"And she has loved me for three, since the day I was born," André continued. "Yes, she is eighty years old this day, *bihan,* and has served my family for nearly all of those years." His lips dropped to Tess's ear. "So quick to jump to conclusions, sea gull? It pleases me, nevertheless. If you are jealous, you cannot be so indifferent as you pretend," he whispered, nipping her ear.

"What have I to be jealous of?" Tess snapped. "I have no hold over you. Nor you over me," she added bleakly.

"Ah, but there you are wrong, *mon coeur.* And before the night is over, I mean to make these bonds tighter still," André vowed grimly. Then his voice changed. "Ah, Marthe, you've come straight from your garden, I see."

"You always did have a terrible notion of time, André, ever since you were a boy. But where are your manners, boy? Who have you brought home to meet me?" The woman's breath checked as she took in the white bandage knotted over Tess's eyes. She clucked sympathetically.

Tess's lips curved at the thought of this hard, brawny Breton being called a boy.

"I've brought a friend, Marthe. She was hurt and will stay until the doctor arrives from Vannes. As for her name, you may call her *bihan,* as the rest of us do."

Even now there were to be no names, no details, Tess realized. In André's line of work, names—at least real ones—were too dangerous. With that thought came the cold realization that her time here would be only brief.

It must be so, for her mere presence brought danger to all of them.

"Very well," the old woman said complacently. "Now come inside and rest, while I fix you a proper meal. I'm sure that good-for-nothing Le Fur has given you nothing but cider and omelettes for the last week," Marthe added with a sniff.

"But his omelettes were very good," Tess could not help but protest.

"Ah bah, you have yet to taste mine, *bihan*. Or even André's. He has a fine hand, so he does."

"But then I had the best of teachers, Marthe." The Frenchman laughed. "Very exacting. *Diaoul*, I still wince to remember how you whacked me with a spoon when I spoiled one."

"Don't curse before me, young man," the old woman said curtly. "Forgetting all your manners, that's what you are. Soon you'll have the young lady believing I'm some sort of ogre." She sniffed shortly. "Now I go to cook. Your room is ready. The sheets have been aired."

Tess felt heat stain her cheeks. Vainly she struggled against André's chest. "Put me down," she whispered. "Whatever must she think?"

"Marthe? She is delighted to see that I've brought a female home at last. She was beginning to think me unnatural in my tastes, I fear. And you are the first woman who has ever come here, *gwellañ-karet*. Do you believe me?"

Tess could not doubt him, not when there was so much fierceness in his voice. Suddenly she seemed to have difficulty breathing.

"Tell me, sea gull—tell me that you believe it. Tell me that you have learned to trust me." There was an edge of desperation to his voice.

"I—I do believe you, André. As for trust—" Her voice checked. It was too soon to ask that of her.

"Who hurt you in such a way?" the *Liberté*'s captain demanded harshly. "Tell me and I'll rip his heart out."

"It—it was a long time ago, André. Please—let's not speak of it. Not now, while there is so much beauty around us."

His fingers tightened on her ribs; Tess felt his eyes search her face. A low curse erupted from his lips. *"Diaoul,* woman, you are a stubborn creature! But you will see that I, too, can be stubborn!"

They sat in a little, sun-warmed garden with the humming of bees and bird song for a lulling background. From the kitchen came the smoke of the fire and the sharp *tap-tap-tap* of a whisk as Marthe beat feather-light omelettes. After those were gone, they feasted on buckwheat pancakes lightly sprinkled with sugar. Tess discovered she was ravenous.

"Here, *me kalon.*"

Tess frowned, cocking her head.

"Open your mouth."

When she did as André asked, Tess felt him place a delicate bit of seafood on her tongue. It slid down smoothly with a faintest taste of lemon. "Carp?"

"Istrenn." His voice was dark and rough. "Oysters, *Anglaise.*"

Tess felt her cheeks burn crimson. Her heart pounding, she swept her tongue across suddenly dry lips.

André growled. "No more of that or I'll forget my good intentions. Now eat." Once more he slipped a delicate Belon oyster onto her tongue, then took another for himself. A long sigh escaped his lips. *"Gwerhéz Vari,* but it is good to be home. To smell the camellias in bloom. To hear the bees droning, just as they have done here since I was a boy." Regret clouded his voice for a moment. "Yes, it has been too long . . ."

"Since what?"

"Too long since a great many things, *bihan.* Since I went hunting for oysters in the bay. Since I climbed along Trech Point and walked the Forest of Sighs. Since I saw the thirty-six standing stones of Kergonan. But enough of these incessant questions. Here is Marthe with more food, and we must eat or she will be very angry."

Tess could barely hold back a groan of protest at the thought of more food. But there it was, more sweet rich cakes of buckwheat and butter, cider, and creamy, washed-rind cheeses.

Finally Marthe pronounced herself satisfied and returned to the kitchen. With a sigh of relief, totally replete, Tess lay back against the pillows André had scattered over the ground. Drowsy from sun and food and wine, she allowed herself to drift off.

When she heard Padrig's deep cough a short while later, she barely stirred.

The two men spoke for a few moments in Breton, and then André's hand brushed her cheek. "I must go down to the ship, but not for long, *bihan.* Stay here and rest. Marthe will be nearby if you need anything."

Tess yawned, nodding, and somehow managed a sleepy smile.

When she woke the bees had gone and the air was cool. She had just sat up and was combing awkward fingers through her hair when she heard Marthe come out from the kitchen.

"Had a good sleep, did you?" The old woman began collecting dishes from the ground, not waiting for Tess's answer. "Yes, there is something special about this place. Food, sleep—everything is better here. Flavors are sharper, colors brighter. André says it's because we're up on the cliffs, where the sun and sea wind scour things clean. Myself, I say it's because of the flowers. They grow everywhere here—camellia, fuchsia, hydrangea, and rhododendron. We even have lemon and orange trees." The rattling ceased. "You're the first one he ever brought here, you know."

Tess swallowed, suddenly dry-throated. "Truly?" she managed to ask.

"Oh, there was that other one. From Morlaix, she was. André brought her to the island, but never overnight. I always thought the whole thing was more *her* doing than his, but never mind that. She died six months ago, poor creature. André was gone to sea, and the soldiers came, damn their black souls to Hell eternal. No one even knew until it was too late." The old woman's voice shook, and she rained down a string of Breton curses. "When they were done with her—well, she was not right somehow. Her mind was never the same. She carried a baby, and lost it three months later. When André came back, she barely recognized him, though the sound of his voice seemed to comfort her. She died not long after the babe." Tess heard the old woman turn, looking out to sea. "She was buried down there in the churchyard, in the lee of the wind, not so far away from my own dear Pierre."

Tess heard a sniff, then the rustling of cloth.

"But I've talked enough, even for an old and very foolish woman. You have a way of making people talk, *bihan.* It's the way you listen, I think, all still and bright. I see why he loves you."

Tess's heart began to hammer wildly. A thousand questions rushed to her lips. "But why—" she began uncertainly.

Marthe's next words cut her short.

"Ah, here he is now."

Tess started, feeling like a child caught in the act of eavesdropping. She heard his quick step on the grass and caught his distinctive smell, a mingling of crisp sea air and the tang of a citrus soap.

"Has Marthe been talking you to sleep?" the captain demanded. "If she's been recounting all my boyhood exploits, I'll—"

"No, truly," Tess said quickly, afraid Marthe would tell him exactly what they *had* been speaking of.

"Enough of your bullying, young man. Listen to your lady, that's my advice to you. As for me, I go out to my garden, where I can think of my poor dead Pierre and how I will soon be with him." Her footsteps moved slowly away.

In the sudden silence, Tess could feel André nearby, studying her face.

"Spread your skirts, *Anglaise,* and prepare to receive your tribute. These are from Le Braz." A cluster of roses plummeted into Tess's lap, scenting the air with dizzying sweetness. "These from Le Fur." The scent of mimosas drifted up next. "And these are from me."

Camellias, Tess thought, enveloped in their haunting perfume. Her throat grew suspiciously tight. "Oh, André," she breathed. "How lovely."

Warm and thick as honey, the last slanting rays of the sun touched her shoulders. Somewhere in the bordering hedge a bird began to croon contentedly. Sitting down beside her, André sang an old Breton song, then translated the sad, sweet words verse by verse while the sun melted in fiery glory over the calm waves of the gulf.

Later, much later, when she could again think with anything like clarity, Tess was to realize that the whole day had been a seduction. With the rich beauty of his rough voice, the Frenchman had seduced her; with his laughter, with his stories, with the potent Breton foods he had fed her, using his own fingers.

Seduction—every part of it. And she had tumbled into his trap totally, caught before she had any notion she was being pursued.

Even the doctor's arrival soon after this had not broken the spell —not at first.

The fingers that probed her bandage were light and deft. Taut with expectation, hoping that the recent pains in her head signalled the return of her sight, Tess could barely endure the mounting tension.

The doctor hummed and clucked, listening carefully to her account of the accident. With careful fingers he released the knot holding her bandage in place. "Look at me," he ordered.

Tess tried; with all her might, she tried. But only darkness was there to meet her.

A choked moan escaped her locked lips. Ashen-faced, she fought the disappointment that slammed through her like a fist.

Nothing. Nothing but blind.

Why had she dared to hope?

Her breath came and went in jerky gasps as she listened to the doctor speak words of hope and encouragement, with André interrupting often to ask a question or clarify the doctor's advice, meager though it was.

But in the days since her blindness Tess had come to know a great deal about voices—and she heard the regret in the doctor's voice now, even though he spoke of the necessity for optimism.

"—never too late—"

"—impossible to say—"

The words began to blur. A great black shape rose over Tess, sweeping its dark wings wide to cover her and crush her.

After the doctor left, Tess did not move, still seated in the shadows of the now-chill garden. Her body tense, stretched taut as a bowstring beneath an archer's fingers, she looked up into the shadows that separated her from André.

"Please," she rasped. As was their habit, she spoke in French. "Dear God, André—you must—" Her voice caught for a moment. "Take me to your bed this night. Take me to the light and make me burn. Oh, please, make me forget this nightmare!"

She did not even realize her mistake.

But André heard, and his face hardened at the word. Even now, he realized, this woman could not bring herself to use *tu,* the more intimate form of address, to him. A small slip, but telling nevertheless.

Particularly in view of what she was asking of him.

Tess's heart was pounding so furiously that she barely heard the rough growl that broke from his throat. The next moment his hard hands seized her wrists and jerked her stumbling to her feet.

"Is this what you ask of me, *Anglaise?*" he snarled. "Then this is my answer. No! As God is my witness, no! This I will never do!"

32

Tess shivered, ashen-faced, as she heard the flat fury in the Frenchman's voice.

Gone, all gone, she thought, feeling her mind grow numb, as if all that had happened was no more than a dream.

Or a nightmare. Suddenly it was exactly that, the same nightmare she always had, the one that had haunted her since those days and nights spent locked in the tunnels at Fairleigh.

Already the darkness had wrapped her in its gleaming coils when she heard André's low curse.

"Even now you cannot say it, can you? *Tu—tu!* Say it!" His fingers, where they bit into her wrists, began to shake. "Stubborn creature, you think you are safe—that these walls can protect you. But they only enslave you, *Anglaise*. Say it!"

Tess whimpered, her thoughts awhirl as she struggled away from the cold shadows. *"T-tu. Vraiment."*

You. Though it was madness itself.

The trembling in his fingers ceased. With a low, savage growl André bent Tess back in his arms until her wine-dark hair spilled down her back and cascaded to the ground. "That way, *gwellañkaret*. That way I'll have you. Not to bed but to love. *Diaoul*, but I'll love you, *Anglaise*. Until you forget where you end and I begin. Until you shudder and whisper—my name. Not his." His fingers splayed apart over her ribs, dragging her into the hard cradle of his thighs, where even now the angry line of his arousal jutted boldly. "Starting now. Say the words, *bihan*. Tell me what you want, and how, and from whom."

"Toi, André. Aime-moi." Somehow she could say them now, the words he wanted, needed even. "Love me—now."

With those simple syllables everything changed. The fires in André's eyes burned brighter, fed not by rage but by desperation and a fierce, devouring need. Without another word he began to tear at the mocking row of buttons down her back.

One. Two. Dimly Tess counted their muffled snaps, her blood pounding.

Three. Four.

With a low, feral growl, André hooked his fingers into the cloth and sheared off all the rest, then tugged the gown from Tess's shoulders until the perfect white sweep of her body was revealed to him.

"But M-Marthe?" she whispered.

"Is gone," André finished. "And we are alone, my beauty. My sweet *sauvage*." His big hands moved to cup her full breasts and circle the dusky crests, now pebbled and urgent. "My heart's own heart."

"Take me, André," Tess heard someone whisper, wondering at the strange, hoarse sound of that female voice.

Her voice?

"Touch me—all of me. With all of you." With frantic fingers she pushed at his collar, tugging at the buttons that separated their skin so cruelly. Finally, with a little moan, she savaged the row of them just as he had done to hers.

They fell with a muffled *ping* onto the green carpet at Tess's feet.

Tess fell a moment later, gasping as André's hard, hot body strained against her. Her fingers tore at his breeches; his hands jerked the float of velvet from beneath her hips and tossed it in a crumpled heap at her side.

She was beyond words now, beyond thought, driven by a fierce, nameless hunger for him. Her lips could only curve and pant, her tongue only slide, restless and hungry.

When his mouth crushed down upon her, she whimpered and

bit, fighting for more, always more, tongue hot against tongue just as his velvet shaft searched for her softness.

When his hand found the warm tangle of curls at her thighs, André growled, low and dark, slipping his fingers deep.

Pleasure burst through Tess in solid, jolting waves. Somehow he knew exactly where to tease and where to drive fiercely. How many women, she wondered dimly, had he touched this way? Only a vast experience could have taught him how to arouse her with such unerring certainty, as if her body were well-known terrain.

Suddenly she stiffened, fighting him. "No, André, not that way. I—I want you with me this time. I want to feel you inside me, to wrap myself around you when the pleasure comes." She could have that much of him, at least. To know he was inside *her*, thinking of *her* and not one of those other women.

"Good sweet God." With a ragged groan, the dark-bearded Frenchman pulled away to knee apart her thighs. Even then she could not bear to let him go, arching her back and straining upward until her lips found the salty line of his throat.

André's whole body went rigid as he fought the urge to plunge home ruthlessly within her. "As God is my witness, *bihan,* any more of that and I'll not be able to wait. I'll take you here and now, without any preliminaries, with all the fanfare of a dockside whore."

"Yes, *now,*" Tess moaned, hearing nothing of what he said but that one word—needing him inside her, bathing her in molten quicksilver.

Anything to find the fire, to still the cruel thought of the darkness that stretched before her always and forever, until the end of her days.

"No," he raged hoarsely, struggling to ignore the sweet wild thrusting of her hips beneath him, the choked whimpers that drifted from her throat, the flush of passion that slicked her skin wherever their bodies met. "No," he gasped again, and knew he was losing.

"An-*dré,*" Tess pleaded, nipping his neck. "Please! Oh—now!"

Her back arched like a bow, her taut nipples scraping his chest like small, sweet buds.

Somewhere in the back of her mind Tess hated herself for responding so completely—and hated him for knowing how to touch her so perfectly.

But it was as if those thoughts belonged to another—her body a stranger's, which she could no longer command.

And then the Frenchman gave her what they both wanted. With a dark groan he reared above her and cupped her hips. "I can wait no more, *bihan*. Are you—ah, God—sure?" His voice was hoarse with his fierce effort at control.

Her answer came without words, in the wild stirring of her hips and the restless arch of her back.

"Take me then, sea gull," he cried, plunging Tess into paradise as his hot engorged shaft swept home deep inside her. "*An Aotrou Doué!* Take every hungry inch of me!"

Tess did.

Wildly. Fiercely. In sweet, mindless abandon. Always wanting more—searching and shifting, digging her fingers into his tensed shoulders and wrapping her long legs around his waist to draw him even closer.

Then her Frenchman took her into the storm, just as he had promised, plunging fiercely and withdrawing in long strokes of endless, exquisite friction, every hard, rocking thrust wrapping her in ineffable, heart-stopping splendor.

She shivered, cast upon a strange, restless sea, following each wave to its crest and then sliding down into a dizzying pool of pleasure. Somehow Tess found light there, just as André had promised, a dancing phosphorescence that drifted up and wrapped about their slick, heated bodies.

Dimly she heard someone groan. Herself? she wondered. Or him? Somehow Tess could not say—they were so close now, pore fixed to pore, nerve fused to nerve, inch against every straining, love-slick inch, locked in a oneness Tess had not believed possible.

His heart hammered, its pitch deep, the same as hers. Their pulses throbbed, drumming in unison. And their bodies—oh, sweetly, perfectly in tune.

Fire and shadow.

Rhythm and counterpoint.

And always the searing pleasure when Tess slid down the wave's dark face to rock in the trough, each climb higher than the last as she was driven gasping and panting toward the mountain of water that rose up from nowhere before her.

Mindless, empty, wanting to be filled completely. By him. Now.

"An-André?" she gasped, suddenly uncertain, feeling a wild convulsive tremor shake her where their bodies joined.

"Yes, that way, *bihan*. Say—ahh—my name so always!"

"Andr—ohhhhh."

Suddenly, trivial things like names and countries and words were forgotten, as a great blinding wave of pleasure crashed through Tess, shocking her speechless, making her arch her back and dig her toes into the soft green grass and whimper.

Hard hands dragged her close, savoring the wild tremors that shook her, drinking the little, breathless moans from her lips.

She fell.

And fell . . .

And found him waiting.

"Aghhh! Tight—so sweet. Yes, again! Again, my wild sweet love. Hold me this way forever." His lips locked, his face taut with strain, the Frenchman began to move anew, balanced on his elbows, filling her with fire and wonder once more.

My God, but she is beautiful, the *Liberté*'s captain thought dimly through a haze of pleasure, feeling her ripple and contract in her ecstasy, each tremor burning through him with an exquisite torture.

Yet, still he held himself back, his whole being focused on her pleasure, filling her fiercely until she arched and then fell back once more.

Fighting his own release, he watched her, until the breathless pleasure sounds died away and she ran slow, questioning fingers up his chest to cup his taut shoulders.

"André?" Tess whispered, swept with sadness that she had not had him with her when she fell away into the sun. Not once but twice.

His only answer was a savage, half-choked grunt.

Dear God, he must have found her unattractive, Tess thought wildly. Too gauche, too—everything! After all, he had known so many women. What if . . .

Tess's eyes widened, dark with embarrassment. White-faced, she tried to pull free, shoving blindly at his chest. A single tear worked its way from beneath her bandage.

"L-let me go, damn you! It's all so easy for you, isn't it? Just another game—just another thing for you and Padrig to joke about during your leisure hours at sea!"

More tears followed, spilling down her pale cheeks in a cold, angry rush.

A ragged sound, half laugh and half roar, exploded from André's lips. "Easy, is it, halfling? *Easy?* To hold back when I'm on fire with wanting you? When all I can think of is that sweet burnished triangle, and how you sheathe every inch of me?"

Tess froze, her features caught in lines of ludicrous surprise. "It isn't? You are?" Laughing raggedly, she brushed at her damp cheeks.

"Yes, and yes again, my witless mer-creature. And now, as Heaven above is my witness—"

André never finished. Not with words, that is, for somehow his taut body grew tired of waiting and interrupted, meaning to do the rest of the talking for him.

His thighs tensed. His belly flattened.

Liquid and hot, he slid home to the hilt in her sweet, trembling velvet—and almost died of the bliss she brought him when she began to convulse around him once more.

Tess gasped. Somehow even then questions burned on her lips. "But you—have not, that is, you did not—"

"The first time was for forgetting, sea gull. And the second— ahhh—was for burning. While the third—" The Frenchman groaned as her clever fingers dropped, discovering the aroused male nipples hidden in a dense tangle of wiry hair. With a low, feral growl, he swept them over as one, catching her above him, his hands cupping her bottom. Around them her hair glistened, falling like a dark curtain of flame. "This time is for loving, *tu comprends?* How could it not be so, *me kalon,* when you fill me with a thousand suns? I will never have an end to wanting you this way. Skin to skin against me—taken in love."

But now it was Tess who did not listen, her heart on fire, her eyes wide with wonder, her full lips curved in a smile of aching beauty.

Delighting in the unimpeded feel of him driving against the very heart of her, exulting in the dark growls of pleasure her slightest movement seemed to wrest from his lips.

From somewhere came the harsh thunder of the surf, echoing in her ears and in her blood and in her heart itself, as wild and untamed as the man who moved against her so fiercely.

This time when the wave began to lift her, she felt André rise with her, muttering dark Breton love words against her neck and breasts as they burst together into the storm's full fury.

Darkness turned to light; for a moment emptiness found solid form. A strange, phosphorescent glow seemed to flow through them, visible even to Tess's blind eyes.

And then they shattered, their molecules spread thin and then mingling, sown wide and together over the vast distance of cloud and water where love's fierce storm hurled them at last.

Sleep came almost immediately. They lay together, limbs entwined, dark hair tangled amid burnished auburn, white skin soft against bronze.

Replete, they dreamed and drifted, while the warm winds whispered over the granite cliffs, stirring the gulf waters to restless silver in the moonlight.

Even the nightingales did not sing that night, for fear of waking them.

Something pricked him, deep in his mind. Some overlooked responsibility?

The Frenchman shifted, mumbling.

Half asleep, his quick mind darted through a hundred preparations awaiting his attention. There were the *Liberté*'s stores to be refilled, and the coppered hull to be scoured free of barnacles and tiny marine borers; the topgallant sails would have to be resewn where the storm had left sections badly frayed.

A soft hand touched his chest, combing through the dense fur.

André's breath caught sharply, fire flooding through his groin. His eyes flashed open.

Slowly his hard features relaxed in a smile full of primal male triumph, a smile as old as man himself.

She was his now. *Gwerhéz Vari*, but with what fire she took him! And how beautiful, André thought, mute with wonder. Every day she seemed to grow more so. His eyes were smoky with passion as he looked down at her auburn hair, flung out against the pillow like a dusky flame. One pale hand was tucked under her cheek as she slept, the faint, haunting scent of lavender surrounding her.

As beautiful as the day he had first seen her.

And he wanted her now just as badly as he had wanted her then. A vein pounded raggedly at his temple as his arousal reached painful proportions. Yes, right now he could think of nothing he'd like better than to bury his fingers in that fiery mane and kiss her lovely skin from neck to toe until she awoke beneath him, flushed and slick with desire.

But he did not, knowing she needed at least a little rest after the exertions of the hours before. And his chivalry was killing him.

Find some distraction, fool, he told himself sharply, slipping from the bed to pick up a small piece of pine and a narrow knife. Soon his fingers were flying over the wood, fashioning a miniature figure; as a boy, he had picked up the skill and never forgotten it.

But as he whittled, André found he had to face questions that before he had always managed to avoid.

Questions about what he meant to do with the beautiful Englishwoman. Questions about what sort of a scoundrel he was to keep her here. What had he to offer her, after all? Only hardship and danger, punctuated by a few brief hours of pleasure.

Only lies and more lies.

Even now they were surrounded by danger, though she could not know that. His dark obsession made him take risks he should never have even considered.

There were so many things he needed to ask her, so many things she deserved to know in turn. But it was far too soon for that, he knew. Not when her trust in him was still so tenuous.

The captain's bearded face twisted in a bitter smile. Tenuous? *Diaoul,* it was nonexistent! She trusted no one and nothing, it seemed.

How deeply, he wondered, were her thoughts still tied to her English lord?

Suddenly he stiffened, smothering a curse. Looking down, he saw that his knife had slipped and blood was welling across his palm. *Clumsy thing to do, my friend,* the Frenchman thought, brushing away the crimson streaks with his other hand.

Blood and more blood.

André closed his eyes, remembering his past with painful clarity. Yes, he had spilled blood—not once but many times. It seemed that those angry ghosts lay in wait for him—now and always.

His eyes opened, smoky slits. Perhaps he more than anyone could understand the Englishwoman's need to sleep with a lit candle.

Would not this savage obsession of his lead to more spilling of blood?

Suddenly he froze, all his seaman's instincts aroused. From outside the door there came a faint creaking of wood.

Slipping from the chair, he threw open the door.

"Sorry to disturb you, my friend." The rough whisper was Padrig's.

"*Diaoul,* man! I nearly gulletted you!" Frowning, André dropped the knife he had been gripping at his side. "Have you ever been told that your sense of timing is execrable!" With a jerk of his head, André motioned the first mate into the hall and then followed him out, sublimely unconscious of his magnificent nakedness.

"Well, there was that time at Morlaix, when the gendarmes burst upon us most inopportunely. I believe you said something of the sort then. And of course, there was that day I came upon you panting and stumbling about in a hayrick with that merchant's daughter from Vannes."

"*She* was doing all the panting, believe me, my friend. Yes, I'd forgotten about that. But what is so important that you come here now?"

Padrig's ruddy face darkened. "French soldiers—a whole detachment, checking every vessel in the harbor. It seems they've an eye to appropriate anything that looks like it might float. I didn't think you'd care to lose the *Liberté* to one of Napoleon's admirals."

"You're right about that, my brawny friend. Give me a few moments and I'll follow you."

Silently the bearded captain slipped back to the candlelit room and stood looking down at the sleeping woman. Her hand reached out, curving around the spot where he had lain moments before. A frown creased her face.

"Sleep, *bihan,*" André whispered. "When I return, believe me, I shall give you more to do than sleep."

He found Marthe in the pantry, setting away the last cleaned dishes. "Watch her, Marthe. I'll not be gone long, but if she should wake . . ."

"I'll see to your woman," the old servant said briskly. "Just you go before Padrig bursts his seams with impatience."

In the quiet night hours that followed, the old woman fought a valiant fight, pacing a bit and then sitting down to mend some of André's torn shirts. When her eyelids grew too heavy, she stood up to pace once more.

But somehow she kept seeing the lined, smiling face of her dead husband drift before her tired eyes. Before Marthe knew it, she was asleep.

"You still have had no letter from her?"

Lord Lennox sank into a chair in the Angel's front parlor, disappointment creasing his handsome features.

Impassively Hobhouse shook his head, continuing to lay out silver trays, cutlery, and spotless linens for tea.

The earl sighed audibly, shaking his head. "It is only that she was promised to attend a small fête we are having two days hence. There is a party coming down from London—I was anxious to introduce her, you see." His voice trailed away.

"She did not plan to make her trip a long one, your lordship, that much I do know. Beyond that I would not make myself so bold as to speculate."

He was handsome enough, in a pattern-card perfect sort of way, the Angel's majordomo thought. Well respected, titled—which amounted to the same thing, didn't it? Yet Miss Tess continued to delay giving Lord Lennox the answer he sought.

It couldn't be that she was still grieving for that bastard Ravenhurst, could it? The man was an out-and-out bounder! The tales of his infamous exploits—both on land and at sea—had reached even Rye. In London, so Hobhouse had heard, the Devil of Trafalgar still figured in a great deal of very spicy gossip.

Although no one ever dared call him that name to his face, of course.

"If you do hear anything, you will let me know, won't you?" Lord Lennox asked, interrupting the majordomo's reverie.

"Certainly, your lordship."

"Ah, Simon, there you are." Lady Patricia stood silhouetted in the doorway, surveying the room with her small, sharp eyes. For a moment disappointment and petulance darkened their emerald depths. Then, with a sharp twitch of her taffeta skirts, she moved inside and sat down. "I shall be grateful for your escort home, to be sure, Simon. There are such tales being bruited about."

Lord Lennox's blond brows rose to questioning slants. "Tales? What sort of tales, my dear?"

Lady Patricia affected a shudder, pressing pale hands to her silk-clad bosom. "The very worst sort, I'm afraid. It seems this Fox fellow has tired of smuggling and has now turned to assaulting defenseless females upon the marsh."

Hobhouse's shoulders stiffened fractionally. What in the devil was the woman blathering about now?

"This is more of Hermione Tredwell's gossip, I take it." Lord Lennox came to his feet and began to pace the small room, his air abstracted.

"Nothing of the sort," his sister countered sharply. "I had it from the vicar himself. And we were having such a nice chat up until then," she purred.

Aye, and so can pigs fly, Hobhouse thought sourly, reaching to offer her a sweetmeat.

Lady Patricia waved him away brusquely. "Yes, it seems a young woman of his parish was assaulted last week as she returned from a visit to her ailing mother in Applegate. Being a country girl familiar with these parts, she had little concern for her safety and decided to take a shortcut through the marsh. A very bad notion, as it turned out, for a tall figure, caped and masked all in black, burst from the darkness and swooped down upon her." Her voice quivered delicately. "He ravished her most cruelly, the vicar said, and after that the brute tossed something onto her bruised body. 'Take it and remember me,' the girl recalls him growling before he rode away. When they found her several hours later, muttering and incoherent, a single black rose lay beside her. The Fox's very sign!" Lady Patricia added triumphantly.

Lord Lennox frowned, his pacing halted. "The vicar himself told you this?"

"Not five minutes ago."

Silently Hobhouse bowed and withdrew from the room, his thoughts in turmoil.

It could not be! Jack could never do such a thing, Hobhouse told himself. But where was the man? No one had seen hide nor hair of the smuggler since he'd left Fairleigh.

The majordomo's grizzled face darkened with worry as he moved down the hall. So absorbed was he by this startling news that he scarcely heard the merry shout from the front steps.

"Why so glum, Hobhouse? Don't tell me you've invested your money in the funds and lost it all?"

Frowning, Hobhouse looked up; an instant later his features froze in a look of comical dismay. No! It could not be!

"Well, you needn't rush to kiss me, of course, but I rather hoped for a warmer greeting than that." A slim, auburn-haired gentleman stood slapping a pair of fine leather gloves against his thighs, making a great effort to maintain an air of studied casualness. He was garbed in the height of fashion, from his polished Hessian boots and tight buckskin breeches to an embroidered yellow waistcoat and wasp-waisted green jacket.

Hobhouse felt his blood turn to ice. "Master—Master Ashley," he stammered. "What—what are you doing here?"

"Doing? I've come to see the contessa, of course." The name was an old childhood joke between the two young Leightons, bestowed upon Tess for her ability to cloak herself in cold disdain when the need arose.

Which it often had, given the sort of childhood they had been made to endure.

A faint titter echoed through the passageway at Hobhouse's back. "Yes, Mr. Leighton, what *are* you doing here? And where, pray tell, is that so charming sister of yours?"

"Sister? What makes you think—*ooow!*"

Somehow Hobhouse was across the corridor before Ashley knew it, his foot grinding into the young dandy's instep. "Lady Patricia has been awaiting Miss Tess's return from visiting you with great keenness," Hobhouse said impassively, turning slightly so that the woman could not see the warning look he sent Tess's startled brother.

"Visiting me?" The pressure to young Leighton's instep increased. "Agh, yes, that is—visiting me. Of course."

"Then where is she now?" Lady Patricia hissed.

"Who?"

"Your sister!" The blond beauty's voice was growing decidedly shrill.

"My sister? Oh, you mean Tess. Well, that is—damned if I know! With me one minute and gone the next. You know how women are," he added lamely, shrugging.

"No, I am afraid I do not know," Lady Patricia snapped. "And I quite fail to see how you could *misplace* her so easily."

Growing up with a father whose whims were always unpredictable and very often cruel, Ashley had learned something of the skill of improvisation. He called upon those lessons, unfortunately rather rusty, again now.

"Well, not to say misplace. Just overlooked," the young man emended carefully. "Yes, stap me if I didn't go off and leave her up at—at Fairleigh. Knew I'd forgotten something," he added with a bright, guileless smile.

Hearing the commotion, Lord Lennox stepped out to join his sister in the hallway. "Ah, good to see you again, Leighton. But your sister does not join you?"

Ashley tried, not quite successfully, to keep the coolness from his eyes when he looked at the immaculate earl. "Left her up at Fairleigh," he said flatly, tired of this interrogation.

"Then I shall wait for her," Lady Patricia announced.

Hobhouse and Ashley exchanged quick looks.

"Er—don't think that'd be a good idea."

Three pairs of eyes looked at Ashley, asking why.

"Well, er . . ." For a moment his inventiveness failed him. Damn, he was hungry and dusty, aching from long hours of travel in a cramped coach. Not right that a fellow should be subjected to an inquisition on his own bloody doorstep—not right at all!

At this moment all he could think of was taking off his new boots, which were pinching his toes raw. But Hobhouse's eyes looked at him pleadingly, and Leighton caught back a curse. "Er, that is—angry, that's what."

"Angry?" Lady Patricia prompted impatiently. "Whatever are you talking of?" *Fool.* She did not say the word, but she might just as well have, considering the scorn in her voice.

Ashley's slim shoulders immediately froze in stiff, defiant lines. "Angry as a hornet, by God. Won't want to see anyone. Not for hours! Maybe even weeks. Devil of a bad temper, my sister has. Yes, you'd best steer clear of her, Lady P., if you know what's good for you." With a little smile, Ashley delivered his coup de grace, using this childhood name, which Lord Lennox's sister had always detested.

"My name is Lady Patricia, and I'll thank you to remember it," the blonde snapped, her cheeks flaming dangerously. "And I don't believe your story for a moment!"

"Please, my dear," Lord Lennox interrupted, pressing hard fingers into his sister's arm. "I am sure Miss Leighton will contact us at her earliest convenience. Let me escort you home, now, so that young Leighton can renew himself after his travels."

"But what about Pierre? He can't have finished speaking with Edouard yet, and he promised to get me the recipe for *pâtés garnis* before our fête on Friday. I really must have it," she added sharply.

"Don't worry your lovely head about Pierre, my dear. He can find his own way back to Lennox House, I should imagine." Slanting a last, polite nod at Hobhouse and Ashley, the earl began to steer his sister out, one hand clamped to her elbow.

"Whatever are you about, Simon?" she hissed, the sound clearly audible as they moved toward the door.

"Enough, Patricia." Lennox's voice was suddenly harsh.

Very interesting, Hobhouse thought, wondering if he had been wrong in grouping the pair together in the enemy's camp. His eyes narrowing, he made a mental note to go check on that ferret-faced chef of Lennox's, before the man wormed all of their best recipes out of Edouard.

"Now, maybe you'll tell me what in the devil all *that* was about, Hobhouse. And don't give me that farrago about—"

Hobhouse caught Ashley's hand in a hard grip. "Not here," he warned, already guiding the new arrival off toward his rooms, down the hall from Tess's own. "I'm afraid something has happened," the servant explained softly. "Something you'd better know about right now."

Engrossed in their soft conversation, neither man noticed they were not alone. Behind them a slim figure stepped back into the shadows at the rear landing. There the Duchess of Cranford remained, careful to make no sound as she studied the two retreating figures, her eyes sharp and very thoughtful.

33

A branch was tapping at the shutter when Tess awoke. Tugging at the cold coverlet, she sat up, trying to place where she was and the source of that dry, restless hammering.

A tree, she thought, its bough tapping against the window. Only a tree. But where?

For a moment fear skittered up her spine. Then she remembered who had brought her here—and why.

With a rich sigh, she lay back against the bed and stretched slowly like a lazy, contented cat.

Lovely, so lovely. All of it. His hands, his mouth, his hard body.

Warmth infused her at the mere thought of the things he had done to her.

But where was the Frenchman now? Frowning, she sat up again, searching for her velvet dress, which she found lying where he had tossed it earlier. Absently she realized she would never be able to secure the buttons now, for he had sheared them all off.

The tapping at the window grew louder. Shivering, Tess picked her way over the bare wood floor, searching for the window. Her fingers met cold metal and she pushed open the door; immediately a cool breeze brushed her cheeks.

Somehow she was not afraid anymore. As if by magic, André's strength and powerful presence permeated the room, wrapping Tess in warmth.

No, she was not afraid. For the first time in years, she had learned to trust.

Still drowsy, she stood before the open French doors, her face turned to the playful night breezes. Her auburn curls swirled about her shoulders as she listened, unmoving, to the sweet lilting song of a nightingale.

She was right to trust him. Somehow Tess knew it without question.

Through the doors drifted the fragrance of roses and night-blooming jasmine. From the darkness something called to Tess, coaxing her out to explore the night's beauties.

In her newfound confidence she did not hesitate.

Just for a few minutes, she promised herself—just until she discovered the source of that magic fragrance.

She found the rose hedge by scent alone, dipping her head to draw in a long breath of its dusky sweetness. She had just reached out to break off a stalk heavy with blooms when she heard the crunch of gravel nearby.

Tess froze.

Someone was approaching. Two men, she realized. In the clear silence of night, their words carried perfectly.

"Almost done here, thank God. *Dieu,* but this stinking piss-pot of a town makes me want to throw up! If we leave tomorrow, it won't be soon enough for me!"

It was their accent that held Tess's attention. Curiously enough, they spoke in rapid Parisian French, not the slow, thick tones of the local Bretons. "Even the women are cows, wrapped head to foot in black, till you can't see a cursed inch of skin."

"Just as well you don't, Marcel. They've all got thick ankles and fat asses! No need to see them anyway. A man can plow a fat ass just as well as he can a beautiful one! All the same in the dark, eh?"

Hard, cruel laughter ripped the quiet night. Tess shivered, feeling their malice, their restless hunger for violence.

For a while there was silence. The acrid odor of a cheroot drifted over the hedge.

"Ugly bitches or no, we leave when the Eagle says we leave, and not before."

"Eh, he's a cold-hearted bastard, true enough. But he's efficient, I'll grant him that. You couldn't pay me to do the work he does. No, I don't plan to dangle at the end of an English noose."

The other man snorted in agreement. "At least the next shipment should be here shortly. The Eagle was acting restless last week at camp, and that means we'll go out again soon. We must have brought in ten thousand pounds in English guineas already. *Dieu,* but what I could do with so much wealth!"

"Still hoping to buy yourself a bordello and settle down for life, eh? Not me. I've had my fill of sweaty, heaving females!"

The other man snarled a curse under his breath. "What does it matter, anyway? We'll never see a single cursed English guinea! Chest after chest, and not a single one for us, who do the real work!"

Tess did not move, feeling the blood drain from her face. Her hands began to tremble. Stop! she wanted to scream. No more! I don't want to hear any of this!

But the men did not leave, and so she was trapped, forced to listen, knowing that some dreadful revelation was about to come.

"I bet that bastard the Fox doesn't put up with any of the Eagle's crap! He's a tough one, I hear. Damned good at what he does, too."

"Which is to help us," the unseen companion answered.

Bitter waves of denial swept over Tess. She swallowed, choking. No, it could not be . . .

Suddenly she had to get away. She couldn't stand to hear even one word more.

Wild-eyed, she turned and began to feel her way back along the hedge. She was very careful—or at least she thought she was. But not careful enough, as it turned out. Her foot brushed a fallen twig, and the dry wood snapped. In the crystal silence of the night, that small sound exploded with all the fury of a pistol shot.

A startled curse erupted from the other side of the hedge. "There's someone over there, by God! Get him. If the Eagle finds out—"

Tess stumbled forward, praying she was going toward the house. Behind her came the crash and snap of underbrush and the hiss of muffled curses.

Dear God, where was André? she wondered wildly.

Her foot slipped and she stumbled to her knees, but somehow managed to struggle back upright. Three steps more and she felt the edge of the flagstone terrace. *Almost there!*

"Not so fast, you!"

Tess gasped as hard fingers jerked her around.

"*Dieu,* but this bitch is a beauty. And half dressed, eh, Marcel? Waiting for your lover, little rabbit? Well, since he's delayed, I'll just have to take his place."

Wildly, Tess clawed the air, trying to find her assailant's face.

The man grunted, seizing her hands. "No need to fight. I've got a tool as hard as any man's. I'll give you a good ride—better than your clumsy Breton peasant would!"

Dimly Tess felt her fingers rake naked skin. Panting and sobbing, she clawed, again and again, knowing she dare not speak for fear the pair would recognize she was English.

"Infernal bitch! I'll teach you to—"

The man's open palm cracked against Tess's face, sending a burst of lights exploding behind her eyes. The world spun wildly, and Tess felt her knees begin to buckle.

Eager fingers dug at her dress, jerking the fabric from her shoulders.

Swept with waves of dizziness, she tried to fight, only to feel her hands knocked away.

The man's startled gasp seemed to come from a vast distance. "Eh, look at that, my friend. This one's a real beauty, by God." Stabbing fingers dragged the velvet down to her waist. "Look at that skin—like milk. And these!"

Ruthlessly the man grabbed at her breasts, pinching her nipples cruelly. Her dress tore in half, the shredded fragments falling to her ankles.

Dear God, she had to get her wits about her! If she didn't get away, they'd soon be astride her.

Fighting to steady her ragged breathing, Tess forced herself to relax beneath those cruel hands, willing herself to listen and wait for an unguarded moment. With a little sob, she caught her lips between her teeth, biting down to stifle her revulsion as the hungry fingers swept over her.

"So the rabbit likes that, does she? Jesus, I'm so stiff I'm about to explode!" The fingers tightened, pushing her to her knees, searching between her legs.

Dimly Tess heard the other man curse, grabbing for her. A moment later her captor fell back.

"I take her first, damn it! You always get everything before I do. But not this time!"

Tess heard a thud, then the sharp sounds of a struggle. Suddenly she was free!

Blindly she pulled herself to her feet and began to run, while behind her the angry, fighting sounds continued.

She reached the terrace and stumbled inside, jerking the French doors closed behind her.

"She's getting away, you fool!"

Ashen-faced, she ran her fingers along the wooden door frame, searching for the bolt. Finally she found it and jammed the cold metal home.

"She's locked the door, the bitch!"

Rustling—more grunting.

With a terrible crash, the glass burst, raining in a shower about Tess's feet. Dear God, what was she to do now?

"Damn, I've cut my hand. Bitch! It will go all the harder for you now," her unseen assailant snarled.

Heavy feet clambered over the door frame and crunched across the glass.

Cold with terror, Tess stumbled back toward the door to the kitchen.

And ran headlong into a rock-hard body. A man's body!

Her heart hammering wildly, she flailed the air, biting back the sobs that threatened to suffocate her.

"Hush, *bihan.*"

With a moan, Tess fell into the powerful arms that reached out to circle her. "Oh, God, André—"

But the *Liberté*'s captain pushed her behind him. "Go inside, woman."

Tess shivered, hearing the harshness in his voice, the barely suppressed violence. The voice of a stranger, almost.

The voice of a man who could kill, and kill easily. Happily, even.

Behind her the crunch of glass abruptly ceased.

"What do you think you're doing, Breton pig? The bitch is ours. Maybe after we've finished with her, we'll leave something for you. Get out of our way."

In the narrow doorway Tess turned, hearing a quick, muffled thump and then a soft gurgling.

After that there was nothing.

"What about you? Want to stay around for what your friend just got?" André growled softly.

"Fuck you!" the unseen man snarled back, already retreating through the shattered doorway to the garden. "Fuck all of you stinking Bretons! You'll pay for this, just wait and see!"

Stumbling and cursing, the man dragged his semiconscious friend behind him across the grass and crashed through the hedge the same way he had come.

Straining to hear, Tess waited, frozen, her breath coming and going in little jerky gasps.

"More blood," André whispered. "Will it never end?"

Tess heard him turn, his feet crunching on glass as he moved toward her.

"You've cut yourself, *bihan.*" His voice was harsh, his movements unsteady as he cupped her hand and traced the wetness that stained her fingers.

Tess felt the light brush of his lips. A wild shudder ripped through her. "Thank God you came."

"What in the name of heaven were you doing out there, woman? Did you go looking for them?" Suddenly his voice was different, cold and hard as a knife. "Has the novelty of my body faded so soon?"

Tess froze, disbelief tightening her face. *What was he talking about?*

Calloused fingers gripped her wrist, painfully tight. "Answer me," the Frenchman ordered flatly.

Anger blazed through her. "Release me," she hissed. "You have no right—"

"On the contrary, *Anglaise,* I have every right. To bed you, to break you. To do whatever else I want with you. I've shed blood for you, you see, and that makes you mine," he growled. "To take whenever and wherever I choose." His fingers tightened, drawing her implacably toward his chest. "Starting right here."

"Stop it!" Tess cried, shoving vainly at his iron fingers. "I should have known you'd be just like all the others!"

"Have there been so many, then?" His voice was soft—infinitely dangerous.

"Too many," Tess breathed, feeling tears slip down her pale cheeks. "I—I thought *you* were different."

With a growl, André crushed her against his hard length, cupping her hips to drive her into the saddle of his thighs. "I'm just a man, *bihan.* A man hungry for you. *Diaoul,* I don't mean to lose you—not when I've just found you!" His mouth came down savagely, grinding against her lips with angry friction. He drowned her protests stillborn, careless of the pain he caused her.

On and on he kissed her, with cold, calculating fury, until Tess swayed from lack of air and tiny flares exploded behind her blind eyes.

Suddenly, without a word, André released her, pushing her away sharply. "Go on!" he growled.

Ashen-faced, Tess turned, trying to run, ordering her feet to move—finding it somehow impossible.

"Go, *Anglaise!*" he said hoarsely. "It will only get worse, I promise you. Much worse. A little time—that's all I wanted. But—"

He bit off what he would have said next.

Still Tess stood, paralyzed by the pain in his voice.

Through the shattered, paneless window the moon cast down a shimmering bar of light, painting her skin silver; to André she seemed a creature from another world, hauntingly beautiful, a mermaid poised uncertainly between the worlds of man and sea.

Tess heard his strangled cry a heartbeat later, and then the thunder of his feet.

"Forgive me, *bihan,*" he said harshly, cupping her cheeks in his strong fingers. Moving closer behind her, he slowly turned her face to meet his gaze, almost as if afraid to face her directly. "It was rage and fear and —" His breath swept over her cool skin, his lips following an instant later. "It doesn't matter what it was, if only you can forget. Yes, I must somehow make you forget."

Hard thighs grazed her soft bottom. With a dark groan, André pulled her against him, arching her back until her head fell onto his shoulder. Slanting his face, he searched for the wild pulse that throbbed at her ear.

"Sheathe me in your dark silk, sea gull. Take me where the storms rage. With you it will always be storm and shadow, then the sweet forgetting."

Dimly Tess felt her body grow liquid and weak; with a little choked whimper she turned, seeking his heat and hardness.

But some shred of sanity made her halt.

Dear God, had she no pride left, no remnant of reason where this man was concerned? Even the cursed Viscount Ravenhurst had never left her so mindless, so desperate.

Her hands tensed, shoving at his arms. "No!" she cried furiously.

"So close," he whispered, as if she had not spoken. "I might have lost you. That I could not bear, *bihan.*" His hands swept over her hungrily, as if to reassure himself she was well. "Did they harm you? Did they hurt you in any way?"

Tess moaned, her head dropping back as his hands began to work their drugging magic over her bared skin. She should fight him, she knew. But it was so slow and good and new, what he did to her. Just this once, she would not fight. Next time—yes, next time.

His strong fingers circled her waist, turning her to face him. "Tell me!" There was fear and desperation in his voice now.

"No, they—you—just in time," Tess managed to answer, the question already half forgotten. She whimpered, her throat raw, her blood flowing thick and hot in her veins.

Already she was on fire for his touch.

Dimly Tess heard his dark groan of relief. With a growl, he kicked away an errant fragment of glass, then knelt on the floor and pulled her down beside him, keeping her locked against him, chest to chest, thigh to thigh.

Tess's eyes widened as she felt him draw her down astride his hard thighs to face him. Hot and achingly engorged, his manhood strained against her bottom.

A low moan escaped Tess's lips, and then another, as he arched her back in his arms so that his tongue could graze a dusky nipple.

"Fly for me, sea gull," he muttered hoarsely. "Let me see your pleasure. Then perhaps I can believe this is more than just another empty dream."

She heard him mutter something beneath his breath, and then his lips closed, suckling her fiercely.

Tess whimpered, squirming at his touch, aflame with furious desire. Dimly she felt his fingers move, combing through the wild curls where their bodies met and strained.

When he parted her, he found her slick and hot, already melting for him.

"An Aotrou Doué," the Frenchman breathed. His fingers teased the velvet bud of her desire and slipped deep to explore her sweetness.

"Now, André," Tess whispered raggedly. "Please."

Muttering a dark curse, he struggled with the buttons at his breeches.

An instant more and the offending garments were shed, but to Tess it seemed a long and cruel eternity. Dimly she heard the sharp rustle of cloth, followed by André's harsh breathing.

Then only pleasure, sweet aching pleasure as he fought free to find her and fill her, sliding home to the hilt inside her.

Cupping her soft, rounded bottom, he showed her how to move against him, matching each silken thrust to her breathless descent until Tess thought she would die of the building pleasure.

Moaning, she pressed harder against him, urging him to hasten his pace, but he would not, fiercely determined to prolong this slow, sweet slide of exquisite friction.

Her nails curled, biting urgently into the rippling muscles at his shoulders. "An-*dré!*"

"*Doucement,*" he muttered. "This time is forever. Ah, *bihan,* I could go on and on, for filling you this way is Heaven."

Wild with need, Tess rained frenzied blows over his forearms, fitting herself to him with wanton abandon. Some ancient woman's instinct made her tighten when he would have pulled back, and that silken contraction finally pierced the iron armor of his control.

"You don't—*Gwerhéz Vari!*—play fair, *bihan!*"

"The devil with—ohhhh—fair. I want you, André. Now!" Again she tightened, shot through with fire when she felt him groan and shudder against her.

"Then take me, *bihan.* Take me now and know that it is forever."

Strong and hard, his hands opened to anchor her, pulling her down to meet his driving thrusts, all caution and restraint cast to the wind. With savage mastery he loved her, with dark fury, with everything that he was and ever would be, muttering rough, unintelligible Breton words as he filled her with aching beauty.

Her head thrown back, Tess listened and felt herself take flight, knowing he was inside her and that he felt all the same dark magic she did. This time when her silken tremors began, her lover drove hard and true, splashing her with sunlight just as he had promised.

Trembling, Tess clutched at his rigid shoulders, drowning in waves of pleasure. Dimly she heard him groan as he rose to meet her again and again, piercing her with beauty.

Gasping, she tensed deep within, wanting to hold him tight when his ecstasy came.

The movement drove André over the edge. "Yes—ahhh! My sweet love, hold me!"

With a harsh groan he stiffened and then arched fiercely, rising up to meet her, pouring all of his hot man's seed deep within her.

And Tess held him endlessly, joining him in wild, soaring pleasure, anchoring him until the shudders stopped, until his fingers loosened and her knees buckled. Then together they tumbled, sprawling, down onto the cool wooden floor.

* * *

Even spent, André did not leave her, only drawing her against him while they drifted, wordless, on golden streams of drowsy contentment. Throughout the long night they discovered each other again and again, laughing like wild children, touched and touching, rapt with this rare, fierce splendor they had found.

When they were hungry, he made plates of fluffy omelettes and fed her with his fingers.

When they were thirsty, she filled a steep crystal goblet and held it for him to drink.

Only once did André leave her, after settling her in his big bed. When he returned, he pressed a tiny, carved mermaid into her hands. Carefully Tess ran her fingers over the polished curves and delicate tresses, knowing she would treasure this gift forever.

"For you, my wild sea-creature. For all the joy you've brought me. And this, too." He pressed a small, hard object into her hand. "Marthe found it in the pocket of your cloak."

With a little cry Tess closed her fingers around the edges of her forgotten hairpin. She had lost its mate sometime during her ordeal at Ravenhurst's town house. Of carved tortoiseshell, the ornaments were among the few possessions of her mother's that had escaped her father's greed. Though small and insignificant, they were of inestimable value to Tess.

"Oh, André—it was my mother's. I'm so glad it was not lost." Her fingers clenched for a moment, then opened, with the brown hairpin balanced on her palm. "Please take it," Tess said, her voice suddenly urgent.

"Your mother's, was it, bihan? Then yours it must remain. Only promise me you'll let me take it from your hair now and then." His voice darkened. "Along with whatever else I choose to remove."

At his husky request, Tess's heart lurched and passion began to flower through her once again. "But I—I have nothing for you, André," she whispered.

"Not so, bihan." The Frenchman's voice was dark and smooth as rum. With startling rapidity, his arousal made itself felt anew.

"André!"

"Ummmm?"

"Again? But—so soon?"

"Are you complaining, *Anglaise?* Yes, move . . . just so. That's it."

With a low groan, he drew her down atop him until she sheathed him completely. Long, breathless moments later he tensed, then shifted them together until they lay side by side, their thighs intertwined as they found the exquisite rhythms of love once more. "Nothing to give me?" he murmured.

"But—"

"Still complaining, *me kalon?*" André asked hoarsely, with each stroke wrapping her in new splendor.

"Complaining? M-me?" Even as she spoke, Tess felt the dark suns begin to burn inside her anew.

Outside, the moon rose and the stars gradually faded. A soft wind teased the camellia petals. A lone bird began to sing.

So the night passed, lit with their warmth and laughter, which spilled out and filled the little rose-trellised cottage on the edge of the cliffs.

"I don't even know what you look like." Sometime near dawn Tess stretched and sleepily traced the hard line of André's face, the thick mat of his beard. "Are you fair or dark? Green-eyed or blue?"

"Guess," he whispered, reaching up to guide her slim, searching fingers to his mouth.

Bold in the aftermath of passion, Tess sketched their full curve, teasing the edge of his moustache. "Golden-haired, I think. With eyes like the night and a face that makes women shiver and make promises they ought not to." Tess's teasing fingers dropped lower, following the line of his neck down to the wiry fleece of his chest and then circling his small, flat nipples.

André growled, fire jolting through his groin.

Tess's lips curved into a dark, secret smile as she felt him swell and harden. "A big man," she breathed huskily. "Oh, very big, I think," she purred.

"And you are making me bigger every second, witch," André

growled. "Painfully so! For that, you'll pay dearly, *Anglaise,* since I'm no sweet-faced knight with chivalry on my mind. This night my vessel is out for plunder and my cannons fully primed. My black flag warns all who see to beware." His voice turned dark with bitterness. "Nor am I what you imagine. My fingers are rough, *bihan,* the scars on my body myriad and deep. Will they repel you, when your sight returns?"

"If," Tess corrected, smoothing the hard lines of his face. "And still the answer is no. I will always love you, André—seen or unseen."

"Prove it," he rasped, already hungry for her again.

And so she did. Not once, but twice. To their total, gasping satisfaction.

34

"*A*nglaise."

Tess frowned, turning her head into the pillow, seeking her haven of dreams. Ah, but what dreams—sweeter than she had ever imagined possible.

"You must wake up, *bihan*." Cold fingers shook her shoulders.

Tess mumbled a protest, trying to shake them away. "S-sleep. *Je veux dormir.*"

"Not now. You must wake!" The hissed urgency of that low voice finally penetrated Tess's haze, and she sat up sharply.

"Wh—"

"Hush." It was Marthe. "Come outside." With trembling fingers the old woman pressed a thick woolen robe around Tess's shoulders. "But you must hurry!"

Tess tossed back the thick cloud of her hair and shoved her hands into the scratchy wool sleeves. Frowning, she slipped from the bed, hearing André mumble and shift behind her.

The old woman's fingers tugged her ruthlessly, forcing her into the kitchen. Beneath her bare feet the stone floors were frigid; the shock of contact cleared the remnants of sleep from Tess's mind. By the time Marthe pushed her into a chair, she was wide awake.

For a moment there was a strained silence.

Tess cocked her head, straining to hear. "Marthe?"

"She's gone out, *bihan*."

"Padrig? What are you doing here?" Already cold splinters of fear began to work deep into Tess's heart.

"I've come for you—we must leave immediately. It is no longer safe for you here. The soldiers have discovered their wounded comrade, and they are on their way here right now. Le Fur managed to slip out from the dock several hours ago; right now he is waiting for me on the far side of the island. But we must go now."

Every word was a deadly arrow sent unerringly through her heart. "And—and the captain?"

"He will never let you go, *bihan*." Padrig's voice was harsh. "As it is, he will murder me when he learns." Nearby came the rustle of cloth. "Ah, there you are, Marthe. Help her dress. I will wait outside. But be quick about it!"

As if in a trance, Tess felt herself rise, Marthe's rough fingers stripping away the robe and replacing it with a sturdy dress of wool. "The wind will be cool, so you'd better wear this. It's one of mine—not fine enough for soft skin like yours, but it will be safer this way. If they should search the wagon . . ."

With a raw, choked moan, Tess caught her lip between her teeth and bit down hard to keep from crying. Marthe fastened the row of buttons and began to push her out the door.

"My—my mermaid!" Tess cried.

"Very well, but hurry!" Padrig said roughly, keeping watch just outside the door.

It was there where she had left it, on the small rosewood table beside André's bed. She tucked it into the pocket of her dress and hesitated, listening to the deep, regular sound of his breathing.

So this was to be their good-bye, then. No whispered vows. No valiant efforts to stifle her tears.

Just a raw, silent farewell, followed by infinite, suffocating sadness.

Go, fool. What else is there to say, anyway? You had him for a while, and for that time you held his heart completely. Be glad of that. For such a man as this could never be held for long. He must always roam, following the sun, seeking the next horizon, wherever his untamed heart takes him.

And always there would be the fear—of the danger you brought him, of the dark secrets of his trade, secrets he must always conceal from you.

No, you knew it could not last. Your worlds are too far apart. And by leaving this way you might anger him into forgetting you. Otherwise, his passion would bring him into gravest danger.

"You must go, *Anglaise.*" Marthe's voice rose, shrill with fear. "In staying, you bring danger to us all!"

Good-bye, my wild love. White-faced and silent, Tess sent him her last farewell from the deep, grieving hollow of her heart.

Perhaps one day, when this bitter war is over and the Channel stretches smooth and silver like a mirror, I'll take a boat and come looking for this isolated corner of Heaven. Yes, and for you, André Le Brix, winging home like the sea gull you named me for.

In his sleep, the bearded Frenchman groaned softly, running hard fingers over the cold quilt. *"Trop tôt,"* he breathed, awash in restless dreams.

Too soon.

Not too soon, Tess thought numbly, already drowning in the sea of loneliness that stretched before her to the end of her days.

Too late. Maybe it had always been too late.

Her father had seen to that. That was his one legacy to her. And what small corner of hope he hadn't succeeded in destroying, an arrogant English officer with lapis eyes finally had.

And now Tess was left with nothing to guard her from her pain, for the Frenchman, though well intentioned, had destroyed her forever by sweeping down the walls that had protected her heart for so long.

"Think of me sometimes, André Le Brix," Tess whispered, brushing away the first hot tears from her cheeks.

Then she turned and stumbled after Marthe.

The cart was small and bad-smelling, the trip over rutted roads interminable. But the *Liberté* was waiting just as Padrig had promised, hidden in a narrow cove that no one but a madman such as Le Fur would ever dare to enter.

Even with Padrig's careful planning, it had been a near thing. A mob of French soldiers was already pounding at the cottage door by the time they crested the first hill.

"Don't worry about him," Padrig said shortly. "Marthe will have him well hidden by now. There's a cave beneath the cliffs that no one knows about, save the three of us. He will be safe there until—until they forget."

Forgetting. The first time is for forgetting, bihan.

Oh, André, I can't do it. I'm not strong anymore, not like I used to be.

The memories choked her, unbearable torture.

The second time is for burning.

Oh, yes, she was burning. Was he too?

And this time is for loving. . . . Dieu, how I will enjoy loving you.

Gone. All gone.

Padrig pulled away the oiled cloth covered by vegetables and helped Tess down from the cart. Nearby she heard the roar of surf and the creak of timber.

Almost before she knew it, she was on the *Liberté*'s deck, listening to—but not quite hearing—Padrig's quiet orders and the snap of canvas as the sails were unfurled.

Bare feet hammered over the deck; high overhead Tess heard the wind sing through the rigging.

And every sound was a sad one, heavy with the ache of goodbye.

Time passed in a blur. The voyage was swift and uneventful. Every wave they crossed and every gust of wind brought Tess fresh pain, for she knew they carried her away from her sleeping captain.

She prayed for lightning and rain to rent the sails and bar their way. But this night the seas mocked her, flowing smooth and swift to England.

Nor was the weather the only thing that mocked her during that agonizing passage. Somewhere mid-Channel she felt her stomach quake and her head throb, she who had never known a moment's seasickness in her life.

Then an explosion ripped through her head—a tempest of merciless colors and wild drumming.

She staggered, her white fingers clenched on the *Liberté*'s cold rail as the night burst into violence and color.

Suddenly she saw a distant wall of silver cliffs beneath the round, unblinking eye of the moon. With a harsh sob, Tess turned, rubbing her throbbing eyes in disbelief.

Blackness, yes, but suddenly it was the blackness of night, tempered by a thousand shades and textures. Dun gray. Slate. Velvety jet.

"Oh, André," she whispered brokenly. "How much I would have loved to share this with you. To turn and see every hard plane and hollow of your face for the first time."

The wind whipped her hair in a wild, burnished veil around her pale face. Unheeded, tears began to slip down her cheeks.

"So close—so close to seeing you."

Then she frowned, brushing away her tears with impatient fingers.

There it was again—a faint paleness to the north, somewhere near Winchelsea. A Revenue cutter!

"Padrig!"

But the brawny Breton had already seen. He shouted an order to Le Fur, amidships, then strode to the rail, where Tess stood.

He was big and ruddy and fair-haired, just as André had told her.

"I'm afraid there'll be little time for good-byes, *bihan*. I'll drop you near Fairleigh Cove and send two men with you. I can spare no more, I'm afraid, not when this cursed English cutter will soon be nipping at my heels. But Le Fur will go along, and he'll see you safe inland." His eyes narrowed. "What is it?"

Tears were streaming down Tess's face. She had lost her captain this night and regained her sight. She thought—no, she was certain—that she would far rather have had the man and lost the sight.

"Nothing, Padrig. Just—just give him this, will you?" With trembling fingers Tess removed her mother's tortoiseshell hairpin and pressed it into the first mate's hand. "Tell him . . ."

Tell him what? What was there to say, when she must go and he must stay? When there were wars and countries to divide them?

Behind her the spray fell back in solid sheets as the sleek brig sped north to England.

"Just—just tell him that I won't ever forget."

"Gone? Gone where?" His face dark with rage, the *Liberté*'s bearded captain glared at Marthe in disbelief.

"It was too dangerous, you must know that. Padrig came while you slept. He said they should be back in England by the morrow, if the winds blow fair."

"Padrig did this thing?" His voice was raw with shock.

"It was the only way, André. You would never have let her go."

The old woman spoke only the truth—perhaps that hurt most of all. His obsession had brought the Englishwoman here, endangering them all.

Somehow that realization only made André angrier.

Grim-faced, the captain thundered toward the door.

"Where are you going?" Marthe demanded.

"To find a boat. *Any boat!*"

Nicely done, the man thought, his face hidden in shadows. Very nicely done. Neither too much blood nor too little.

His opaque eyes narrowed as he studied the woman's unmoving body and the single black rose slanting across one bloodied breast.

Yes, it would serve his purpose perfectly.

What of Tess Leighton, a cold voice asked. What if she chose to turn prying eyes?

Then she, too, would be swiftly eliminated. Nothing could be allowed to interfere with his plan, not even the beautiful Miss Leighton.

And Lady Patricia?

His lips flattened. Lady Patricia would have to be made to see the light. She had her uses, of course, but no woman was indispensable to him, as she would soon learn.

Suddenly his cold eyes hardened. The ring! Why hadn't he noticed it before? Smothering a curse, the man in the shadows stared down at the dead woman's cheek.

It was only a slight miscalculation, but he was not a man who made mistakes. Indeed, his caution was the only thing that had kept him alive so long.

From beyond the flimsy door came the sound of drunken voices. "Oh, aye, she's here, Digby. Just keep your breeches buttoned!"

Damn! No time to correct his oversight now!

His face a snarling mask of fury, the tall figure clothed head to toe in black replaced his whiskered fox mask and moved soundlessly to the open window.

They were mere specks of black against the shifting play of gray and jet where the foaming sea lashed England's proud cliffs. Le Fur went first, moving with a quiet ease that spoke of his familiarity with this place. At any other time Tess would have asked him a thousand questions, but tonight she said nothing, concentrating on finding a precarious handhold on the narrow path that ascended from the beach. Behind her trotted a short, powerful seaman whose voice she recognized from the *Liberté*. She soon was thankful for his presence, for whenever she slipped, he seemed to be at her side, offering a strong hand to assist her.

The wind combed through her hair as she finally clambered over the cliff edge and stood on Fairleigh's rolling green downs. With every minute that passed, her vision sharpened. Although there was still a great deal of blurring and pain, Tess barely noticed; her heart was too hollow and cold, numb with sadness in the wake of her farewell to André.

Turning back, she looked out to sea just in time to see the *Liberté* leave the pursuing English cutter far behind and fly south, sails full, toward home.

Tess's vision blurred, and this time it was from the hot tears that fell in a silent rush down her cheeks. Unmoving, she fixed desperate eyes on that fleeing speck darting toward the horizon.

Taking all hope and happiness with it.

At her back, Le Fur coughed uncomfortably. "We—we make

too clear a target here, *bihan*. Never know who might be watching."

Recalled to her surroundings, Tess made a furtive pass at her eyes and choked back the sob in her throat.

Le Fur turned away, making a great business of scanning the slope. "We'll get you back, but best that we not delay. The sun will be up soon, and we have a boat to meet."

"How—"

Le Fur smiled faintly. "Better that you don't ask, *bihan*. But rest assured, we'll be back in the Morbihan before three tides have risen and turned."

"Will—will you be safe?"

Le Fur's look was shuttered. "Don't worry about us. We've done this before."

He would give her no answers, Tess realized. No details. No names, dates, or places. All these were too dangerous. She of all people should have known that.

Le Fur's caution only reinforced the cruel sense of distance Tess felt from André, one more example of how far apart were their separate worlds. She realized how useless it was to hope that they could ever bridge the chasm between them.

A shudder swept through her. A moment later her fingers met the polished outline of André's mermaid. Slowly Tess drew it from the pocket of Marthe's dress, where she had thrust it for safekeeping during their journey.

Beautiful and fragile, the creature stood poised in mid-flight, forever frozen in a moment of restless indecision—living in one world and dreaming of another.

Achingly beautiful. Ineffably sad.

Behind her Le Fur swung about, muttering something in Breton to his companion, who immediately slipped off into the night.

Her heart hammering, Tess turned, facing the shadows. "Wh—"

"Silence," Le Fur breathed, unmoving.

As the pair stood searching the slope to the north, a tall figure, black-garbed, slipped from the face of the cliff at their right, part of the darkness itself.

" 'Tis no night for you to be abroad, lassie."

With a glad cry Tess spun around and stumbled toward the man in the black cloak, who waited, arms outstretched.

"Tell me what you were doing on the cliffs, lassie." The big, silver-haired man thundered across the room, cupped Tess's shoulders in his powerful fingers, and pushed her into a chair. "Only this time it's the truth I'll be having, starting from the very beginning. No more of your deceit will I tolerate!"

A single candle flickered in Fairleigh's nearly empty salon. The curtains hung in shreds, and scattered dust motes danced across the bare wooden floor. Somewhere outside in the night an owl hooted, the sound low and piercingly sad.

In a low, quiet voice Tess told the smuggler what he wanted to know. About everything, from the night Hawkins's men had surrounded her on the beach up until the moment that he had encountered her on the cliffs, André's men at her side.

She did not look at her friend as she spoke, afraid of the condemnation she would read in his eyes. Instead she fixed her gaze on the faded damask settee pushed against the far wall.

Speaking was a relief, she discovered. But there was one thing Tess did not tell Jack, and that was how she had found love, only to lose it again. No, the wounds upon her heart would remain her secret; she was careful to tell Jack only about those that had afflicted her eyes.

Grim-faced, the Fox paced back and forth before her, listening intently, interrupting her several times to ask a tersc question.

When at last she had finished, Tess found her burden was somehow lighter for the telling of the tale. Slowly she looked up at Jack.

Pinpoints of light flared in his dark eyes. He cursed long and low under his breath. "It was too little for you to sneak off and join my men. No, you had to do something wilder. You had to set up your own runs, usurping my role, by all the saints above!" His pacing stopped abruptly. Scowling, he faced her, an angry question in his eyes. "Why, damn it?"

Tess stiffened before that dark glare. She swallowed once, her eyes haunted. "At—at first it was only a lark, Jack," she said softly, finding it almost impossible to remember that first time she had gone along as one of Jack's men. "It was the challenge, I suppose. And then, when my father's propensities for gambling and whoring bled Fairleigh dry, it was for the money. That's when I got the idea to take your place. By then I knew all I needed to know about the business, for I had watched and listened carefully."

Jack winced at her harsh words but did not correct her. How could he, when she spoke the perfect truth?

"I needed the money for Fairleigh, don't you see?"

"Are you daft then? Naught is worth your taking such mad risks, lass—not even Fairleigh! I would have given you the money. All you ever had to do was ask."

"What difference does it make, then, whether you won the money or I? I'm no hypocrite, Jack. I never thought that you would be one either."

The silver-haired man smothered a curse, his fingers clenched at his side. " 'Tis hardly the same, damn it, don't you see that? You're a female, young and innocent—gently reared. You've your whole life before you, lass. Someday soon you'll marry and have children. Why would you risk all that for a few hundred pounds?"

Tess stifled a sob. "Marriage?" she repeated, her voice brittle, on the edge of hysteria. There was only one man she would ever consider marrying, and now she could never have him. "No, not for me marriage and a pack of mewling children, Jack," she said flatly. "Nowhere in England could you find the man born to hold me."

That, at least, was true, Tess thought. The only man who could comfort her, the only man she loved, was far away, sleeping in a perfect, sheltered harbor studded with hundreds of sun-kissed islets.

When she looked up, Jack was studying her with narrowed eyes. "If only . . ." he breathed, cutting himself off with a smothered curse.

"If only what?"

He shook his head sharply, his silver hair bright in the flickering candlelight, dispelling old dreams. "Nothing, lass. It was—nothing of importance."

"So you are to keep your secrets, but I am not." Tess's lips settled in a mutinous line. "Is that how you would have it, Jack? After all these years?" She could not keep the hurt from her voice.

"Damn it, lassie, that's unfair and well you know it!"

Tess shrugged stiffly. "I'm afraid I don't. What's sauce for the goose, and all that. . . ." Her eyes glinted. "I won't lie to you, Jack. Not even for you will I give the smuggling up." She couldn't, Tess realized, not now. Her deadly masquerade was the only thing that could take her mind from the long, bitter years of loneliness before her.

"Oh, yes you will! If I hear of your ever again donning mask and cloak in my absence, I'll flay your bottom so well, you won't sit down for a year!"

A burst of gray-green flame flashed deep in Tess's eyes; her chin rose in mute defiance.

But Jack did not notice, already turning to pace again. "Aye, I've too damned much on my mind to be worrying about you, lassie. Not while a madman haunts the marsh, brutalizing any female luckless enough to fall in his path. And leaving my own calling card behind him, damn his soul! By God, I'll garrote the bastard when I find him."

Tess's breath checked sharply. "What are you talking about?"

"You truly do not know then? Things have not been exactly quiet in your absence," he muttered grimly. "I could hardly believe it myself, when I first heard of it. Aye, I put it down to Hawkins and his old mischief." Frowning, he dragged a large hand through his hair. "The Fox is now a figure of terror. Already three women have died from his cruelty, each left with a single black rose beside her. Dear God, how many more until I catch the villain?"

"But you would never—"

"Of course I would not. But someone dares, and he dons my disguise to do it. Very careful, the scum is, too. He allows himself to be seen, but never too closely—just enough that there are witnesses to his crime. Even that fool Ransley dared to task me with the offenses today. He said my boldness made him respect me more than ever." A low curse exploded from the smuggler's lips. "Respect me? For murder—for the cruel violation of a woman?" he said harshly. "God knows, I never thought it would come to this. But it's made Hawkins look a fool for boasting far and near that he'd murdered me on the beach." Abruptly his features creased in shock. "Never tell me that was you, lass?"

Tess simply shrugged. "So it was. He very nearly succeeded in his boast that night."

With a startled exclamation, Jack strode to her chair and seized her in a harsh grip. "Are you mad, Tess Leighton?" he demanded, shaking her fiercely. "By God, I'll—"

"Don't, Jack." Tess closed her eyes, overwhelmed with the memories of all that had followed that ill-fated run. Remembering the fire and fury of the Frenchman who had saved her life, plucking her from the stormy Channel seas.

Suddenly hot tears spilled down her ivory cheeks.

"Ah, lassie, none of this. 'Tis a cruel brute I am, for sure. Hush, now—hush. Don't cry." He knelt beside her, his big fingers drawing her to his chest.

Shuddering, Tess gave herself up to the emotional storm that had been building ever since Marthe had awakened her long hours before.

"What did he do to you?" Jack growled, after her sobs abated slightly.

Tess stiffened. "Who?"

"That bastard Ravenhurst, of course. I know what happened the night Lady Patricia came knocking at his door, purring like a cat with a bowl of cream she's just itching to taste. Aye, more than one person saw you darting down Mermaid Street the next morning."

Tess flinched before the raw fury in Jack's face. "It wasn't—" She swallowed. "He isn't—"

"Don't tell me I lack a proper set of eyes in my head, Tess Leighton. Now nor five years ago." He shot her a sharp, probing look. "Aye, if the man's so much as touched a hair on your head, I'll—"

Tess pulled away slightly, brushing away her chill tears. Ravenhurst had touched a great deal more than a hair on her head, Tess thought bitterly, and she had a fairly good idea of what Jack would do if he had any notion of that fact.

Lies. Disguises. Deception upon deception.

Suddenly she was tired of it all, mortally tired. "Ravenhurst means nothing to me, Jack."

"Lennox, then? I never had much liking for that bloody exquisite—too cool and careful by half. Just tell me what he's done to you and I'll—"

Tess sighed faintly. "Nothing, Jack. I swear it." She swept tired fingers across her eyes.

"Then who—"

"It doesn't matter. He's—he's gone. I shan't see him again, not for a long, long time. Perhaps . . ." Her voice caught. "Perhaps not ever. So I beg you to stop this interrogation. From all you've said, you must have far more important things to consider than the status of my unruly heart."

Tess would tell him no more than this. André must remain her secret, the embers of his memory to be clutched to her heart, guarded protectively, so the cold disapproval of others could not drown its faint flame.

And there she could hide her own dark fear—that the bold Frenchman was in league with the very spy Ravenhurst had come to track down.

Wiping away a final tear, Tess sniffed and sat up straighter. "Tell me instead what can I do to help you."

Jack's look of concern fled, replaced by fierce exasperation. His silver eyebrows flew together in a scowl. "Naught, lass! Absolutely naught. And I want you far away from Fairleigh when I spring my traps, do you hear?" he blazed, his eyes hard and challenging. "The murderer might be any one of a score of men, each more desperate than the last. I've made a wheen of enemies in my life, just you remember that. Aye, men who would stop at little to see me brought down to grovel in the dirt. My own fault, perhaps—or the fault of fate." His fingers tightened on her slim shoulders. "But I'll be damned if I see *you* fall prey to their sordid schemes!"

Tess did not speak, frightened by the flat violence in his voice. It struck her again how many things she did not know about this man, for that had always been how Jack had wanted it. Shivering, she wondered about those enemies he had spoken of and just how dark his secrets were.

"You're not involved in gold shipments, are you, Jack?" She had to ask, for the question had been burning inside her ever since Ravenhurst had spoken of it to her. And of course there had been that terrible conversation she had overheard in Brittany.

The smuggler whirled about, his face hard. "What do you know of gold shipments from the Romney Marsh?"

"Nothing much. I—I only heard it hinted at."

His eyes narrowed. "You know a great deal more than that, lassie, but I can see 'twill do no good to ask you to tell me."

Tess studied him in chilly silence.

"And equally little good to task you with the rest of what happened during those days you were in France, I see. Aye, you've told me naught but half, lass—you've not a hope in Hell of hiding your feelings from me," he added gruffly.

The line of Tess's mouth grew even tighter.

Jack snorted. "Hobhouse and that motley crew up at the Angel have set it about that you were up at Oxford visiting your scapegrace brother. Which," he said flatly, his eyes keen on Tess's guarded face, "is only a little bit more daft than this story you've fed me."

Tess could only smile at her majordomo's loyalty. "On the contrary, I had a lovely visit. Ashley showed me all about the Botanic Gardens, Radcliffe Camera, and the Church of St. Peter-in-the-East."

Jack's eyes grew blacker, snapping furiously. "I've half a mind to turn you over my knee, lassie, so don't go pushing me."

Tess returned his angry look with cool defiance. "Don't push me either, Jack. I'm—tired." The word came out like a sigh. "So tired. Can I go up to sleep now?"

The smuggler's face immediately relaxed, his eyes softening with concern. "Never one to give an inch, were you? Nor do I wonder at it, considering the way that bastard of a father treated you."

Tess did not answer. The only sign that she had heard him came in the whitening of her fingers on the arm of the chair.

Smothering a curse, Jack waved his hand in resignation. "Very well, then. I've affairs of my own that need tending. But I'll be back tomorrow at sundown. Wait for me at the priory ruins. And then, Tess Leighton, I mean to have some answers, I warn you!" Still scowling, the smuggler turned and swept up his black tricorn and cloak.

For a long moment he studied her, his eyes unreadable, the whiskered mask dangling forgotten from his fingers.

"Tomorrow up at the priory. And try, if you please, to stay out of trouble until then, lassie." With that final gruff utterance, the Fox strode from the room.

Long after he had gone, Tess sat staring at the empty doorway. A vein pounding at her temple, she reached into the pocket of Marthe's woolen dress and pulled out the little wooden mermaid.

For a long time she studied the sculpture, her eyes bleak with pain. Then slowly she rose to her feet, lifted the guttering candle, and walked mechanically toward the stairs.

35

It was nearly midmorning by the time Lord Ravenhurst slid tiredly from his horse, a battered leather satchel wedged beneath his arm. The trip from Dover had been a nightmare. He had nearly been run down by a drunken coachman; then, to make matters worse, his horse had thrown a shoe.

His face was etched with exhaustion, and a thick stubble darkened the unyielding line of his jaw. His last hurried, near-dawn meeting with the Admiralty's agent in Dover had been brief and entirely fruitless, raising more questions for which he had no answers.

Ravenhurst shook his head, slanting a disgusted look at his mud-spattered boots and dusty greatcoat. Yes, the only bright spot in his day so far had been his anticipating the consternation on his valet's face when Peale saw the viscount's disreputable state.

As well as the shock on one other person's face, Ravenhurst reminded himself grimly.

His eyes were opaque as he hammered the knocker impatiently, knowing the delay was his own fault, since he had given his servant no expectation when he would return.

The door opened to reveal Peale's startled face. "My—my lord!"

The way they were spoken, the words might have been a blasphemy rather than a direct address, Ravenhurst thought grimly, moving inside. Without a word he shrugged off his greatcoat and tossed it down on the banister, then continued upstairs without any check in his stride.

"That is—you're back!"

Unseen by Peale, one jet brow climbed to a point. "Your eyesight remains reasonably acute, Peale, a fact which delights me, of course. Since it has been nothing short of a hellish morning, however, I beg you to restrain your effusions and bring me water and towels in my room, instead."

"Of course, my lord." The valet's impassive mask was firmly back in place. "Immediately."

Quick, that man, Ravenhurst thought, deciding he would have to increase his valet's salary. Long, fluid strides brought the viscount swiftly up the stairs. At the threshold to his bedroom he halted, remembering it as he had seen it two weeks before, glass shards scattered across the floor, his sheets bloodied and knotted, hanging through the casement.

For a moment he did not move, his face an impenetrable mask. Not a trace of the wreckage remained, of course. Peale was far too efficient for that.

Only the shard-sharp memories haunted Ravenhurst still.

Slowly he crossed to the far wall, stopping before a massive pedestal desk of burnished mahogany with brass fittings. The viscount twisted a key in the ornate brass keyhole, opened a drawer, and lifted out a small object. His eyes were bleak as he studied the carved hairpin, which Tess had dropped in this room a fortnight ago in her frantic effort to escape him. He had glued it back together as carefully as he could. *Why* he had done so, he refused to consider.

Unconsciously his fingers tightened. He tensed, awash in painful memories, trying to forget the way her hair had floated in a wild auburn cloud on his pillow.

The way her skin had burned against his naked arousal, all softness and woman, lavender-scented.

The way her eyes had pleaded with him, dark and haunted, while she twisted in the grip of Lady Patricia's foul drug.

Desire knifed through him, sharp and insistent.

Forget her, a harsh voice warned. *By now she has almost certainly forgotten you.*

With a low, hoarse growl, Ravenhurst replaced the hairpin, then slammed the drawer shut.

Pain and more pain. Desire and deception. Why couldn't he let it go? Especially now, when he knew that the memories could bring him only torment.

Because he could not, even though it seemed it was their lot in life to cause each other nothing but pain.

He had just finished removing the last of the stubble from his cheeks when a light tap sounded at the door behind him.

"Come."

Peale's face was impassive as he held out a cream-colored envelope. "This just arrived, my lord."

Ravenhurst sniffed the air suspiciously. "What, no perfume? It is, however, a trifle early for *billets doux,* I suppose." His smile faded as he took the vellum missive, noting the spidery handwriting.

So the Old Man was back at his cloak-and-dagger tricks, Ravenhurst thought, frowning. Still, he supposed the stiff-rumped old martinet had his reasons.

"Thank you, Peale. That will be all."

The valet cleared away the basin and towels and left, closing the door softly behind him. As soon as he had gone, Ravenhurst strode to his bookshelf and took down an old, dog-eared volume of Shakespeare's sonnets. For a moment his long fingers riffled the pages until he found what he was searching for.

His lapis eyes narrowed. With a faint sigh, he carried the open volume to his desk and began the laborious process of converting the Admiralty's coded document.

It might have been worse, he supposed. His next mission might see him brushing up his Greek with a volume of Homer.

Twenty minutes later, the sheet before Ravenhurst was full of scribbled text. Once again the viscount read the message, his face hard.

So the push in the Peninsula was to be very soon then. If only there weren't so many questions, so many pieces of the puzzle that did not fit.

Ravenhurst's face hardened as he recalled the strange, slanting mark on the right cheek of the dead woman he had examined earlier that day in Applegate. Bile filled his mouth at the memory of those pale limbs, the dark bruises mottling her naked flesh.

All the time he had found himself thinking it might have been Tess lying there, her lifeless body crisscrossed by bloody welts.

With a smothered curse Ravenhurst tossed down the coded document and jerked to his feet. His plans were made, his traps laid, and yet. . . .

Something was wrong—bloody everlasting wrong. Somewhere deep in his mind he felt the old familiar tingling, a feeling he had learned never to ignore. But he could not stop now, not when everything was riding on his success at trapping the elusive Fox.

When the viscount looked out the window toward the distant hills a moment later, his eyes were hard, the color of sleepless nights and broken promises.

Tess was almost at the Angel's front steps when the hastily scrawled notice nailed to an adjoining fence caught her eye. She moved closer for a better look, her face darkening as she read its contents.

TO THE INHABITENTS OF RYE ROYAL
AND PLACES AJACINT

"Wanted by his Majesty's Customs and Revenue Service,
for crimes against the Crown, including,
but not limited to, the smuggling of conterband,
the asalt of Crown offacers, and the brutil murder of
three innocent females,

The villin known as *THE ROMNEY FOX.*

Reward for information leading to the villin's capture:
ONE THOUSAND POUNDS.

Reward for information about the identity and wherabouts

of the Fox's accomplisses and comrads:
FIVE HUNDRED POUNDS."

Tess's heart slammed against her ribs as she read the ill-spelled notice, recognizing it as Amos Hawkins's work.

With angry, trembling fingers, she ripped down the sheet and crumpled it into a tight ball, then marched up the Angel's steps, two bright flags of color in her cheeks.

How dare Hawkins post such a sign on the very steps of her inn?

Her head held high, Tess strode through the oak double doors and past the intimate little breakfast room whose bay windows overlooked Mermaid Street; all she could see before her was that scrawled notice.

If it was war that Amos Hawkins wanted, Tess swore silently, then it was war the brute would get!

Three pairs of eyes flashed up in surprise as the auburn-haired beauty marched furiously up the Angel's polished steps.

So the little bitch has returned after all, Lady Patricia Lennox thought, swirling the last amber residue in her bone china teacup. Seeing the Duchess of Cranford smiling at her across the room, she answered with a polite greeting of her own, but the warmth did not penetrate to her sharp emerald eyes.

Yes, I know exactly what you're after, Tess Leighton, for all you try to pretend you are indifferent. But you won't have him, do you hear? He's mine. He's always been mine. I shall teach you that very soon—and delight in watching your face when he betrays you.

Again.

With a cold, secretive little smile, the blond beauty rose to her feet in a swirl of topaz skirts, dropped her napkin on the table, and moved gracefully toward the door.

Across the room, the Duchess of Cranford studied Lady Patricia's retreating back. The woman was really quite lovely, of course; it was easy to understand why Ravenhurst had been attracted to her.

He had always had a taste for beautiful things, even as a little boy, and in recent years he had earned a singular reputation as a connoisseur of female beauty.

The duchess's eyes darkened. Even she had heard the stories circulating about his opera dancer. After that, there had been a voluptuous pair of twins, whom he had plucked from the slums of Shoreditch. Yes, there were always "friends" only too eager to carry the duchess all the latest sordid gossip about the man known in *beau monde* and tenements alike as the Devil of Trafalgar.

The duchess's frail fingers tightened on her teacup for a moment, pain seeping through her. If only his mother had lived. If only she could turn back the clock and do things differently . . .

He had lost so much in this wretched war, after all—parents, brother, and fiancée. It was no wonder he had become so hard. If he ever learned that . . .

The slim fingers trembled, and the duchess's cup lurched.

But there was no going back. She knew that better than anyone.

Which left only Lady Patricia Lennox, and she, the duchess decided, would make a very ill sort of wife for Lord Ravenhurst. Shallow, vain, and petty, the woman had a lush sort of beauty that went no deeper than her silken skin.

A man of keen intelligence, wit, and good breeding, the viscount required far more in a wife, the duchess decided. But was he, in fact, seeking a wife? Perhaps her sources had been wrong, and he was merely pursuing more transitory pleasures.

Still, there was something wrong here, the duchess thought, feeling a slight frisson of fear. She was not a woman given to flights of fancy, but she could almost feel a vortex of emotional undercurrents swirling around her.

Her cool eyes narrowed. Every instinct told her that Ravenhurst needed her help and the exasperating boy would have it, whether he liked the idea or not.

Meanwhile, he was a fool if he did more than amuse himself with the imperious blonde, and the Duchess of Cranford well knew that Viscount Ravenhurst had been a fool only once in his life. It was not a mistake he would ever repeat.

* * *

At a table near the window, the room's third occupant delicately buttered a wonderfully airy pastry and nibbled a piece appreciatively, sensuously flicking a tiny crumb from the corner of her full lower lip.

The Angel's chef must be French, of a certainty, the woman decided, taking another bite. *Bien sûr,* no one but a Frenchman could do such justice to *pâtisserie.*

For a moment the woman's perfectly sculpted brow creased in a frown.

Par Dieu, this place was not at all as she had expected. The staff were most superior, the rooms comfortable and elegant. Fresh flowers decorated her mantel each morning, and spotless white napkins her table.

And what of the so elusive owner Danielle had glimpsed striding down the hall only minutes before?

Quite lovely, the Frenchwoman conceded—in a *farouche* sort of way, of course.

Yes, Mademoiselle Leighton was a force to be reckoned with, Danielle decided. She was fire in ice, a woman who could be made to burn with rare passion.

In the hands of the right man, of course.

But the English viscount must not be allowed to become that man.

Danielle could not wait forever, after all. She had been careful with her money, managing to save up a tidy sum, but her resources were not so great as to permit more than a week's time here.

But she had invested too much to give up just yet, the emerald-eyed beauty decided. For her virile English lover was most certainly worth a gamble, Danielle reminded herself, moistening her crimson lips as she recalled some of their more passionate encounters in London.

Nor did the amount of money involved escape her.

Abruptly her lips curved in a slow, sensuous smile.

Oh, yes, Danielle would snare Ravenhurst and soon. Her methods could not fail. She hoped the viscount enjoyed his remaining days of freedom.

They would be very few.

Unaware of her place in these various ruminations, the Angel's owner sped up the rear stairs toward her private rooms, thankful that she had not been waylaid en route.

Her eyes were blurry, her head throbbing when she sank down onto her bed and pulled off the old, frayed bonnet she had worn from Fairleigh. Not that anyone had blinked an eye to see her in a hat so démodé. She was, after all, the eccentric Miss Leighton.

Tess's lips tightened, her eyes straying to the distant blue line of the Channel. With you it might have been different, André, she thought bleakly. With you I might have pulled up my sandy skirts and gone hunting for oysters along the rock-strewn coast. With you I might have donned breeches and climbed to the top of the highest rigging. And one day, a small head, soft with curling silken hair, might have rested against my breast.

Our child.

Tess caught back a sob. She must not think of that, for the thought of her loss would be too painful to bear. Brushing away the tears that leaped to her eyes, she dug deep into her pocket and pulled out the Frenchman's sculpture. Quickly, as if the touch burned her, she pushed the object to the back of her writing table, where she could not see its haunting beauty.

Not yet. Not until the hurting stopped. Which, Tess thought bleakly, would probably be never.

From the hall came the muffled thump of feet, followed by a burst of laughter quickly stilled.

Someone tapped sharply on the door.

Tess sighed, wishing only to be alone. She was not yet strong enough to begin dissembling, hiding her pain.

Once again the tapping echoed in the quiet corridor.

"Who is it?"

"Only your most faithful admirer, Contessa."

Tess's heart lurched. Gasping softly, she ran to the door and threw it open. "Ashley? Is it truly you, you rogue?"

She could not believe it. The young man standing before her in a maroon satin waistcoat and bottle-green jacket seemed too tall and elegant to be her brother.

With a swift, warning smile, Ashley pushed her back inside and eased the door shut. "Wouldn't want to trumpet it about that you're seeing me for the first time, now would we? Not when Hobhouse has been at such pains to make everyone think you spent the last two weeks up at Oxford with me." His pale green eyes narrowed. "But why—"

Tess interrupted, pulling him to a chair beside her desk. "First you must tell me everything, Ash. Are your quarters comfortable? Have you found amiable comrades? And what of your studies?"

The young man laughed shortly, his eyes darkening. "What sort of interrogation is this?" Seeing his sister's brow furrow, he shrugged. "All well enough, Contessa, so stop fretting over nothing. I'm no sort of scholar, but I suppose you had no expectation of my being that. My fellows are a good enough sort. As to my quarters—I see them seldom, so their lack of comfort bothers me little. But I mean to know what you've been up to, Tess. I warn you, none of these tactics will deter me; I know you too well, my dear. I confess I could not believe it when Hobhouse told me you were still at your wild masquerades."

Tess turned and began to toy with a letter opener on her desk, her eyes carefully averted. "What exactly did Hobhouse tell you?"

For a moment Ashley's delicate features tightened. "Damned little, as a matter of fact. Only that you'd been engaged in some business of a clandestine nature, received an injury, and were rusticating somewhere while you recovered." His voice turned dry. "Odd, you look the very picture of health to me."

For a moment Tess could not speak. "It—it was my eyes, you see. I lost my sight after a—a fall. It all happened so suddenly that . . ." She was babbling, Tess knew. Taking a deep breath, she tried for calm. "It sounds fantastical, I know, but up until last night I could see nothing. Then it was as if a veil were pulled from my eyes." She gave a shaky laugh. "I can still hardly believe it myself."

Ashley studied her intently, his legs crossed as he sat in a little damask armchair. "There's more to it than you're telling me, Contessa," he said softly. "I know you too well to be put off the scent. What really happened while you were away? And with whom did you pass those leisure hours—recuperating, that is?"

"It is better that you do not ask, Ash. There are dangers—so many questions, still. Believe me, I would tell you if I could."

The elegant young man before her looked unconvinced. "Tell me at least who took care of you. I hardly see the Fox in the role of nursemaid."

With a ragged little cry, Tess spun about, one pale hand flung across her mouth. Her eyes, when she finally turned back to her brother, were gray-green pools of pain. "Don't ask me anything more, my love. I—I cannot talk of it. Not yet, while the scars are still fresh. Perhaps not—not ever."

Her brother's lips curved in a thin, self-mocking smile. "It never changes, does it, Contessa? Always you must be the strong, silent guardian, and always I the weak, foolish schoolboy, to be coddled and protected at all costs. Well, I'm bloody tired of my juvenile role, do you hear? Just for once, why don't you let me grow up? By God, I've enemies who treat me with more respect than you do!" He pushed unsteadily to his feet, shoving his fists into his waistcoat pockets. "When you can see me for what I am—a man, Tess, not a little boy—then I'll be happy to talk further. Until then, just—just don't bother to look for me!"

Without a backward look, he turned and flung himself from the room, leaving a stricken, white-faced Tess to stare after him.

Was it true? Had her brother grown up without her noticing? Her eyes fixed on the empty corridor, Tess asked herself how she could have made such a terrible muddle of things, when all she had meant to do was be kind.

"Her Grace, the Duchess of Cranford." Peale's face was a lesson in impassivity as he opened the door of Lord Ravenhurst's study.

Behind him stood a frail, white-haired lady, her bearing stiff and regal. Her gloved fingers tightened on a fold of gray, watered silk. Motionless and silent, the two people stood studying one another.

"My dear boy," the duchess whispered finally, fierce joy lighting her pale face. Even as she spoke, her hands reached out to him.

"Aunt Victoria," Ravenhurst murmured, moving to grip her slim fingers and lead her to a chair. "What are you doing here in Rye? The last time I saw you, you were caught up in the whirl of the season, with barely enough time left for your various charities."

"What am I doing here, indeed?" the old woman chided, her dark eyes keen on his face.

"Tending to your nephew?" There was a hint of resignation in Ravenhurst's voice.

"Tending to my nephew."

Dane's dark eyes studied her lined face fondly, if exasperatedly. "With no more marriageable females in tow, I devoutly pray."

The duchess made what sounded very close to a snort. "One fête at Ranelagh and you never let me forget it. I suppose an old woman can see to the well-being of her only surviving relation without being called an interfering old harridan!"

Ravenhurst's face broke into a smile, which had the immediate effect of softening the hard, chiseled lines of his jaw. "Ah, but I was so very careful not to call you an, er, interfering old harridan, Aunt." An irrepressible light of mischief gleamed in his lapis eyes. "Would it do the slightest good if I did?"

The duchess only glared. "Not an iota, and well you know it."

"So then a truce it must be. We shall have tea and then you may tell me all that has happened in London since my departure."

"I rather hoped we might talk of you," the duchess said, briskly smoothing her skirts. "At least you've put on some weight since I last saw you. But you've not been sleeping well—I can see it in the lines about your eyes."

Ravenhurst threw up protesting hands. "Come, Aunt. I am nearly six and thirty. You must know I'm past praying for."

"No one is *ever* past praying for," the woman said sharply. Her eyes probed his face. "Is it very dangerous, then?" she asked softly.

Ravenhurst stiffened. "Overseeing the Royal Military Canal is a great nuisance, but the terrain can hardly be called dangerous, Aunt."

"*Bosh.* I'm talking about your real purpose in Rye."

Ravenhurst's eyes were fathomless. "And what mission would that be, my dear old dragon?"

"Don't flummox me, boy." The duchess's face was hard with challenge. "I've my own friends at the Admiralty, don't forget. You're no more here to inspect the fortifications than I am—"

"To see the quaint sights of Rye," Ravenhurst finished darkly. "Although I would, of course, be more than happy to show them to you."

"You are a practiced liar, my boy. Yes, you've inherited your father's wit and your mother's charm, and that woman could charm a miser out of his gold, I think. In you it is a deadly combination, I fear."

Ravenhurst's eyes darkened as bitter memories swept over him. But the emotion disappeared almost as fast as it had come, and his mask of lazy indifference dropped back in place. He made the duchess a slight, cool bow. "Such praise is unlike you, Aunt. I quake to imagine what will come next."

The duchess paused in tugging off her long kid gloves. "If I asked for the truth, would you give it to me?"

Ravenhurst's lips tightened.

"I was afraid of that. But, like a fool, I knew I must ask." The duchess's brow creased in annoyance. "Bah, if a woman cannot grow loose-tongued in old age, then what value is there in living so long?" Her fingers freed, she folded her gloves and studied Dane fixedly, one white eyebrow raised in an imperious slant. "When am I to meet her?"

"*Her?*"

"This woman with whom your name is eternally being linked."

A muscle tensed at Ravenhurst's jaw. "Perhaps you will be so kind as to enlighten me, Your Grace. I am lamentably behind in the season's gossip, I fear."

"Lady Patricia Lennox, of course. Lady Jersey would have it that the banns are to be posted any day." The duchess smiled, not missing the irritation that flared in Ravenhurst's face. *More and more intriguing,* she thought.

"Of course—Lady Patricia Lennox. How remiss of me not to realize immediately."

"Really, Dane, whom else could I have been speaking of? Never tell me you are dangling after more than one female!"

"Come, Aunt, surely I cannot be held responsible for the sidewalk prattle of idle people with small minds and large tongues." His lips twisted in self-mockery for a moment. "After all, I am the Devil of Trafalgar. Without me, the *ton* would find little to gossip about. In fact, I rather think I am entitled to some sort of remuneration for all the amusement I provide them."

The duchess's slim fingers rose as if to reach out for him, then fell, tightly laced. "Wretched, exasperating creature!"

"I might say the same of you, madam." Ravenhurst's eyes narrowed, faintly mocking.

"So you mean to tell me nothing at all?"

"Absolutely nothing. 'Twould destroy all your pleasure in ferreting out the truth for yourself."

As he spoke, the duchess's eyes began to sparkle with a faint, wicked gleam. "Yes, I rather believe it would, you rascally creature."

36

The sun glowed molten fuchsia over the dark crest of the distant Wealden hills as Tess climbed the steps leading to the priory's crumbling stone towers late that afternoon. In her hands she held two silver épées, which had belonged to her maternal grandfather, their chased silver hilts glistening like fire in the light of the setting sun.

So few things she had left. So few things her father had not taken from her. These, at least, Tess had not allowed him to find and pawn to pay for a night's pleasures with one of his drunken whores.

Her eyes burning with jade fires, she tightened her grip on the cold metal.

Defiantly she tucked the foils under her arm, climbing the last steps that took her to the half-ruined parapets. At the corner tower she stopped, leaning upon a pillar of sun-warmed granite while she stared out over the sweeping green lawn and woods of Fairleigh.

As far as the eye could see, all was Leighton land, fertile, emerald acres running down to an azure cove. *Her land,* or at least her land to care for until Ashley was able to care for it, for everything had gone to her brother, of course. Tess realized now that her brother was closer to being able to shoulder that responsibility than she had known. Perhaps it was only her own obstinacy that had delayed the process.

What would she do then? she wondered. Dwindle into lonely old age, her energies devoted to tending the Angel? Arrange charity functions for wounded soldiers back from the war?

Her expression turned bleak for a moment. There might have been more, so much more. A different world glimpsed, a future lost—not once but twice.

A moment later her chin rose defiantly and she swept back the long auburn strands coiling about her face. At the least she would see the Angel made into the very finest, and the most expensive, hostelry in the south of England. At the very most—

Suddenly her breath checked, her grand schemes forgotten as she watched a tall shadow slip through the thick tangle of trees near the white garden. *Jack,* she thought, hoping he might have some answers, for she seemed to have only questions.

And then something else caught Tess's attention, a low, muffled drumming coming from the opposite direction. Frowning, she turned to the south, her eyes sweeping across the distant spires of Rye and the lush fields crisscrossed by canals glinting crimson in the sun's last fiery rays.

She tensed, seeing faint puffs of dust float up over the serpentine ribbon of the Winchelsea road.

It was a solitary figure on horseback, coming fast.

One of Hawkins's men?

He was nearly at the Fairleigh turning, reining in his mount for a moment, before surging forward up the graveled drive.

Coming directly toward her.

Dear God, what if it were Hawkins? Jack would be emerging from the trees at any moment!

With a sharp cry of alarm, Tess spun about, her foils clutched tightly as she darted back down the way she had come, scattering gravel in her flight. She took the steps two at a time, still carrying the foils beneath her arm.

Too late she saw the erect bearing of the solitary, dark-clad rider, too late the broad sweep of his shoulders.

The white wing of hair glinting at his temple.

The one man more dangerous to the Fox than Amos Hawkins, Tess thought wildly.

Viscount Ravenhurst. Her lover. Her betrayer.

Then that lean, hard-angled visage was before her, his eyes heavy lidded as he scrutinized her face. A crisp fall of white linen gleamed at his throat, pristine against the form-fitting lines of his emerald coat.

A face from her dreams. Nay, from her nightmares!

No time! Tess told herself desperately. Jack would be out of the safety of the coppice at any second.

Her face fierce with challenge, Tess raised her glistening foil. "Take yourself off, blackguard! I've known enough of your villainy." She made her voice shrill, hoping it would carry a warning up the slope to Jack.

Dane's eyes returned the fire of her gaze, all lapis and smoke. "So rumor was right, for once. You have indeed returned. Looking every bit the hoyden, as usual. Your stay—in Oxford, wasn't it?— did little to tame your wildness, I see." His eyes scoured her face, and Tess had the odd feeling he was plumbing her very soul, noting her panic as well as her attempts to conceal that emotion.

"Turn around and go back the way you came, my lord. Thomas is just over the hill, and his pistol will soon bring you to your senses, if my foil does not!"

"Brave words, Miss Leighton, but I believe I shall not leave just yet." His eyes flickered over the vein that throbbed at her neck. "Were you so ably seconded you would not clutch that foil so desperately. Yes, once already you have escaped me, but no more. This time you will not be so lucky."

"Luck, my lord, had nothing to do with it!" He had a cut near his left eye, Tess noticed vaguely. Good. She only wished his opponent had been more thorough. "The truth is that you were outwitted. By a mere female. But I can see you will never admit the fact."

"You showed a certain resourcefulness in your escape, my dear. I will grant you that much. But what I most particularly recall is the remarkable sight of your naked white thighs flashing down Watchbell Street." His lips curled in a sneer. "I suppose that half the male population of Rye shared my enjoyment in the sight."

Tess smothered a gasp. "You arrogant, black-hearted—"

"Your intemperate tongue, too, has not changed. Wherever you spent the last weeks, it was not in tame company. Nor, I think, in Oxford," he added silkily.

Tess tasted the acrid bite of fear, knowing Jack would appear on the slope at any second. She must find some way to distract this damnable interloper!

Without taking time to consider exactly what she was doing, Tess hurled one of the épées up to the mounted Ravenhurst. "Fight me then, and we shall see who is entitled to arrogance and who is not. Know that you do not come onto Fairleigh lands unchallenged!"

Strong fingers caught the hilt of chased silver, curving to test the rapier's weight and balance. "I could think of better contests between us, Tess."

"I seriously doubt that."

"Can you doubt it? Even now?" he countered, his voice deep and gravelly.

Something about that harsh voice made Tess shiver and think of distant rumbling thunder. Of storm-swept seas. Of dark passion spent and rekindled, again and again.

She shook her head sharply, her gray-green eyes flashing. "Are you a coward beneath that stiff military demeanor, my lord? Were all those tales of bravery simply so much nonsense? Or are your heroics only at sea?" she taunted, desperate to draw his eyes away from the expanse of open lawn above them.

Ravenhurst's mouth set in a rigid line. "That was most unwise of you, my dear."

"Brave words, my lord. Do you care to suit actions to speech?"

Hard eyes the color of midnight narrowed upon Tess's face, then slipped lower, studying the sharp rise and fall of her chest. "And if I win? What prize to me?"

"The privilege to walk on Fairleigh land unmolested."

"An interesting choice of phrase." Dane leaned back in the saddle, a mocking smile upon his lips. "But not good enough, I'm afraid."

"Then you may name your prize," Tess countered quickly. "It

matters little, since you have not a snowball's chance in Hell of winning it." Dear God, he must accept her challenge!

Ravenhurst's eyes darkened as he considered her words. "Very well," he said at last, slipping down from his horse and looping the reins over a stunted hawthorn tree.

Immediately Tess's foil rose. *"En garde."* The words were barely out of her mouth before she was driving him back across the grassy slope and around toward a gravel-strewn terrace at the far side of the priory, out of sight of the place where Jack would emerge from the coppice. Her movements were fluid and swift, metal crashing upon metal as he met her lightning strokes.

"You fence well, my dear, even hampered by skirts. Your wrists are light, you eyesight remarkably keen. I can only wonder," he said shortly, between parries, "what other—abilities, shall we say? —you hide."

"You might be surprised, my lord."

"Oh, I doubt that. And you forget the very first rule of warfare," he said shortly, as she backed him toward a narrow curving stairway, which rose to the roof. "Never underestimate your enemy."

Without warning he sidestepped and then lunged in a lightning maneuver. Tess barely managed to twist aside as his foil drove forward over hers.

"Very clever, my lord. But I have yet a few tricks in store." Even as she spoke, Tess disengaged, spun about, and flew up the steps to the parapet, her kid half-boots crunching on the loose gravel.

Ravenhurst followed relentlessly, driving her to the top of the steps and across toward the roof's far wall. Their swords ringing, he pressed her back. All too soon Tess felt her strength begin to wane.

Still he drove her, showing not the slightest sign of strain. He was, Tess saw, both a brilliant strategist and a strong and fearless adversary.

Perdition! Did the man never check his pace to draw a breath? Tess could feel beads of sweat break out on her brow, but she could not slow down to brush them away. Her wrist and forearm began to throb, but she refused to relent.

Suddenly the viscount lunged again, engaging her foil with a loud crash, only to twist his arm deftly and send the gleaming length of metal flying high in the air. Stunned, Tess watched the silver blade twist end over end, flashing in the molten sunlight. Instinctively, she lunged for her lost weapon. . . .

And fell into empty space, as without warning a section of the decaying wall gave way and she found herself plunging toward the ground thirty feet below.

A hard hand shot out, seizing her wrist with a strength that seemed to drag her shoulder from its socket. Strong fingers dug into her palm, hauling her up what was left of the wall. Gasping, Tess kicked wildly, trying to find a toehold but meeting only smooth, weathered stone at her feet.

Through a haze of pain she felt his other hand grasp her forearm and slowly begin to maneuver her across the gaping hole where once the parapet had stood.

"Steady," Ravenhurst ordered, his voice taut. "Try to move to your right. There's a ledge no more than six inches from your right foot."

Gritting her teeth, Tess pressed sideways until she felt her toe nudge an outcropping slab. Her rib was burning with pain but she ignored everything except that narrow ridge of rock. Grim-faced, the viscount moved with her, maneuvering her into position closer to the ledge. Then at last her foot eased onto the slab.

A moment later Ravenhurst hauled her onto the roof, where she collapsed coughing onto the loose stones at the rim of the ruined wall.

Ravenhurst's face was white with anger as he bent over her. "You little fool!" he roared. "You might have been killed!"

Barely recovered from her fear, Tess flinched before the force of his fury, only to feel her own spark in turn. "And what business would it have been of yours if I had?"

Roughly the viscount grabbed her forearms and hauled her against his chest, anger flaring in the tense set of his face. "You are every inch my bloody business, woman! There are too many things left unfinished between us for me to let you jump to your death. Or is the chance of winning worth any price to you?"

"I would have won!" Tess countered. "Any moment I would have routed you!"

"You never give up, do you?" her captor growled. "You remind me of myself, unfortunately—of the headstrong and damnably arrogant fool I was, when I was a great deal younger. When victory still meant something to me."

"You f-flatter yourself in seeing any resemblance between us!" Tess sputtered. Suddenly her protests died away as she saw the viscount's dark intent. One hand tightened in the small of her back, drawing her close while the other forced her face up to meet his gaze. But before he could do more, Tess's hand cracked furiously across his face.

Ravenhurst's eyes went cold and unreadable, studying her with savage intensity. Straining wildly, Tess jerked free and wiggled backward across the gravel until she felt the wall bite into her back. "Stay away from me!" she warned. "I'll not fall into your filthy hands ever again."

His lips tightened. "The drug was not of my doing, Tess, something you would realize if you gave the matter any thought. As for leaving you alone—that's the very last thing I mean to do, little hellcat." Slowly Ravenhurst stood up, his long body throwing her face into shadow. His boots crunched over the loose pebbles, coming closer, ever closer.

Tess shrank back against the wall, realizing there was no way to escape him. Her hands began to tremble, and she raised her chin in mute defiance.

Without a word Ravenhurst dropped to one knee beside her, burying his long fingers deep in her auburn hair. Inexorably his grip tightened, forcing her head back while his eyes devoured her face—flashing eyes, crimson cheeks, and moist, trembling lips. In vain she tried to jerk her head free, but his grip was unyielding. Every movement of her pinioned head burned like tiny knives plunged into her scalp.

"I'll make you sorry for this!" she blazed, as his hands found her wrists and forced them back against the rough wall. Tossing her head from side to side, she struggled to escape his cruel grip as he slid closer and closer.

Suddenly there was no more room between them, no haven from the searing heat of his big body.

His mouth ground down across her sputtering lips, cutting off her defiant words, her air, and finally, her reason.

Wildly Tess fought as he deepened the kiss and plunged his tongue between her lips to test the barrier of her teeth.

His touch was smoke and fire—his mouth all angry, demanding male. She could feel the rippling play of his forearms at her back, the taut strength of his thighs locked against her hips. She shuddered, feeling the heat of his body lick her skin through her dress.

Everything about him was hard and hungry.

And infinitely dangerous.

A choked cry broke from her lips. "Stop it. You're—you're mad!"

Dimly, her blood on fire, her heart thundering madly, Tess heard him groan far back in his throat.

"Yes, mad—mad for the taste of you! I ought to take you here and now," he growled against her mouth, his lips nipping and kneading and stroking her fiercely. "I saved your life, woman. You owe me something for that!"

"I owe you nothing, sea slime! Let me go!"

His eyes narrowed. "You feel it, don't you, Tess Leighton?" he growled. "Every bit of the same fire that I feel."

Tess's only answer was to twist her head from side to side, struggling vainly to find some part of his anatomy to sink her teeth into.

"Yes, I see the glaze of passion in your eyes, the wild beat of your pulse. This flame burns you as keenly as it does me." Capturing her wrists in one hand, Ravenhurst cupped her flushed cheeks; slowly his thumbs traced her full lips, wet and swollen from his kisses. "All woman—hot and hungry. For me. For the pleasure only I can give you. Why won't you admit it?" he demanded hoarsely.

Tess struggled desperately, but she felt him everywhere, hip to thigh, breast to breast, her frantic squirming only driving their bodies closer together. And then she gasped, feeling the rigid, heated length of his sex brand her thighs like searing steel.

Ravenhurst's eyes flashed darkly from their lapis depths, narrowing as he watched color stain Tess's cheeks. "You give me an ache, woman, an ache that knows only one release—and that is to be quenched in your sweet fire."

Slowly, hypnotically, he lowered the calloused pad of his thumb, rubbing her swollen, sensitized lips. Somehow Tess couldn't control the shiver that knifed through her at his rhythmic strokes.

Immediately his eyes flamed, missing nothing of her response.

Sobbing, Tess closed her eyes, fighting his keen scrutiny, fighting the erotic image of their bodies joined, as they had been that night not so long past.

Impossible! her mind screamed. He was ruthless enemy and heartless betrayer.

Even as she focused on that thought, her traitorous heart began to slam against her ribs. Her pulse surged, wild and hot, through her veins.

"That you'll never have!" she cried, fury and terror warring with the gnawing rise of desire. Along with that came a terrible, harrowing guilt that she could betray André so. " 'Tis only my hatred you'll ever feel, blackguard! A hatred like the Channel wind, so cold it sears."

"Liar," the viscount whispered harshly.

Her breath coming fast and jerky, she fought to put a distance between them, anything to clear her head. At the same time her eyes moved of their own accord, fixed on those hard lips only inches from hers.

A vein beat at her temple.

Her mouth went suddenly dry. Unconsciously her tongue crept out to moisten her bottom lip.

Immediately Dane's fingers tightened, biting into her slender wrists. "I'll have all your fire and more, Tess," he growled. "And the pleasure will be yours as much as mine!"

"Never! 'Twould be taken by force, coward, and no other way."

But all along she knew it was a lie. Dear God, how could she have any feeling left for this man?

Ravenhurst's eyes darkened. "I'm a sailor long at sea, my dear. You taunt me at your peril."

"Taunt you? My only wish is to be free of you!"

Grim-faced, her captor stared down at Tess's moist, swollen lips. "Then stop moving against me, or I do not vouch for the consequences. 'Tis been far too long since I've lain with a woman," he added bluntly, his voice harsh with desire. As if to prove his point his thighs tightened, driving against her hips.

The shock of that intimate contact made Tess gasp and flinch back as if burned.

Sweet Heaven, he was like dry tinder, waiting to be kindled by the tiniest spark! Right now, she realized, her body was blazing with a thousand hungry fires, any one of which could send them both up in smoke.

But it would be the wages of anger and revenge, not the stunning intimacy and total belonging that she had known with her Frenchman.

The realization was like frigid water dashed into her face.

A tiny smile twisted on Ravenhurst's lips. "Since I've lain with a woman of your raw sensuality, that is. A woman who has the face of an angel and the body of a Whitechapel whore."

"Beast!" she cried. "I'll no more be the object of your cruel sport."

"But why all this outrage? You are, my dear, by your own account well accustomed to the amorous attentions of men. Let us be frank then. I want you—and I mean to have you." His eyes scoured her face, dark and inscrutable. "Quite obviously you feel the same, though you work hard to deny it."

Tess struggled helplessly, sputtering incomprehensible invective. "I—I feel nothing for you—nothing except contempt!"

His eyes only mocked her. "So it's back to this fiction of the ice maiden, is it?"

" 'Tis no fiction, you bastard. Just the firmest fact!"

Ravenhurst made a clucking sound. "Such language, my dear. You will never find a husband that way. But why don't we put the matter to the test?" His fingers tightened, stretching her arms until they were anchored to the stone wall behind her head. Slowly, inexorably, he fitted his hard body against hers until she was trapped between inflexible stone and implacable muscle.

A queer, choking noise tore from her throat. "S-stop!"

"Perhaps, my dear, if you first tell me where you really were. For you were in Oxford just as surely as I was"—Ravenhurst's eyes darkened for a moment—"on the moon."

He knew! Tess thought wildly, studying the hard line of his jaw. *Somehow he knew!* "What makes you believe I—I was not in Oxford, you arrogant scoundrel?"

"Well done, my dear, played with just the right touch of indignation. But every flicker of your eye, every leap of your pulse proclaims your guilty secret." His fingers tightened. "With a man, of course. But did he make your skin burn as I can? Did you flame at his touch the way you do beneath me?"

"I'll tell you nothing, cur!"

"Did he tire of your silken body so soon? Or did *you,* perhaps, tire of his attentions? Which was it, Tess?"

"What I have done, you bastard—what I do—is none of your business! You lost any right to interfere in my life five years ago, when you stormed away without accepting any explanation for what you saw—for what you *thought* you saw—in that gate house!"

"I saw you in bed with another man, Tess," Ravenhurst rasped, his words clipped, as if dragged from the very depths of his soul. "With his hands on your naked skin, the marks of his teeth across your breasts. You were barely seventeen years old, yet I saw you writhe with the passion of the most hardened harlot. By God, what was I supposed to think?"

"You were supposed to think that you loved me—with all your soul, beyond even life itself. Or was that promise, too, a lie, my lord?"

"At the time I believed it to be true. But I had no idea then how gravely my feelings would be put to the test." His voice dropped. "I'm listening now, Tess. Tell me what happened that night."

A wild sob rose in Tess's throat, threatening to choke her. Vague images and clawing shapes twisted around her. "I—I can't remember! He—he must have drugged me, don't you see?" She shuddered, feeling once again the press of hurting fingers, the swift, searing pain at her thighs. "Oh, why can't you just leave me alone?" she sobbed. "Why must you come back now and dredge up the whole sordid business all over again?"

Ravenhurst's eyes were opaque, unreadable. "Because, my dear Tess, I have discovered that once a man has you in his blood, he can never be free of you again. And because I have dreamed of nothing else but this moment for five long and bitter years." His voice was low and hoarse, as if the admission cost him a great deal.

Suddenly, through the chaos of her thoughts, Tess noticed the slim blade of a foil glistening at the base of the wall, where Dane had dropped it when she fell.

Immediately she averted her eyes, afraid he would notice the hope that must be glinting there. Fixing her gaze over his shoulder, she stared out over the sweep of lawn toward the sea.

She stiffened, her breath catching audibly.

"What is it?" Ravenhurst demanded, scowling.

"There—there in the cove! 'Tis the French brig, dropping anchor in broad daylight."

"The devil it is!" Dane growled, releasing her to whirl about sharply.

Breathless, Tess lunged, triumph singing through her veins. *She had it!*

The next moment the sharp point of her foil nudged the viscount's chin.

"You treacherous little—"

"I'd advise you to choose your words carefully, my lord. My wrist is remarkably tired, and I would hate to lose my grip, accidentally marring those handsome features."

"You play a dangerous game, woman. More dangerous than you know."

"As you once told me, this is no game. Now, move forward slowly and keep your hands where I can see them."

After a moment's hesitation, Ravenhurst shrugged and did as he was directed, feeling the weapon trail across his throat.

Moving just behind him, her eyes trained on his face, Tess guided him across the roof and then step by step down the rear stairway. "I underestimated you once, Lord Ravenhurst, but it is not a mistake I mean to make ever again."

White-lipped, the viscount moved before her, his shoulders rigid, fury licking at his blood. Taken in by a slip of a girl, damn it! And by such an obvious ploy! He must be losing his mind.

A scowl twisted his lean face. That much was certainly true. His mind was decidedly unstable whenever it came to Tess Leighton. Five years had done nothing to change that.

"You'd better start walking, my lord. It's a long way back to town." The foil dropped, playing over his taut stomach. "But only think how much good it will do you. 'Twould be such a shame for you to run to flab, wouldn't it?"

"You won't always have your foils about you, Tess," Ravenhurst growled. "Watch your back, I warn you. One day you will forget, and that's precisely the day you'll find me waiting."

Tess forced a laugh, trying to mask a prickle of fear at his words. "You would accost me in broad daylight at an inn full of people? I think not," she scoffed. "I believe not even you are so brazen, my lord."

Her captive stared at her, his eyes hard with menace. "Then you are gravely wrong, my dear."

A piece of gravel skittered across the flagstone terrace, with a sound so faint that neither Ravenhurst nor Tess paid any attention, their eyes locked in bristling challenge.

So it was that the voice ringing out from the twilight shadows behind them took them equally by surprise.

"God's teeth, now this is a rare sight!"

37

"**L**ord Ravenhurst, I'm thinking," the tall, silver-haired man on the terrace murmured. A black tricorn sat rakishly back on his wavy hair, and a dark, whiskered mask veiled his features.

The only part of his face to be seen was a pair of keen black eyes, which were just now trained on Ravenhurst.

So this is the man who's been combing the countryside looking for me? the Fox thought. Perhaps it was just as well that they finally met, for Jack had a few questions of his own to ask.

"I believe I'll take that from you now, lassie." The smuggler extended a hand for Tess's foil.

"But—"

"*Now,* Tess. The viscount's come a long way to speak with me, and the least we can do is listen to what he has to say, don't you think?"

Reluctantly Tess handed over the silver foil to the Fox, who lifted it slowly to Ravenhurst's throat. "So we meet at last, Lord Ravenhurst." With his free hand, the smuggler doffed his tricorn and sketched the viscount a little bow, careful to keep his foil poised before the officer's neck. "Do your duties as commissioner of the Royal Military Canal leave you such leisure that you've time to pry into my petty affairs?"

"You are part of my duties, you scoundrel, as you well know,"

Ravenhurst snapped angrily. "Can you wonder at it, when you add murder to your crimes?"

"My crimes, as you term them, may include many things, but murder is not one of them." The foil advanced, grazing Dane's throat. "And you'll be mindful of that fact, laddie, else our conversation—and maybe more than that—will be at an end. Start moving—we'll talk in the tunnels, where we will not be disturbed."

Ravenhurst's jaw set in a stony line. "You might just as well run me through right here, you bastard, for I've no intention of moving one bloody inch."

"Oh, is that the way of it? And here I was, fancying you had something important to say to me."

Ravenhurst's lips tightened as he fought the urge to tell the smuggler to go straight to the devil. But the Fox was right; he had come in search of this man, more's the pity, and Admiralty orders took precedence over any personal wishes he might have in the matter.

For that reason, and that reason alone, Ravenhurst swallowed his curses unspoken and nodded curtly. "Very well. But what I have to say is for your ears alone." His lapis eyes flickered over Tess's rigid features. *"She* stays here."

Tess crossed her arms mutinously over her chest. "I have no intention of leaving. This matter affects me as much as it does either of you."

Jack's eyes narrowed within the slits of his mask. "The lass has a point, Ravenhurst. Something tells me you've discovered her mad masquerade already. Keeping her out of this discussion would probably only goad her to do something even wilder. Which, lassie, is something you'll give up any notion of doing," Jack growled, "else you'll feel the heat of my palm on your backside."

Tess began to mumble a protest, but Jack's hard, warning look cut her off. "It's over, Tess. You might as well begin to accept that fact. There'll be no more midnight runs for you! If you take it into that hard head of yours to disobey me in this, I'll make you very sorry."

Ravenhurst's brows rose fractionally. As much as he hated the fellow, Ravenhurst had to agree with the Fox—in this matter, at least. But this was hardly the loverlike talk he had expected. No, the man treated Tess with the gruff concern of an uncle rather than the tenderness of a lover!

"I make my own choices," Tess snapped. "Just as I've always done. You've no hold over me."

"Perhaps not. But you'll do as I say anyway, lass." The Fox's voice changed, harder now, cold with command. It was a voice he had never used to her before, Tess realized, and she could not suppress a little shiver at the sound.

"The blackguard's right," Dane said flatly. "Next time Hawkins won't miss. And if it isn't Hawkins, it will be someone else. A young Revenue officer itching to get his hands on that thousand pounds of reward money, perhaps. Or maybe a loose-tongued neighbor who has seen one strange occurrence too many. I hardly think you'd relish a night spent in Hawkins's care, Miss Leighton." He pronounced her name with cold formality. "He is the sort of man who would enjoy inventing ways to see you pay for making him look the fool."

"I have no intention of—"

"That's just it. No criminal ever does. But somehow it happens. One night your reflexes are off. You make a mistake, even a slight one, and then you're taken. The odds are against you, you see. Even *he* will tell you it is true."

Jack's lips thinned to a narrow line. After a moment, he nodded gravely. "He's right, lass. Much as it pains me to admit it."

Ravenhurst shrugged. "Are we going to talk or are we to stand here arguing the night long? The entrance to the tunnel must be very close, I think." His lapis eyes searched the granite wall. "Over there, I would guess."

Tess checked a gasp. How long had he known her secret?

The viscount smiled grimly. "I and my men have been watching this place for weeks now, Miss Leighton. There's very little I don't know about Fairleigh. Or about you," he added darkly.

"Go and open the tunnel, lass," Jack muttered, after a brief hesitation.

"But he'll see—"

" 'Tis a bit late for that. He'd have discovered the way of it himself soon anyway."

Tess snorted, mumbling beneath her breath. Leave it to men to band together against a woman. Only give the two a few more hours together and they'd be thick as thieves!

Turning her back, she searched until she found a small rectangular stone near the base of the wall. There was a faint click. A moment later a door opened in the wall of stone.

Ravenhurst's eyes followed her, missing no detail, including her attempt to conceal her movements. "Very clever, Miss Leighton, I applaud you. I might have stood directly before the stone and never even have seen the catch."

Tess permitted herself a tight little smile. "But that is exactly what you *have* done, my lord. On two occasions, I believe."

Ravenhurst's eyes flashed back at her, dark with a promise of revenge.

Tess merely shrugged, tossing her auburn curls over her shoulder and tugging open the door. Cold, stagnant air rushed up out of the tunnel. As always she shivered, feeling tiny fingers of fear play over her skin.

Why could she never forget? Why did the nightmares keep coming back to haunt her?

Frowning, she shook her head, realizing the two men had moved past her into the tunnel.

In a few minutes they were below, ranged in the small, granite-walled room, a candle flickering upon an upturned barrel. "So, Lord Ravenhurst," the Fox said softly, leaning back against the cold stone wall. "Now perhaps you'll tell me what is so urgent that you track me over marsh and weald? Or have I read your character wrong? Is it merely the lure of gold guineas that brings you after me?"

For long moments the viscount stood motionless, studying his opponent. His expression was unreadable, but the tightening of his fists bespoke an inner argument of fierce intensity.

Tess's eyes narrowed. She felt a faint prickling in the far recesses of her mind, almost a sense of warning.

But then Ravenhurst turned, his lean, angular face cast in shadows, and the elusive sensation fled.

Smothering a curse, the viscount plunged his hands into his pockets and began to pace the narrow space. "It is indeed gold guineas that makes me dog your steps."

Jack's eyes darkened; his fingers tightened on the foil.

Ravenhurst allowed his lips to twist in a slight smile. "Oh, I don't mean the reward for your capture, man. It's the gold guineas bound for France I'm after, those that leave this coast under cover of darkness. One way or another, I mean to stop whoever is behind that damnable trade, for each cargo prolongs this cursed war by buying bread and arms for Boney's men. Now, especially, we can ill afford—" With a low curse, Ravenhurst bit off the words he had been about to say.

"Don't stop now, laddie. I vow you fair begin to intrigue me."

"I've said more than enough already, you scoundrel. Seeing as you, by all accounts, are the leader of that band of traitors."

Jack's eyes snapped. "Then all the accounts are wrong! My men carry brandy and silks, not the guineas you speak of." The smuggler stiffened. "But you knew that already, didn't you? You simply wanted to see my reaction to the charge." Abruptly the tip of the Fox's foil rose, grazing Ravenhurst's neck. A tiny bead of blood oozed out beneath the unwavering point. " 'Tis canny you are, laddie. But a great deal too brash for a man who might meet his Maker any second."

Ravenhurst's eyes did not waver. "I think not . . . Jack, is it not?" The viscount's lips curled in triumph as the smuggler's foil froze. "You need me far too much to consider murdering me. Not yet, at least, for I'm the only one who can help you find the impostor who is blackening the Fox's name."

"What makes you think I need your help in that?"

"Because if you could have found the man alone, you would have done so already. No, in this our interests coincide, for I'm seeking the same man, the traitor who organizes the passage of gold to the French. Who else would have such a good reason to see you hated and driven out of the marsh? Yes, our man must find your presence a decided hindrance to his free maneuvering here."

The Fox's foil wavered, then slowly moved away from Ravenhurst's throat. The smuggler uttered a dark laugh. "I can name probably fifty men who would like to see me gone, and that number comes to mind without giving any serious consideration to the question. But you interest me vastly, and I'd have you continue." Since the end of the Fox's épée was still scant inches from the viscount's throat, this silky request carried something of the weight of a royal command.

"Very well. But first . . ." In the candlelight, the planes of Ravenhurst's face were harsh, his features seeming sculpted from cold marble. Very carefully, he pushed the foil away from his neck. For an instant his eyes flickered to Tess, who had seated herself on the pallet of straw near the entrance to the tunnel. Then with a faint shrug he plunged into his tale. "I've been searching for the traitor for weeks, but the man is damned clever. He keeps always to the shadows and confides his plans to no one in advance. His men are few, handpicked for their absolute loyalty. And for their ruthlessness, I might add. So far, we have been unable to plant an agent in their ranks. We have sent our own men along with the outbound gold, of course." Ravenhurst's voice hardened. "None has lived to tell what he has seen. All except a young officer named Thorpe, who was found seconds from death in Fairleigh Cove." His eyes rose, seeking Tess's face. "You remember him, do you not, Miss Leighton? He was hardly more than a boy, yet whoever discovered his identity had no qualm about slitting his throat. His last words, as it happens, were of you."

Tess felt a frisson of fear brush over her. Well she remembered the genial blond young gentleman. For a fortnight he had been a guest at the Angel, explaining his presence by an ardent interest in natural science and the marsh's unusual flora.

His act had been good enough to fool Tess, but apparently not the man he had most needed to fool.

"Oh, yes, the Admiralty hushed the affair up soon enough," Ravenhurst continued. "Wouldn't do to have the bastard realize we were on his scent."

Tess swallowed. Had Ravenhurst laid the blame for the boy's death at her door? "But you couldn't possibly believe that—"

"I *believed* nothing, Miss Leighton," the viscount interrupted coldly. "I accepted the possibility of *everything*, however. After all, the body was found washed up on Fairleigh land. And there have been frequent sightings of cargoes landed in the vicinity, everywhere from Pett Level to Camber Sands. What could make a better haven than a nearly derelict house, perched on a rise that commands a view of the entire coast from Winchelsea to Dungeness?"

Tess sprang from the pallet, angry emerald sparks flashing in her eyes. "Enough! You are foul and contemptible! Fairleigh was never used for such purposes. Oh, maybe for a run or two—"

"A wheen more than one or two, lassie," Jack murmured.

"Why are you agreeing with him?" Tess blazed at Jack. "He is your enemy as much as mine! You must see that."

Jack's eyes were unfathomable beneath his mask. " 'Tis naught but death that's certain in this life, lassie. That means the man who is today your enemy may tomorrow be your firmest friend. Let the man continue."

Tess snorted angrily, sinking back onto the pallet.

"You may save your self-righteous tirade, Miss Leighton. I have lately come to the same belief. Had I not, you may be certain I would not be here talking with you. For you, my dear, would be in a Dover jail right now awaiting sentencing."

"Children, children," the Fox murmured equably. "Don't let us fall to squabbling. We'll need all our wits about us if we're to catch this fellow."

Tess's fingers tightened in her lap as a painful memory resurfaced. "He's called the Eagle, isn't he?"

Two pairs of startled eyes darted to her face.

"How did you—" the two men demanded in unison.

"His name was—was mentioned in my hearing. Do not ask me more than this. So he is the man you are searching for." It was no longer a question; the hardness in their eyes had already answered Tess's question. "How do you plan to trap him?"

Neither man seemed eager to answer her, both having secrets to conceal.

Tense seconds passed. Ravenhurst studied the Fox, trying to

assess just how much the man already knew, and how far he could be trusted. "You know about the next shipment?" he asked tersely.

Jack nodded.

"And you have the point of rendezvous?"

"Unfortunately, no. But I have hopes that a certain meeting later tonight may shed some light on the details." His smile was grim.

Abruptly Ravenhurst ceased his pacing. A muscle flashed at the hard line of his jaw. "I'm going with you."

"Impossible, I'm afraid. You'd be spotted a league away and then we'd both be dumped from the edge of a cliff. Nay, this meeting is for me and me alone. But I would not be above accepting a bit of assistance before the event."

"What sort of assistance?"

"It strikes me that since the Fox already has two impostors"—here Jack flashed Tess a dark look—"he might just as well have one more. Aye, a bonny way to put a spoke in the wheel of anyone who might be following with mischief on his mind."

Ravenhurst looked unconvinced. "How am I to know that this isn't merely a ruse—that you don't have your men hidden in some deserted cove waiting to dispose of me?"

"For one thing, laddie, I need you too much to see you murdered now, just as you've guessed. As for the rest . . ." The smuggler shrugged. "You'll just have to take my word for it."

"I suppose I have very little choice," the viscount said curtly.

Tess listened to this interchange in growing disbelief. Did Jack really plan to strike a bargain with this arrogant, infuriating Crown officer? He must be mad!

"To work, then," Jack said crisply, reaching down to tug a stone from the wall. As Tess watched, wide-eyed, he removed a black bundle, which he tossed to Ravenhurst. "You'll be needing these. It should be dark by now, but not yet moonrise. A bonny time for a smuggler to be abroad, it is. Now, listen carefully. Follow the Rye road until you come to a fork just beyond the Level. 'Twill take you to a windmill, and there you can rest before changing back to safer attire. Aye, your timely appearance should draw away anyone who might think of following me."

"I don't believe what I'm hearing!" Tess cried, jumping to her feet. "This whole thing is mad! The meeting you spoke of might well be a trap, Jack. And how do you know that *he*"—she eyed Ravenhurst suspiciously—"hasn't sent a group of preventive men into hiding to wait for *you?*"

"Difficult questions, lassie. Aye, difficult to be sure. But the truth of it is that I have no choice. No more than our viscount does. But either way, you're to stay out of it, do you hear? I will not have your blood on my conscience."

"But—"

Jack's eyes were cold behind the mask. "Enough, Tess. The rest must be left up to us."

Stony-faced, Tess stared back at him. Who was he to issue her orders? She would simply wait until they left and then—

"Don't even think of it, lass. If you do not stay clear of trouble tonight, I'll keep on riding and never return. 'Tis a promise, that."

One look at those hard eyes was enough to convince Tess that the Fox meant every word. If she didn't comply, she would never see him again.

It was probably the only argument that could have convinced her.

Her lips set grimly, Tess nodded, turning furiously to the wall. The wretched man left her no choice.

Dimly she heard the rustle of clothing. She turned around and blinked to see two identical images, each garbed head to toe in black, topped by black mask and tricorn. Her eyes narrowed as she tried to distinguish the two. Yes, Ravenhurst must be to her left, for he was several inches taller and rather broader of shoulder than Jack. But the differences were very slight. And in the darkness, astride a fast horse . . .

"Aye, my garb suits you, I see. I beg you do not take it into your head to usurp it permanently. Now, I'll ask five minutes before you follow."

Jack turned. Slowly, as if in a dream, Tess rose to her feet, her eyes blurring.

"Remember what I said, lass. No more tricks." Jack ran a finger lightly over Tess's pale cheek. "But why so Friday-faced? 'Tis careful I'll be. And back before moonfall, I promise you."

Tess tightened her lips against the sob rising in her throat.

Another good-bye, after so many.

Quickly, as though he might change his mind, the smuggler raised her hand to his lips and planted a hard kiss on her palm. "Don't cry for me, Tess Leighton. I'm far from worth it. Besides, there's nae an English musket made that can bring me down."

It was nothing but bravado, and they both knew it. But perhaps bravado was what had kept the Romney Fox alive all these years, his name already a legend along the southern coast.

Spoken with awe by those he had saved from starvation with an oilskin bag of gold tossed through an open window.

Spoken like a prayer by those who found bread and cheese and a rabbit or two on their doorstep at daybreak.

"Godspeed," Tess whispered, her lips trembling as he turned and strode up the tunnel into the night.

She heard the quiet crunch of his boots on the loose pebbles. High above there came a faint *whooosh*. The air stirred for a moment, brushing her cheek like a ragged sigh.

Then he was gone, only choking silence in his wake as the shadows closed in upon her once more.

Across the small room Dane stood watching, his blood seething in fury. The look the two had shared was enough to convince him that something far more intimate than business bound them together.

He smothered a curse, putting the thought from his mind. Tonight he could afford no distractions. Masquerading as the bloody Fox! By God, he ought to be shot for stupidity, if nothing else.

Grim-faced beneath his mask, he strode toward the dark mouth of the tunnel, where Tess was still standing, frozen. "I shall leave you now also. I'm sure my going will cause you none of the pain that the Fox's did. But like the Fox, I shall see you again. Sooner than you care for, I imagine."

Something flashed deep in the smoky sapphire of his eyes, a

dark flame of inchoate passion that disappeared so quickly Tess wondered if she had only imagined it.

And then the viscount, too, disappeared into the night.

She gave them time to be well away before she followed up the tunnel, her thoughts in chaos, her heart hammering loudly in her ears.

Through the night silence she walked, over the slope and down to the great house, her shoes whispering over the dew-slick grass. Overhead a crescent moon climbed from cloud to cloud, no more than a pale smudge behind a silver veil of clouds. Somewhere nearby an owl cried once. Tess heard wild scratching, and then the shrill, terrified cry of a small night creature.

Abruptly the sound ceased.

The owl had made its kill.

Shivering, she hurried toward the darkened house. Behind her came a faint rustling, and she turned sharply, staring back into the thick shadows. A dark shape rushed toward her out of the night, wings spread, then plummeted down onto her shoulder.

"Safe haven by morning," a shrill voice called.

Tess loosed a long, ragged breath. "Maximilian, you bad, bad bird. Whatever are you doing here?"

But she already knew. Maximilian had escaped from the Angel a dozen times, and each time the wretched creature found his way here to Fairleigh. Tess sighed, studying the bird on her shoulder. At least she would have company through the long hours until sunrise.

She was nearly at the vine-covered steps when she felt Maximilian stiffen. His sharp, taloned claws dug into her shoulder.

"What's wrong now, you rascally thing?"

From the far side of the hill, beyond the gaunt walls of the priory, came a sharp explosion of musket fire.

One shot. Two. Then a third.

"Dear God, no . . ." Tess's fingers dug into her palms.

"Breakers on the lee! Watch your port bow!" Maximilian called shrilly.

But there was no answer from the night. Only the wind heard, murmuring through the grass, rushing through the leaves.

A cold, hard knot of fear twisted Tess's stomach. Weak-kneed, she sank down onto the steps and prepared to wait, suddenly grateful for the comforting weight of Maximilian's body against her shoulder.

She did not know that they had made one grave miscalculation in their plans that night.

And the name of that miscalculation was *l'Aigle*.

The Eagle.

Tess did not have long to wait.

She heard him before she saw him, jumping up at the faint snap of twigs, the muffled pad of feet. He was coming fast, careless of who might see him.

Tess froze, watching the hill.

A tall, lean figure broke from the darkness, black garbed, his tricorn set at a rakish slant. *Jack or Ravenhurst?* she thought wildly, feeling her heart slam against her ribs.

She did not ask herself why both choices left her taut with fear.

He was past the priory now, strangely bent as he ran.

"Is—is that you, Jack?" Her heart was hammering in her chest, so loud that she could barely hear her own question.

The figure's pace quickened. He was close now. Tess could make out the tight line of his lips beneath his mask. *Whose?* she wondered crazily, not daring to breathe.

Sheet-white, she faced the darkness. "Dane?" she demanded raggedly.

The caped figure came to a halt only inches away, then sank slowly to one knee, his breathing hoarse and strained. "Said I'd . . . return, lassie. Moon's yet in the sky."

On Tess's shoulder Maximilian cried once, long and shrill, as the Fox slipped down to the cold ground.

38

Her heart pounding, Tess grabbed the swaying figure and tore the mask from his face. "Jack, oh, Jack, what's happened to you?" Her breath checked at the sight of his white, drawn features. His lips were set in a rigid line, his eyes glassy.

"Took a ball, lass. One ball too many, I'm afraid. Someone—ahh—waiting by the copse. Stopped by the white garden, I did. No time—"

"Hush," Tess ordered hoarsely, half lifting and half shoving him up the steps into the house. She would have to find hot water and clean linens. Now, where had she put them the last time?

"Forget it, lass. My time's run out. Just let me sit for a minute. Must . . . catch my breath. Things to tell you."

His fingers were hard on Tess's shoulder as his full weight sank down onto her. Fighting back a sob, Tess managed to maneuver him onto the shabby settee by the window.

Her fingers trembling, she pulled away his cloak, stiffening when she saw the ruffled shirt, once so fine and white, now soaked black with blood. More oozed out every second, thick and dark, from the jagged hole in his chest.

Tess moaned raggedly, swaying. *No, no!* her mind screamed, over and over.

"Wrap—cloak around me, lass," Jack whispered through gritted teeth. "Must tell you . . ."

Stark and unfocused, his dark eyes found her face. He shuddered fiercely, and then his mouth clamped down in a hard line. When he spoke again, it was with a desperate clarity. "Sit down, Tess. Listen to me now, for I've only a bit of time left." He shook his head, seeing a raw protest rush to her lips. "No time for lies now, lass. Too damned clever, he was. Waiting . . . tell Ravenhurst." He stopped, white-faced, struggling for breath. "Ransley and one other. Watch—watch for the wing. Trust no one."

The smuggler's eyes clouded for a moment, but he shook his head, fighting the creeping numbness. "Not what he seems, your viscount. You could do far worse, lass."

Tess shook her head, not wanting to hear any of this. "Don't talk this way, Jack. You'll . . . you'll—"

"Be gone soon," he finished flatly. "But I'll have naught of tears, do you hear? 'Twas a good life. I've rare memories to take with me wherever I go. And the best ones are of you, lass." Once again his eyes blurred. "And of her. Sweeter than any woman I ever knew, she was. Aye, a finer creature never graced this earth." His fierce, dark eyes settled on Tess's face. "I promised her I would not tell you, but I'm breaking that promise now. You deserve to know." His fingers circled her wrist, tightly, almost fearfully. "You were never his, lass. Nay, 'tis blood of my blood, bone of my bone you are. And I've loved you from the very first moment you drew a tiny, ragged breath. My sweet, sweet Tess. My own, my bairn."

Tess's breath fled. Impossible! Her heart lurched in her chest and a great roaring filled her head.

And yet suddenly nothing else made so much sense. It explained so many things—Edward Leighton's cruelty to her. Her mother's silent pain. The concern Jack had always shown for her.

"It was never sordid, lass. I'd known her long before *he* first laid eyes on her. But like a fool I believed our stations were too different, and so I let her slip away. When I came to my senses and returned for her, she was already gone, forced to marriage by her father's debts." His eyes flickered closed for a moment, and a spasm shook him. "How she would have been proud of you, lass.

You never gave in an inch to him. Aye, you've all the fire she wanted you to have. That much, at least, I could do for you."

A thousand questions sprang to Tess's lips, but she realized with a terribly clarity that she would have no time to ask them.

The silver-haired man groaned, struggling with his pain. After long moments, his eyes opened. "Look . . . in the Angel's flue. Letters—a diary."

"Jack!"

The smuggler sighed jerkily. His fingers began to loosen around her wrist.

"No, Jack! *F-father.*" Tears fell like hot acid on her cheeks. Not yet, please! So much yet to know. So much she hadn't said.

She had only found him, and now she was to lose him.

"Hush, lassie," the man who was her father said softly. "Let me go now. Tired . . . so tired. And I've—I've the strangest feeling she'll be waiting for me." A frown tightened his features for a moment. "Cloak pocket. Take it . . . hers."

With nerveless, trembling fingers Tess searched his cloak, biting back a sob at the thick blood that met her everywhere. Deep in the pocket she felt the outline of a small, hard object. Frowning, she pulled out a ring—a single pearl surrounded by tiny cabochon sapphires.

"She—loved you dearly, lass. Remember that. And if you find love—hold it tight. Don't—ah—don't let it go, like we did."

Tess bent closer, holding him while her tears spilled onto his pale cheek. "I love you, Father. I always have."

His lips curved slightly, then a harsh shudder ripped through him, tensing him like a drawn bow. "Godspeed, my daughter," he whispered. "Safe harbor before moonfall, eh, Max?"

On Tess's shoulder the great bird crooned, low and smooth.

The silver-haired giant trembled once and then did not move again.

Ravenhurst heard the first musket shot just as he rounded the hill. Turning in his saddle, he tried to make out the source.

Again came the distant explosion, then another and another.

Damn! They came from Fairleigh.

With a sharp curse, he reined in his horse and turned back up the road. Even as he hunched into the wind, his fingers tense at the reins, he feared he was too late.

"Tess?"

She had not been in the tunnel. He had gone there first, steeling himself to find blood on the ground and her motionless body beyond.

Instead he had found nothing.

Again he whispered her name, standing at the base of the steps to the priory's roof.

No answer.

His boots sped over the ground toward the silent house. Why no lights anywhere? Had the little fool broken her promise to the Fox and followed him? Were those distant shots for her?

Ravenhurst's hands tightened into fists. For a moment blackness blotted out his vision. Then he shook his head sharply.

Faster, damn it.

He exploded down the slope, his steps like thunder, his eyes fixed on the dark house, which mocked him with its silence.

He took the stairs at a run and yanked at the latch. Why no lights? he kept asking himself. Where could she be?

The entrance hall was wrapped in darkness, and he cursed, stumbling over a small crate just inside the door.

Suddenly he stiffened, seeing a faint patch of gray at the far end of the corridor.

His throat constricted painfully. "Tess?"

Still there was no answer.

His fingers tight on the musket in his cloak pocket, Ravenhurst moved soundlessly down the hall toward that dun-colored rectangle.

Just outside the door he paused, preparing himself for whatever dangers waited beyond.

Or so he thought.

But nothing could have prepared him for the grim picture that met him as he crossed the threshold.

A silver-haired giant of a man, his features ashen and immobile, sprawled on the shabby velvet settee. An auburn-haired beauty, her eyes haunted, cradled his head in her lap and whispered soft words of comfort and encouragement.

Words, Ravenhurst realized immediately, that the Fox would never hear.

A cold stab of regret pierced him, surprising him in its intensity. The man was a criminal, he reminded himself, possibly a traitor to his country. So why did he feel this—emptiness, yes, that was the only word for it. As if something important had been stolen from the world.

Without a sound he moved closer, his eyes on the face that now lay unmasked, a face somehow familiar. Frowning, Ravenhurst studied the Fox's proud nose, his generous mouth, his pale cheeks.

Cheeks even now, locked in death's embrace, not so pale as Tess's.

Ravenhurst's fingers tightened on his pistol as a fierce wave of jealousy ripped through him, burning like corrosive acid. Scowling, he opened his mouth to speak, only to close it again, feeling a razor stroke of self-contempt. Jealous of a dead man, for God's sake!

He could do nothing for the Fox now, nor could he say anything to comfort the woman grieving beside his lifeless body.

No, the only thing Ravenhurst could give her was the privacy of a few quiet minutes with her smuggler, the last she would ever know.

He turned, ready to leave, when a shrill cry from a shadowed corner of the room brought him up short.

A dim oval shape slid out of the gloom, falling onto Tess's shoulder in a blur of emerald wings.

What was that damned macaw doing here? Ravenhurst wondered.

"Go away," Tess said harshly, her eyes fierce when she looked up from Jack at last. "He's sleeping, can't you see? He needs . . . sleep. That's all."

A muscle leaped at the stony line of Ravenhurst's jaw. In that moment he glimpsed through her proud facade to the pain and denial. Too well he knew what she was feeling, as the blood of someone dear stained her fingers, his lifeless body a cold, inert weight in her arms.

Raw remembrance hit him like exploding cannon shot.

He blinked, seeing smoke shroud his vision, hearing terrified screams as a pitching deck caught fire.

Then the image was gone, as swiftly as it had come. And he knew what he must do.

"Sleeping, yes. But he'll sleep better if you put him down, Tess. Yes, like this." Carefully, he lifted her lifeless fingers from the smuggler's chest. "That's better. He'll like that. Just a bit more . . ." Very gently he raised the Fox's head and drew her away, then settled the body back against the faded cushions.

Tess shivered. A long sigh escaped from her clenched lips. Slowly she came to her feet, her face devoid of emotion, a cold mask of perfect pearl. Suddenly Ravenhurst saw the faint silver outline of tears on her cheeks.

"He—he told me to trust no one," she whispered. "It might have been you waiting in the copse." Her hands balled into fists. "Maybe it was your ball that felled him." Her voice rose to a shrill cry. "You've wanted him so long. Dear God, tonight you finally had your chance!"

Suddenly, she threw herself against him, her hands wild and clawing, raining fierce blows across his shoulders, neck, and arms.

A vein hammered at Ravenhurst's temple as her fingers struck his cheeks, raising welts. Yet he did not move nor turn away, allowing her furious blows to fall unimpeded.

"Gone—gone when I'd just found him," Tess cried raggedly. A dry sob tore from her lips. "Oh, God, why can't I die too?"

Ravenhurst's fingers circled her wrists and tightened brutally. "Yes, he's gone, Tess, but I had nothing to do with that. And you've your whole life before you—a life as good as you make it. Let him go. He would not want this of you."

"How do *you* know what he would want?" Tess demanded, her lashes dark with tears. "He was—he was *my* father!"

Ravenhurst's breath caught audibly. Her father? His eyes narrowed, studying the proud line of Tess's chiseled nose and the uncompromising lift of her chin.

Yes, this woman was every inch the Fox's daughter, he saw, now that he was looking clearly. And that meant . . .

Frowning, he tried to submerge the fierce wave of hope that burst through him.

But there were a thousand questions to be answered first, and a traitor to be run to ground. "Who was it? Did the Fox tell you anything at all?" Ravenhurst demanded, gripping her hands urgently.

For a moment Tess studied him, her eyes wild and unfocused. Then, shaking her head, she began to struggle against him. "You —you're hurting me!"

Immediately Ravenhurst's fingers loosened, but he did not release her. "Think, damn it! It's important. If not for me, then do it for him! For your country. I'll get the man who did this, you may be certain of that, but I'll need your help, Tess!"

The barely leashed violence in his voice made Tess blink, her eyes scouring his face. But she could not quite understand what he was saying. His voice seemed to be muffled, as if coming from a great distance away.

Ravenhurst caught his breath sharply. When he spoke again, his voice was slow and very clear. "Tell me everything he told you."

"I—he—" A shudder ran through her, and she squeezed her eyes closed.

For an instant she seemed to catch the faint scent of lavender. Her mother's scent . . .

Blindly Tess shook her head, driving away the seductive comfort of that familiar smell. Her fingers touched the outline of the ring that Jack had given her, now worn securely on the middle finger of her right hand.

I am not mad, she told herself fiercely. *I am not mad.*

When her eyes opened again, their gray-green depths were blurred with tears, but cold and determined. "I'll tell you then. He said it was Ransley and one other. 'Trust no one,' he said. 'Watch for the—'" Her brow creased as she fought to remember Jack's last warning. "'Watch for the wing.' Yes, I think that was what he said." She shook her head. "But it might have been 'ring.' It—it makes no sense."

Ravenhurst's scowl told her he thought the same. "And he said nothing else?" His voice was harsh with disappointment, making him sharper than he meant to be.

"Only one other thing." Tess's eyes were accusing. *"You.* He said you were not what you seemed. What did he mean?"

Ravenhurst's lips twisted in a self-mocking smile. "Perhaps that I am someone you can trust, for all that you try to deny it. Perhaps that . . ." He cursed long and low, biting back the words he would have said next. Too soon, he thought grimly. "One thing I assure you, the Fox will ride again. And he will not stop riding until I have the man behind this villainy. But first . . ." Ravenhurst's fingers settled at Tess's chin, slowly tilting her face up to meet his gaze. "I must bury him, Tess. Later, I will find a priest . . . my aunt will see to that, I think. But for now, where—"

"In the white garden," she answered softly. "He would want that. It was the place she loved most. Yes, in her white garden. . . ." Her voice trailed away. She blinked suddenly, her eyes filling with tears as they searched Ravenhurst's face. "Thank you," she said simply.

They were not the words he wished to hear, not even one tiny fraction of all he ached to hear her say. But they were enough.

For now.

"Do you have . . ."

"I'll find everything you need," Tess said softly, and then was gone.

The eyes he turned on her back were dark and haunted, overflowing with the pain that Ravenhurst was usually so careful to hide.

From everyone. Even from himself.

He came to tell her when it was done.

She was still sitting where he had left her, in a shabby velvet armchair in the middle of the front salon, the room stark and strange with all its fine furniture long sold.

How different the room had looked that night five years ago, Ravenhurst thought. Then candles had burned in their sconces and a row of ancestors had stared down arrogantly from their portraits on the silk-covered walls.

How the proud have fallen, he thought. And wondered in the next instant if the words referred to Tess or to himself.

A bar of silver slanted through the uncurtained window, the only light in this room of shadows.

Tess's face, when he came to stand before her, was translucent and strangely unreadable. "One last favor," she whispered. Her hands trembled where they lay entwined on her lap.

Ravenhurst's dark brow creased. A strange tension gripped him at the darkness gathering in her eyes.

"You—you said I could trust you." For a moment Tess's voice broke, and then she continued in a breathless rush. "Prove it to me."

She rose, her fingers reaching for his muscled shoulders, tentative at first, then bolder. There was a wildness in her face, a harsh torment that set flames alight in his smoky eyes.

"Sweet God almighty—" Ravenhurst's breath fled in a harsh rush as her hands brushed the open skin at his neck.

Fire. Torment on torment. Purest, drugging pleasure.

"Now, Dane."

Ravenhurst cursed darkly. He could not. It would be taking cruelest advantage of her. It would be rankest danger. It would be . . .

Sweet and infinitely soft, he knew, feeling her lips brush the corded arch of his neck.

He felt a savage tightening in his groin, knowing it would be nothing but raw pleasure and aching delight to love her now, after their bitter separation.

Yes, unspeakable ecstasy to have her now, to bridge the chasm between them with wordless, unbreakable bonds.

A shudder passed through him. Her fingers whispered over his chest, opening the first button at his neck. "Tess . . ." he muttered hoarsely.

As if in a dream, she nudged the first ivory circle free, then bent to the next, knowing she could not stop to think about what she was doing. It was a gamble that rested on nothing but an elusive memory.

A gamble and something far more dangerous. But already the stirring in her blood made her unable to think of anything else.

Don't do it! her bewildered mind cried, but her body urged her on, whispering a very different truth. Perhaps her body had always known that truth, even though her traitorous reason had fought to deny it.

Now she remembered. Hours of torment and delight. Hours of trust and sharing.

Two men. Really one?

Calloused fingers gripped her wrist, holding her motionless.

"Why—" With a curse, Ravenhurst cleared his dry throat and began again. "Why are you doing this, Tess?"

Tess's eyes glowed, strange and catlike in the moonlit oval of her face. *"Why?* Do you truly need to ask me that?" Her voice held a hint of mockery. Very gently she slipped closer until their bodies brushed, the touch as faint and seductive as a lover's first kiss.

"Stop it, Tess," Ravenhurst growled, but at her touch the fire in his loins raged out of control. He was aching with the need to drag her beneath him and fill her. Endlessly and savagely and with exquisite care.

Until there were no more words. Until there were no questions and no damning answers.

Above all, no lies.

"Tell me," she whispered, her head thrown back, her hair a shimmering cloud around them.

In the bar of moonlight the harsh, angular lines of Ravenhurst's face seemed chiseled from marble. He could not. He must not— not even now.

Tess waited, deathly still.

"Gwellañ-karet."

The words erupted between them with soft violence, hanging like a dagger in the taut, choking silence that filled the room.

Tess laughed once, a ragged, keening sound. "Or perhaps, André, now that I know your black secret, you don't want me anymore?"

Ravenhurst's rough fingers gripped her wrists, his touch brutal and yet strangely careful. *"Gwerhéz Vari,"* he muttered, dragging her against his chest. "Oh, I want you all right, *bihan,* and have since I first saw you hiding in the rose garden at Fairleigh five years ago, your eyes alive with green fire, your hair like a dark flame about your shoulders. Dear God, I've never stopped wanting you."

His words pounded into Tess, blinding her beneath a mountainous wave of pain and raw betrayal. Up to the very last moment she had dared to hope she was wrong.

But no longer.

Her head fell back; wild, choked laughter flooded to her lips.

"No, Tess," he muttered. "Don't."

But she was beyond him now, and the darkness was worse than anything she had ever known in her days and nights of blindness. Then she had had light, André's light, and the hope he had given her.

"André Le Brix," she spat. "Captain and corsair. Just one more lie, on top of all the others. Dear God, you're no different from my —from the man who pretended to be my father!"

"Not a lie," Ravenhurst muttered. "Frederick Dane André Jordan Le Brix St. Pierre. My mother was a Le Brix, from the Morbihan. The cottage was hers, Tess. And I never took another woman there. Only you." Urgency made his voice harsh.

Familiar now, and dangerously dear, seduction in every syllable.

Wild laughter shook Tess's slim shoulders. Even now he meant to convince her of his innocence, after shattering the last vestige of her hope, stripping away the years of her recovery in one ruthless stroke. In the end he had done just as the French corsair had threatened, she realized dimly.

He had reached into her very soul and ripped the heart from her chest.

It was his, Tess knew it now, to her bitter torment. Whether Dane or André, it made no difference. Her heart had always been his.

Suddenly she exploded into movement, her face slick with tears that shimmered silver as she twisted, struggling, and fell full into the slanting bar of moonlight.

"It wasn't enough to betray me once, was it? No, you had to repeat your perfidy. Filthy, bloody liar! No, a murderer, that's what you are, for you murdered André!"

"Stop it, Tess. André still exists. He is one part of me, the voice of my youth, the joy of a captain at his helm. But you can't have him without me. That's the way of life, Tess: the good can't always be separated from the bad. That's what you can't accept, isn't it?"

She did not answer, her eyes bottomless, dark with an infinity of pain. "It was all a sick game—a way to get back at me and have the answers you needed for your bloody Admiralty. Even if it"—her voice broke in a sob—"even if it meant betraying me with this gnawing torment of hope. Dear God, why did you teach me to hope again?"

Unnoticed, there came a rustle of wings from the shadows nearby. A moment later Maximilian sailed from the gloom through the bar of moonlight, a blur of crimson and emerald as he skimmed Ravenhurst's head. The startled viscount ducked, cursing.

Instantly Tess saw her chance and took it, yanking free of his hard grip and driving her knee wildly upward.

Just as he had done that day in the kitchen, Ravenhurst bent double and toppled before her blow, driven gasping to the bare floor. Waves of agony ripped through his groin, but still he struggled to speak. "Damn it, Tess. *Uhhhh.* Wait—"

"Too late," she cried wildly, her eyes silver with tears. "André —Dane, whichever name you chose to hide behind now, it makes no difference! You've betrayed me for the very last time. I'll see you get no other chance."

His face harsh with strain, the viscount watched her sway, then turn unsteadily and stumble toward the door. *"Wait . . ."* he managed to mutter hoarsely.

But Tess did not, could not, wait. Her slippered feet swept from the room, their echoing rustle too soft to mask the wild sob that escaped her taut lips.

39

The moon was high, a pale sickle rocked on waves of cloud-foam as Tess turned up Mermaid Street. Numbly she noted that a damp fog had crept up from the marsh, loosing a sea of chill, ghostly mist that lapped over the cobblestones.

She had taken Ravenhurst's horse without a second's hesitation, shattered in the wake of Jack's death and the terrible discovery of André's identity. Every angry drum of the hooves, every forward burst of those great legs mocked her.

Too late, they seemed to chant. *Too late. Too late.*

White-faced, she heard the rustle and press of unseen things behind her in the darkness.

Oh yes, the demons were very close this night.

Jem, the young hostler, might have been pardoned for feeling a rush of fear as she burst into the quiet stableyard a few minutes later, her hair a wild auburn tangle about her ghostly face, her eyes dark pools of pain, a Valkyrie herself.

Already she knew what must be done, and that it must be soon.

Ten minutes later Tess threw the last garment into her old leather satchel and then jerked the fastening closed, praying that she could avoid meeting Ashley. Someday she might explain to him, but not tonight, while the jaws of Hell yawned open before her.

Tonight she must think only of surviving. At whatever cost.

"Miss Leighton?"

Damn! Tess stiffened, not turning her head. The voice was soft, imperious, and entirely unfamiliar.

"Please . . . don't go. I—I have something to give you."

"Go away," Tess said flatly.

The voice went on determinedly, as if the speaker was afraid if she stopped she might never begin again. "It is something I have carried for five years, and all that time it has been destroying me," the woman whispered raggedly. "Please—you must take it."

Something about the desperation in that aged voice penetrated Tess's haze of pain. Slowly, stiff with reluctance, she turned, frowning at the tiny, silver-haired woman standing so erect in the doorway. "Who are you? What do you want of me?" she asked tiredly.

The Duchess of Cranford's face was gaunt with strain. "You know my nephew. Very well, I think." Her dark eyes probed Tess's face and beyond, deep into every corner of her anguished soul. "You might have been all that he needed. If only . . ." Her hand emerged from the deep folds of her skirt, clutching an envelope, which she held out to Tess. "Yours. I know now how very cruelly I behaved in keeping it from you."

Tess did not move, staring dumbly at that rectangle of vellum. So this was Ravenhurst's aunt, the Duchess of Cranford. Five years ago he had spoken of her with gruff, protective affection.

The woman's hands twisted and untwisted at her waist. "Take it, please. Even now he does not know that I kept this letter from you. He sent it on the eve of Trafalgar, through an old friend of mine at the Admiralty. I knew it must be very important for him to take advantage of a family connection, something he always so stubbornly refused to do." Her frail hands trembled, and for a moment Tess feared the woman would faint.

Quickly she moved forward, guided the duchess to a chair, and then poured her a glass of water at the side table. "Drink this, Your Grace," she added, after a moment's hesitation.

The keen eyes rose, fixed on Tess's face.

Lapis eyes—just like his. A shiver skittered down Tess's spine, bringing with it a wave of blinding pain.

Slim, fragile fingers gripped Tess's arm. "He never knew, you must believe me. It was all my—my wretched interference. I thought it would make him stronger, safer in the conflict to come, if he thought everything was finished between you. Then there would be nothing to distract him and make him vulnerable. That is why I told him I had delivered his letter personally and watched as you tore it up, throwing the pieces in my face." Her eyes closed for a moment. "God help me, I thought it was the right thing to do. How I have regretted it ever since!"

Tess's face paled. One more shock, after so many.

The lapis eyes, so familiar to her now, flashed open and studied Tess pleadingly. "It changes everything, don't you see? He tried to contact you—to explain, to plan for a future he fervently wanted, in spite of all that had happened. Yes, my dear, he told me even about that. He was half mad that night, I think, and I'm afraid I could only counsel him to put you from his mind forever. It seems I have been nothing but a silly, interfering old fool." The duchess's eyes glazed with tears as she pressed the letter into Tess's hand. "Read it for yourself, my dear. Read it now, for he needs you — more than you'll ever know. He's lost everything else. Perhaps he is near to losing even himself."

Tess's chest rose and fell unsteadily.

Open it, a soft voice urged. *The answer is there, everything you've ever hoped for. Read it.*

Her fingers tightened on the thick vellum envelope. She looked down and saw her name written in strong, slanting script as decisive and firm as the man who had penned it. Dane's handwriting, achingly familiar.

A tear hit the faded ink, smearing it to a gray puddle.

Cruelly seductive, hope flared through her.

With a little choked sob, Tess cast down the letter and shrank back, as if from the edge of Hell, more tempted than she had thought possible.

"It can make no difference," she whispered. "Nothing can be changed. To hope now . . . to feel again . . ." She caught her lip between her teeth as a spasm of regret shook her. "Dear God, no more!"

Catching up her satchel, she shrank back toward the door, each step costing her dearly, her face fierce with strain. "D-don't follow me. Don't—don't say anything more! It's—too late, don't you see? For all of us."

Spinning about blindly, Tess barely noticed the woman standing just outside in the hall.

So close she had come to losing him, the Frenchwoman thought, watching the auburn-haired beauty flee down the hall.

Then Danielle's emerald eyes narrowed.

But here was her chance, dropped into her very lap. She would not miss it, as this silly, stubborn English chit seemed so determined to do.

Grim-faced, she dug her taloned fingers into her palms, pressing until tears sprang to her heavy-lidded eyes. Then, while the silver drops still shimmered there, she moved quickly forward into the quiet room.

"Your Grace, forgive me," she began urgently, her hand at her breast. "I could wait no longer. I must speak or die . . ." A moan trembled on her crimsoned lips. "Not for myself, *vous comprenez?* Not even for your nephew. But it is for the child that I come to beg your help. For *our* child."

At the landing, where she had returned after leaving a note for Ashley, Tess froze, her face going deathly pale at the Frenchwoman's words.

If she had had any doubts left, then those words put them to rest.

Now there could be no going back.

A square of light flooded out from Lord Lennox's study as Tess reined in her horses an hour later. Swiftly she jumped down from her curricle and tossed over the reigns to a worried-looking Jem.

"It will be fine, Jem, I assure you. Lord Lennox will bring me back later." Her fingers were trembling with the combined effects of anxiety and exhaustion, but Tess was glad to hear that none of her uncertainty reached her voice. "Go back to the Angel now."

"A'right, Miss Tess." The young hostler's frown deepened. "If you're sure, that is, though I don't half look forward to what Mr. Hobhouse says when—"

"*Now,* Jem." This time is was an order.

Shaking his head, the youth climbed back into the curricle and urged the horses forward. A moment later they turned down the long, tree-lined drive, their hooves kicking up ghostly waves of fog as they vanished into the night.

In the sudden silence after their departure, Tess felt a wild urge to call the boy back. But it was too late for second thoughts, she knew. Her lips tight, she walked up the broad marble steps and rapped the knocker smartly.

A sleepy-eyed servant appeared several minutes later, looking distinctly displeased at this late interruption.

"I am here to see Lord Lennox," Tess announced imperiously, well aware how odd her presence at such an hour must seem.

Raising one bushy eyebrow, the servant looked her up and down, from her tangled hair and dusty cloak to the worn leather satchel lying beside her on the steps. His eyes were patently mocking. "And who am I to say is calling, if you please? Assuming, of course, that his lordship is at home, which I ain't saying he is."

Tess's chin rose a degree higher, but she was instantly assailed by new doubts. What if the earl was from home? What if he was with company?

It had to be tonight! If she did not act now, Tess knew she would never find the strength again.

The servant did not move, refusing to budge until he had a name.

"Miss Leighton," Tess answered coldly. "Do you mean to keep me waiting here all night?" she demanded.

The dark eyes flickered. Almost furtively, Tess thought, as the man turned and ushered her inside. Without a word, he led her to a small, windowless room off the foyer, then left her, closing the door carefully behind him. But his steps, she realized a moment later, moved off in the opposite direction from Lord Lennox's study. Having been here before for an occasional fête or dancing party, Tess was familiar with the rooms on this floor.

An odd flare of relief warmed her at the thought that she could delay her interview, and that is what convinced her to open the door herself and go in search of Lord Lennox.

For she was weakening, Tess knew. Quickly, before she could change her mind, she darted down the quiet corridor.

She found her destination easily. Too easily. Far too soon.

She raised a slim white fist to knock, a cold knot of regret tightening inside her, squeezing her heart painfully. Go on, she told herself sharply, her eyes bleak with pain.

Far away, down the corridor, she heard the tap of approaching feet.

Her fingers gripped the cold metal latch. Forcing her lips into a bright smile, she opened the study door, an apology ready on her tongue.

With an odd, numbed sort of clarity Tess noted the room's elegant furniture and the man seated before an exquisitely carved rosewood escritoire, pen in hand, several vellum sheets and envelopes spread out before him. He was just putting a red seal in place on one of the envelopes, she saw, using his ring to imprint the warm wax.

Abruptly Lord Lennox swung about, his blond brows sharply slanted. Strange, Tess thought, but she had never noticed before how light his hair was.

"Pray forgive me, my lord, for intruding so late."

The green eyes warmed. "Miss Leighton?" he breathed, almost as if he did not believe that the vision before him was real.

"So it is," Tess said, in what she hoped was her gayest tone. Feeling the sudden intensity of his gaze, she ran her fingers nervously across the bookcase beside the door. "You've changed the room somehow. New curtains, perhaps?"

"New chairs." Slowly the earl pushed the envelope to the back of his desk and came gracefully to his feet. "New desk. New wallpaper. But somehow," he murmured, moving across the room, "I cannot believe you have come here at this late hour to talk about my household furnishings."

Tess's throat constricted, as if blocked by a wedge of linen. *Tell him*, a hard voice urged. *Now, without delay!*

She swallowed.

"Do you mean to tell me why you have come, my dear, or am I to guess?" He reached for her hands, cradling her wrists gently as he searched her face.

Tess jumped nervously as the cold metal of his ring brushed her skin.

Get a hold on yourself, she thought, barely catching herself before pulling away from him.

Lord Lennox's fingers tightened fractionally. "Yes, my dear?" he asked softly.

Her heart began to pound. "I . . . I . . ." Tess cleared her throat. "To see you, my lord. That is, to give you your answer," she finally managed.

A flicker of surprise crossed Lennox's eyes. "I shall not pretend to misunderstand you, my dear Tess. Am I to be made the happiest of men, then?"

Was there the faintest formality in his tone? Tess wondered dimly. No matter. It was all part of this impossible night's events. Tomorrow everything would settle to normalcy. Yes, tomorrow . . .

The blond brows rose slightly.

Tess flushed, realizing he was still waiting for her answer. "Yes. I mean, my answer is yes. I shall marry you, my lord."

Slowly Lord Lennox raised her open palm to his lips, his eyes probing her face. "My dear girl," he whispered, his lips skimming her cool skin. "You positively unman me."

Tess's skin prickled, now hot, now cold. She felt a nervous giggle rising in her throat and barely managed to fight it down. Hypnotized, she watched Lennox's fingers tighten, anchoring her palm while his teeth scored a sensitive ridge of skin.

A tiny shudder ran through her. She looked up to see the earl's eyes upon her, hard with hidden demands.

"This is loverlike, to be sure. To slip to me by moonlight. You fuel my warmest thoughts, my dear, I warn you. I have waited a very long time to hear those words—longer than you know."

"I-it was for that reason—because you had waited so long, that I came, to tell you immediately."

"Very thoughtful of you." The earl's lips brushed little circles on her palm. At each intimate movement Tess blinked, painfully aware that it was not Ravenhurst who touched her so.

She let her eyes close, afraid he would see the black despair that swept over her. But she dared not move away, even slightly, lest she betray herself. *Dear God,* she prayed numbly, *let me convince him. And let it be over soon.*

The quiet rush of his escaping breath made Tess open her eyes. His face was shuttered now, the fires carefully banked. Slowly he released her hand. "You delight me with your answer, my dear. And with your impetuosity in delivering it. Yes, you make me the happiest of men. Indeed, I believe the occasion calls for a libation."

The earl turned and strode to a small chest, from which he removed a crystal decanter and two glasses. Nervously, Tess locked her hands, trying to focus on something—anything—to take her mind off the enormity of the commitment she had just made.

Blindly she looked away, her eyes falling upon the vellum sheet on Lennox's desk. Behind her she heard the clink of glass, followed by the rush of liquid.

15 JUIN, the letter was dated. June 15th. So he was writing to someone in French. Tess's eyes widened as they ranged lower, skimming over line after line of numbers in no discernible order.

Probably some arcane financial transaction, she thought, her gaze shifting to the back of Lennox's desk, where an envelope stood propped against an inkwell. Thick and crimson, its seal caught her attention, a medallion of a bird in flight.

Very lovely, she thought, just as everything the earl had was lovely. Was it possible that he desired her in the same way, as an object to add to his collection?

Pained by that thought, Tess frowned faintly, bending down to pick up a small jade figure from the corner of the desk.

"Admiring my furnishings again?" Lennox's mouth was at her ear, so close that she jumped slightly.

"Just—just this sculpture. It is very lovely. But then, you always did have exquisite taste, my lord."

As if in a dream Tess saw two filled glasses lowered onto the desk. A moment later Simon's hands circled her shoulders, his lips seeking the vein that throbbed at her neck. "Indeed?" he murmured.

His touch was light and teasing at first, but soon grew more demanding. "And is that all you were thinking about, my dear?"

Tess swallowed, trying not to flinch. Her eyes darted wildly about the room. It was only then that she registered the image on the seal. A bird of prey, wings upswept.

This time her stiffening was sharp and unmistakable. Her heart slammed painfully against her ribs. No, she must be mistaken! It could not be. . . .

Slowly Lennox straightened, his fingers gently caressing the ridge of her shoulders. Without haste, he turned her to face him, his eyes unreadable.

"I suppose I should return now . . ." she blurted. "Since I have—since we are—"

"What, you would return so soon? And without so much as a toast to our future happiness? I will not hear of it." Smiling, Lennox pressed the cool rim of a glass into her nerveless fingers.

Blindly Tess touched her glass to his, then lifted it to swallow a tasteless mouthful of what was probably very fine brandy. The drink slipped down her throat in a trail of fire. Quickly she took another.

Lord Lennox's eyes were warm and faintly chiding as he drained his glass. "My dear, dear Tess," he murmured, his eyes never leaving her face as she drained her own.

Gently he removed the long, cool stem from her unsteady fingers.

Tess blinked, swaying slightly. Faint beads of perspiration broke out on her brow. "I don't feel . . ."

Suddenly she was very hot, as hot as she had been cold only moments before. The room, the curtains, Lord Lennox's face, all began to run together, blurring before her eyes.

Watch for the wing, Jack had said. *Trust no one.*

Too late, she understood his warning.

Coolly Lennox toyed with the ring on his left index finger. Rising in sharp relief, a bird gleamed on the ring's golden face. A bird in flight.

An eagle . . .

"Whatever am I going to do with you, my sweet?"

That soft question was the last thing Tess heard before blackness rushed up to meet her.

40

The jolting of wheels on rutted earth woke her.

Why was her mouth so dry, Tess wondered? Why the metallic taste on her tongue? And why was the air so dank and still at her face?

In a fierce, painful burst, memory returned. Simon, smiling faintly. The fiery bite of brandy.

Drugged.

Once more she dipped and lurched, wooden wheels creaking somewhere beneath her head. Where was she now? Tess wondered crazily, opening her mouth to scream.

But she could not, for her lips were raw and bound by a thick cloth. She twisted her hands, only to discover they were knotted together at her waist. The wagon lurched again, and her head dropped with savage force against wooden planking.

A tear slipped from the corner of Tess's eye.

The Eagle—Simon Lennox.

Terror gripped her, her blood running cold as a Channel tide in winter. How could she have been so wrong about the man? After all these months, she had never had the slightest inkling of his terrible duplicity.

Tess grimaced with pain, forcing her thoughts back to his study and the soaring bird on his ring. Jack had known, though, and he had tried to warn her.

But Simon Lennox had murdered the Fox. And now he knew that she had seen the incriminating document in code on his desk.

Frantically Tess twisted at her bonds, tearing at the harsh hempen coils. But it was hopeless, and she knew it. In tying knots, as in everything else he did, Simon Lennox was an expert.

Suddenly the wagon pitched and ground to a halt with a shrill protesting of the brake. From somewhere to Tess's right came the creak of the seat, and then the muffled drum of feet.

Her heart slammed against her ribs as she heard the door of the carriage jerked open. A tall, shadowy figure stood outlined against the unrelieved gloom of the night.

Tess did not move, keeping her eyes open the barest crack, feigning sleep.

Long fingers slid across her brow and cheeks, settling at her chin. "Wake up, Tess."

How had that soft voice ever sounded attractive? she wondered, holding tight to her guise of sleep. Anything to throw him off guard and perhaps gain a few seconds . . .

The fingers at her chin tightened to a painful pinch. "Wake up." This time the words were a flat snarl.

Tess couldn't prevent the shiver that ripped through her. It was a stranger's voice she heard, cold and deadly impersonal. The voice of a man who would kill her without a second's hesitation.

She sighed and twisted her head, opening her eyes slowly as if shaken from sleep. *"Ammmm!"* The gag at her lips prevented her from making more than a sharp, muffled cry.

"That's better," Lord Lennox said shortly. "I don't relish carrying you, my dear. In spite of all that we are to each other," he added, his tone mocking. His hands gripped her wrists, jerking her to a seated position. "Get out."

Wincing, Tess stepped down, her eyes darting right and left. Only darkness met her, unbroken by lights of any sort. Where had he brought her?

Cursing softly, Lennox shoved her stumbling before him. There was softness beneath her feet—grass? Not sand, at least, she thought wildly. Not the beach then. A good sign, surely, for Tess had no desire to be dragged across the Channel to France.

Then, in a chilling rush, another thought flashed through her mind. *He would not bother to take her to France. He meant to dispose of her right here.*

"Not much farther, my dear, only over that rise. But you don't recognize this place, do you? It is my own little secret—or at least it was until the night your father came snooping about. Oh, he played his hand well, I shall grant him that. First he blustered, then he feigned anger, and then he offered me the use of Fairleigh land whenever I wanted, with no questions asked. Yes, I almost considered his offer." Lennox's flat voice hardened. "But it would have been too dangerous. Then there was the question of his lovely, headstrong daughter. You were something of a thorn in my side, I admit. For you, also, the temptation was great . . ."

Tess swayed, walking blindly before him in the darkness, and nearly fell. With a harsh oath, Lennox seized her shoulders and pushed her forward over the dewy grass. Her eyes, gradually growing accustomed to the night landscape, now picked out the dark shapes of nearby trees. At her feet the low-lying mist swirled and coiled like restless, phantom fingers.

The flat, expressionless voice at her back continued. "But then the Fox returned, and I discovered your little masquerade. Very daring, my dear. I quite applaud you. Even Ransley did not realize that there were *two* Foxes. But you could not hope to deceive me, who knows these tunnels even better than your father did." Lennox laughed softly. "Yes, the tunnels made it so easy to watch, to wait unseen—to discover whatever secrets the night might hold. Even to set up some phantom lights of my own."

Bile rose in Tess's throat. *But Leighton was not my father!* she wanted to scream at the man behind her. *The Fox was, though, and you killed him, too!*

Only a muffled sob penetrated the thick binding at her lips.

"Yes, this all must be something of a shock to you, I'm afraid. But when you blundered into my study, you left me no choice. Of course, it was only a matter of time anyway. I would have worn you down finally, and married you with all the requisite pomp and ceremony. Then one day, while on a visit to town, you would have fainted. Your skin would begin to grow pale. At first your friends would whisper of your being in a delicate condition, but you would grow thinner rather than larger. Your mind would begin to wander, and you would imagine . . . oh, terrible things. Then, to my eternal and crushing grief, you would slip away from me forever. A terrible blow, of course. And a very great deal of valuable time wasted. This way is so much neater, don't you agree, my love?"

Tess shivered at his cool impersonality. There was no malice in his voice, indeed no emotion of any sort, only a chilling matter-of-factness.

"It is merely a question of business, you see, of tying up loose ends. For all it takes is one clue, and I am a dead man. You of all people should understand that, my dear, given your own dangerous impersonation. Yes, very cleverly executed. Even my sister could not believe it of you. I can only wonder what became of that bottle of brandy she bestowed upon Ravenhurst. It contained a remarkably potent mixture of herbs and tonics to, shall we say, inspire his affections. There she was, perfectly poised to provide its palliative, with her silken body ready and entirely available. She was quite understandably livid when he would not drink. I, too, was disappointed, for she might have learned a great deal from him in such a state," Lennox added meditatively.

His long, slender fingers pushed Tess inexorably forward up the wooded slope toward a dark, crenelated tower faintly outlined against the leaden sky.

The priory! He was entering from the opposite side, Tess realized, a way she never came, since it was farther from the road and the route bordered a farmhouse with a particularly large, snarling dog.

Her foot slipped on an exposed root and she fell forward onto the grass. A raw sob escaped from beneath the cloth at her lips.

"Get up," Lennox ordered flatly. When she was too slow in obeying, his fingers bit into the soft skin of her forearms, yanking her cruelly to her feet. "You must not delay now. We're nearly at the journey's end." A mirthless laugh burst from his lips.

Tess spun about, kicking at her shadowy captor. But with her hands bound, there could be no contest. Cursing, Lennox shoved her forward until her face met the rough bark of a tree. "You will be very sorry if you try that again, my dear, let me assure you. I have been indulgent with you so far, but I shall be so no longer, if you oppose me in any way." As he spoke, Lennox drove her forward, grinding her cheek into the hard wooden scales until Tess felt her skin stripped away.

"Ammmmmm!"

The fingers did not loosen in their implacable assault. "Do you understand me now?"

Tess continued to kick, driven by raw terror and fury.

A knee settled into the hollow of her back, driving her whole body against the tree's bulk. "Stop fighting!" he snarled.

The cold metal muzzle of a pistol dug into her neck.

Tess shuddered as her breasts were driven against the rough trunk. He was far too strong for her to resist, especially now that she knew he had a pistol. She would have to think of something else.

With a pronounced slump of her shoulders, she stopped struggling.

Slowly Simon's fingers loosened, and his knee fell. "Better, my dear. Much better. We shall rub along together perfectly, I think, as long as you remember your place in the grand scheme of things. Which is rather lower than you like to believe," he added, with a short, dry bark of laughter. "And now we are at our destination, I see. Which means . . ."

Suddenly Tess felt him tug a wide strip of cloth over her eyes and jerk it tight in a knot. She twisted frantically, only to feel the pistol dig into her ribs. "Remember what I said," Lennox hissed. "If you wish to see your lover alive, that is."

Little pebbles skittered over the flagstones as he pushed her over the terrace behind the priory. Tess felt cold tendrils of fog drift about her ankles. Dear God, did Lennox have Ravenhurst in his grasp too?

Up the stairs he drove her, step by stumbling step, while the wind hissed down through the crenelated stones. Black fingers of fear clawed at Tess's mind, her heart drumming as she seized upon her one slim chance of escape.

He thought her sightless and disoriented beneath the muffling cloth. True and yet not quite true, for long days of blindness had left Tess with new strengths. Now her ears were keen, picking out space by sound. To her right she heard faint echoes where a wall rose close by; to the left, the blank stillness of empty space.

Yes, it was all there. She had forgotten nothing. Somehow she must use that knowledge and make it serve her ends now.

The wind hit her, damp and clinging, and Tess realized she was beyond the corner towers, at the center of the roof. Carefully she calculated the distance between the dilapidated wall at her right and the fallen ruin of stones somewhere to her left.

Embracing the blindness, searching the darkness, just as her Frenchman had once taught her to do aboard the *Liberté*.

It was her only chance of survival.

Swiftly Lennox pushed her forward until her back met a high, jagged wall. Then he reached around to untie her gag. "You shouldn't have long to wait, my dear. He should be here any—ah, that must be Ransley now, unless I miss my guess. Yes, the man's swagger would be hard to mistake. He's grown quite unmanageable since I gave him the business of that girl in Applegate. I'm afraid he positively relishes that sort of work."

"R-Ransley was w-working with you?" Tess's lips were dry and cracked, but she forced herself to speak, praying that this might grant her precious minutes of delay.

"An unpleasant sort of fellow," Lord Lennox said ruminatively, "but really rather brilliant at what he does. Unfortunately, the Fox was the one thing Ransley feared. So the business of eliminating him fell to me. Simple enough, however. I merely had to watch in the copse and bide my time. I knew he would come back to see you sooner or later. I admit I did not expect to see Ravenhurst though. The lovely Danielle had her uses, but they did not include ferreting out information about you, lamentably. But of course, how remiss of me. You have not made the acquaintance of the viscount's mistress."

Tess's breath caught. The Frenchwoman at the Angel, the one carrying Dane's child. Jealousy ate through her for a moment, and then something else, which she recognized as fierce, gnawing regret. She had wished for a child of her own some day.

Now it seemed she had lost her chance.

Stop it, lassie. This game's yet to be played.

Tess stiffened, hearing that gruff, chiding voice echo through the chaos of her thoughts.

Jack?

But the Fox was dead. With her own eyes she had seen him die. No one could help her now.

From far below came the muffled tread of feet, interspersed with harsh, smothered curses. Little rocks skittered over flagstone with angry, *pinging* sounds.

"H-how long have you known?" Tess asked. "About my masquerade?" It hurt to speak, but she managed it somehow, her voice dry and raspy.

"Some six months now. Hawkins wanted to take you, shall we say, in hand long ago, but I forced him to wait, for you still had your uses."

"Hawkins?" Tess's voice was flat with disbelief. *"He* is involved in this—this villainy?"

"His admittance to my little secret was a necessary evil. One more weak link in the chain," Lennox mused, almost as if he had forgotten her presence. "Yes, I rather think—" He broke off, his sentence unfinished, as hard boots clumped up the stairs. "So, here they are at last. Efficient as usual, Mr. Ransley. My compliments."

"Aw, this bastard weren't no trouble. Only he weren't where you said he'd be. Picked 'im up on the Rye road, and bloody surly he were too. After a few friendly taps he learnt his manners right enough," the unkempt man added smugly, pushing his captive forward. "Bound his eyes just like yer said, Eagle."

For long moments the two men faced each other, wariness and something darker, more primitive, etched on their faces. Ravenhurst growled something incomprehensible beneath his gag, and Lennox smiled faintly.

"It has been a long and tedious business, Ravenhurst, but at last my plans are near to completion. These last weeks you have dogged me rather too closely for comfort, something I fear I can no longer tolerate." Lennox's green eyes flared, burning against the cool pallor of his face.

"Dane?" Tess asked unsteadily, desperate to know what was happening. "What—what have you done with him, you bloody scum?"

"Your viscount is only a little mussed, my dear. But I think I shall remove his gag now. It will be amusing, I think—for the few minutes that remain to you." Like a shroud, those flat, emotionless words choked Tess.

"Yes, there is a certain aptness to the scene, don't you agree?" Lennox mused. *"He* is muzzled; *she* is blind. Just as you were in Brittany, my dear. Ah yes, I know all about those days. For I was there, too, you see, busy with tasks of my own. Although at the time I did not realize the identity of the *Liberté*'s bold captain. A pity." His voice tightened fractionally. "Now those tasks require my undivided attention. Which, unfortunately for you, means that your continued presence would be a decided nuisance. So it must be, I am afraid, *ave atque vale,* my friends."

Tess stiffened, hearing Lennox turn slightly. His voice became cold and precise. "Toss them over, Ransley. The girl first. A lover's quarrel, I am sad to say. Unfortunate, to be sure, but such things happen, especially with two people so—headstrong—as these. And there is the viscount's instability too. Ah yes, nightmares still haunt the Devil of Trafalgar, I'm afraid. Those, too, I know about, Ravenhurst. Danielle is a very efficient instrument of information."

Tess heard a low, muffled curse, followed by the sputtering of gravel, and then Ransley grunting in pain as bone smashed against bone. There came another thump, and this time it was Ravenhurst who groaned.

"Stop it, damn you!" Tess raged, her blood churning with a desperate urge for survival. After all the suffering she had known, she refused to be cheated of her existence now. Not by a twisted, amoral traitor like the Eagle. "Is that what you did to my father, throw him off the roof? He never had an accident on horseback in his life, for he was a bruising rider. It was one thing I always wondered about." Tess knew she had to keep Lennox talking.

Perhaps then Dane would have time to recover from that last punishing blow of Ransley's.

Yes, talk was their only hope.

"Really, my dear, you are so patent," Lennox chided coldly. "Talking will avail you nothing. However, since it is something of a deathbed request, I suppose I must answer the question." He laughed, low and humorlessly. "No, as a matter of fact, I simply set a small and rather vicious spiny shell beneath his horse's saddle. He always favored that big black mount, and the brute went berserk, tossing your father from the cliffs. The whole thing was accomplished in a matter of minutes, leaving me the unpleasant task of bringing him back up closer to Fairleigh, since the discovery of his body so near the mouth of my tunnel would have been inconvenient in the extreme. Yes," Lennox added thoughtfully, "your father died as he had lived—sweating and swearing to the very last."

Tess's lips pressed in a thin line, imagining that final, gory scene. "But he did not die."

"Nonsense, my dear. I saw him with my own eyes. I carried him up the cliff path, remember?"

Was there a hint of tension in Lennox's voice? Tess wondered. "But my father did *not* die that night. He died only hours ago."

"What pathetic attempt at deceit is this? You'll get nowhere with this nonsense, I warn you."

Tess cocked her head, hearing a faint rustling somewhere to her left. Was Ravenhurst coming around at last? "Leighton?" She managed a cold laugh. "That man was not my father."

She allowed the tense silence to stretch out, able to imagine the faint flattening of Lennox's mouth. Yes, he was a man who would not like untidiness or surprises. "No, my real father was a man of rare talents, of hidden skills. He taught me everything he knew. He was the Fox, you see, and it is his pistol that points at you right now from my pocket," she finished coolly.

"You are a liar." But there was an infinitesimal hesitation before Lennox spoke again. Tess could feel the cold fury of his gaze upon her. "Yes, a liar—for all that you do it superbly."

"Shall we conduct our own little experiment then? Not a fair bargain, certainly, since I am blinded by this cloth," Tess added viciously. "But then, you were never fair with any other of your victims, were you? The true mark of a coward."

"Life would have been interesting with you, my dear," Lennox said softly. "I am almost sorry that I must deny myself that pleasure. And as for experiments, those, too, I must decline. The hour grows late, and I have—investments, shall we say—to protect." His boots crunched toward Tess. "Give it to me," he snarled.

"I think not." Tess's heart slammed wildly against her ribs. For God's sake, where was Dane? Why did he not assist her? They had so little time left.

Tess went still, hearing a faint noise. Was it the distant drum of horses' hooves? Thomas, perhaps, or Hobhouse?

"In that case your friend the viscount goes over the edge—rather sooner than I had planned."

Perdition! Tess swore silently. The villain held all the cards and he knew it. But why was Ravenhurst still silent? Had his wound been graver than she realized?

Outside in the darkness the drumming grew louder, a rider approaching.

Tess's throat went dry. There were no choices left. "Very well. Leave him here and I will hand over the gun. Then you can do what you like with me. By the time he can work his way free, you and your precious gold shipment will be far away from here."

Lennox laughed softly. "Very cool, my dear. I've always admired a woman who knows how to play a poor hand, even when it's quite hopeless. Now give me the pistol and then we'll discuss Ravenhurst's fate."

Tess tossed her head and laughed. "You must consider me a great fool to ask such a thing. Without this pistol, I am powerless."

Silently Lennox inched closer. "Even with this much mentioned pistol—which I have yet to see, by the way—you are still powerless, my dear. For one sign from me and Ransley throws the viscount over that crumbling wall." A strange tension entered Lennox's voice. "By God, you really do love him, don't you? So much that you would give up everything for him?"

"That is none of your affair, I think," Tess said flatly. "Love is an emotion you could scarcely comprehend. I see that now. To my eternal shame, the discovery came too late."

Lennox made a dry, clicking sound. "Don't upbraid yourself for that, my dear Tess. My act was a very good one, and it has been honed on far more worldly creatures than yourself." His boots inched closer, rustling over the little stones between them.

"Stay back," Tess hissed. "I warn you, I shall shoot. I am sightless, but my hearing is most acute."

"And I begin to grow bored by this masquerade."

Tess felt faint drops of sweat bead her skin beneath the thick linen at her eyes. "Do you care to risk your life on that gamble?"

"I believe I do."

A horse neighed somewhere down the slope toward the great house. Hope surged in Tess's heart. "Very well. Since you leave me no choice . . ."

Suddenly, with a muffled snarl, Ravenhurst exploded from the wall where Ransley had been holding him, his grip growing ever looser as the viscount continued slack in his hold. With a sharp jab to his captor's unguarded stomach, Ravenhurst broke free and spun about toward Lennox.

Then nothing but silence.

Ashen-faced, Tess strained to hear the slightest whisper of movement. It came a moment later, two pair of feet crunching over the rock-strewn surface at the center of the roof.

Dimly she heard the wind sing down over the hill. Somewhere an owl cried, short and shrill.

There were no hoof beats now, she realized, only an ominous silence.

Wildly she wrenched at the bonds that held her captive, squirming and twisting in an attempt to reach the linen at her eyes. But her hands remained locked as before, the knots as firm and unyielding as ever. With short, careful steps she moved along the wall, her back to the cold stone, working her way toward the steps.

If only she could reach Thomas . . .

Behind her the boots crunched on pebbles, circling slowly. Neither man spoke, intent on this last, life-and-death struggle.

Almost at the steps, Tess calculated. One more foot and then . . .

Dull thumps echoed up the stairway. "Thomas?" she whispered.

A hand cupped her shoulder softly, then squeezed.

"Thank God," she breathed, sagging against that short, powerful body.

Shoulders too broad for Thomas's? Fingers too hard?

Warm, damp breath played across her neck. "Gave it to ye good, did he, this Thomas? I'll give it to ye even better, lovey. Don't ye worry none about that."

A moan wrenched from Tess's throat as those stubby fingers probed her neck. Dear God, it was Amos Hawkins who held her —and Hawkins was one of the Eagle's men!

41

Whirling about, Tess tried to run, only to stumble on a fallen slab of granite. The next minute Hawkins dragged her to her feet. "Let them bastards fight their battles in peace. Me and yerself got more important things to keep us occupied, eh?" His hard fingers pinched and probed, ruthlessly exploring breast, thigh, and stomach.

Dear God, she had played right into his hands!

From behind Tess came the harsh thump of a powerful blow landing on flesh. Lennox grunted, snarling a curse.

Hawkins jerked her hand from her pocket, revealing nothing more than a rigid fist. "Fooled him well, didn't ye, wench?" His mouth was hot and wet at her ear. "About time someone taught that bastard a lesson or two. But now I mean to take ye in hand. God, I'm near to exploding already!" Brutal and jabbing, his fingers wrenched at her skirts, seeking the secret recesses of her body.

Wildly, Tess twisted, kicking and panting until one foot met solid muscle.

Hawkins grunted in pain. "Ye bloody little bitch! I'll teach ye to—" His open palm cracked across Tess's jaw, sending her reeling to hands and knees. "Aye, here and now I'll take ye. Rough like, on all fours, until ye beg me to stop. Only I won't stop, d' ye see? I'll ram myself inside ye again and again, until ye learn to soften yer tongue! Aye, on me, wench." His voice rose, hoarse with lust and the image of his own vile pleasures.

Tess bit back a sob of pain, working her feet beneath her and struggling to stand.

From the open circle of stone behind her came short, muffled curses. Once more a blow was landed, and this time it was Ravenhurst who grunted in pain.

Stumbling, she inched back along the wall, hearing Hawkins stalk closer.

"Aye, I'll get ye, bitch. And when I do—"

Suddenly a ragged cry exploded behind them. Desperate fingers dug at scattered stones; twisting feet kicked against the granite slabs.

Then a harsh cry, followed by the sound of a body bumping over the ruined parapet and plummeting to the ground, a hail of gravel and loose stones raining down in its wake.

Tess stifled a scream. *Dear God, which one?*

Hawkins stopped moving.

She heard the rustle of clothing.

"Ah, a bracing bit of exercise."

Lennox! Tess thought, blackness flooding over her. Once again he had won.

"Nooooo!" Wildly she threw herself toward the spot where Ravenhurst's body had made its muffled descent.

But Lennox caught her at the edge. "Not quite yet, my dear. I still have one more thing to finish." He drew out the eagle-crested ring from his pocket. "Soon everyone will be talking of Ravenhurst and the shocking things he did to those poor females. Yes, who would have dreamed he would take advantage of his office in such a way, indulging in such depravity? And a smuggler as well." The earl made a clicking noise. "Terrible business, indeed. And you, my dear Tess, you must wear his mark. Then I will slip the ring onto his finger, where it will be easy for the investigating magistrate to find."

The earl's hand tightened on Tess's waist. Cruelly he began to drive the sharp face of the ring into her right cheek. "The first time, with the boy, it was a mistake. I forgot all about the mark this ring would leave. Now, what was the fellow's name? Thorpe, yes, that's it. I found him nosing around the end of my tunnel. A calculated risk to dispose of someone who was so obviously a government agent, but in the end his death proved remarkably useful. When his body was discovered at Fairleigh Cove, where I so carefully left it, it would be certain to throw suspicion on you, my dear. Of course, I saw to it that the boy received a message which appeared to come from you, and so his suspicions were passed on to the riding officer who found him just before he died. So sorry, my dear, but a rabbit needs must have more than one hole, you know. Or an Eagle, one nest." Lennox laughed coldly. "Then the idea came to me—quite a brilliant one, I think. Why not leave the same mark on all my victims? Or on all the *Fox's* victims, I should say. Which means Ravenhurst's." Lennox continued to chuckle as the cold metal bit into Tess's soft skin.

"Let me have her first, Lennox," Hawkins pleaded hoarsely. "I've waited for six months, damn it. Ye promised—"

"You'll do as I say! I've business to finish, and more important things to consider than how you slake your crude appetites. Go down and check on the last chest. Ransley's already gone to see that the schooner is secured and ready to sail within the hour."

Hawkins made a low growl, deep in the back of his throat. "Not this time, I don't, ye bastard! This time I'll have her, damn ye!"

Suddenly Tess was flung wildly across the roof, the force of the blow loosening the ropes at her wrists.

"Get away, fool!"

In the night silence the sounds of their struggle erupted with startling violence. Snarled curses and sharp grunts echoed over the ruined roof.

Her heart pounding, Tess shrank in a crumpled heap against the scattered stones. Too late, her mind whispered bleakly. It had always been too late.

Somewhere to her left the struggling continued, but now the outcome held no interest for Tess. Like a dank fog, pain lapped at her mind, icy fingers squeezing her heart. There was nothing left for her now—she had lost two men in the space of one, muffled shout.

'Tis not moonfall yet, lassie. Do you not remember my promise to you?

Her thoughts unfocused, Tess twisted her hands, working the knots free and tugging off the length of bloodied rope. She should have felt pain, but now she felt nothing at all, only a terrible, choking emptiness.

Numbly her fingers fumbled at the linen knotted over her eyes. *Ah, Jack, if only I had known sooner. If only . . . if only . . .*

High overhead came the whispering of air currents. Tess heard the faint *whooosh* of wings. The owl about to find its prey, she thought dimly.

The great wings rose and fell, their beating louder now.

A shrill avian scream erupted over her head, followed by Lennox's shocked shout, Hawkins's raw curse.

Tess froze, hearing the wild flailing of arms, the thump of shadowy wings. An instant later the whole ragged edge of the parapet gave way, exploding in a cloud of gray dust, burying the two stunned men beneath a ton of smoking granite.

It is over, Tess thought.

Fragments of gravel bit into her hips and calves, and her wrists stung where Lennox's rope had stripped the tender skin raw, but she felt none of it.

Her only real sensation was of a terrible, draining emptiness, as if someone had bored a hole deep inside her and the contents of her body were slowly spilling out onto the cold, hard stone—blood oozing warm and thick, heart still pumping, synapses quivering.

Yes, it was over, but the truth was that it was just beginning. Now time stretched before her, an endless, harrowing stream of leaden days and gnawing nights.

Minutes. Seconds. Hours. Choking her in a great black tidal wave of time.

At least before, she had been able to console herself with thoughts of André, off chasing different dreams on the far side of the horizon. Now even the faint comfort of that image was denied her . . .

Her eyes bleak with pain, Tess sank back against the remaining stones beside the parapet's gaping hole, totally dead inside. Listlessly she reached up and tugged the dusty scrap of linen from her eyes. Overhead Maximilian circled, then came to sit on the wall beside her, whistling softly.

Far to the east, she saw, above the black spires of Rye, the sky was beginning to grow light, smudged with grays that would soon bleed into streaks of pink and aquamarine. The sun would slip from the marsh and climb over steeple and rooftop, dragging another day behind it in a fiery resurrection of light from darkness.

But for now the leaden shadows remained, Fairleigh's lush acres concealed beneath ghostly tendrils of fog, which lapped in drifting swirls about the hedgerows and trees right up to the dark stones of the priory.

As chill and numbing as the pain in Tess's heart.

So how was she to go about this process of living, Tess asked herself, when all she could think of was Dane? When her thoughts cried out to be with him, even in death?

On the top of the ruined wall Maximilian flounced his wings, crooning and whistling softly, enjoying the play of the wind through his feathers. Slowly Tess ran a finger down the macaw's chest, stroking those downy inches. It was little enough to do. The bird had saved her life, after all.

Or Jack had, she thought, remembering the strange words that had echoed through her mind.

But that was the merest fancy, of course.

Dead men did not speak. And they certainly did not climb walls.

"Safe harbor before morning, lassie," Maximilian chanted, stamping upon his perch of stone.

No, there would be no safe harbor for her, Tess thought. But there would be life and at least usefulness.

Yes, one began, she supposed, just by beginning. By putting one foot down and then the other, again and again, until all the complex, comforting habits of living were relearned.

A cold, sea-damp gust of wind hit her face, tossing the auburn curls about her cheeks and shoulders. *Dane, Dane,* her soul cried, tormented. Struggling to find equilibrium, Tess closed her eyes and inhaled deeply even as she drowned beneath a crushing wave of regret.

Knowing this time there would be no rakehell Frenchman to pluck her mid-Channel from the dark waters of her grief.

The wind soughed through the white garden and the dark wood, shaking the oak leaves, tossing petals of nightshade and anemone. And in that soft, restless wind came the faint hint of lavender and the sound of chiding laughter.

Open your eyes, lassie, the night whispered. *Find your heart and follow where love leads. Don't let it slip away, as we did.*

White-faced, Tess dug her fingers into the cold, unforgiving stone, oblivious to the tears spilling down her cheeks in a silent rush.

Up the hill she heard the wild scuffling of a night creature, pressed to finish its hunting in the last minutes before light returned. The rustle grew louder; bits of gravel *pinged* across the flagstone terrace far below.

Suddenly Maximilian raised his wings and soared off through the jagged hole in the parapet, a slash of crimson and emerald against the leaden, predawn sky.

Once more Tess heard the skittering of pebbles. Rousing herself, she inched closer to the jagged scar of stone, peering down over the edge into the swirling fog.

What she saw there made her heart twist convulsively, her fingers clutch the sharp granite.

A black shape detached from the mist, rising slowly, laboriously, along the priory's weathered stone face.

With a choked cry, Tess slipped farther out over the rim, sending a rain of gravel spilling over the wall.

"Enough, *bihan,*" the man below rasped. "Do you seek—once again—to kill me?" He was well above the mist now, making a laborious ascent over the gray, cleft slabs.

Her face translucent, her eyes shimmering with joy, Tess inched farther, reaching out for him. *"Dane!"*

His face slanted up, a vein pounding at his temple. Blood matted his forehead; his eyes, she saw, were glazed with pain. "Help—help me up, love."

Catching his arm, Tess helped him struggle up the last foot, then across the rim and onto the roof.

"Never—ahhhh—give up hope, *me kalon*. It's the one thing that separates us from the beasts," Lord Ravenhurst panted as he fell sprawling beside her, one hard thigh slanted across her legs.

After a moment he twisted onto his side and drew her down against him, her hair spilling like a dark curtain around them. His fingers found hers and laced tightly together, as if he needed to reassure himself that this moment was real and all else before had been the dream.

"It—it was Simon," Tess gasped. "All along, it was Simon. He killed my . . . my . . . Leighton—when he discovered that the tunnel was used for transferring gold to the cliffs. It was Lennox who killed Jack, too." Her hands tightened convulsively. A salty tear fell over their clenched fingers. "Forgive me for thinking it could have been you."

"Hush, sea gull," Dane whispered. "It's—finished now." His fingers moved, slipping deep into her hair and cupping her neck protectively as a tremor knifed through her.

So close they had come to dying, Tess thought. So close to losing the only thing that was good and lasting in this world.

Oh, yes, Jack, I've found that love and I will follow wherever it leads me, I promise.

Dane's fingers moved gently, stroking and kneading the tension from her shoulders. "Hush, my heart. All that is behind us now. The Eagle will never fly again, for he has been slain by our strident dove. Besides," he added, pushing back a long strand of Tess's burnished hair, "you did not think to dispose of me so easily, did you? After all, I've two men inside me. And right now both of them are demanding to spend a lifetime with you," he added huskily.

Tess studied him through a veil of tears, her love spilling out in a fierce wave potent enough to engulf them both. "André or Dane, I mean to have you, my lord. Even if it means three to share our bed."

Ravenhurst's eyes turned smoky. "I mean to put that vow to the test very soon, *bihan*. But first, witch, there is the little matter of your running away from me in the night, without so much as a

word of farewell. And there I was—applauding myself on taming
my beautiful shrew."

"I could not stay, Dane. Padrig was waiting; French soldiers
were already on their way to the cottage. It would have been
dangerous for all of you had I stayed."

"All quite true, but it would have made no difference to me.
And then your sight returned on the voyage home." His eyes were
faintly chiding. "Yes, I had my ways of learning that, too. Dear
God, how sorry I am that I was not there to share it with you."

Green glints danced in the depths of Tess's eyes. "Ah, but a
lusty corsair has more important things to do than tend to debilitated females."

"Debilitated?" Ravenhurst muttered something in Breton beneath his breath. "Were you any more 'debilitated,' *bihan,* you
would have been the death of me! Either by épée or granite block
or the gravel you kept strewing down upon my poor head."

Despite a very great effort, Tess found a smile snaking across
her lips. "Such a poor head, you are quite right. I apologize for the
gravel. But for nothing else, you realize."

A pair of smoking lapis eyes narrowed upon her lips, and Tess
felt the fire and power of the man break over her in hot waves. "In
Brittany, we have ways of dealing with intractable women, did you
know that?"

"Indeed, my lord?" Tess's smile widened. "You terrify me. Do
you Breton men use whips, or knives?"

"Oh, something far worse," Ravenhurst murmured darkly.
"And your punishment, *me kalon,* will be long and very agonizing, I assure you. Hours and hours of it," he rasped, slanting his
face to brush his lips against the line of her throat, the ridge of her
high cheekbones, the soft arch of her upper lip. "Weeks and
weeks." His velvet tongue traced her lips' shadowed center, teasing, seeking admission. With exquisite control, he swept inside
her, hot and sleek and demanding.

Deep in her throat, Tess moaned, aflame with an aching need,
her body melting beneath him like wax hungry for the imprint of
him everywhere.

Dane caught the sound with his mouth, answering with a dark

groan of his own, shaping and stroking her lips hungrily. "Oh, I can see it lasting for years, woman. And you will find me infinitely inventive in my methods, I warn you."

Shivering, Tess gave herself up to his sensual demands, seduced by heated images.

Of two men. Each one fierce and proud, each tortured in his own way.

But those are wounds I mean to heal, my love, she vowed silently. A second later even that thought fled as she was swept away in the vortex of desire he unerringly aroused.

When the first rosy fingers of dawn broke over the rooftops of Rye a short while later, filtering down over this quiet corner of England, there were two people who gave no notice, too intent on the dawn they had already kindled, secure in the knowledge that their love would resurrect a thousand such dawns, nay a thousand thousand of them.

Above them, Maximilian stamped gravely, looking smug and very wise for a moment before soaring off over Fairleigh's green slopes, well contented. Already he was tasting the delicate morsels of fruit he would coax from Edouard for his breakfast.

Epilogue

They were married from the old church at the top of Watchbell Street two weeks later, to the deafening peal of bells tolling over marsh and weald. It was the height of summer, the trees girded in crimson blooms, the grass in boldest greens. The air was as clear as crystal and the azure sky was cloudless, running unimpeded all the way to France.

Perhaps even running as far as a rocky, wind-swept peninsula in Brittany, where a tall ship rocked at anchor, its crew busy mending shroud and canvas.

All people like a good scandal; and nearly as much, a good wedding. So it was not surprising that on this day all Rye turned out at the old church in appreciation of an event that held every promise of being both.

The ceremony completed, the bridal couple stepped out into the sunlight. Whispers ceased and nudging arms stilled as the two turned to look at one another.

The bride's hair spilled like a burgundy flame against the tiny seed pearls covering her satin wedding dress. Even more luminous was the look of love that lit her piquant face. The green glow in her curious, uptilted eyes halted more than one matron in mid-speech.

In a gray rush of wings the fan-tailed pigeons fled south, stirred by the wild peals that spilled over the old city walls and down to the marsh, which rolled like a green sea, lapping at the foot of the town.

But the man on Tess's arm noticed none of this, his whole gaze, his whole being focused on the vibrant beauty beside him. Suddenly his long, calloused fingers tightened, as if he feared he might lose her, as if he feared the weight of so much happiness.

His new wife saw, and smiled, running gentle fingers across the dark comma of hair that fell onto his scarred brow. *"A jamais mon coeur,"* she whispered softly, smiling at the fire that her words kindled in his fine cobalt eyes. "Forever, I swear it."

"And I hold you to that vow, *me kalon.* Not even a sea battle right there at Dungeness would take me from you now." His mouth hardened slightly. "Nor would a very superior cargo of silks and brandy persuade me to let you slip away to Camber Sands one more time."

Tess managed to make a little moue of discontent. "Not even once? Faith, how the lion doth roar once he has cornered his mate."

"A bad example, love, for it is the lioness makes the kill, while her lazy lover simply profits by her exertions. And you, my sharp-tongued wife, will do nothing more strenuous than feed me tea and omelettes in bed for the next month." A muscle flashed at his broad brow. "Along with other sorts of exertions, of course, which I have been planning for five years now. Yes, witch, I mean to leave you with no energy at all for joining your disreputable friends upon the marsh."

"In that case I shall need to be kept *very* busy," Tess said silkily, her finger dropping to sketch the curve of Ravenhurst's full lower lip. "Are you up to that, I wonder?"

The growl that burst from her husband's throat was answer enough.

The sound made Tess's smile break free, luminous and unrestrained, as her joy poured like molten sunshine from her radiant face.

Behind them they heard a sharp little cough. "Any more of this celebrating on the church steps and even my considerable social skills will not be enough to keep you two from ostracism." The

Duchess of Cranford, elegant in gray watered satin, stood at the door of the church, studying them severely.

Only the faint gleam in her blue eyes betrayed her happiness.

Tess was the first to move, lifting her long skirts and moving back to take the old woman's hand in a warm clasp. "You've done so much already, Your Grace. How can we ever thank you?"

The old woman's eyes blurred for a moment, and she shook her head abruptly. "As if I expected thanks! No, just see to the domestication of that volatile nephew of mine. He's yours to control now, my dear, thank the good Lord." Her fragile fingers tightened on Tess's for a moment, and she blinked back tears.

Tess's voice dropped. What she said next was meant for the duchess's ears alone. "It did make a difference, Your Grace. More than you can know. And as for the letter, that shall remain our secret. What you did was done out of love. How can I ever fault you for that?"

The duchess's fingers shook, and a tear slipped from her eye as Tess bent down to kiss her cool, papery cheek. "My dear, dear girl," she whispered.

A moment later Ravenhurst was beside them, his eyes dark with concern as he clasped the duchess's other hand. "Plotting some new devilry already, are you? And you not five minutes married, my wife. I can see I shall have to keep you on a short leash."

"Impudent young puppy," the duchess said sternly, pulling her frail fingers free of his and rapping him sharply with her fan. "This poor girl will have her hands full domesticating you, I can see. Now off with the pair of you, for you've more important things to do than stand here tormenting a frail old woman."

Her stern look lasted while Ravenhurst bent down to plant his own kiss on her pale cheek; then he straightened and looked down at his wife, with all the fire of his heart, all the force of his yearning soul written clear upon his face.

Another tear slipped from the duchess's eye, joining its cousin on her cheek as she watched the couple turn and walk hand in hand down the gray, weathered stones where so many other eager feet had trod before.

"Godspeed," the duchess whispered, her eyes suddenly filling with hot, salty tears. Sniffing sharply, she plunged her hand into the reticule dangling from one arm and pulled out an elegant scrap of embroidered lawn.

Her face carefully averted, she allowed the white square to float to the ground, all the time fighting the tears that threatened to spill onto her face at any moment. People were streaming out of the church now, their hushed comments overheard in snippets as they passed.

"—quite, quite, lovely. Yes, marriage will do her a great deal of good. Children, too, of course—"

"—Lord Lennox, of all people. I always said there was something a bit too polished about that fellow—"

"—the Devil of Trafalgar, don't you know? But the man looks to have settled down at last. Not that that bride of his will let him kick up much of a dust. Be a regular fool if he did, anyway, with a woman like that waiting for him at home—"

The duchess sniffed sharply, reaching for her handkerchief with one hand and brushing her eyes swiftly with the other. Suddenly a blurred image of shining black boots swam before her averted eyes.

The white square was lifted onto her shaky fingers.

"If I may be so bold."

Slowly the old woman straightened, her eyes narrowing on the tall, blond man who stood before her, his broad shoulders eased into a bottle-green jacket topping charcoal breeches.

"Your Grace." His keen blue eyes swept her face quickly, missing nothing.

"Wretched thing." The duchess's opprobrium left it unclear whether the handkerchief or the man was the object of her censure. With a defiant little sniff she pushed the white fabric back into her reticule. Then her head tilted back, and she studied the man before her thoughtfully. "Tony Morland—you young scapegrace!"

The man before her winced. Only a few people in England dared address him in such terms, but the Duchess of Cranford was one of them.

And she knew it.

A shrewd smile lit the old woman's gaunt features. "I don't believe I've seen you since that lackluster affair at Lady Harewood's last year. Dreadful bunch of people. But my nephew didn't tell me you were coming." Her tone made it clear that Morland ought to have presented himself to her directly upon his arrival.

"I arrived only last night, I'm afraid." The earl coughed slightly. "Urgent business, you understand."

The old woman snorted. "Came down for a last farewell fling, eh? Good burgundy and bad women, most like." She tried to look stern but failed lamentably, ending up looking like an old and very frail fairy godmother.

Morland smiled, then turned to slant thoughtful eyes on the new viscountess's retreating back. "I believe that Ravenhurst has found all the woman he can handle right there. And as for celebrations, it was no more than a shared bottle of brandy and a slow, savored cheroot." His smile broadened. "Be glad you were not there, Your Grace. A filthy habit, I assure you."

"Which one, the women, the tobacco, or the brandy?" the duchess shot back. Her eyebrows rose suddenly. "And speaking of bad habits, weren't you dipping rather deep at faro at Lady Harewood's?"

"It was piquet, as a matter of fact. And the place was Lord Lemmington's."

The duchess waived her hand airily. "Close enough. You won a great deal of money from me that night, my boy."

"Three hundred and sixty-one pounds," Morland murmured.

"So you've a head for cards, have you? And for other things, too, unless I miss my guess." Shrewd lapis eyes studied Morland for a moment. Why had the boy never married? the duchess wondered. "The sort of things with long legs and a copious quantity of blond curls. Do you continue to play today?"

Morland's expression was all innocence. "At which? The women or the cards?"

"The cards, you impudent young jackanapes."

"I might consider a game. If the stakes were right, of course."

"Cheeky brat." Suddenly the duchess took Morland's arm.

"But I've nothing better to do today, as it happens." Already she was marching down the walk, her expression bright, her confident posture restored. "I'm certain that that clever Hobhouse can scare up some cards and a dealing box for us."

Morland slanted a secret smile down at her white-haired head. "I dare say."

The old woman's pain and loneliness had not been lost on him, nor her fierce attempts to conceal them. Watching the laughing bride and groom disappear around the corner, Morland rather thought he understood the duchess's sentiments exactly.

Some fleeting emotion skittered across his lean face. Then he shrugged slightly and turned keen eyes upon the duchess. "Very well, Your Grace. But I play to win, I warn you."

"Of course you do, boy. Why else would one play, except to win?"

The duchess's eyes narrowed as she studied her companion's chiseled, handsome face, her mind already busy at its calculations. Yes, it was high time that the earl married and produced an heir. That father of his had been a very ramshackle sort, but this young man was made of sterner stuff, she decided.

Let's see, she thought, there was the eldest Stedfield chit. Lovely figure—he would like that. But no, the creature was insipid in the extreme. This man would never tolerate boredom in a wife.

There was the season's current incomparable, of course, the dark-eyed Amelia Egremont. Very taking little thing, and could converse on any number of topics. Still, there was a certain coldness about the girl that might put a man off.

Her mind happily absorbed in a host of matrimonial speculations, the Duchess of Cranford allowed her tall companion to slip her hand more securely into the crook of his arm and steer her off toward Mermaid Street.

Yes, it was a lovely day for faro, the duchess decided.

"Marry in haste, repent at leisure!" a shrill voice cried as Dane and Tess turned down West Street.

Gaudy green wings lashed the air, and a moment later Maximilian dropped to his perch on Dane's shoulder. His sharp face slanted, the bird peered up at the viscount. "Needles and pins, needles and pins," the macaw screeched companionably. "Let a man marry and his troubles begin."

Ravenhurst threw back his head, laughter thundering from his chest. "By God, you've the right of that, Maximilian!"

Green sparks flashed from Tess's eyes. "I believe I see Edouard now. He's proposed adding roast pigeon to the Angel's menu, but I think I shall suggest something more tasty. Something with green wings and crimson breast, you wicked bird!"

Feathers ruffled, Maximilian stamped upon Ravenhurst's shoulder. "Bloody Frenchman!" he screeched, then swept off, a blur of color against the dark, tiled roofs.

Laughter tumbled from Tess's lips. "Impossible creature," she murmured, shaking her head. "He was Jack's bird, you know. They were very close. I feared for a while that he would never spring back after—after Jack died. It's strange, but sometimes I almost think—"

"No, don't tell me," Dane muttered. "I don't think I want to hear."

Tess's eyes searched his face. "But if it hadn't been for Maximilian getting free when he did and coming out to Fairleigh . . ."

Dane's fingers tightened on her waist. "Don't think of it, *me kalon*. All that is finished. Lennox is gone and his wretched sister has fled in disgrace. I think she knew only a small part of what her brother was doing, in fact. But none of that matters. Yes, now there will be only sunlight and laughter for us, I promise. And no more need for you to sleep by candlelight, I hope."

Tess smiled tremulously, imagining how she would love and grow with this man through the long vista of happy years lying golden before them. Fighting, sharing, caring, their hearts bound irrevocably—even when it hurt to care so much.

Yes, Tess could think of no better way than this to spend the next sixty years of her life. Although she decided not to tell her imperious husband that.

Not yet, at least.

"Tess!"

At just that moment Tess's brother crossed toward them from the far side of the street.

"Soon the whole town will be dogging our steps," Ravenhurst muttered, pulling Tess to a halt and clapping a semblance of a smile on his face.

But this meeting was important, the viscount knew, feeling the sudden tension in Tess's arm. And if the young whelp hurt her, by God, he'd—

"Bloody lucky I caught you! That wretched Tredwell woman cornered me on the steps and wouldn't let me go. Before that, there never seemed to be the time to . . ." Ashley's eyes narrowed, studying Tess's face. "I'm a bloody fool, Tess. After all you've done . . . I . . . I don't know how to ask you to forgive me."

But I do, Ravenhurst thought. *Very quickly. So I can be alone with my wife.* But he said none of these things, for he could see Tess's lip quiver.

"I understand now," her brother continued gruffly. "About our —about Edward Leighton. About Jack. By God, he was a trump, wasn't he just?"

Tess smiled at Ashley, only a hint of sadness in her eyes now. For Jack would always be with her, she knew, always the brash silver-haired smuggler who'd captured her heart ten years ago.

"So he was, Ashley," Tess said softly, giving her brother's hand a quick squeeze, immeasurably glad that their fighting was over.

"Now go on with you," the elegant young man ordered. "And whatever you do, be happy. For once." His eyes searched out Ravenhurst's. "You'll see to that, won't you, my lord?"

If I could ever find a minute alone with her, I would, Dane thought irritably. But the smile he turned on Tess then was full of warmth and an infinity of promise. "That I will, Ashley," he said softly, never taking his eyes from Tess's face. "That I will."

"Very well, I'll be off then. You both must be wishing me at Jericho."

Beneath his fingers, Dane felt Tess's arm begin to relax. He smiled as he heard her sigh. Now, if only his own problems could be solved so easily.

Suddenly his eyes hardened. He growled a low curse.

"What is it?" Tess asked worriedly.

"That bloody Tredwell woman! With her bloody son and her bloody husband. Heading this way. By God, if she says one word, I'll—"

Tess's eyes flashed to the left and a secret little smile played about her lips. "Follow me," she ordered, pulling her husband into the narrow mouth of the alley before them.

"What—"

"Hush, or they'll see us."

There in the lee of the fine summer wind, she pressed her back to the cool, shadowed wall of the Needles passage and pulled her husband into her arms, drawing his head down to meet her kiss. "Kiss me, André Le Brix. Or have I given my heart to a fickle man?"

A frown worked its way across Ravenhurst's handsome face. "What are you up to now, woman?"

Tess smiled vaguely, then slanted her lips across his.

The next moment Ravenhurst forgot his question and everything else but the warm softness of his wife's lips. With a groan he buried his fingers in her hair and crushed her to his hard chest. "Ah, *gwellañ-karet,* how I've missed you. I told you we'd have no more of this before parson had us firm in his mousetrap, for I wanted no chance of your escaping me again. But now . . ." His strong fingers curved over Tess's back, smoothing and stroking, rediscovering the thousand joys of merely touching her.

Dazed with a need of her own, Tess let her head fall back, her eyes dreamy on her husband's bronzed face. "But I don't want to escape, my love," she breathed unsteadily. "And now that we *are* married . . ." Her head tilted, she studied him beneath lowered lashes. Her pink tongue swept gently across her soft lips.

Ravenhurst growled, feeling desire twist through him like a burning blade. "The thought of all the things I'm going to do to you is adding inches to my anatomy, *bihan.* Very painful inches."

Tess shifted her hips, confirming the awesome heat of his arousal.

"No more, woman," he rumbled warningly.

With a laugh, his green-eyed wife spun out of his grasp and darted down the passage.

"What in the name of—" Dane's angry voice echoed loudly as he plunged into the shadows after her.

With a clang, Tess freed the concealing brick and raised the hidden trap door to her tunnel, sweeping up her skirts and slipping down into the darkness.

Her husband dropped beside her a moment later, a scowl upon his face. "So this is how my soot-faced urchin eluded me. I thought it must be something of the sort. You're too clever by half, witch." Ravenhurst's eyes darkened as Tess stretched out her arms to him, a sweet hunger burning in her radiant eyes.

"It was the shortest route, my love. And I find I am become most terribly wanton and wish to spare no seconds until I can do all the things *I've* been dreaming of."

With a raw groan, Ravenhurst pulled the door shut, then walked slowly toward his wife. "Is this what you want, sea gull? Truly?"

"Of course, I *have* been meaning to open the old chimney as Jack instructed. My mother left a diary there for me, you see. I suppose we could go upstairs and—"

With a fierce oath, Ravenhurst hauled her against his hard body, his eyes hot and devouring. "Bloody blazing hell, woman. You would try the patience of a saint! You know very well what I meant."

"Do I?" Tess eye's darkened with sudden uncertainty. "You could have had your pick of the *ton,* Dane. I'm sure there must be dozens of well-bred females desperate to have you. I wouldn't have stood in your way, you know." Only the faint tremor in her voice betrayed these fine sentiments.

"Stood in my way? *Stood in my way?*" the viscount roared. "I don't *want* anyone else, by God! One green-eyed, brandy-haired temptress is all I can handle. *More* than I can handle, I begin to think." His eyes narrowed to dark slits. "Has that Tredwell woman been at her meddling again? Has my aunt—"

"No, none of those things, my love. It is only that—"

With a smothered oath, Ravenhurst hauled his wife close and

silenced her in the same way men have silenced their women since time immemorial. His lips hard and hungry, he took her mouth beneath his, parting her with his tongue, groaning when he felt her soft heat feathering over him in answer. *"Gwerhéz Vari,* but you're sweet. More, *bihan.* Let me die of this sweetness!"

His deft fingers began to probe the row of tiny buttons at her back. At the same moment Tess attacked the perfectly starched folds of her husband's neckcloth. Satin rustling frantically against crisp broadcloth, they fought to free each other, hungry for the touch of skin against naked skin.

"My sweet love," Tess breathed.

"Si douce," Ravenhurst muttered.

Right there in the cool tunnel, with his elegant jacket wadded into a shapeless mass and ground into the dust, Ravenhurst took his wife beneath him and filled her with all the fire and fierceness of his love until she dug urgent fingers into his back and whimpered.

"Yes, sea gull. That way . . . ahhhhhh . . . I'm dying!"

"Sweet heavens, Dane, I—ohhhhhhh, *please!"*

And there, too, in the shadowed tunnel, the hard-faced hero of Trafalgar finally came home, finding all the sweet welcome he had ever yearned for. Guns, traitors, and vessels forgotten, he whispered dark Breton love words against Tess's ivory skin and discovered that his tormenting memories were gone, burned away by the luminous fires that glowed in his wife's eyes as she shuddered and convulsed beneath him, taking them both plummeting into the storm's whirling vortex.

Drowning in love.

Thanking their Creator for giving them a second chance.

Hours later, just as the moon unfurled silver sails and slipped over the horizon, old Thomas made a final trek to inspect the shaky remains of the ruined priory wall.

The servant stiffened, his bushy brows knitting in a frown. There it was again, the sound of laughter, up near the white garden.

He spun about, his eyes narrowed. But he saw nothing, just as he always saw nothing.

Pulling off his battered hat, the old man scratched his head irritably. Bloody bunch of nonsense, this talk of voices and light.

'Twas only the wind soughing through the oak grove, of course. Aye, no more than the old stones echoing beneath stray pieces of fallen gravel.

With a little shrug, Thomas turned down the hill toward his cottage.

Queer place, this, he thought for the thousandth time. At least the young mistress was married now, and that sea captain of hers would give her little time to be prowling about up here in the shadows. Aye, a marriage long past due, the old servant thought, a smile lighting his grizzled face.

His eyes busy searching for the lantern in his window, Thomas did not see the faint shimmer that seemed to rise over the top of the hill.

"Padrig and the crew of the *Liberté* sent you this, along with their regrets that they could not attend the ceremony. 'Twould have been a bit too dangerous even for such rogues as they."

The moon was drifting through a cloud-swept sea as Tess and Dane crossed the green lawns below the priory's ruined wall, hand in hand, the caressing summer winds soft upon their faces.

Her eyebrows raised, Tess took the leather box Dane held out to her. Inside, nestled on a bed of crimson velvet, she found a re-poussé pendant strung from a heavy silver chain.

"Qui voit Groix voit sa joie," Dane read. " 'Who sees the Isle of Groit sees his own joy.' Not even Danielle's tricks will take this from us." His eyes narrowed suddenly. "My aunt told me of that talk about a child. Simply another lie, in her great arsenal of lies. You know that, don't you, my heart?"

Tess smiled up at Dane. "The duchess told me something of the sort, although she found it devilish hard going. I do believe it was the first time the old dear was ever tongue-tied in her life."

Dane's lips curved with laughter. "I only wish I might have been there to hear."

"Impudent young puppy," Tess scolded, capturing the duchess's tone exactly.

"What joy you bring me, *bihan,*" her husband said huskily as he carefully lifted Tess's glinting hair and slipped the silver ornament around her neck. "And these, too, are yours," he said softly, pressing two tortoiseshell hairpins into his wife's soft palm. "I'm afraid I had to repair the one you dropped in my bedroom. But it seems you are prodigal in your gifts, my love—you left your tokens for two men." His eyes darkened. "And both of them offered their hearts in return." His fingers tightened, crushing her hand within his. "They are both me, I'm afraid, Tess. At sea I am alive and happy, but too often I grow restless kicking up my heels on land. Yes, ashore I become a monster, *me kalon*. And soon the Admiralty will come knocking once more, with some urgent business or other or perhaps the offer of a new command. Will it be too much to ask for you to join me?"

Tess's fingers traced the delicate outline of the hairpins. "I would sell Fairleigh and follow you aboard the *Liberté* tomorrow, my love." She did not hesitate, though her heart quivered slightly at the thought of giving up that beloved old wreck.

But stone and clay were not what Tess needed; she knew that now. "I suppose your crew will have to become accustomed to a female disturbing their cables and canvas."

Dane studied her face, still unconvinced.

"Let's just say," Tess added, her eyes glinting with mischief, "that life with André Le Brix will have certain, er, compensations." One soft finger nestled in the dark mat of hair at Dane's neck. "Very pleasant compensations."

Her husband growled deep in his throat, his eyes going smoky. "You make me a man of infinite happiness, *gwellañ-karet*. And it's satisfied I mean to keep you, every day of our lives."

Tess's mouth curved. "Oh, it's well you do, my lord, for I know a dashing French sea captain who would be only too glad to take your place."

A little laugh gurgled on her lips as her husband caught her up into his strong arms and began striding up the hill toward the white garden.

"Dane?"

"Enough of this teasing, wife," he growled. "Before I'm done this night, I'll have you a biddable female."

And there beside the ancient grove of oaks, beneath the moon's unblinking silver eye, he made her his wife anew. Not in the way of man and church, but in the old way of nature and earth, claiming her totally and irrevocably until their breaths mingled and their pulses beat in time, until she became heart of his heart and blood of his blood.

The first time was for forgetting, Ravenhurst whispered to the woman in his arms. The second was for burning. And the third, silver-swept in moondust and marsh fire, was forever.

Around them drifted the heady perfume of lilies and night-blooming jasmine, and, queerly enough, the scent of lavender, though no lavender grew anywhere nearby.

Caught in their own joy, neither noticed the faint gleam that shimmered around the garden.

"At long last, my beauty," the wind seemed to whisper. "Let's go home, lass. We've long years to catch up."

Sweet, lilting laughter trembled on the wind for a moment, then gently faded.

And in the fullness of time a tree grew up in the center of that peaceful ground, and from that tree there grew a rose.

Of a cool summer's night, when the wind blows up sharp and steady from the harbor, the leaves seem to heave and tremble, whispering in the steady currents.

And sometimes, when the fog swirls up from the marsh like the ghosts of old lovers, travelers swear they hear distant laughter and catch the haunting scent of lavender.

On just such nights, when the trees are lit by strange, shimmering lights that play across the marsh, a nightingale comes to sing in the dense branches of that tree, its voice sweet and sad beyond description, so that any passerby must still his steps and listen in dreamy awe.

And the roses beneath the bird's feet, one could almost swear, are black.

Glossary of Breton Words

(With warmest thanks to Evelyne Cucmener and Marie Jaffrenou, who graciously reviewed—and corrected—the Breton phrases below.)

Aman	here
An Aotrou Doué	God in Heaven
Bihan	little; little one
Diaoul	the devil
Duzé	over there
Gwellañ-karet	dearest one
Gwerhéz Vari	the Holy Virgin
Istrenn	oysters
Karet	dear
Mamm de Zoué	Mother of God
Me kalon	my heart

Dear Reader:

I hope you have enjoyed Tess and Dane's story as much as I have enjoyed the telling of it. In it I have tried to be faithful to historical fact and represent the differing points of view about smuggling during the Napoleonic Wars.

Public opinion was often with the free-traders, especially in poor regions like Wealden Kent and Sussex, where smuggling offered a route out of poverty. In 1823, the writer Charles Lamb expressed the view that the smuggler was the only honest thief, for he robbed "nothing but the Revenue—an abstraction I never greatly cared about."

Public opinion was also tipped in favor of the smuggler because of popular reaction to increasingly high import duties on such items as tea, French brandy, gin, tobacco, and silk. These duties provided the necessary revenues to fight England's long and costly wars with Napoleon.

The smuggling of gold guineas to France was an extremely lucrative—as well as dangerous—occupation; the smugglers of Deal and Folkestone specialized in this trade. Their light, swift galleys could be rowed from Deal to Dunkirk in five hours under optimum conditions.

It was a violent age, however; smugglers could be found in virtually every coastal area of the country, and large, powerful gangs did not hesitate to attack any who dared oppose them. The Romney Fox is, of course, a fictional character.

The secret Peninsular action that Lord Morland refers to is an historical fact. When Sir Arthur Wellesley landed in Portugal in 1809, his troops of 25,000 faced a French force of some 200,000. In a brilliant maneuver, the English commander (newly created Viscount Wellington) ordered completion of two great lines of fortification at Torres Vedras, where he ordered his army to retreat in October 1810. There, well provisioned, Wellington waited while the French died from starvation, sickness, and ambush. When the

French retreated four months later, they had lost some 20,000 men.

Wellington's action at the Lines of Torres Vedras was crucial to the outcome of the Peninsular campaign. Had details of this plan reached French ears in advance, the outcome of the war might well have been very different.

Exciting people in an exciting age.

I hope I have done them justice in *The Black Rose.*

If you would like to receive a signed bookmark and a copy of my current newsletter with information about upcoming books, characters from prior books, and curious facts unearthed in my research, please send a legal-size stamped, self-addressed envelope to me at:

111 EAST 14 STREET, #277
New York, NY 10003

I would love to hear from you.

With best wishes,

Christina Skye